the Fledglings

the Fledglings

A NOVEL

DAVID HOMEL

Cormorant Books

The publisher gratefully acknowledges the support of the Canada Council for the Arts
and the Ontario Arts Council for its publishing program. We acknowledge the
financial support of the Government of Canada through the Canada Book Fund (CBF) for
our publishing activities, and the Government of Ontario through the
Ontario Media Development Corporation, an agency of the Ontario Ministry of Culture,
and the Ontario Book Publishing Tax Credit Program.

The author wishes to thank the Conseil des arts et des lettres du Québec
for its ongoing financial support.

LIBRARY AND ARCHIVES CANADA CATALOGUING IN PUBLICATION

Homel, David, author
The fledglings / David Homel.

Issued in print and electronic formats.
ISBN 978-1-77086-382-8 (pbk.). — ISBN 978-1-77086-383-5 (epub). —
ISBN 978-1-77086-384-2 (mobi)

1. Title.

PS8565.06505F54 2014   C813'.54   C2013-907897-5
                                                 C2013-907898-3

Cover art and design: Angel Guerra/Archetype
Interior text design: Tannice Goddard, Soul Oasis Networking
Printer: Friesens

Printed and bound in Canada.

The interior of this book is printed on 100% post-consumer waste recycled paper.

CORMORANT BOOKS INC.
10 ST. MARY STREET, SUITE 615, TORONTO, ONTARIO, M4Y 1P9
www.cormorantbooks.com

For my mother,
the original

ONE

Death Benefits

ON A WEEKDAY MORNING, A working day, in plenty of time for an early breakfast, Joey Krueger stood waiting in the lobby of his mother Bluma's apartment building. The elevator was agonizingly slow, programmed to run at the speed of an eighty-year-old hobbling up a flight of stairs. He didn't need an elevator to make it to the second floor, but the stairway was alarmed to prevent theft from the outside, and wandering from the inside.

The beauty salon off the lobby was empty. For a woman to maintain her self-image in the face of aging seemed to Joey like a good strategy, but he wondered about the sign that hung above the panel of mirrors. I'm a hairdresser, not a magician, it read.

The elevator doors slid open, admitting him to his mother's floor.

Her residence was the kind of place he might have designed in his days as an architect. Even when he was in training, he felt all the important buildings had already been built, and that he had arrived too late. The result was a sense of melancholy that had him turning out buildings that were a reflection of his condition, structures functional to a fault, spaces that left people physically exhausted the minute they stepped through the door — buildings like this one.

He had the good sense to get out of architecture years ago. His buildings would have risen up and destroyed him with their feelings of heaviness had he stayed in the business. Now he was an environmental catastrophist, and he had made a killing at it. Years ago, he played a hunch: the ecology fad would seep out of health-food stores and spread across the nation into conventional workplaces. He borrowed money from his mother and launched an all-natural air duct cleaning business that fed on fears of Legionnaires' disease. All-natural, because he didn't use fungicides — or not very many. Once the business was thriving, he got bored with it. He sold it for a dizzying profit, and started a mould-removal business with the proceeds. Lady Luck smiled on him by delivering Hurricane Katrina and other smaller storms. Suddenly everyone wanted into his business, and he obliged by selling the operation to the highest bidder. A good thing, since El Niño arrived, or was it La Niña, and put the kibosh on hurricanes for several seasons. Mould went out of style.

His business sense was the fruit of childhood upset. Early on he learned how to anticipate the next big thing. When he was a boy, the next big thing was never good, so it was better to be prepared.

On the second floor, he went down the hallway that was fitted with stabilizer bars bolted into the gyprock. It was easy to spot his mother's door. Bluma was a maximalist when it came to decoration. She had plastered every inch of her apartment with souvenirs and memorabilia, and had moved on to the door, pasting cut-out pictures of puppies and kittens and flowers on it. He knocked, then let himself in with his key. His mother was in her easy chair. He bent and kissed the corner of her mouth.

"You're looking beautiful today."

"Oh, you stop that!" She waved her hand in the air, dismissing his usual compliment.

"You're still the looker you always were," he insisted.

"Then look at me," she told him.

He did. There was something feverish about her.

"Feature this — it came yesterday! I could have called, but I wanted to tell you face-to-face!"

She waved an envelope in the air so energetically it flapped like a pennant in the breeze. He couldn't read it.

"It's from the government."

"I thought I was handling your affairs," Joey said.

"You are. But some things slip past you."

"Apparently." Joey put out his hand. She did not surrender the letter. "So what's the good news?"

"Death," she declared triumphantly. "Or, more to the point, death benefits. I never thought I'd see the day, but why not? It makes sense."

Joey drew up a chair next to her, close enough to steal a glance at the envelope that was now at rest. It came from the Social Security Administration.

"We can go to the casino now!" she enthused.

"Good news," he agreed. "Do you want to clue me in, or are we going to play Twenty Questions?"

"Sometimes you have no sense of humour. That's the businessman in you. You want to control everything, you have to know what's going to happen before it happens. All right, I'll spill the beans. I had a husband, you know, a long time ago. He was your father."

"I'm aware of that."

"And we separated."

"I remember that too."

"I told him to go find himself, and come back when he did."

"You told him to find himself?"

"Those were my very words. You don't think I could say something like that?"

"Of course you could. You can say anything you want. It just sounds, you know, like a 1960s expression."

"People have been trying to find themselves forever. Anyway, don't

3

interrupt me, I'll forget what I was saying, and you're the one who wants to know. I told him to come back when he found himself, and he never came back. Draw your own conclusions. Now I get this letter from Social Security. They're giving me his pension."

"So you never got a divorce," Joey concluded.

She waved the same dismissive hand in his face. "I didn't have time. I was too busy getting away from him, with you in tow."

Joey considered her wrinkled hand clutching the envelope, a piece of the past she hadn't solicited, from his father who apparently was using the federal government to send his final regrets.

"I don't know anything about you," he told his mother.

"Those weren't happy times. I'm sorry."

"Don't worry, I turned out all right in spite of it all." He took her hand, the one that wasn't holding the envelope. "At least I think I did."

"At least you're making a living for yourself."

So there's my mother, Joey thought, relinquishing her hand, telling my father to go find himself, long before it was the fashion. What kind of woman said something like that to a man back then? She must have known the chances of him succeeding were pretty slim.

Unless go find yourself was a more polite version of another common expression with the letter F.

"You probably know more than you think you know," his mother told him.

"Of course. But it's not enough."

"Don't flatter me. Anyway, you might not like it," she warned him. "Careful what you wish for."

"I'm a grown man, I can take it."

"Then read this, for starters."

Pursuant to such-and-such an Act, the late Eddie Krueger's pension, through direct deposit, would henceforth be paid to … Joey stopped reading. The sum was symbolic, especially in the world he moved in. But the money wasn't important. It was a message from another world, one he knew only scraps of gossip about. And gossip isn't very satisfactory when your origin is at issue.

"I'm going to write your life story," Joey announced.

She stared at him incredulously.

"You, write something?"

"Okay, no, I won't write it. I'll record it — that's different. I'll get it down on paper."

Bluma flushed a little. "Well, I can't stop you. Why would I? Everybody wants to be in a book."

Not a book, Joey thought, but he didn't contradict his mother. Why put the brakes on that little rise of excitement that brought some needed colour to her face? It wouldn't be a book, since, as his mother reminded him, he was no writer, and a book needed a writer. It would be something truer than a book: a life story — hers, told by her. What could be more straightforward?

It was also the perfect pre-retirement project, fitted to a man his age.

"I'll put it on CD," he explained, unsure whether she knew what a CD was. "But materially, CDs don't last forever. Think of everything that's gone before: 78s, 33 1/3 long-playing records, 45s, reel-to-reel tapes, cassette tapes … Every medium was supposed to last forever. Who knows what eternal ways of preserving memory are doomed to disappear?"

That's just like him, Bluma thought. Her boy was worrying about preserving something that didn't exist yet.

"You tell me," she said. "What form of recording has been around the longest? What form is everybody always going to know, no matter what crazy things technology comes up with?"

Joey didn't have to think too long.

"Pencil and paper," he answered.

His mother clapped her hands in approval.

"What a smart boy!"

"Acid-free paper," Joey made a note for himself.

"If that's what you think is best. I didn't know paper had acid in it."

"I could explain it," he offered.

"Not now."

"The safest thing would be to put your story in a time capsule."

"What in the heck is that?"

"A sealed tube that protects what's inside. But you can open it whenever you want to. Usually they're buried in the ground."

"Like, six feet under?"

"No, not six feet. Deep enough to be protected, but shallow enough to retrieve in the future, so people can learn how wonderful you are."

"That's enough!"

She shooed away his devotion as if it were a troublesome fly.

"But what if somebody wants to read my story, and they don't happen to have a shovel on hand?"

"I'll have paper copies available."

"Thank goodness for that."

He got up from his chair, eyed the envelope on the table, then let it lie.

"Do you want breakfast?"

"Let my stomach settle first."

"How do you feel this morning?"

"The usual: lousy."

Lousy or not, he went to the refrigerator and got out the eggs. Bluma liked the classic American breakfast, minus the bacon. After one of her cancer scares, she went vegetarian. Maybe a lifetime of toxins could be harried out of her body, even at this late date. Out of empathy, Joey had become a vegetarian too, most of the time. That meant turning his back on his wife Elke's roasts, which she ended up sharing with the dogs.

When her scrambled eggs were before her, awash in ketchup, Bluma told him, "About this life story business, I'm warning you, my memory isn't what it used to be."

"I'll help."

"You'll help me remember? How will you do that?"

"I remember things."

"You remember stuff from my childhood?"

"You told me things. I never forget anything you say."

He carried away the breakfast dishes when she was through and quickly rinsed them. The helper he paid to look in on his mother would finish washing them. She slumped forward expectantly, ready to receive the massage that was the crowning point of every visit. Joey had no hesitations about touching her, though it had taken her some time to get used to their rite. At first she squirmed away from his hands, unaccustomed to touch. The only contact she had was with doctors, and most of the time they used cool metal probes, not their hands.

"You're my sleeping pill," she told him with closed eyes.

"You should try sleeping at night," Joey chided her.

She opened her eyes and considered his naiveté. "Sleep doesn't want me. Who cares? I'll sleep when I'm dead."

"That will never happen."

"What a silly boy you are!"

Her bones were more fragile than the thinnest china. With her, he was as delicate as a man could be.

Once his mother was asleep in her easy chair, her legs steadied on a hassock, Joey crept out the door and locked it. He carried his sense of rightness out into the morning freshness of the Branfords, and back to the workings of Ecological Solutions.

OZZIE HAD LISTENED TO ANY number of his partner Joey's revelations, but this was the first one that had nothing to do with business. That was a revelation in itself. He was almost as enthusiastic as his friend. Here was a defence against Joey's tendency toward melancholy that, Ozzie suspected, was getting worse with age.

"This is great; it'll help you get your energy back," Ozzie said after Joey laid out his ambition to record his mother's story. "You need to get your younger self back."

At the words *younger self,* Lia the office manager wrinkled up her nose as if she'd detected a bad smell.

"What was so great about you when you were young?" she wanted to know.

"And for that to happen," Ozzie pushed on, "you need a project, something else besides the business. You're too good at it. There's no challenge anymore. So take all the time you need. This place practically runs by itself."

"Thanks for the credit," Joey told him.

"Don't worry, I don't get credit for anything either," said Lia.

Joey gave them a sly look. "Wait a minute! You two aren't planning a palace coup, are you?"

"Go on!" Ozzie laughed. "You know I love you too much for that. So start — start today! Get on the phone and tell Bluma you're starting on Monday, first thing."

Grateful, Joey headed for the door. It was Friday afternoon, he really didn't need to be at the office, and he could use a little time by himself to digest just what he was getting himself into — though what he would do with that time, he wasn't sure. He left the Ecological Solutions office and drove into the roiling suburban Connecticut traffic with the explicit blessing of his best friend, and his mother's scratching voice on his cellphone.

Half an hour later, he stepped onto the wraparound porch of his house. From beyond the hedges and trees, the traffic was in rush-hour mode, but the greenery muted its agitation, and the noise was distant enough beyond the vegetation to be almost comforting. Everyone was rushing off somewhere, but he was beyond all obligation. He wondered if that was what people meant when they used the expression *peace of mind.*

TWO

A Man's Secret Garden

FIREFLIES. JOEY KRUEGER DIDN'T EVEN know he had them on his property.

He was enough of a man of science to be interested in their patterns as they flew across his back lawn. Some stayed low, just above the grass, dragging their lit bellies over the leaves. Others spiralled up to the lower branches of the trees, putting on an aerial show. If the insects were going to all that trouble to stage a display, he assumed courtship was the reason.

"All that beautiful singing, and it's only just for sex."

He smiled in the twilight at the way his mother criticized the song-birds every spring when they returned to raise a racket in the ravine beneath her window. Did Bluma really think birds sang for the sole beauty of their songs? Apparently, if it turned out that nature cared only for copulation, she wasn't going to pay it any mind. Not that a woman in her eighties could be expected to get interested in the call to wooing.

My mother's love life, Joey thought. With or without my father. Indecent territory, best avoided as if it never existed, despite the evidence — his own existence. But he would have to attend to that issue if he was going to record the life story of the most extraordinary woman in his world.

He would have to pay careful attention to everything about her, though he didn't think he could be more attentive than he already was. Mornings, he drove to her apartment in the seniors' block and made her breakfast, the kind of errand that had his wife calling him a mama's boy. He followed each breakfast with a massage that sent Bluma drifting off to sleep, as she claimed insomnia had kept her up the night before. He used her brief capitulation to peek into the medicine chest and make sure the level in the pill bottles was descending at the right rhythm. He went on all her excursions to the gerontologists who marvelled that a woman with so many things wrong with her could be so tenacious in her grip on life.

But she deserved his attention. Everything he could do would not be enough. Getting down her life story, preserving it for the world — that was the least he could do.

His ambition tormented him, and he hadn't even recorded one line. He'd been trained as an architect, a man of techniques, and technically, he wondered how the recording process worked. The issue of the proper medium — pencil and paper, what an original idea! — was easy compared to what came next: where did his mother's story begin? And since he was no writer, something they both agreed on, and since he didn't intend to become one, how could he record her story without actually putting pen to paper?

Earlier that afternoon, in the midst of these anxieties, his neighbour Caroline wandered into his field of vision. He didn't know the woman, although their lawns touched. They must have spoken at some point, but he couldn't recall when or what they might have talked about. The colour of her dress intruded on him. It was orange, like the flame of a gas barbecue, and scarcely more substantial than a handkerchief. He had never seen her in something like that.

A woman's secret garden. The words entered his mind as Caroline bent over her geraniums and began snapping off the heads of the faded flowers. He had heard of that place. Sheila, who tended bar at the Italian joint on US 1 where he and Ozzie met, used that expression all the time. He was sure he'd never been there. The way Sheila said those words made him mildly envious, and he wondered whether a man could have a secret garden, and if so, what would grow there.

The secret garden of Joey Krueger. The idea was laughable. But he shouldn't laugh. He should be searching for the place.

His neighbour picked up a watering can and began attending to a flower Joey could not identify. A delicate and fussy one. The particular alliance of the red petals of the geraniums and the shimmering orange of her dress began to work on his attention. Her watering can was green metal. She would not have used plastic; he knew that much about her. That, and the fact that her property had no leering garden dwarves or ceramic squirrels frozen in cute poses. She bent low as she watered, softly speaking to her flowers, he imagined, saying their secret flower names. Gardeners, according to his experience, were usually nuts.

The flame of her dress was attached to her shoulders by two nearly invisible straps, and her skin was deeply tanned. Apparently she hadn't heard the news that the sun is poison, or maybe she just liked to pick her poison, and the sun was it.

It came to him as a complete surprise: he was coveting his neighbour's wife.

Out jumped a joke from his mother's endless collection of antique humour. The Ten Suggestions, she cackled in her raspy voice, deeply pleased by the world's iniquity. He acted like the Ten Commandments were the Ten Suggestions.

Caroline straightened, touched the small of her back with her right hand, then began rubbing the skin of her forehead above her right eye with her dirty fingers. He watched as she worked her skin into a welt he could see all the way from his porch. He felt like striding across the property line, full of that righteous feeling you get from helping people, and stopping her. Taking her hand from her face and scolding her like a girl, since her routine obviously had its roots in childhood.

But he didn't. He watched her instead.

Where's the husband? Joey wondered. He ought to be keeping her from harming herself. Caroline was married, he assumed, though he had no picture of the man who went with her, or her children if there were any, which he doubted. Satisfied with the work she'd done on her forehead, she moved on to a spot on her neck, just beneath her jawbone. A welt, sister to the first one, soon blossomed there. It was painful to watch. Maybe bugs were biting her. Maybe she had an allergy. Suddenly Elke was standing next to him. He hadn't heard his wife step onto the porch.

"Get your eyes off the chick next door."

Joey turned away from Caroline. Elke was shaking her finger at him like a schoolmarm.

"I saw you staring. Bad boy! I know what's on your mind."

"Nothing's on my mind," he told her. "Or at least nothing that I know of."

"Nothing that you know of," Elke mocked him. "That sounds like defence by reason of insanity."

Then she walked off the porch, more noisily this time. She had made her point, and now she had something of greater consequence to do, probably brushing the dachshunds.

"I didn't know you cared," Joey spoke to her departing form.

Across the property line, Caroline was dangling her watering can from one bony finger. She smoothed her dress carefully. Joey wondered if she knew he'd been watching her.

She turned and looked across their two lawns straight into his eyes. A worry line ran between her eyebrows, or maybe it was just the effort of squinting into the last rays of the setting sun. She gave him a half-smile of acknowledgement. It was a permission of sorts. Then, with her watering can dangling casually from one finger, she disappeared into her house.

He wouldn't have known she was there if Elke hadn't pointed her out.

No, that wasn't right. He wouldn't have understood he was watching her so attentively without Elke telling him as much.

I am a prisoner of myself, Joey thought as he stared at his neighbour's empty lawn. He wasn't sure what that meant.

He returned to Ozzie's advice about recovering his younger self. Was it sage advice or a self-improvement cliché? It was hard to summon forth a younger self. Life as a carefree student, the college parties from wilder days. He could only dream of those kinds of parties now, and maybe that was just as well. When he thought about the Halloween bash for the architecture students and the woman in attendance named Christine, he wasn't sure he wanted to go back to those days. Christine was a hard-edged Swiss-German girl hell-bent on showing the boys she could be as vulgar as they were — better still, she could beat them at their own game. Those were the days of the battles for women's liberation, and many fell on that field of combat. He had no idea what Christine had become since then. There were ways of finding people in his former profession, but he'd have to want to find her. He remembered the costume she wore to the party. She was completely naked except for her dancing shoes, and swathed in layers and layers of Saran Wrap twisted into translucency over her body. Christine had designed a work of genius; she was more artist than architect. Every man could see she was naked, but none could make out a single detail of her body. The packaging, a domestic convenience made by the same Dow Chemical Company that manufactured the napalm used in Vietnam, a sister product to Saran Wrap — that wouldn't have been lost on anyone in those days — made her look like a corpse in a winding sheet.

At the party, at the height of the evening in the frantic kitchen that was quickly becoming a pigsty, a girl named Elaine slowly lifted her dress the length of her endless thighs. The men watched in breathless suspense.

"Oh, my goodness, I forgot my panties," she announced in case anyone missed her act. Every man gazed avidly at her demure bush, a brushstroke of auburn, a gesture by a Zen painter. The males did what they did best back then: they whistled and applauded.

Then Elaine lifted her dress further to reveal what she had been intending to show all along: the colostomy bag attached to her right flank. The kitchen fell silent as a church. This Elaine — he never saw her again or heard anything about her — was a gifted performer, a dedicated member of the advance guard of sexual horror. What man would want to spend the night with her after that performance? In expert fashion, Elaine stopped the party.

What had become of Christine and Elaine? It was hard to imagine them working as architects, though they were definitely women of technique. Why hadn't he paid more attention to them? He'd been like every other guy at the party. Shouting and whistling with admiration for their daring, but scared dickless by their reality.

NOW HE WAS BACK ON his porch again, Sunday at twilight, mulling over his anxieties about his first session with his mother the next morning. There would be breakfast, but no soporific massage. Bluma would need to be alert for the heavy work of memory.

He looked across his darkening lawn. Lightning bugs. That's what they called fireflies when he was a kid, living on Mary Barone's farm, after they'd left his mother's sister's place, after some upset he dimly remembered. But his mother's sister wasn't her sister, but her cousin, though he'd been encouraged to think of the woman as his aunt, at least until whatever went wrong had gone wrong. There had been no lightning bugs there, though there had been clouds of them at the farm. Suddenly he was doing the remembering, which was not the idea. But like it or not, there they were, the swarms of lightning bugs, great fistfuls of them, mirrored by the heat lightning that scared him until Mary Barone told him it wasn't lightning at all, but the earth's warmth escaping into the sky at the end of a hot summer's day. Why hadn't his own mother told him that to shield him from his fear? She must have been working. In the evening? Why not — people worked in the evening when they had to, and everything she did back then was because she had to. She was working for him. So what if Mary Barone told him what heat lightning was? A boy could have several mothers. Maybe it was better that way. He had no brothers or sisters to torment, but there were the Barone boys who were better than brothers, who would drag him along when they ventured into the field to pick tomato worms off the plants and crush them between flat stones.

The music of ice cubes made him put aside his memories. So evocative, a scene in a movie: ice tinkling in a glass on a warm summer evening. He wasn't much of a drinker, but no one can resist that music.

He stepped off the porch as quietly as his weight would allow, then walked across his lawn to the property line. From that point onward, he was entering another man's territory. The line was invisible in the night, but he could tell he'd crossed it from the change in the pile of the grass.

Caroline's flame-coloured dress was a dark beacon among the fireflies. She was standing by the geraniums as if she and Joey had set a rendezvous there two evenings ago, at an hour somewhat earlier than this one. The flowers glowed with the same muted orange colour as her dress. Joey scattered fireflies as he moved barefoot in her direction. He felt invisible, a foolish thing to feel in the Branfords, the seat of Puritan America where every heart was supposed to be as transparent as a glass house.

As he came near, Caroline shook the ice cubes in her glass.

"You don't have your own," she said, seeing he was empty-handed. "I thought you would."

"I'm unprepared."

She held up her glass.

"Have some of mine. You know what they say about ladies drinking alone."

He took her glass tentatively in the darkness and drank, then returned it.

"Hmm. Better stuff than what I'm used to."

"Why not the best?"

"That's what they say. Nice garden you've got."

Caroline laughed. "It's best admired in the dark."

"No, really, it's nice. You put a lot of work into it."

"Actually, neighbour, you've never paid much attention to it."

"I know. I'm a slow guy. Slow on the uptake."

"That's just as well."

This was the kind of talk he was bad at: when you don't say what you mean. It was called flirtation. He doubted he could have had this conversation in the light.

"The fireflies brought me," he said. "The lightning bugs."

"Ever since they stopped spraying for mosquitoes, the whole ecology has returned."

"I work in ecology," he told her.

That was the right thing to say, and he knew it. So he wasn't that slow.

"But I'm afraid I'm not much for gardening."

"I know," Caroline reassured him. "Your wife does it."

"She likes order."

"I can tell. But nature doesn't."

Joey didn't know what nature did or didn't like, and he suspected there was always order behind its most tangled exuberance. He thought of telling Caroline that, then decided against it.

"I suppose you're married," he said instead.

"You have to be married to live in the Branfords."

"It's a requirement?"

"Of course." She pointed at the wide lawns and trees under the cover of the settling darkness. "All this room, these expensive houses, the whole set-up ..."

They stood in silence a while. Caroline handed Joey her drink again.

"If you drink from someone's glass, you can read their thoughts."

"Read away," she told him. "I'm an open book."

The drink was mostly melted ice by now. The fireflies were disappearing. Darkness covered the lawn and the flowerbeds.

"So much for the lightning bugs."

Caroline smiled at the word. "They come out at dusk," she told him. "When night falls, they fly off to bed."

"Firefly bed. That sounds like a line from a poem."

Caroline laughed. "Right — a poem written by a teenage boy under the influence of hormones."

"That's me," Joey said.

To prove that illogical claim, he did something with Caroline that he couldn't bring himself to do with his wife. He put one arm around her and pulled her gently to his side. Gently enough so she could resist. She didn't. He felt the thrill of knowledge: all there was to know about her that he didn't know, and probably never would, all the layers of her resistance.

"Are you married like I am?" she asked.

"How married is that?"

"We could compare."

"I'd lose."

Caroline took his hand and led him toward her front door. He brushed off his bare feet on the welcome mat.

"Don't bother. I never do."

Inside the living room, the lighting was low. They kissed by the coffee table. Caroline closed her eyes and her features softened, her body leaned into his. Who am I to her that she would surrender this way? She must be giving herself to something else. To hope, maybe: hope for a cure for the deep Branford loneliness that filled every one of these big houses.

"You're beautiful," he told her.

She opened her eyes and smiled. She plainly did not believe him.

"A woman who closes her eyes is always beautiful. It's not particularly me."

He pushed her hair away from her forehead. The welt from the day of the watering can had completely disappeared.

"You can go back later," Caroline told him. "You can even go back now."

"Don't talk about later."

"I'm just trying to make it easier."

"Thanks. But it won't be easy. It isn't easy. Not for me."

Caroline held him close, comforting him ahead of time.

"It's all right. We don't have to do anything."

THE DACHSHUNDS SET OFF A mighty racket of detection when Joey opened the door from the porch into his house. The door was unlocked, as he'd left it. With the dogs, a lock was unnecessary.

When the dachshunds understood it was only him, they stopped barking, though they did follow him into the bathroom, snuffling with interest at the fresh smells on his bare feet. He put on the light, and in its harsh glare he peered into the mirror to see if his resurrection was visible.

Why you? he said to the man in the mirror.

Then he bared his teeth and cracked a smile. The dye job on his hair was the only part of his new self that didn't fit. Then he went into his room.

The separate rooms had been Elke's idea, a punishment, so she hoped, for his excessive devotion to Bluma. If you spend more time with your mother than you do with me, I'm not sleeping with you — he could still recite her line, word for word, though it wasn't the sort of thing he could tell anyone about, not even Ozzie. He had grown used to the arrangement, since he was not going to change his care-giving routine. Tonight, separate rooms struck him as the most adult invention in the world.

But really — why you? he wondered. He had done nothing, and Caroline, everything.

But that wasn't true. When does a love affair begin? Long before it seems to have. He went onto his porch in the afternoon in a moment of truancy and she was there among the flowers, though it took time to see her, even if she was dressed in flame. Then he stepped out a second time at twilight and she was there again, wrapped in fireflies. He climbed down from his porch and crossed the line of demarcation between their two species of grass — he, barefoot, the guy who wore shoes on the beach.

Admit it, he told himself. You took giant steps. That's not like you.

THREE

Guardian Angel

EVEN WITH HIS INFALLIBLE SENSE of catastrophe, Joey Krueger wouldn't have succeeded without his partner. When melancholy appeared out of nowhere and paralyzed his ability to act on his hunches, Ozzie Georgandas would whip him back into an entrepreneurial frenzy like a college football coach, setting him on the rails of commerce again.

There was no telling why Ozzie decided to be Joey's guardian angel. Like angels, he was just there; there was no explaining him. "Somebody has to look after you," he would tell Joey. Ozzie didn't necessarily hope to cure Joey of his melancholy permanently, not that he had any idea what that might entail. He just wanted to keep his partner operational.

The two men had met on neighbouring bar stools over a conversation about women. The cliché ended there.

Elke's son and daughter were adults by the time Joey "teamed up" with her, as he referred to their marriage. Children would not be an issue with Elke as they had been so painfully for him and Debra. His marriage with Debra had been an extended debate over whether or not to have children. Though it was no debate at all, because there was no exchange of views, and no amount of rhetoric he deployed could have swayed her. He wanted; she did not want. She controlled the means of production and would not surrender that control for an instant: a birthday, an anniversary, the few times they toddled home from a restaurant after some occasion. There didn't seem to be any moments of surrender in Debra. Either that, or Joey couldn't make them happen.

His sense of rejection sustained him for years. It was a noble role and it fit him well: the unappreciated, the neglected — it fit with his childhood sense of himself. Then, one day, the pleasure he took in it collapsed in dramatic fashion. Out of the blue, he didn't want to be the rejected person anymore. After another long night of sterile debate, he understood something that any other man would have seen years before. Debra would never change her mind, no matter what he said or did, no matter what promises he made to be the most perfect father in the world, to change diapers and wake up for bottle-feeding in the middle of the night — he would have promised breastfeeding if he could have delivered. Most of all, he swore he would provide her with more of that mysterious thing called space than she could have possibly used in a lifetime. Space was at the heart of her not wanting kids. Her body was her space, her ultimate private property, and she didn't want to share it with anyone, even for nine months.

After years of Debra telling him just that, and in so many words, over and over again, Joey finally got it. In a rush of disappointment and self-loathing, he raised his hand against her. It was the first time he'd ever done such a thing, and not just with his wife, but in his entire life as a man. He hadn't hit anyone since the grade school playground.

Debra stood before him, her cheek reddening. She stared at him with a look he'd never seen. It was disbelief. She hadn't thought he had it in him.

Whatever astonishment she felt, and with it the possibility that she might have to rethink her husband, vanished the next moment. She could read it on his face: he hated himself for what he'd done. Contrite wasn't the word for it. If he'd accepted that thing in himself that had made him lash out at her, things with Debra might have been different. But that wasn't the kind of man he was.

Debra seized on his transgression and launched divorce proceedings the next day. He had struck her once. He would strike her again. It didn't matter how many times he insisted it would never happen again. His violence couldn't be an isolated case. Every survey, every article in every magazine said as much, and she would not be one of those foolish women who come back for more. Doing that would be an insult to victims everywhere — victims like her.

"You're lucky I'm not calling the cops," Debra told him as he rubbed his hand against his pant leg to erase the stigma. "You'd be in the slammer in no time. Domestic violence isn't a joke anymore. Us victims are speaking up."

You, a victim? But he couldn't say that. He'd slapped her, and that deprived him of his rights. He, the real victim — at least that's how he saw himself until a minute ago — was suddenly standing on the absolute wrong side of the fence.

In those miserable days, he was a melancholy architect, designing schools and civic buildings that looked like they'd come from a kid's plastic building-block set. That was before he met Ozzie. And he'd met him because of his foolish mistake with Debra.

Too ashamed to hang around the house, he drove to the bar at the Italian place on US 1, where he and Debra occasionally went in the days when their conflict was better managed. The restaurant was the only piece of real estate he was allowed to keep. He was staring at a Red Sox game on TV, though he was no sportsman, and he couldn't summon up the necessary identification to get interested in the players and what they could or couldn't accomplish on the field. He had no stomach for food in those days, though he was able to keep down liquids. A lonely guy sitting at a bar exerts a powerful negative force field, and into it came a man who seemed to be on his own too.

Ozzie Georgandas gazed at the game for a while. He was no fan either. He looked across at Joey and nodded toward the TV.

"Takes your mind off your troubles," he said.

It was one of those times when a man will say the opposite of what he thinks to see if the other man is open to conversation.

"Hardly," Joey answered.

Male misery loves male company, and the two found each other that evening. Ozzie Georgandas was a happily married real estate agent, though he wouldn't have admitted his happiness to Joey, who was steeping in a pool of confusion and self-hatred. Ozzie was at the bar because his wife's sisters had summoned her to a family council of war over what to do about their mother who could no longer be trusted to turn off the taps when the sink was full. He didn't like eating alone at home, with the unnaturally loud clatter of dishes and silverware in the sink and on the counter, as if it were the herald of some future loneliness.

Ozzie listened to the tale of Debra's wilful sterility. He winced at the part where his new friend slapped his wife. Then Ozzie did what any man would have: he told Joey he was better off without the wife. After all, he was living in the here and now, with a plate of antipasto at the bar and a glass of good wine, making new friends — when was the last time that happened? By the end of the night, Ozzie was Joey's new best friend, the one he'd never had time to make until now.

Joey wanted to know how he could ever repay him.

"Friendship," Ozzie declared, the Chianti making him sententious, "has no price."

Joey looked showily at his watch.

"You want to know what happened tonight?"

"Shoot," Ozzie said.

"My lawyer and my wife's lawyer butted heads like a couple of bucks in heat to see what'll be left of me. Even if I put my business out of her reach."

"Good move," Ozzie approved. "They're just play-fighting. That's all lawyers ever do."

"I will never follow my heart again," Joey declared.

"Still," Ozzie countered, "you look like someone who's not afraid of risk."

"I took a bad risk with my soon-to-be ex. Otherwise we wouldn't be here."

"See, risk gets you something after all."

"Okay, so you're right. There's a property for sale not far from here," Ozzie said, changing registers. "You can practically see it from the front door. But no one's biting."

"What's the problem?"

"It used to be a gas station. Maybe the traffic level is too high."

"No," Joey said, suddenly sobering up from his self-pity. "Decontamination. That's what they need."

"That hadn't occurred to me," Ozzie admitted. "I'll be damned. So that's why no one will touch it."

"First, tank removal," Joey said, in a sudden state of grace. "Then decontamination. It'll move, you'll see."

Just like that, decontamination became Joey Krueger's next ecological enterprise, and Ozzie Georgandas became his partner. Ecological Solutions was born that evening over eggplant antipasto and California Chianti. The petri dish on which it grew was one man's bitterness and sense of abandonment, but that didn't matter; the company was in tune with the times. At the bar, Joey explained his catastrophist vision to Ozzie. The principle was simple. People are afraid. They're afraid of the air. They're afraid of the world they themselves made. And with good reason — it's toxic, there's no disputing that. They're afraid of what's invisible. Radon gases seeping up through their basements, bacteria collecting in the ducts that deliver warm air or cool air depending on the season, clumps of microscopic mould that accumulate in their lungs and choke off their air supply. The dangers are as real as they are invisible. Decontaminating the soil, once you pulled those rusty old gas tanks out of the ground, followed in the spirit of everything he'd done up till then.

A handshake was all it took to make Joey and Ozzie partners: the ex-architect and the soon-to-be ex-real estate agent. Joey imparted his vision, and in return, Ozzie kept Joey's melancholy at bay. Ozzie kept him sharp and curious and wondering about what was going to happen next. As everyone knows, the ability to project yourself into the future is one of the pillars of good mental health.

THE TANK REMOVAL BUSINESS WAS Joey's first foray into the visible. You could actually see the tanks being pulled from the ground, nasty-looking and rusty, dripping with carcinogens. The decontamination that followed played on the invisible at the heart of his clients' fears; they could see the dirt but not the evil it contained. The tank business had another advantage. It responded to the recycling fad — and Joey did consider it a fad, as he did all the fears his successive businesses were built on. Tank removal involved two catastrophes: economic and ecological.

It worked like this. Take the neighbourhood gas station. Once upon a time, those places dotted the landscape like so many oases. Like the man behind the bar at the corner tavern or the medical doctor, the station attendant, who was usually the owner in those days, received his customer's anxieties. The attendant could ensure you a safe journey, and look into the body of the car you depended on entirely, given the suburb you chose to live in, and diagnose what would go wrong next, and what had already begun deteriorating. On a busy corner, often there were three or four stations representing companies that appeared to be competing with their bright logos and slogans and mascots. You can trust your car to the man who wears the star. Those companies gave you the pleasure of choice.

Then came the end.

Gas stations began to close. More and more men decided there was no future in a margin of a few cents a gallon. The old Italians who had stations on US 1 in the Branfords were tired of customers busting their balls over high gas prices they had no say in, not to mention the environment people who charged them punitive taxes to dispose of used motor oil and bald tires. Their sons weren't naive. They weren't going to follow the old man into a dying business no one had any respect for. If people wanted gas, they went to the 7-11 where prices were cheaper. No one cared about trust anymore.

Though the gas station business was going to hell, the land the stations stood on was worth gold, and contractors were eager to build condos on it. But first the tanks had to be extracted and the land that once held them in its embrace decontaminated. That's where Ecological Solutions stepped in. Joey was paid good money to pull the tanks safely from the ground and cart them away. No one knew exactly where they went. He promised his clients they would be cleaned, then sold to a concern that recycled them. And he wasn't entirely lying. He sold them to an Asian company that put them on a slow boat to China, where they would be fashioned into something else.

There were two things Joey never did. He never mentioned China, a country that served milk flavoured with powdered lead to its children when it wasn't running over them with tanks in full view of the world. And he never used the word sell. He didn't sell, he recycled. You could pawn off sandbags full of shit on people as long as you called it recycling.

Not that he would ever do something like that. He didn't need to.

IN THE MORNING, JOEY HEADED for Bluma's apartment for their first session. He imagined that Caroline still lay upon his skin; in his boyish elation, he imagined many things about her: she was his reward for something he hadn't done yet, she was his permission. Though talk of Bluma had not figured into his wooing of her.

What did he know of his family story? There was a bad man, his father, who was bad in an ordinary way, and a good woman, his mother, who was extraordinarily good. Other than that simple scheme, he knew nothing of what had come before them, outside of a few rumours about the previous generation, grandparents he'd never met, shadowy people who came from some obscure place in Russia. But these people would have to step out of the shadows, since they were his mother's parents. If he was going to begin at the beginning, that meant Bluma's childhood, didn't it?

FOUR

A Schoolgirl's Prayer

EVERY DAY AFTER SCHOOL, AS she pushed her way through the tall grass of the prairie she had to cross to get home, Bluma Goldberg, who had learned very little about God in her house, would whisper a prayer. Please, Almighty, let there be no fighting when I get there. To give her prayer extra power, she crossed the fingers of both hands.

The kids in Burnside all did that. They crossed their fingers and tightened up their faces when they were hoping really hard for something and wanted it extra-bad. But sometimes when you crossed your fingers, it meant the thing you were saying was a lie. It all depended. On what, she didn't know.

But it didn't much matter what she did, how many fingers she crossed or uncrossed. The Lord was busy elsewhere. He hardly ever answered her prayer. That was all right with Bluma. The real reason behind a prayer was the feeling you got when you said it, and not whether it was answered. Prayers aren't made to be answered, but spoken.

The Lord probably had his eye on Lexington Street where her cousin Bella lived with her family, her father and mother, who was Bluma's Aunt Taube, and all of Bella's raucous, joke-playing, automobile-driving, dice-shaking brothers. The Lord's people lived in city neighbourhoods.

He probably didn't even know where Burnside was, where she lived, a triangle-shaped district hemmed in on three sides by railroad tracks, the last stop on the streetcar line, just past where Hell froze over. Burnside wasn't on city maps, so how was the Lord supposed to find it? But it was an excellent place for her father, Abe Goldberg, to run his business, which was why he moved his family there as soon as opportunity knocked.

Bluma pushed through the tall, prickly grass of the prairie and onto the sidewalk that ran along 93rd Street. She cast a look behind. Her brother Laurie's lean-to stood somewhere in the middle of the vacant lot, invisible from the sidewalk. She never went there unless she was invited, when Laurie needed her. The lean-to was made of grass and branches in a prairie covered with grass and branches. Disguise was something her brother was good at, not like her.

She knew some kids on the outs with their families lived full-time under the railroad bridge, or the front stairs of two-flats until it was safe for them to return. She heard of one gang that had hollowed out caves in the banks of the new shipping canal, and they lived there. But Laurie didn't need the lean-to for a roof over his head. He had a house with his own room, the way she did. Laurie's lean-to was for the times he couldn't stand their father.

Bluma walked along 93rd toward her place with her books tied in a strap. They banged against her right leg as she walked. The covers were scraped and raw-looking and the pages dog-eared. She didn't have much use for books. She wasn't a good learner. Whenever she went to read a page out of a book, her stomach started to churn.

The Goldberg property had two buildings on it. There was a frame house that faced the street. According to law, wood frame constructions weren't allowed in Chicago, and hadn't been since the Great Fire of 1871. But Burnside was the wild frontier, and the inspectors weren't too picky, the few times they came around.

The house was narrow and had a tall wooden fence in front of it, built on orders from her father. The house measured twenty feet across and was drafty in winter, and the windows rattled when the freights passed in the yards down the block. Life in Burnside was ruled by the railroad tracks. When three freight trains came by and closed off all three level crossings at the same time, they might as well have been living on an island.

Behind the house, down the gangway and across the yard, there was the Chicken Coop. It could be reached by going past the house, or directly from the back alley, a track with deep ruts worn into it. There were no chickens in the Chicken Coop. Chickens weren't the reason Abe Goldberg had wanted the property.

This afternoon, it looked like Bluma's prayers would be answered. Peace reigned in the Coop — at least that's what it sounded like as she came up the gangway by the house.

Her father stepped out the back door. He must have been watching for her. He pointed to the Coop.

"I need you in there."

"I have schoolwork."

"Go serve them. I got the supplier."

He spoke to her in Yiddish, which she did not want to speak, though the word supplier he said in English, since apparently it couldn't be said in Yiddish. That was why she wanted no part of that language. It was too weak for all the things that had to be said in Burnside.

Her father turned and strode back into the house. He slammed the door shut even though it was a warm spring afternoon. Abe Goldberg was afraid of drafts. A draft can kill, he believed. A man as big as a horse and as strong as a bull, and he's afraid of the breeze.

Bluma liked to say she wasn't afraid of anything, and sometimes it even looked that way. She wasn't afraid of the things other girls her age were, like the dirty words boys said when they talked about them. She liked pushing and shoving with the boys, and they liked pushing back because she was the most developed around. Not like Bella, her best friend and cousin, a scrawny tomboy with no breasts. Breasts were okay, Bluma supposed, but not for her. She wanted to be a boy. She wanted to go with Laurie and sleep in his lean-to in the prairie.

The problem was the thick crabgrass and nettly weeds that covered the prairie. Bluma was afraid of them. She couldn't stand the way the grass pulled at her legs as she pushed through it, like it was trying to get her to lie down in it.

Bluma did what her father told her. She crossed the yard where the crooked apple tree was flowering for no reason, since it never gave fruit once the flowers fell off. She went through the screen door and into the Chicken Coop. Four Irish cops were sitting in the room in a circle, in straight-backed chairs, singing.

> *Old Hogan's goat was feeling fine*
> *He ate four red shirts off the line*
> *I took a stick and broke his back*
> *And tied him to the railroad track*
> *The five-fifteen came flying by*
> *Old Hogan's goat was sure to die*
> *He gave a cry, a cry of pain*
> *Coughed up the shirts and flagged the train.*

The cops hadn't bothered taking off their uniforms and putting on their street clothes. Maybe they were still on duty; that happened too. Bluma watched them. They were exceedingly happy with their song. It was one of those songs that was hard to figure out: full of cruelty to the goat that only did what goats do, eat things, then celebrating the goat because it managed to come out alive in the end. The cops hadn't noticed her. She'd hardly made a sound.

They don't need me, Bluma thought. They can go ahead and serve themselves. They know where the hooch is.

Like everyone else, she used another word for alcohol. You couldn't say drink, even if that's what was on everyone's mind. The euphemism business produced a million and one words for the forbidden thing, and that was all because of the strange invention called Prohibition. Alcohol wasn't allowed, even if it was everywhere, and that was the subject of no end of joking in the Coop, the policemen and everyone else agreeing that there was way more to drink now than before this Prohibition thing had been invented by a bunch of country bumpkins they called nativists, people who made the law that was no more and no less than an attack against the immigrants who were building this country, and who had the right to take a drink after their hard day's work. Going to the Coop for a nip was their revenge.

Bluma got an education at the Coop just by listening, which was easier than cracking a book and trying to follow the print that swam before her eyes. She learned there was a war going on between people in the country and people in the city, between people with English names and people who had names like hers. But that kind of knowledge wouldn't keep her from being the class dunce in Miss Reilly's homeroom.

Listening was part of her job at the Coop, but she had to do more than just that. She had to agree with the people who were speaking, since the Irish policemen took these things very seriously, and the Irish were essential to her father's business. When they started talking, you'd think you were at a political meeting, not in a speak-softly shop.

She had her own idea about euphemisms. Even with all their laughter and singing, the men who came here knew they were doing wrong. But who wants to admit that? If you don't say the word for the thing you shouldn't be doing, and say something else in its place, especially a funny-sounding word like hooch, that'll take the sting off.

"What do you boys want?" she asked in her practised voice.

The red-faced men turned in her direction. They were absolutely delighted to see her.

"She snuck in quiet as a mouse!"

"We struck it rich today! To be served by this pretty girl!"

"How about one of your daddy's special coffees?"

The percolator was on the stove, keeping warm on a hot plate. She poured four cups of coffee to the halfway mark. Then she topped up each one with whisky from a tightly capped bottle from the cupboard. You could leave coffee standing around, but you couldn't do the same with whisky. A bottle uncorked loses its power. The genie gets out through the opening.

The whisky came from Canada. It wasn't a country anyone ever came from, like Lithuania or Poland or Ireland. In Canada, you didn't have to make up funny-sounding words for drink, which meant there was no need for men like her father. One day, Bluma swore, she would go to Canada and never come back.

The Irishmen lifted their cups and toasted her. Then they began to talk about drinking. They said nip and pick-me-up and eye-opener, even though it was late afternoon and everyone's eyes should have been open by now.

"Deal us the cards, sweetie," one of the policemen said. "Last time you brought me a great spot of luck."

Playing cards was part of her job too. When they drank at the Coop, the coppers wanted her, a fifteen-year-old schoolgirl, to be their dealer. Maybe they imagined they were her father, and she their dutiful daughter. Maybe her cutting the cards and dealing made drinking seem like a family affair.

Bluma cut the cards and dealt. Her fingers were nimble, and she dealt like a pro. The policemen adored her, though she had no particular use for their affection, and no favourites, since she couldn't tell one from the other. What would it be like to have a copper for a father? A policeman's lot is not a happy one. She'd heard that expression, but these specimens didn't look too mournful.

Because she was a kid, and a girl on top of it, once they had their hands and their drinks, the cops didn't pay her much mind. They began to talk shop. They talked murder, solved and unsolved. The second kind made for better stories. Who got taken for a ride. Who bought his lunch. Who was wearing concrete overshoes and who was sleeping with the fishes. Who took the Ten Commandments for the Ten Suggestions. More euphemisms — they never ran out of them. Most of the unsolved crimes could have been solved if the right people had the gumption. She could have solved half of them with what she heard in the Coop, and then forgot, because who was she going to tell these things to? Burnside might have been at the far edge of the world, off the Almighty's map, but it had its share of murders. There were probably more crimes in Burnside than on Lexington Street, where everyone looked after each other, and no one slept in the prairie because they couldn't stand their fathers.

Her nervous stomach pulled at her. That's the way it felt: a pull, like the story of gravity Miss Reilly told her class. It came from her middle, and she couldn't separate herself from it. She didn't dare touch the place that hurt, not in front of the men who weren't like school-boys she wasn't afraid of. She started working over the leather strap that bound her books. A policeman looked over his cards at her.

"You've got homework, is that what you're trying to say? Then go on and study your lessons. We'll make ourselves at home."

"Your studies are important," one of them told her.

"Especially if you want to make something of yourself," the first policeman said. "If you do well at school, you can be a teacher or some such thing."

"Well, it's true, I do have homework."

"Go, my child. Your father will show up soon enough."

She topped up their coffees and chalked up what they drank in her father's ledger book. That was just for show, because policemen rarely paid for what they drank. She crossed the yard to the house. Her father wasn't in the kitchen, but the blue cigar smoke hanging like a cloud above the table told her a meeting between men had taken place.

Upstairs, her half-sister, Libby, was singing tunelessly to herself. Her father could send Libby to do the chores at the Coop next time. Bluma laughed at the idea. She was daring for even having thought it. Sending a half-wit girl to pour hooch and keep the coppers charmed — now how would they like that?

Bluma unstrapped her books and set them on the kitchen table. The lesson in her exercise book was no particular challenge. She had to list the requirements to become a citizen. The Americanization worker had been to the school, and her visit was the subject of the homework. Besides the Irish and her, there were plenty of Polish and Ukrainian kids in Burnside, some of them citizens, others waiting to be. Bluma didn't see their fathers in the Coop. It wasn't because they didn't drink. Her father wouldn't let them in.

She sat down to her homework. The cigar smoke hanging over the table sifted down and alighted on the skin of her forehead and kept her from concentrating. Where was her father? Out front, maybe, testing the fence built to keep Libby out of sight. Tomorrow, maybe she would find a body in the prairie. What would it look like? She would gaze into its face, unafraid and unsurprised. No one can avert their eyes from that sight. What does a dead man look like? Astonished, probably, because no one ever thinks it's going to happen to them. And mad too, really pissed off as hell at it being over already, even if it was never so great in the first place. The crows would have gotten to it. There were bound to be worms if you believed the song all the kids sang, and she did believe. The worms crawl in, the worms crawl out, they crawl in thin and they crawl out stout ...

She saw the ruin of her father's face in the prairie.

She shook off that thought. She never wished for that. So why think it?

Bluma couldn't do her lessons, and not because she didn't understand the simple thing the teacher asked of her, writing down the list of citizenship requirements, but because she was busy waiting for something terrible to happen. Waiting took all her energy. Half the time she couldn't finish her homework. Miss Reilly would pin donkey ears on her and make her wear the pointed hat and sit facing the wall, as if the punishment would help her learn.

BLUMA'S FATHER, ABE GOLDBERG, WAS a bull of a man: heavy-minded, slow-moving and determined. He was a plodder, the kind who could walk through a brick wall. His life had taken him from the village of Shukyan in Lithuania to the Burnside district of Chicago, and he never once weakened a decision through second-guessing or excessive thinking.

In those days, people were streaming into the country by the boatload. Abe Goldberg was the pioneer who'd moved the family to America. Abe Goldberg — it was a joke of a name, a Jewish joke, a joke played on a Jew. The story was almost too familiar to bear repeating. Goldberg's real name was Tabiliak, but Tabiliak was too big a mouthful for the customs man, so Tabiliak magically became Goldberg at the point of entry. Or maybe the man before him in the line was an authentic Goldberg, and said his name and had made it through, so Tabiliak figured the name would work for him too. The change didn't take place on the grand stage of Ellis Island, but at a government counter in Milwaukee, Wisconsin. The name was just fine with the newly baptized Goldberg. Immigration could have called him O'Malley, and he would have answered. He was alive, and he'd made it in. That was all that mattered.

After he sent for his wife and family, Abe didn't stay any longer than necessary in the comforting, fraternal poverty of Lexington Street. He didn't see the point of hanging around his wife's family, her sister Taube and her noisy, nosy brood. He didn't choose these people, they'd been handed to him; they were total strangers he had to make room for, and when he saw an opportunity, he took it. Opportunity knocks, that's what people said, and it doesn't knock in places where everybody is busy minding everybody else's business.

Confused and frantic impulses beat inside the newly minted Goldberg's brain, and he had the size and bulk to give them free reign. Sometimes he wondered, in the one or two moments of reflection he allowed himself upon waking, a luxury he couldn't afford during the rest of his working day, whether his change of name hadn't put him on the wrong track. He had been a Tabiliak, a man with a name, a family, a village. Then he became a Goldberg. A nobody, a generic immigrant, somebody else's invention.

He tried to think back to his life in Shukyan. The past lay behind curtain after curtain of experiences that needed to be forgotten, the big humiliations and the small daily ones he'd suffered despite his size. The past was like waves of heat rising from a dirt track in summer, distorting what needed to be seen. Had he always been this way? It was hard to remember. Memory was just another luxury he couldn't afford, but he didn't think he'd always been careless with other people. He never had the patience for those pale, birdlike boys hurrying to the synagogue to read their books. Maybe America had turned him into a monster; maybe it had happened on the way there. Something had happened. He began to do things because he could. Something had freed him.

ABE GOLDBERG CARRIED A SECRET that touched what was supposed to be nearest and dearest to him: his wife.

Abe Goldberg was not the first man his wife knew, though he had been her first betrothed. At the age of thirteen, Rachel was promised to him in the usual way. A group of men including her father met in a room in the rabbi's house to conclude the agreement. In attendance was the man who was promised to her, who lived in a hamlet outside the village. At the time, before marriage took its toll on her spirit, Rachel was a spunky, mischievous girl, disobedient within reason. At the solemn meeting at which her fate would be decided — though fate had stranger things in mind for her — she crept into the rabbi's house after sending in a playmate to distract the rabbi's housemaid. She stole up to his office door and peeked through the keyhole in hopes of seeing the man she would be spending the rest of her life with. Her disappointment was bitter, considering she had to pay off her playmate with her entire cache of sweets. Through the keyhole, she saw a room full of bearded men dressed in black. They all looked the same. Her father was the only one she recognized. As for the man designated to be hers, she couldn't tell which one he was.

But what the men of Shukyan had pieced together, the Czar in Moscow tore asunder. One day, a recruiting party of three soldiers on horseback rode into the hamlet not long after Rachel's betrothal and without warning, Abraham Tabiliak, her intended, was made a soldier in the Czar's army. When his parents protested that the boy was only sixteen and too young to kill, the press-gang leader had a ready answer.

"Look at the boy — a giant! If that isn't a man, then I'm not one either."

"I don't know why you're talking about killing," a second soldier told Tabiliak's mother. "All we do is sit around and peel potatoes. If he kills anyone, it'll most likely be at a card game."

"I don't play cards," Abraham offered.

The third soldier leaned down from his horse and patted him on the shoulder. "We'll teach you, my boy. Now get your things."

His family knew the routine. It was part of living where they did, and everyone had a kit packed for an occasion that you hoped would never come. A change of foot-rags and underwear, an extra sweater: a survival pack, always at the ready. His mother wrapped a piece of poppyseed cake in a paper. Once the strange-looking party — three soldiers on horses and a strapping boy on foot — got past the last house in the hamlet on the way to the barracks in Vilnius, Tabiliak opened the paper and shared the poppyseed log with the soldiers. He liked to identify with the strong.

When Abraham Tabiliak did not return after his first year in the Czar's army, as expected — who even knew where he was? — and when he didn't return after his second, and considering he did not answer a single letter Rachel's family sent him at great expense via the public letter-writer, her family began to worry about her future. She was nearly sixteen, and time was running its cruel course. Even worse, a young unmarried woman in the village with her dark hair bouncing freely on her shoulders was potentially a catastrophic force. After the second anniversary of the boy's disappearance, the same consortium of men in black met and decided that Rachel would be married off to another man. An older man she was instructed to call Mr. Reisz. She had not seen or heard of him before.

She continued to call him Mr. Reisz even after their wedding night, and the subsequent nights that little by little became less trying. It was true what the women of Shukyan had intimated to her before her wedding: she did get used to it. May you never have to get used to what you could get used to — that was village wisdom she'd heard from a dozen women's mouths about a dozen things that could happen. The thing that happened to her in the marriage bed could not have been as bad as what happened to her betrothed Abraham, who had disappeared without a trace. In bed, as Mr. Reisz went about the business that he didn't seem to enjoy very much, she made up wonderful tales about her intended's tragic fate at the hands of the Czar and his army. She devised stories of wolves, blizzards, birch forests and extraordinary courage, and she and Abraham were the heroes of every tale.

Soon her stories stopped sustaining her, and she blamed Abraham for disappearing and casting her in with Mr. Reisz. If he didn't want Mr. Reisz doing this thing to her, that he was supposed to do, and presumably would have done with greater affection, then Abraham should have answered one of her family's letters that inquired if he was still intending to return and claim his prize. True, she knew nothing about him, except that he wore a black beard and black clothes and was three years older. The biggest advantage he had over Mr. Reisz was that he wasn't there.

In her eighteenth year, Rachel gave birth to a girl. That meant the end of her secret stories about the miraculous return of her intended. The baby had vaguely Oriental features, which didn't surprise anyone at first. Even in this far corner of Europe, the Mongols and Kazakhs had left their imprint. From time to time, a brown-skinned, almond-eyed child with high cheekbones and a somewhat flat nose would appear in a family of fair-haired children. A member of the lost tribe, went the joke.

But Rachel and Mr. Reisz's daughter was not one of those. As the months went by, the village women made her understand that her Libby was a tribe unto herself.

Mongoloid children, the gossips told her, are visited upon women who wait too long and conceive too late. These children come as a punishment for their mothers.

"But this is not your case, my child," the women told Rachel.

She waited for the next piece of advice. It did not come. In the market square where the women had taken Rachel for their talk, away from the authority of men, they stood in a circle around her, arms crossed over their breasts, their shawls tightly drawn around their heads.

"If it's not my fault, then it must be his," she deduced.

"So you understand," they told her.

"He's too old," one of the village women said. "His seed is worn out and feeble."

The women laughed, then elbowed each other in the ribs as atonement for their laughter. But all this was less funny to Rachel.

"Then why was I married to him?"

"That we cannot say."

"It is a question best put to the men."

"That is, if you dare."

"It's a question you'll be chastised for asking."

The message of the Shukyan women's chorus was clear enough in its own cruel way. Mr. Reisz had put this thing in her, a poor creature who would never take her place in the village or know the joy of having children of her own. Rachel had nothing to do with it. She had committed no fault. It wasn't a mistake of nature; it was a mistake of man. She was a child thrust too early into the functions of womanhood, before she could possibly understand what was happening to her. Don't worry if you can't love or console or defend this man, even if he is your husband, the women counselled her in so many words. You scarcely know him, and he has nothing to do with you outside of the few minutes he spends camped between your thighs.

Why are they telling me this? Rachel wondered. What am I supposed to do?

The village women were long on bitter commentary, but short on useful advice.

It turned out that Mr. Reisz wasn't without feelings. Though enough time had passed to make her approachable again since Libby's birth, he began to practise sexual intercourse in the manner of Onan to ensure he wouldn't cause another child to be born. Onan wasn't a masturbator as the poor man is unfairly accused of being. He was a withdrawer. He withdrew and spilled on the ground, depriving the Lord of additional members of his tribe. From on high, all-seeing, God spotted this insubordination and had him destroyed, though not before giving him fair warning. Mr. Reisz came to be destroyed too, though he had never been disobedient toward his masters, on earth or in heaven. On the contrary: he obeyed them fully, to the letter. He did everything he was told to, including marrying a child. But his sense of obedience changed after Libby was born.

THE GIRL BLOSSOMED INTO A deeply retarded, affectionate child whom all of Shukyan cared for. She was a screen upon which the village cast its fantasies. For some, she was a mysterious blessing, or a wandering spirit looking for a dwelling. Whatever she was, the village was not so large or powerful that anyone could be neglected, even a Mongoloid girl.

But Mr. Reisz was blind to the kindness people showed his daughter. An old man's seed — do you know he's nearly forty? He heard those words in the market and they poisoned his mind, which is why men should not go to places where women congregate. They didn't mean him any harm, not personally. They were bored. Life in Shukyan was full of an unbroken, heavy sameness. From one crone's comment, Mr. Reisz built a universe of condemnation. He heard imaginary whisperings about his cock and how he'd used it. If thy right hand offend thee. That began to sound like a solution. No one spurned Libby or blamed Rachel. He was alone with the weight.

Mr. Reisz began to separate himself from life. The village whisperings sounded like thunder, though no one heard it but him. Slowly, people stopped thinking about him. He'd been blamed at the start, when Libby was a new phenomenon, because no one had seen a child like her in a generation. Gossip loves novelty, and the gossips of Shukyan soon turned to newer misfortunes. But for Mr. Reisz, forgetting never came.

He lost all affection for his wife. The little appetite he had for her body faded. Rachel noted the loss, but did not complain. What examples did she have of lasting tenderness between man and wife? There weren't words in her vocabulary for that kind of thing, and no law said affection was necessary for marriage. She thought of asking the village women for advice, then pictured their arms crossed over their breasts and thought better of it.

In the meantime, she was busy enough for three women. Libby needed constant care, and would not learn small skills, like how not to put her hand on the stove when it was hot. Rachel kept a stall on market days, where she sold food from the countryside. She travelled out to the farms unaccompanied to bargain with the peasants. A harder and more obtuse lot of human curses could not be imagined, and she had to drink glass after glass of vodka with them before they would begin to negotiate with her. A wonder they didn't make her eat pork. Her head spinning, nauseous with fatigue and alcohol, she could not bargain down these mud-people to a price that allowed her a small profit. Well, then, who cares? she told herself as she rose uncertainly from the kitchen table in some peasant's hut that, like hers, had a dirt floor. What more do you want from me? This is man's work.

During the second winter after Libby's birth, Mr. Reisz walked onto the ice of a fishpond that belonged to a wealthy merchant who raised brooding, sluggish carp in the unmoving waters. A weak spring fed the pond, weak but strong enough to create a current and keep the ice from knitting together securely. Mr. Reisz was a dozen steps from the bank when the ice began to give way. He didn't hear the sighs that would have warned any sane man to get off. The fishpond was not deep, but a man can drown in a bowl of soup if he's determined. In the Lithuanian winter, the cold kills before drowning does.

Rachel found herself back where she started. She was a young woman, unmarried, trouble and mischief just waiting to happen, worse now that she'd known a man. Something had to be done quickly. Shukyan had witnessed the birth of this strange child, and then an inexplicable accident. Anything could happen next.

THEN A MAN APPEARED TO marry her.

At the end of the winter of Mr. Reisz's death, a broad-shouldered young man with an empty look in his eyes turned up on the outskirts of the village. He wore a Russian army coat that looked as though it belonged to a dead man. On his legs he had something that was a cross between puttees and riding breeches. No one had ever seen such trousers. His boots had been nibbled on by rats.

Here was the man who was meant to marry Rachel in the first place: Abraham Tabiliak, who now stood not far from the spot where he had been spirited away by the Czar's men. His appearance had changed so much that no one recognized him. Reflection, humility, observation, a timorous, ironic nature — these things identified a Jew. Tabiliak had lost all of them.

He looked as if he had returned from the dead.

The villagers gathered around him. Slowly they figured out who he was. A boy was sent to alert his family.

"Where have you been?"

"What happened to you?"

"Why didn't you write?"

Tabiliak didn't answer. He had lost the ability to understand logical questions. When the villagers considered him more closely, they understood. Tabiliak had had to get used to what he could get used to.

Finally, he spoke.

"Rachel."

His voice was a monotone, but there was plenty of determination in it. He wasn't asking a question. The crowd pointed him toward her house, then followed after him. They were eager to see what would happen next.

He pushed open the front door without knocking. He came upon Rachel sitting alone in the room in a rocking chair, making soothing noises at a small child, who responded with high-pitched yelps of incomprehension.

Rachel looked up at the intruder and screamed, then muttered the prayer that protects humans against monsters, even as it acknowledges that they are part of God's creation too. She abandoned Libby on the chair and hid behind the partition that separated the former marriage bed from the rest of the room. Unlike the villagers, she had no trouble recognizing Abraham.

He moved around the partition and advanced on her as she cowered in a ball on the bed. A dead man had returned, the man she betrayed to marry another. Now he was back to claim his due. No one would reason with him on her behalf. She deserved everything that happened.

But Tabiliak didn't lay a hand on her. He had had enough brutality for the time being. He stared at her, one ghost gazing at another, and did not say a word. His long empty stare, his emaciated body·that still remembered its old strength, the way he could go forever without talking in a village full of blabbermouths — everything about him terrified her.

"You are my intended," he told Rachel.

She nodded. Tabiliak turned and walked out of the house. He crossed the fields toward the hamlet where his parents lived. He was satisfied. He had done what he'd come to do. When his parents made him understand that the strange-looking girl in the house with his betrothed was the fruit of another man's loins, a dead man at that, and that his intended was a widow, none of that made any difference. He wanted Rachel.

On their wedding night, Rachel could not help but display her knowledge of how bodies are supposed to mate. In return, Tabiliak tried out some of the caresses that the public women he'd used while in the army apparently liked, but Rachel didn't take to them. She turned and twisted in his arms as if trying to escape.

He spoke the words he had rehearsed, hoping they would sound gallant.

"I will plow the field anew," he told her as he lifted her nightgown, "so you will forget the harrows that were once laid in the dirt."

Rachel answered his crude poetry with something more down-to-earth.

"I was never plowed very deeply," she told her second husband. "So you won't have to work too hard."

What wife would talk to her husband that way, he wondered, and on their wedding night? The world had not waited for him. His wife had been with a dead man. He had been with army whores. They were even. That's all he could expect from life.

Tentatively, Rachel put her arms around his back. She had never gone that far with Mr. Reisz, but Tabiliak didn't feel her tenderness.

HE WAS SATISFIED WHEN RACHEL gave him children. First Laurie, then Bluma, born of his vengeful plowing. But he didn't know how to act when the babies were presented to him. He reached out to take Laurie as he was expected to, but drew back his hand.

"He has blue eyes. How can that be?"

"Foolish boy," Rachel's mother told him. "All babies are born with blue eyes. They'll change soon enough."

His mother-in-law was right. But even after the baby took on his colour, and began to look like him to a reasonable degree, he still didn't know what to feel. There was a word he'd heard when he was a boy, playing in the muddy road in front of his house: *nachas*. It meant the pride you felt in your children. That feeling was a complete abstraction to him. But at least he had made his mark; he had reclaimed the woman who'd been promised to him. And Rachel had been served too; the normal children were a relief. The blame had been erased, if not forgotten. Mr. Reisz was no more than a dark eddy in the stagnant water of the fishpond.

Now that he had his own children, the women of Shukyan expected Tabiliak to disown Libby, send her back to his wife's parents, or murder her under the cover of an accident. The village was already preparing to forgive him for an act that would wipe away the trace of that unfortunate match. But Tabiliak did no such thing. He could have crushed Libby's throat with one hand. Instead, he coddled her and played with her, and when he thought no one was looking, he took real delight in that small, otherworldly creature who seemed to need his love so desperately. Libby reached a secret part of him and gave it a voice. He kept his devotion hidden; he was more tender with her than his own children.

It was a simple case of one monster recognizing another. And Libby loved him back. Handicapped or not, she knew what was what, and where survival lay.

TABILIAK HAD BEEN SUCH A good soldier for the Czar's army that it kept him long past his normal period of service. He knew how to obey orders, and the Czar's men noted that quality. When it came time to use Tabiliak again, they figured he would be at the exact same spot he was the first time, some years older, but still completely useful.

This time, the Czar would want him to do more than consort with whores, play cards and peel potatoes. He would send him to fight the Japanese on the eastern front, a place from which no one returned. The point was not to win the war, but to get rid of the soldiers who, one day, would rise up against him.

Tabiliak wasn't vain enough to think It can't happen to me, and go on living his life until it was too late. And he didn't think he couldn't be who he was in any other place, the way some people in Shukyan believed, probably because he didn't know who he was in the first place and didn't much care. Unknowing turned out to be his advantage.

He left Shukyan on foot one day before dawn. No violins played. There was no singing and no one philosophized about America. No one even saw him go, though he did tell his wife about his plan the day before.

"When I get to America and get a job, I'll send for you and the children," he told her.

Every man who walked west into immigration said that. Rachel didn't believe a word. She wasn't particularly upset about her husband leaving. She liked Shukyan; it was all she knew. Besides, immigration was for men, not women.

TABILIAK WAS AS GOOD AS his word. Two years later, he summoned Rachel and the children. He was in Chicago, which could be found in America, and his name was Goldberg. He was waiting for her.

Don't forget, he had the letter-writer write, to bring Libby.

When the rabbi's wife read her the letter, Rachel was astonished. So was the rabbi's wife, though she tried to be discreet. Rachel had expected no such letter. She knew that men sailed off to America, full of promises to their wives, and were never heard from again. They found new wives and had new children in the new world. Not only did she expect Tabiliak to be one of those men, Rachel would have been happy with the arrangement.

Can a woman refuse a summons to America from her husband? She'd never heard of that happening.

Rachel wanted to ask the rabbi's wife if there were precedents for such a thing, but she lost her nerve.

"What's with the Goldberg?" she asked instead.

"This happens all the time. Think nothing of it. It's only a name. You'll still be who you are."

The rabbi's wife fidgeted with the strands of her shawl.

"He is asking for your first child too. That is unusual. Praiseworthy."

"Yes, of course," Rachel had to agree. "But it doesn't seem normal. Every time he has the chance to get rid of her, he does the exact opposite."

"And what is wrong with that?"

The rabbi's wife got to her feet and pulled the shawl tightly around her shoulders.

"If you can't do something yourself, don't count on others to do it for you."

Then Rachel found herself on the front step of the rabbi's house with the door closing behind her. Ahead of her lay America.

BLUMA'S BROTHER LAURIE NEVER SERVED in the Coop. As far as he was concerned, his father was a ghost, a bad smell on the breeze, a spider-web that stuck to him on his way to a more important destination called the future. Laurie had a sensitive streak from some earlier genera-tion. There must have been a book-reader or a musician or an amateur poet in the family past. No one knew what was hiding there. The ancestor's genes must have hopped across the generations and landed on him.

The list of things Laurie couldn't stand about his father grew longer every day. He couldn't stand his vulgarity. He couldn't stand the mishmash of English and Yiddish he used, neither one language nor the other. He couldn't stand the way he toadied up to the Irish cops. He couldn't stand the way he kept the Ukrainians and polacks out of the Coop, as if they were any different from the Irish. He couldn't stand the way he doted on his retarded half-sister. He couldn't stand the way he pushed around his mother when he wasn't ignoring her.

After every fight they had, once the name-calling and chest-thumping were finished for the evening, Laurie would storm out of the house with his own trademark dramatic flourish and hole up in the lean-to in the prairie, across the street. The fights usually happened at suppertime, when the five Goldbergs were thrown together for a meal — four and a half Goldbergs, Laurie thought, but he kept that insult to himself. If a fight didn't break out one day, it would the next.

Laurie was seventeen and nearly as big as his father, though he hadn't learned his father's violence, and didn't intend to. His father would shout at him about something, anything, an unobeyed order, and he would shout back, because Laurie believed in giving as good as he got, though it never went further than that. He played his father for what he was: a cracked fiddle that produced a single sour note.

"You don't respect me, do you?" Abe would challenge him. "Go ahead, say it! I dare you!"

Laurie hated this masculine vaudeville, this fake pageant. He came up with a better insult than the one his father was asking for. Laurie would stand in front of him and stare at him with a little smile on his face and say absolutely nothing. Then, slowly, he would turn his back and walk out the door. He headed across the prairie to the lean-to he had built with his own skill.

Laurie had built the lean-to after his first fight with his father. All over the city, boys his age and even younger understood they needed places of their own, hideouts they could count on, clubhouses for their gang. Laurie was different from them. He built his clubhouse for himself and invited no one. He was a one-man club and he liked it that way.

The location was designed to mock his father. Abe couldn't see his son in the lean-to, but Laurie could watch him. Laurie could look into the upstairs of his house, above the fenced-in front yard. Through the uncurtained window of his parents' room, his father paced and gesticulated and shouted at nobody in particular, and otherwise behaved like an overwrought clown.

The most important thing was not to become like his father. That was the first thing he understood. If I stay and fight him, he reasoned, I'll kill him. Sooner or later, I will. That's only normal. The story has to end that way.

But if I do that, I'll become just like him. And I don't want that.

Better let somebody else do it, Laurie concluded. Sooner or later, given the business he's in, someone will bash his head in with a pipe, or smash the end of a bottle and slit his lousy throat with it. Or maybe it'll be professionals, a shotgun from close range or a rain of bullets from one of those new mechanical guns. And with that satisfying thought, Laurie settled into his lean-to for the night, wise beyond his years and comfortable with his decision, and much more at ease than if he'd stayed in the house.

LAURIE WASN'T JUST TALKING BIG to himself. He knew that violence was in him. He'd taken it out and used it before.

When he first heard about junking, it sounded like a fair enough way to make some pocket money. It didn't involve hurting anyone, or at least not anyone he could see. Of all the possible crimes, it was the softest. He stole electric wire from building sites and public utilities, took it back to his lean-to and stripped the insulation off with a jack-knife, then sold the copper to a man he met by the train yards. The insulation ended up under a clump of bushes in the prairie.

It didn't take Laurie long to understand that the man he sold the copper to, who would fence it to someone else, made a lot more money than he did, even if he was at the origin of the deal. He went along with it until the injustice galled him too much, which didn't take long.

"I'm doing the hard part — the thieving," he said to his fence, a ferret-faced man whose name he never learned. "How come I'm getting such a small cut?"

"I'm taking the biggest risk here," the fence told him. "You're just hooking a little wire if you happen to see some lying around. If you don't like the job, get yourself another one."

Laurie did.

One of his high school buddies told him about a sweet deal with absolutely no middleman to take a cut from your efforts. There were places on West Madison Street where drunks hung out. When they got too high, it was easy to roll them. They always had a little something on them, and they were never in a position to call the cops.

Laurie followed his buddy Harry to a hotel on West Madison. They went in through the back, into a blind pig so dark Laurie wondered how he'd ever be able to find a mark. His buddy knew his way around. He told Laurie to sit at a table. Then he moved slowly across the room toward the bar, walking in a floaty kind of rhythm that Laurie had never seen before, and returned to their table with two drinks.

Soon men appeared from out of the darkness, drifting in slow motion, the way Harry had. Laurie put that down to them being drunk. Harry chose a pair of them as marks, and the four of them climbed the stairs into the darkness of a hallway. It seemed too easy to Laurie. There was no suspense, no risk. The two men were eager to walk into the trap. The rooms along the hallway were no more than stalls, with walls that didn't go up to the ceiling, like a changing room at a swimming pool.

It was a tight fit with all four of them in one hutch. Laurie looked to his buddy for the sign. Harry was busy yanking his mark's pants down to his knees so the man couldn't run. Laurie did the same. He looked to Harry for the next sign. His buddy had his dick out of his pants, and the mark was working it over. Then the mark kneeled down and took Harry's dick in his mouth.

That was the sign, Laurie decided. He slammed his mark in the gut with his fist. The man crumpled over without a sound.

"What're you doing?" Harry yelled, but Laurie was too busy going through his mark's pockets to answer.

"Help! The bastards trapped us!" Harry's mark screamed. Harry popped him in the mouth. There was no more out of him. He went through his pockets too fast to get everything, and the two of them ran for the stairs. Their victims' shouts echoed down the hall, but no one tried to help out.

Harry caught up to Laurie further down the alley.

"Don't run. A fellow running looks guilty."

Laurie knew his buddy was right, but he ran anyway. They got up to Halsted and caught a streetcar. It was going in the wrong direction, but Laurie didn't care.

"How come you let him do that?" he demanded when they were sitting in the back of the car.

"It's got to look real. Otherwise they get suspicious."

"Those weren't drunks."

"You got to be drunk to do what they do," Harry assured him.

"You went along with it."

"If I can get my dick sucked along with the cash, why not? But I'm no nancy boy."

"You're worse," Laurie told his friend.

"Count your money and be happy."

"I'm not counting. And I'm not happy."

"Suit yourself. You're awful particular for someone who has nothing."

"Right. Beggars can't be choosers. I've heard that before. But I don't believe it."

Laurie didn't count his take till he was back at the lean-to. It was good, but no amount would have convinced him to go back to rolling drunks, especially since those men weren't drunks. They were something else. He pictured Harry smashing the guy in the mouth, where his dick had just been. That was enough to make Laurie look for an honest job, not that there were any of those.

He was no better than his father. He lay back on his horse blanket and waited for his sister to show up, the way he knew she would, sooner or later.

Bluma had a sense for when her brother needed her. She would slip down to the kitchen and make sandwiches. Tongue sandwiches swimming in horseradish, or sardine sandwiches with oil blooming through the bread. She would wrap them in wax paper if there was some, or a clean dishrag if there wasn't. Laurie's hideaway depended on Bluma and her sandwiches.

BLUMA TALKED TO HER STOMACH as she worked on the breadboard. She kept one ear on the door in case her father came back and caught her. What's eating you? she asked her stomach. She got that from the Coop. The men would ask each other that when they were in a bad mood. She asked her stomach, but she got no answer, so she had to supply it herself. Nothing's eating me. I'm eating myself.

She cut through the prairie in the darkness, holding the sandwiches so tight she left thumbprints on the bread. No matter how fast she moved, the grass had time to grab at her bare legs and give her cuts and scratches. That was one more reason to go live on Lexington Street with her cousin Bella. There was no prairie. The houses were built close together, with no room left for unwanted things. Darkness had settled while she was making the sandwiches. It hid her from her father, but it could hide things in the prairie too. Bodies, living and dead. Men from the Coop ended up sleeping it off here when they drank too much. Laurie never knew how much effort it took her to bring him food. He was in the righteous grasp of his revolt, and had no feeling for his little sister. Sure, he knew she was nervous; everyone in the neighbourhood knew about her nervous stomach. That was just who Bluma was, like the colour of her hair or the shape of her face, or how she was a pretty girl who was developing fast.

The things she wouldn't do for her brother.

She called his name low, then crawled through the lean-to entrance. A candle was burning in a saucer, and the ground was swept as clean as the floor in their home — cleaner even, with the way her mother was getting. For a man, Laurie could really keep house.

He took the package off her. There was a red smear on the crust.

"There's blood on the bread," he told Bluma.

She looked at her hands. "Sorry." She sucked the blood off her thumb. "The knife slipped. I thought I heard our father sneaking back to the house, but it was only Libby."

"She won't tell on you."

Laurie fell on the sandwiches. A minute later they were gone. He tipped the wax paper into his mouth for the crumbs, then handed her the paper. She refolded it.

"Thanks," he said. "I could use a couple more."

"You're a growing boy. You need nourishment." That was just something to say. "Where've you been?" she asked him.

"How come? What's up?"

"You don't seem right."

"I was out job-hunting. Getting refused. That'll do it to you."

They sat a moment in the candlelight. Romantic, Bluma thought. People said candles were romantic, though she didn't know why. She wondered where he got them. They couldn't have come from the house.

"When are you coming back?"

"When he's dead."

"You can't say that. Take it back!"

"You're defending him?" Laurie laughed. "Okay, when he's out." He tapped himself on the temple. "Out cold."

"He doesn't drink."

"Like hell."

"He serves. They drink."

"He drinks. Afterwards. Take my word."

"That's what you say. I've never seen him drunk."

"I see things you don't."

Bluma wanted Laurie back in the house as a shield against loneliness, but it was useless hoping for that. Laurie hated their father. She started in folding and unfolding the wax paper.

"Leave off with that already, you'll put holes in it. And you're making me nervous," he told her. "Talking about people not seeming right, what's wrong with you?"

"Nothing's wrong with me."

"You look all clenched up."

"I'm playing a game."

"Yeah?" He waited for her to name it, but she didn't. "Can I play too?"

"No. I play it with myself."

"Sounds like a blast." Laurie watched her a minute. "You know, there are doctors for that. Pills and tonics and stuff."

"There's nothing wrong with me. I can't stay too long, it's night."

"Night's for getting away with things."

"Yeah — for you."

"For everybody. Ask anyone."

"Night's when people are afraid."

"You can be afraid during the day," Laurie said.

"Tell me about it."

Bluma stood up.

"Okay. Gotta go."

She stashed the wax paper in her shirt pocket. She brushed off her pants even if she didn't need to. She never thought dirt could be clean, but it was here. But the pile of horse blankets in the corner where Laurie slept looked itchy.

"I could never stay overnight here."

"You don't know what you could do," Laurie told her.

A heap of rough blankets stacked like burlap sacks, a dirt floor, no door you could lock — she didn't think so.

"I'm a girl," she said.

"I figured that out myself."

She pointed to the stack of blankets. She didn't know where they came from either.

"Girls don't do that."

"Girls do anything they want to. At least I hope so."

"Come back to the house, will you? Not for him, for me."

She begged him to promise and he did in a low, mumbled voice. It was better than no promise. She went out into the darkness, and across the prairie. A lamp was burning yellow and wan in Libby's room across the way. Her half-sister was allowed to leave the light on.

MISS REILLY WAS BLUMA'S SOCIAL studies teacher, the caring, compassionate, solicitous kind who can cause no end of trouble. Motherly, but unmarried; her students were her children. The teacher made her class dunce, then gazed at her with longing eyes. Bluma made the mistake only once, but it had stuck: she smiled back at her teacher. She didn't know what else to do. What are you supposed to do when someone looks at you and smiles? You can't look away forever.

The afternoon of the smile, Miss Reilly took Bluma by the arm as she was trying to make her getaway with the rest of the kids. She asked her to stay after class. It wasn't to beat the erasers or suffer any of the usual punishments. This time the torture was more sophisticated.

"I see the pain in your eyes," Miss Reilly told Bluma.

Bluma stared unblinking at her teacher. She was smart enough to see that this woman was setting a trap, but she didn't know how to escape it. The door that led to the hallway and freedom was miles away.

Bluma shrugged. "I don't know." She shrugged again. Her shoulders hurt from all that shrugging. "I don't know what you mean."

"You're not doing well in school. I know you can do better. You're not working up to your capacities."

That was the diagnosis she received four times a year, with every report card. Not working up to capacities. What did that mean? That she wasn't as stupid as she seemed? She knew that. Her parents didn't understand the words, and the first time her mother wanted her to translate. It wasn't easy explaining, and the job took all her inventiveness.

"Is something the matter? Something that's preventing you from working up to your capacities?"

"Sometimes, maybe; my stomach hurts."

"Where? Show me."

Bluma pulled her shirt from the band of her skirt and raised it an inch. She did the same with her undershirt. She made sure not to lift too high.

She pointed to her stomach.

"It hurts here. Sometimes."

Miss Reilly ran her fingers lightly over Bluma's skin, as if she could divine something beneath it. Her skin was as white as a sheet of paper from a notebook.

"Here?"

Miss Reilly rubbed a slow circle on her skin. Her fingers were cool. It felt good to have someone pay attention to her.

"Yeah, there."

The teacher straightened up and withdrew her hand. Bluma tucked her shirt in.

"It hurts all the time?"

"More after school than during. But during, I know it's going to hurt later. That's why I can't work up to my capacities."

ON THE WAY BACK ACROSS the prairie that afternoon, Bluma realized she'd been tricked. The worst part was that she'd tricked herself. She gave Miss Reilly what she wanted because the teacher was paying attention to her for once instead of putting that stupid dunce cap on her head.

What the hell was I thinking? Bluma wondered.

It was true. Her stomach did hurt. If some part of her hurt, she must be sick. But she didn't feel sick. Being sick is being incapacitated. Capacities and incapacities. Maybe she wasn't working up to her capacities, but she wasn't sick. Her stomach hurting was just who she was. It was only when she squealed on herself, the way she had, that people like Miss Reilly thought she was sick.

She didn't feel sick, but she wasn't well either. There was no one around who could help her puzzle out what that meant.

THE SCHOOL DOCTOR WAS A small man with a nose like a turnip and sandy hair sprouting out of his ears. A smell of formaldehyde hovered over him. When she sniffed him the first time, Bluma figured it was booze. A lot of doctors drank, just the way a lot of policemen did. But the smell was too medicinal to be whisky.

The man got the job of school doctor because his office was close to the school, and whenever there was some emergency, a playground tussle that produced a cut that wouldn't stop bleeding on its own, he got the call. Otherwise, his patients were single men who stayed in the railroad hotels and worked for the South Shore Line that ran east toward Indiana and the steel mills, and west into the Illinois farmland.

Bluma was being held in the waiting room of the principal's office when the doctor came bustling in, self-important with his worn alligator bag. She had pleaded responsibilities at home, family chores, but Miss Reilly told her it was too late. She had called the doctor, he was on his way, and in the meantime she insisted on staying with her and stroking her hand. At one point she slipped into the inner sanctum of the principal's office, and returned a few minutes later to tell Bluma she'd called her parents and told them their daughter would be late. Bluma knew it was a lie. Her mother didn't answer the phone and her father would have been in the Coop. Bluma was a prisoner of Miss Reilly's kindness.

"Tell Dr. LaRue what the matter is," the turnip-nosed man instructed Bluma. When he talked to patients, he referred to himself in the third person, as if he were Santa Claus.

"I'm here," Bluma told him, "and I don't want to be. That's what the matter is."

"But there must be something wrong. Otherwise I wouldn't be here either, right?"

Bluma pointed a finger at her teacher. "Ask her. She called, not me."

"This girl's stomach hurts," Miss Reilly said. "It hurts her so much she can't work up to her capacities."

"It hurts you all the time?" the doctor asked.

Bluma nodded.

"If you ask me, it could be appendicitis," Miss Reilly put in.

Just as Miss Reilly had done, but with considerably less gentleness, he had Bluma lift her shirt and undershirt. Where Miss Reilly had stroked, he probed. Bluma winced.

"Does it hurt you there?"

"When you do that, sure."

Dr. LaRue turned to Miss Reilly. When it came to teachers, he was the eternal pupil, still trying to curry favour to make up for his mediocre talents.

"It's swollen. Sensitive too. I believe that's what it is: appendicitis. We'd better take it out."

"We?" Bluma asked.

By that time, no one was paying attention to her. Even if I'm wrong, Dr. LaRue reasoned with himself, there's no harm taking out the appendix. It's not like something more important for a girl. The doctor had not forgotten his Hippocratic oath: at least do no harm. In his case, that meant applying the most cautious diagnosis that was least likely to kill the patient.

"LET ME SEE THE STITCHES."

"Yeah, let's see where they cut you."

Bluma was standing on the sidewalk in front of her house after school, the first day she was allowed out. She was bent from the surgery and walked like an old woman, which impressed the swarm of kids, the sons and daughters of Chicken Coop customers. She was a celebrity. No kid had ever been to the hospital before.

"Did you feel it when they cut into you?"

"No," Bluma told them. "They put you under."

"Under what?"

"They give you gas. You don't feel anything."

"That's no fair!" one kid told her.

"Let's see what they did to you!"

Leaning against the tall fence, she lifted her shirt and undershirt. The kids were disappointed. All they saw was a bandage.

"I want to see the cut," an older boy named Tommy complained.

"Later. When the bandage comes off."

"I want to see the other cut," Tommy insisted. "Further down."

That set off a storm of laughter among the boys. Bluma rolled her shirt down and tucked it tightly into her jeans. Then her father started bellowing from inside the house and the Irish kids scattered like crows on a train track. Her celebrity was brief.

The stitched incision, the bandage and the sickness from the gas had spared her from work at the Coop for a while. Her father got along the best he could, though the unwashed cups piled up and the sticky spots on the tables went unwiped. Abe tried to get his wife to do the cleaning, but she claimed the smoke gave her a headache. He needed Bluma at the Coop. When there was a girl around, the drinkers were less likely to get out of hand. Bluma didn't have to say anything. Her being there was enough to make men mind their manners.

At first the operation put her in a state of grace, and not just because it kept her out of the Coop. Alone in her room, with Laurie out in the world and Libby singing to herself from behind the front fence, Bluma could concentrate on the superficial pain of the surgery that replaced the deeper work of her body. Against Dr. LaRue's orders, she would peel away the bandage halfway, then tease and prod the young scar into a half-smile. I had an operation, she told herself. That means I'm cured.

A FEW DAYS LATER, BLUMA's vacation was over: turnip-nosed Dr. LaRue gave her permission to go back to school. She returned for the last week, which she spent gazing out the window and thinking about the summer. She had no vacation plans; escaping Miss Reilly's covetous looks would be vacation enough. The teacher seemed to think Bluma was her personal property since the phantom appendicitis attack and the operation. She'd discovered the girl's pain and diagnosed her trouble before the doctor did. She'd helped Bluma when the girl needed it most. In return, she expected appreciation and gratitude. Bluma was in her debt, and the debt was called love.

Bluma wanted no part of it. Every gaze Miss Reilly sent her way made her skin crawl. The teacher's kind considerations, like letting her take off the dunce cap, only made her stomach more nervous. She told it to shut up but it didn't listen. Bluma expected as much. She was waiting for the pain, and it did not disappoint. Her real self soon emerged from behind the superficial itch and ache provided by the healing incision.

One more week, she told herself as she walked up the alley behind her house. Her unread schoolbooks banged against her side from the end of their leather strap. She didn't care about grades or whatever revenge her teacher might dream up. One more week and her cousin Bella would be there. The going would get easier. No more having to explain. With Bella she didn't need to explain.

With all her worrying about Miss Reilly, Bluma forgot to say her secret prayer. Now it was too late. When she neared her house and got in earshot of the Coop, she heard men shouting.

Bluma began to run. She felt a fight brewing, and something drew her to fights. As she ran across the yard toward the screen door, her incision split open. Dr. LaRue was no more skilled with sutures than he was with diagnoses, but she didn't notice. She wanted to be near the action.

The Coop was crowded with men. She couldn't tell who was who, and at first she didn't see the Irish policemen who were kind to her. Men she'd never seen were throwing wild punches. Watch that haymaker! someone shouted. He was wearing a trainman's uniform. She had seen fights before, plenty of them, and the fighters always looked like they were enjoying themselves. They were fighting for the fun and joy and friendship of it. This time they were fighting to kill.

She pushed into the crowd and got to the middle of the melee. A man with a flat square face and straw-coloured hair was trying to punch her father.

"I tell you, you're open for business!" he yelled.

"I am closed to you!" her father yelled back.

The man was a Ukrainian or a polack, she could tell by his looks. There were a lot of both in Burnside, on the other side of the train yard, but they weren't allowed in the Coop.

They'd forced their way in, and they were trying to fight her father. They hated Jews, and Abe was the only one around. Hating Jews was a habit they'd brought over from Europe, and they couldn't get rid of it just because they were in Burnside now. Bluma was afraid of her father — most of the time she hated him too — but she wasn't like Laurie, who wanted him dead.

"Stop that!" she screamed at the man. "Stop fighting this instant!"

"He's going to get his clock cleaned!" a man shouted next to her.

"About high time too!"

"Where's the whisky key? That's what I want to know!"

Her father and the Ukrainian stood face to face, with their legs planted. They grunted when they took a punch, otherwise they were silent. The punches didn't seem to have any effect. The men were like train cars banging together in the yards. Bluma made a fist and punched the man in the thigh, but he didn't notice. She thought of hitting him where it hurts, but she was too scared to find the spot. Blood splashed onto her face and shirt.

"Stop it, you! All of you!"

She might as well have spit in the lake. Her shrill voice made no impression. The Coop was full of people she didn't know. They don't belong here, let them find their own Coop. Suddenly she was protective of the place that was the plague of her life. She pushed her way free and ran out the door, down the gangway and across the prairie, all the way to 95th Street. She was out of breath by the time she reached the police station.

A policeman was standing at the massive wooden counter, trying to change a tube in a radio with his fat sausage fingers. He looked up, annoyed, then got curious when he saw a girl.

"There's a fight at the Chicken Coop," Bluma told him, panting for breath. "You have to come and stop it! Ukrainians are killing my father!"

The man set down the tube. Two cops drifted out of their offices down the hall when they heard a girl's voice. Maybe she'd have a tasty story for them.

"What chicken coop is that? We don't know from chickens."

"Hurry up! You have to come and arrest them!"

The cops looked at each other. They knew the Coop she was talking about, and they knew her too.

"You go home now. This isn't your business. And it's not ours either. It's a private home, and we don't get involved in simple fights in private homes."

Bluma put her hands on her hips.

"You're just saying that because he gives you free drinks. That's why you won't help, Irish copper. I'll have to break up the fight myself!"

Bluma ran out of the station with the policemen's laughter in her ears. In the middle of the prairie, halfway home, she stopped. How was she going to break up the fight? She made a fist and pictured hitting the Ukrainian in the balls. What were balls like, anyway, and was there a special way to hit a man there? Multiply that by a dozen drunken men. She would have to slug every one of them in the balls, as hard as she could, one after the other.

She felt silly standing in the middle of the prairie with her right hand in a fist.

She veered off the path toward Laurie's lean-to and slipped inside through the low opening. It was empty. Laurie was out working, doing something he wouldn't tell her about, unless he was at school, which happened sometimes.

Bluma sat on the folded horse blankets. She thought of lying down, and almost did. She leaned back on her elbows, but wouldn't let herself go.

Leaning back made her stomach muscles hurt. She looked down and saw the blood, spatters of it from the fight at the Coop, and fresh blood from her stomach. She pulled up her shirt. The turned-in pucker of her scar had split and was leaking. She felt satisfied. She'd bled too. She was part of the fight.

The next minute she was cutting through the prairie toward the house. She couldn't remember where her books were. Maybe she dropped them in the Coop. The last time she remembered having them, she was running up the gangway. No wonder she was class dunce. She was always losing her books. No wonder she was always losing her books, living in the house she did.

The Coop was dead quiet. The prayer she'd forgotten to say had been answered.

She crossed the yard and looked through the screen door. Her father was sweeping the floor. He didn't look any worse for wear.

She knocked.

"What do you want?"

"Maybe I left my books here."

"This is no place for books."

Bluma took the hint. "Maybe in the house."

She turned away. She looked across the yard at her house but didn't go inside. She knew that one day Laurie would leave and never come back. She'd be alone without anyone to bring sandwiches to. Alone with her mother, who made believe she didn't notice that her husband was a bootlegger, a gangster, and that there were drunkards passed out in the yard. Alone with her half-sister Libby, that eager, affectionate animal she was jealous of.

I could leave, she thought. I could be the one to leave.

That was a great idea. But who would take care of her?

Who was taking care of her now?

She thought about marriage. It was a solution. But she was too young, and to get married, a girl needed a man.

THE KIDS AT BURNSIDE PUBLIC wouldn't be free to run wild in the streets until they'd had one final visit from the Americanization worker. It was

Miss Reilly's last attempt at correcting their deviant immigrant ways before they ran off into the heat and dust of their neighbourhood, the prairie, the banks of the new shipping canal and the bridges under which some of them camped for the summer.

There were a number of things you could not be, Bluma learned that afternoon from the Americanization worker — an earnest, big-bosomed woman with short, gun-metal grey hair and frameless glasses — if you wanted to be an American. You could not be a disbeliever in organized government, or associate with people who disbelieved in organized government. Why did the Americanization worker say "disbelieve" when she could have said "not believe"? She talked like a book Bluma didn't want to read.

The other thing you couldn't be was a polygamist or believe in polygamy. The Americanization worker paused to let the ripple of giggles subside, but there were none. No one knew what polygamy was, and no one cared enough to ask.

Then there were the things you had to do and be. You had to be attached to the principles of the Constitution of the United States. You had to renounce absolutely and forever all allegiances and fidelity to any foreign prince or potentate. Bluma liked the word potentate: the Hottentot potentate of Harlem. And you had to be able to speak the English language.

"Who among you was born abroad?" the Americanization worker asked the class.

Because everything the woman had said so far seemed harmless enough, with conditions easy to satisfy, Bluma lifted her hand. She looked around. No one else had their hands up. Even the kids she knew full well were born in the Ukraine or Poland weren't raising their hands. They were all lying low.

The Americanization worker pointed at Bluma.

"Do you have citizenship?"

"Sure. I guess."

"You don't sound very sure."

"I'm here, aren't I?"

"Do you know how to achieve citizenship if you were born abroad?"

Bluma reached her tolerance for answering questions. She slumped back in her chair, crossed her hands over her scar and stared at the Americanization worker and her chubby, homely face.

"Your parents obtain it on your behalf."

Bluma paid no attention to the rest of what the woman told them about dead presidents, glorious naval battles, the fight against King George of England — here, the Irish boys cheered — and the natural westward movement of the brave pioneers. She was waiting for the bell to ring.

Once she'd exited that building of nightmares she ran home and waited for Laurie. He went to high school when there was no offer of a paying job, and luckily for her, this was one of his school days. He walked into the house just after four, instead of dragging in at ten o'clock or midnight, depending on what he was doing for money.

Bluma intercepted him in the kitchen before he could go up to his room and hide, or take the sandwich he was making out to the lean-to with a bottle of milk.

"Let's go over to 95th Street," she told him.

"I just got here. What's your hurry?"

"I'll buy you a soda," she answered.

"You don't have the money."

"I'll kiss the soda man. He'll give me one for free. And one for you too."

"Do I have to kiss him too?"

"No. I'll take care of it."

"You're a girl, not a woman. You can't compete."

"Says who?"

Bluma thrust out her chest so her brother could feast his eyes on her cleavage.

"Stop that," he told her.

"See? I'm right! Admit it!"

"I sure won't."

Laurie was glad to get her out of the house and onto the street where she wouldn't advertise like that. He carried the bottle of milk and his sandwich as they walked down the gangway and onto the sidewalk. Bluma had no particular destination. The idea was to be out of their parents' earshot.

"What's your problem?" Laurie asked.

Bluma stopped on the sidewalk and looked back at the house.

"Are we citizens?"

"What are you talking about?"

"Citizens of the United States of America. In God We Trust and all that crap."

"I don't get it," Laurie complained.

"Are we American citizens?" she demanded. "How hard is that to understand?"

"Oh, that! You bet I am! One hundred percent American, through and through. You can't get no more Americaner than me!" He put his hand on his breast and began to sing. "My country 'tis of thee, sweet land of liberty ..."

"How do you know you are?"

"How do I know I am what I am? Is that what you're asking?"

"Yeah!"

"You're out of this world! How did I ever get a sister like you?"

"You don't choose your family, that's what I heard. So how do you know you're American?"

"Because my name's on the paper. I got a paper that says so, all right? The old man got it for me a long time ago. He put my name on that paper. He signed me up."

"All right." They began to walk down the sidewalk, a lot slower now, away from the prairie and toward the row of stores. "A paper.

That's what I wanted to know."

"Happy now?"

"Where's the paper?"

Laurie shrugged. "Search me. In the house somewhere."

"Is my name on it?"

"Sister, I really couldn't tell you."

Laurie lifted the milk bottle and drank off half the contents. It was amazing how food went into him and stayed there. He handed her the bottle and went at his sandwich. Bluma was fascinated. She stopped and watched him. He was all health, in full possession of his body.

He took back the bottle.

"I'm going to look for that paper," she told him.

His mouth was full of sandwich.

"You can help."

He washed the bread-and-meat mixture down his throat with milk.

"What can I do?"

"For starters, you can keep the old man busy while I go looking."

"I got an idea, Bloom. Why don't you just ask him where it is?"

"No can do. It won't work."

Laurie shook his head. There were times he pitied his sister. What was the point of worrying about the old man anyway? He was in the Coop most of the time. Their mother was the one who never seemed to leave the house.

"What's with you and this piece of paper all of a sudden?" he asked.

"The teacher had this woman come to class and talk to us. A real homely thing. She made me feel like I wasn't American."

She turned and started walking back to the house. She left Laurie standing on the sidewalk, with the bottom of the milk bottle pointing to the sky. He had to run after her to catch up.

When they got back to the house, their mother was sitting in her chair in the kitchen. Rachel looked at the two children she'd had with Abe. "Up to no good," she said. She could have been talking about anything. Laurie did something he never did, and it wasn't just to cover for his little sister's search upstairs that he thought was foolish. He pulled out a chair and sat down next to his mother at the kitchen table. He had no use for his father, and normally he had no use for the woman who married him either.

His mother looked at him suspiciously. "What's with you?" she asked.

"I can't sit with you?"

"Since when do you do that?"

"Since now."

Rachel and Laurie had no natural subjects of conversation, and it was a sacrifice for him to speak her language that he hated to speak. They sat in silence for a moment. Boredom drove him into daring.

"What do you do here all day? I don't get it."

She stared at him. Was someone asking her opinion? That never happened.

"I think about what used to be."

"Was it better than here?"

"I'm here. What can I say? Have you ever heard of anyone who went back?"

"No," he admitted. "Never heard of that."

"Some people must want to. I can tell you one thing: the journey isn't made for everybody."

"Then why'd you do it?"

"He sent for me. That was supposed to be an honour. He sent for you too."

"Is that so? I was how old? I had a say?"

"Did I have a say? Did I have a say when I married Mr. Reisz?"

She stared at him, hatred in her eyes, as if Laurie were the rabbi who married her off to that old man.

"Who in hell is Mr. Reisz?" Laurie asked.

"My first husband."

"You were married before — before him? I can't believe it!"

She waved her hand in his face. "That's what I get for talking. No one believes me. I should keep quiet? You're a man now, at least you think you are, so you can hear the truth. He's Libby's father. Mr. Reisz. The poor man drowned in a fishpond. Went through the ice, don't ask me how. There, I told you a secret. Now you can go away."

Laurie looked at his mother and thought *disorganization*. The Americanization workers used that word to talk about people who'd lost track of themselves somewhere along the journey. And here he had a case of disorganization under his own roof. But it wasn't that simple. He sensed his mother's cunning. She was building another woman to keep her company, a character like in a book, and she'd crawl into her skin to hide.

"Is Mr. Reisz my father too, or just Libby's?"

"Look at yourself. Then look at your father. You figure it out."

She shooed him away like a fly trying to land on her food. Laurie got up and walked out of the kitchen. It was the first time he'd let her boss him around in years.

He went upstairs. Libby was singing to herself behind her closed door. It was a kind of self-devouring. She liked to chew on the inside of her cheeks, and when she did, she made a sound he and Bluma called singing because they didn't know what else to call it, and singing sounded like something a normal person would do.

He knocked on her door, then opened it and walked into her room. She looked up at him, delighted. She could never get enough company.

She came and threw her arms around him.

He broke off her embrace and looked at her. She basked in his attention. Her fat, heavy features and sleepy eyes came from another man. What that meant, Laurie realized, is that his mother did not belong absolutely to his father. She'd had another man before him. He liked that. She moved up a notch in his esteem.

BLUMA CREPT INTO HER PARENTS' bedroom. Her mother was the only one who slept there, which meant that most of the forbiddenness had leached out of the room. If I had a secret, where would I keep it? Once Bluma asked that question, finding the paper was easy. She opened the chest of drawers. The first drawer held her mother's bulky underthings. She closed it fast, and as quietly as she could manage. She didn't like the smell of abandonment in that drawer.

The second drawer held her father's things. It smelled like smoke from the Coop, which was better than her mother's intimate apparel. Bluma closed her eyes so she wouldn't see her father's underclothes as she slid her hands along the rough wood of the drawer. He hadn't gone to much trouble to hide the paper.

Bluma drew it out and opened her eyes. "Petition for Naturalization," she read. It was addressed to the Superior Court of Cook County, Illinois. None of that interested her. She could read fast and understand everything when the subject mattered to her. Halfway down, Point Seven, her mother's name was inscribed. And below her, the children: Libby and Laurie. Her name wasn't there.

She put the paper back in the drawer. She could have left it lying on the bed for all it mattered now. The secret was out, and she felt a grim satisfaction. She would have been surprised if her name had been there.

Her mother was on the paper. She was there because she could work. She needed to be a citizen to get a job, but she ended up not working after all. All she did was sit in the kitchen and whisper curses to herself. Laurie was there because he was a boy, and that counted. Even Libby the retard was there. She might have been a retard, but she was an American retard.

Laurie came out of Libby's room and Bluma came out of her mother's and they met in the upstairs hallway. Libby's song droned on from behind her closed door.

"She's on the paper." Bluma pointed to Libby's room. "The retard's on the paper. I'm not."

"Don't call her a retard," Laurie said.

"You knew I wasn't on the paper. You knew it."

Laurie looked at his shoes.

"It's not my fault."

"Did I say it was your fault? But you knew it. You knew something about me I didn't know."

"That happens a hundred times a day. Maybe it doesn't matter."

"What are you talking about?"

"Maybe the paper doesn't matter. I mean, you're here, that's the important thing, right? You live here. And no one's the wiser, so it doesn't matter. Life goes on."

"Yeah, without me. American life goes on without me." She thrust out her breasts because she knew he hated that. "Do you see anything that's not American about me?"

"Actually, no."

Actually, yes, he thought. She didn't have that American quality called self-confidence. She didn't take up enough space. She wasn't a fighter. She was a mouse, and mice aren't American.

"Let's face it," Bluma told him. "He's got no use for me. Otherwise he would have signed me up."

"I got no use for him either. And you can take that to the bank."

"It's not the same thing and you know it. For all you're supposed to hate him, he still signed you up."

"I told you, it's not my fault."

"Stop saying that!" Bluma screamed.

She couldn't stand his excuses. His excuses, or anyone else's. She went down the stairs two at a time, through the kitchen and into the yard. On the way out she nearly took the screen door with her.

BLUMA CROSSED THE YARD AND pulled open the Coop's door. She went inside, letting it slam behind her.

Her father was in the side room, fiddling with a barrel of whisky.

He was holding a hand drill, and he didn't look especially happy to see her.

"What do you want?"

"Look at me," she told him.

"I'm looking."

"Do I look American to you?"

Abe Goldberg wasn't much for riddles. He lowered the hand drill to his side and breathed out noisily.

"I'm not."

"What of it?"

"Why didn't you sign me up for citizenship?"

Her father squinted at her. "Why are you bothering me about this?"

"How come you signed up Libby? I saw the paper. You care more about Libby than you do about me, even if she's hardly a person at all."

Her father didn't react. She didn't even have the satisfaction of his rage. He probably didn't understand a word she was saying. All that bravery, wasted on him.

"How come you didn't sign me up?"

"What are you talking about? I signed you up."

"You signed up one daughter."

"Yeah. I signed you up. Not Libby. That's the way your mother wanted it."

"That's not what I saw on the paper."

"Then somebody made a mistake with the names. Somebody wrote one name when they should have written another. But whoever did that, it wasn't me. I don't know how to write, and you know it."

Her father went back to his hand drill.

FIVE

Somebody Else's Memories

JOEY COULD BARELY DRIVE TO his office after his first conversation with his mother. It was early Sunday evening, and he was tremendously excited and monstrously fatigued, with a keen need to be alone. The afternoon provided him with everything he'd hoped for and more. His mother seemed to be afraid of nothing. He wasn't sure he could say the same about himself.

He massaged his right hand with his left as he pulled into the Ecological Solutions parking lot. His right hand felt like a claw, and if it hadn't been Sunday evening, their night off, he would have driven over to the massage joint operated by the Asian girls in the strip mall and had his hand worked on.

That afternoon, he had sat down across from his mother in front of a host of mementos and tchotchkes of every description, and pressed Record on the old cassette recorder he'd unearthed in his basement. She gave him a disapproving look.

"What's that thing?" she asked.

"A tape recorder. I can't believe I still have one. Let me just make sure it's working."

"I can see it's a tape recorder, Smarty-Pants." She shifted on her chair as if she were sitting on a tack. "That machine is going to do the listening for you? Aren't you going to listen?"

"That's the point. I can listen better."

"No," she declared. "You have to write it down. Otherwise you won't be paying attention. Not really. Write it down. Otherwise it won't be real."

He let out a breath of exasperation and clicked off the recorder. He rewound to zero and hit Play. You have to write it down, his mother repeated on the tape, as petulant as a little girl who won't believe she's not a princess.

Otherwise it won't be real, she repeated, as if on cue.

Joey hadn't written anything more than a thank-you note or a grocery list by hand in years. He scribbled away that afternoon, lagging behind by several anecdotes and anxious about missing something important, his mother watching his efforts. You'll never catch up to me, she seemed to be saying.

He unlocked the front door of Ecological Solutions and deactivated the alarm system. The office, mercifully, was empty. One thing he could count on was that his happily married partner Ozzie would not be moping around the office on a Sunday evening, pretending to be working, and surfing the sports sites on the computer. He was home, doing whatever happily married men did: nibbling on his wife's ear, running his fingers through her wavy locks, watching a Helen Mirren drama on PBS with her, their hands tightly locked.

Bless him, Joey said to himself. To each his happiness.

He opened his attaché case and pulled out an overstretched Office Depot file folder. The stack of canary pads was inside. Page one, chapter one: at least he had a beginning. His handwriting was a childish scrawl. He had forgotten how to write cursive, a skill his grade-school teachers had spent years drumming into him and the other boys who grasped their pencils like ice picks.

The problem with his mother making him write everything down, besides the cramps, was that writing turned him into a writer — physically, at least. That hadn't been the plan. He'd intended on dumping a pile of cassettes on Lia's desk and telling her to transcribe the whole mess. The armour-plated office manager — that's what he and Ozzie called Lia, since she had the gift of being able to fend off the few disappointed clients that any business produced. Whether Lia was going to do the job on Ecological Solutions' time or her own, with Joey paying her hours, was a detail. She lived by herself on a retired sailboat in dry dock facing the Sound. She had a golden retriever, she told Joey and Ozzie, and didn't need a man. Forty-five years old and through with love — that's what she told them the evening they invited her out to celebrate the first anniversary of her employment. Neither took her claim as a challenge.

On the other hand, did he really want Lia, the classic tough broad, listening to Bluma's life story? He wondered if she would have identified with her, or dismissed her as just another clueless victim.

She'll never have the chance to find out, Joey thought ruefully as he gazed at the pads covered in scrawled writing.

He went to the decorative wood cabinet that stood beside his and Ozzie's desks. It was the only piece of furniture made of solid material; everything else was particleboard and veneer from the Swedish import store. He reached inside the cabinet and drew out a bottle of Scotch and one of the thimble-sized glasses that stood on a tray, the whole arrangement a prop to be taken out when hospitality was called for to solemnize a contract. The glasses held no more than what it took to moisten the tongue, the message being that Ecological Solutions, though it thoroughly mastered the masculine art of hospitality, was a serious, sober operation.

There in the dim office, the disarmed security alarm blinking a friendly green and the wash of traffic on I-95 laying down a continuous oceanic soundtrack of restless movement, he raised his thimble in a toast. To himself, the guy who got more than he bargained for. And to his mother and her endless well of stories that described a childhood no one should have had.

Joey wheeled his chair back to the cabinet for a second thimbleful. A deep conviction lay behind his project, and he had no trouble stating it in so many words. Not only was Bluma nobler than he was, personally, experience for experience, blow for blow, but her entire generation was nobler than his. His generation was mediocre, and he along with it. It wasn't personal, he wasn't wallowing in self-denigration — it had to do with the challenges each generation had to face. Was there any grandeur in his mediocre ranks? He didn't see any. No grandeur, because no struggle. Name the battles of your life. Let's see … He submitted to a liberal education in the field of his choice. When that was done, he joined the march toward prosperity, with time out to engage in personal liberation. A trip to a third world country, perhaps, with a case of hepatitis being the only risk. And even when the promised prosperity went bust, the way it was doing nowadays, he made money off the decline.

That was Joey Krueger's America. Bluma's was a rougher, wilder place. Her generation built the country with no instruction manual. Immigration, the Depression, the attempt by some women to become persons in their own right, the war, the terrible settling in of the fifties with its anxieties about conformity … He had no confrontations like that.

Just as well, Joey thought. Nobility leads only to suffering. An afternoon spent gathering his mother's life story proved that much.

He wiped the thimble dry with a Kleenex and set it back in the cabinet. Then he went and stood over Lia's workstation. Brassy Lia. He bent and sniffed the top of her chair back, a rare and perverse form of sexual harassment. A perfume did linger there: the scent of brass. If some man cared enough to apply himself, he might find that Lia had a story as noble as his mother's. But for that to happen, the man would have to love her with the same devotion he had for Bluma.

He laughed out loud in the empty office. Well, why not? Why

shouldn't Lia have the same opportunity, or for that matter, why not Sheila, the waitress at the Italian place on US 1 who kept the Red Sox games at just the right volume, Lia's sister in brassiness, both of them armoured in a way he could never be? The thought was noble. All of a sudden he was being noble. One day every brassy babe would have her story told.

THE EYES OF THE GARDEN dwarves lit up in the sweep of the Volvo's headlights, their smiles leering out of the darkness in reflecting paint like Cheshire cats. What was it with Elke and garden dwarves? Not just dwarves, but ceramic rabbits and does and fawns and whole families of masked, lifelike raccoons making their way unfettered across the lawn. It must have been the European in her. People from the old continent love domesticating nature.

Joey switched off the headlights and the leering dwarves faded into darkness where they squatted, figments of the subconscious purchased at the garden supply depot. He stepped out of the car and smelled the fruit of Elke's labours. Freshly turned flowerbeds. Cedar chips broadcast over manured plots. He turned and gazed across the lawn toward Caroline's place. Her property was dark, inside and out, and it was too late in the evening for fireflies.

The two dogs, mother and daughter, began howling even before he put his key in the front door. By the time he got it open and entered the living room, they were beside themselves with anxious joy at the prospect of hoisting their sausage bodies the length of his calves.

"You missed them," Elke said from the kitchen, looking up from the dishes.

On Sunday, them could only mean early supper with her kids, Sabrina and Stefan, out of the house and in their own apartments. They had moved so quickly through the obligation of Sunday supper that the extra set of dishes in the sink was the only record of their visit.

"Sorry. I needed to think."

"Is that so? About anything in particular?"

"Today was my first conversation with my mother."

"Mama's boy," she said.

"For me, that's no insult."

"Of course not. You're a model for sons everywhere. A man so attached to his mother — we don't see that every day in this modern world."

"She supported me every time I needed support. This is the least I can do."

"I know all about it. She supported you when your first wife left you. She supported you when you couldn't find work. You slept on her couch. I know that story."

"I refuse to feel shame for those things."

Elke thrust her hands into the sink and began scrubbing the dishes her children had eaten off. Roast beef had been served, he observed. Elke served it as often as possible, the former European displaying her American prosperity.

"Don't tell me," Elke concluded. "Your mother was a saint."

"Oh, she wasn't that, not for a minute. Not now and not then. If you want to read her story, you'll see what I mean."

"No, thanks. Family doesn't interest me. You know that. My own family doesn't interest me, so why would I care about someone else's, unless they were serial killers or something unusual like that."

"I can't help you there. We're not ambitious enough for that. But don't worry, it turns out there's plenty of violence."

The dachshunds came into the kitchen, their toenails clicking on the wooden floor. They milled around their owners' feet and began barking, drowning out all conversation. The dogs had a nose for conflict. Whenever Joey and Elke were on the cusp of a disagreement, they galloped into the room in their sausagey way and laid down a carpet of noise.

"The dogs need a bath," Joey noted.

"I gave them a bath. Well … they gave themselves a bath. They played with the hose."

"Then they rolled in manure."

"That's possible," she admitted. "Though I call it fertilizer."

The dishes washed, Elke wiped them dry and set them in the cupboard. Satisfied, the ever-vigilant dogs filed out of the room. Joey considered the bare table and the wiped counters, and understood he would have to forage for his dinner. He went exploring for leftovers in the fridge. A slab of roast beef lay in its congealed juices. He left the door open as he cut a slice off the roast. Leaving the door open was designed to drive Elke crazy. She grew up in Germany in the desolation after the war, and refrigerators were objects of veneration. Any outrage to their precious, temperamental nature made her cringe.

"Please don't dirty what I just cleaned."

"I promise, *liebling*."

"You know," she said to his back, "a lot of men love their mothers too much. It's a current social trend."

"Are you trying to tell me you think I'm gay?"

"Well, you are dying your hair. Isn't that gay?"

"I'm trying to look young. Younger. That's a current social trend too."

"Miss Clairol doesn't suit you. Especially not that charred aubergine colour."

"How do you know about Miss Clairol?"

She sized up the damage he'd done to his hair. "We do live under the same roof," Elke reminded him. "Even if I have to share you with your mother."

Like magic, the dachshunds appeared again, barking and snarling at each other in their play fighting, a kind of canine parody of what their masters were attempting to do.

She headed into the living room and the dogs followed, mother and daughter tussling with each other. The racket didn't stop until Elke was safely seated in front of the television, the place of no talk.

He chewed his beef in the kitchen in the ensuing quiet. The dog smell lingered in the air, dampening his appetite. He, Joey Krueger, gay? No one would mistake him for that. He was too sloppy, too unconcerned with his appearance despite the Miss Clairol, and far from handsome enough. How could someone so messy have been an architect?

He looked up from his plate to see Elke in the doorway.

"You eat standing up, like a horse."

"Horses don't eat meat."

"I'm going to tell your mother you're eating meat."

"How could you? You don't speak to her."

"Mother — always mother. I don't get it. Maybe if she weren't always in your thoughts, I would feel more like marital intimacy."

"I don't believe I've come scratching at your door for some time."

"Such a way with words. You're just as happy like that. You won't be distracted from thoughts of your mother by your wife's body next to yours."

"Don't be ridiculous. One has nothing to do with the other."

"Say that again," Elke advised, "and you'll hear how wrong you sound."

When she saw that Joey was not going to co-operate with her experiment, she turned and went up to her room. Her husband might as well have been an elephant she was trying to provoke with a twig.

In the quiet kitchen, Joey listened to Elke move around upstairs. Marital intimacy — where had she found that one? He preferred this form of marital intimacy: following his wife's footsteps on the floor upstairs after another unheroic spat as he dreamed of being elsewhere, in the house next door, where there was everything to learn. Mother — always mother. Elke was right. Even when it came to their marital friction, he thought of Bluma and how she fought with his father, though he remembered nothing of all that. But she must have fought with him, since they broke up. That deadbeat, the bastard was ruining my life, he remembered her telling him as they carried their belongings out of the house. They had taken a taxi, a grand occasion and a noteworthy expense, and that thrilled Joey.

A hair separated itself from his scalp and landed on his plate. He picked it up and examined it in the glare of the ceiling fixture. Miss Clairol had been the economical choice, and buying a product off the shelf meant he didn't have to go public with his secret New Year's resolution to begin doing something about his appearance. Maybe Elke was right. Miss Clairol did not flatter him. On his head, the dye underwent an unfortunate transformation and took on the colour of charred eggplant, as if he had fallen headfirst into a plate of antipasto.

He opened the cupboard door where the trashcan was and dropped the hair into it. Trust Elke to locate his weakness. Joey peered at himself in the little mirror above the kitchen sink. Maybe he should have asked for lessons at the cosmetics counter.

Then it was his turn to move around upstairs. He walked past the laundry hamper, opened it and looked inside. Nothing but his rarely used jogging suit, rolled into a ball. He reached in, pulled it out and shook it. No ladies' socks or panties flew free. She had washed her clothes and left his in the hamper.

He continued to his room and sat on the single bed, a boy's bed. He tried to remember the scene that would have led to his mother putting him into a taxi with their suitcases, on their way to her cousin's apartment, but nothing appeared. Nothing but his single boyhood memory: the picture of himself in Mary Barone's lettuce patch, muddy tears running down his cheeks as the Barone kids ran off to some place he could not follow. He sat bawling on the ground until he got bored with his own crying, then began pulling the outer leaves off the lettuce plants and eating them, out of spite, not out of hunger, one plant after the other, in a destructive rage. He did not stop until a snail shell shattered beneath his teeth and woke him to what he was doing.

A FEW EVENINGS LATER, AS Joey and Ozzie Georgandas sat eating tight rolls of capicollo at the bar at the Italian joint with their elbows in puddles of condensation, Joey made an unusual admission. He mentioned that his wife was refusing to wash his clothes.

Ozzie gave him a careful, evaluating look.

"So what?" he asked. "The machine does the washing, not your wife. Do you really think Elke's scrubbing away with a washboard and a bar of laundry soap?"

"I should have your common sense."

"I'm just not into the symbolic stuff. I mean, if women went down to the river and scrubbed out our underwear on the rocks, I could see the value. You do know how to use a washing machine, don't you?"

"I used to go to the laundromat when I was a student. Good place to meet girls."

"Right — let me help you fold your sheets, baby. Those were the days." Ozzie knocked off the nostalgia and told Joey, "You don't have to put coins in the one in your basement. Just turn the knobs."

"I'll give it a try."

Sheila stopped by their spot to refresh their drinks with her legendary loose wrist. She saw that male bonding was taking place, and lingered just out of range. Once she figured discretion was no longer needed, she fell upon them.

"How was Day One with Mama?"

"Exhausting. The hardest work I've done in years. I don't know who was more beat, her or me."

"Getting old must be terrible," Ozzie commiserated.

"The opposite of getting old is dying. That's what she says."

"Isn't there any other choice?" Sheila asked them.

Both men laughed uneasily.

"Take all the time you need with her," Ozzie told him.

Joey shook his head in disbelief. "How come you're so good to me? I can't get used to it."

Ozzie played dumb. "Used to what?"

"I don't know. Friendship. Affection. Whatever."

"Don't be afraid! Look at me, I'm not afraid to show the love," Ozzie told his friend.

He turned to Sheila, who was trying her best to look casual. But when men started talking emotions, she couldn't help but eavesdrop. It was part of a study she was undertaking — that's what she told men who caught her in the act. She suspected that men had feelings after all, and she was gathering evidence to prove it.

"Show me the love," Ozzie told her.

She smiled, and every line in her face burst into honest, delighted beauty.

"Oh, you're such a young and tender thing!" she said happily.

She wiggled the fingers of both hands in his direction, sending out waves of endless love.

"If you weren't married, I'd take you home and make you my special pet."

"I've never been anybody's pet," Ozzie admitted. "I wonder what that would feel like."

"You'd get used to it fast," Sheila promised him.

He rose from his stool and got his bearings. Brassy Sheila and her free-pouring hand had propelled him into intoxication. He patted his coat pockets for breath mints in case a patrolman should cross his path.

"Your problem," he said to Joey, "is that you think you have to deserve love to get it. That's absolutely false. Love is not a meritocracy. You just have to find somebody with the capacity for it."

He stuck his finger in Joey's face. "The biochemical capacity. And now, talking about love, I'd better be heading for home."

Joey put his hand on the bill. "I'll pick it up."

"You got the last one."

"Who's counting?"

"You ask me why I'm so good to you, Joey. But you know the answer."

"I do?"

"Sure you do. Because you're that way with your mother. You're a better man than you think. Get used to seeing yourself differently."

Ozzie clapped Joey on the shoulders. From the TV screen, the Red Sox players looked on in envy at their show of emotion.

Then Ozzie turned to Sheila. "The love." He wiggled his fingers in her direction.

"Go on, now! You're too young for me."

She swatted away his imaginary roaming hand, imaginary because Ozzie would have never tried to get fresh with her. The restaurant was family: forgiveness for small foibles was ever abounding, but there were limits. And like any good mother figure, Sheila didn't want to favour one customer over another. Ozzie over Joey. Especially since Joey needed the love hardest.

IN THE MEGA-WALGREEN'S AT the Branford Super Plaza, Joey understood his mistake. It came from a combination of inexperience, which he couldn't be blamed for, and his unwillingness to ask questions, which was a personality defect.

He stood in the hair-colour aisle and glared at the rows of pretty women on the Clairol boxes. He had a problem: he couldn't remember the shade he bought that had given him that eggplant look, so he couldn't be sure he wasn't buying it a second time.

Don't be one of those men who won't ask for help, he lectured himself. Communicate with the appropriate person. It's not a shame not to know, but it is a problem if you won't admit you don't know.

Powered by that post-masculinist philosophy, he stopped a teenaged stock girl with a nose ring. He pointed at the Miss Clairol babes.

"Do you have hair-colouring products for men?"

She gave his head a sidelong look. "I see what you mean. You're in the wrong aisle."

"But there's all this stuff here ..."

"Aisle three. Next one over." She found him totally clueless. "Do you really think they'd put men's products and women's products in the same aisle?"

And with that information bestowed, the stock girl walked down the aisle.

Aisle three contained shaving products, deodorants with athletic names and hair colouring in the basic male shades of brown, black and blond. Words like "shimmering highlights" and "sheer glossy colour" were noticeably absent. And there wasn't a dizzying array of choices as there was in the women's section.

Joey opted for brown. Then he chose Clairol Natural Instincts. Of course instincts are natural, he scoffed silently. If they had to be learned, they wouldn't be instincts.

He wondered if it was instinctual to colour your hair. Probably not. But it was instinctual to want to appear young. Or younger, in any case. It had something to do with procreation. The more vigorous a male appears, the greater his chances of multiple mates, and the more seed he can broadcast. That's instinct, isn't it?

He headed for the cash, his hand wrapped around the box, hiding the dye.

SIX

The Two-Girl, All-Girl Gang

THE FIRST SATURDAY MORNING AFTER classes ended, a giant, lurching, nine-passenger Packard pulled up by the fenced-in yard in front of Bluma's house. The horn sounded, as if the Packard needed any further attention. Bluma's cousin Bella was at the wheel, sitting on a telephone book.

"I'm here!" she shouted out the open window.

She took her foot off the clutch too quickly and killed the motor, but that didn't matter. She had arrived. At sixteen, Bella didn't have much experience at the wheel. One of her gang of brothers had driven down from Lexington Street, and a half-block from Bluma's house, they decided to sit her on the phone book and have her drive the rest of the way to make a stirring entry into her summer vacation.

Bluma watched the scene from the upstairs window. The phone book made her jealous, the way Bella's brothers had taken the trouble to put one in the car, and driven it all the way from Lawndale on the West Side, just to make a joke that would last a few seconds. Now that was family love.

Her brothers piled out of the car. There were five of them, but they moved so quickly and were so busy doing so many things at once that it seemed there were twice as many. They were named Harry, Rudy, Sam, Jack and Izzy, but they had a way of changing their names on a whim, sometimes in the middle of the day and without telling anyone, so it wasn't easy for Bluma to know who was who. Her cousin Bella never had any trouble. Her brothers flowed around her and protected her, knowing where to be and what she needed and when she needed it. They moved and thought as one person, a single big brother with five heads and ten arms. They were wise guys, guys who knew what was what. They pooled together to buy the Packard, each according to his means and needs. Though they were socialists at heart, they had nothing against accumulating capital, but only to spend it, preferably as quickly as possible. They wouldn't do just anything for money, except maybe change their names, because their names weren't who they really were. And they didn't believe in the banking system. Unspent money was wasted money.

Bella jumped down from behind the wheel and the phone book tumbled down after her like the walls of Jericho. Two of her brothers were busy lifting her bicycle from the rumble seat where it had been riding shotgun. The others were unloading crates of fruits and vegetables that Bella's mother Taube had put up, since she had divined long ago that her sister Rachel was unskilled at keeping house. Just because Rachel couldn't cook shouldn't mean that Bluma and Bella would go hungry. Her brother Rudy, who had recently changed his name from Adolph, dug into a compartment deep within the Packard, came up with Bella's kit bag and handed it to her.

Bella grabbed the bag from her brother and ran down the gangway, shouting all the way. She charged into Bluma's house; it would have been an insult to knock first. The family commotion attracted Laurie, who came walking across the prairie from his lean-to, twigs in his hair. It did not look like he had slept well.

"How do you like that? It's the hayseed!" Harry shouted happily. "Farmer Layb is here."

"Where's your corncob pipe?" Rudy wanted to know.

The five brothers embraced Laurie, not before industriously working the twigs out of his hair and brushing off his clothes. The brothers were in their zoot suits. It wasn't even noon, but they looked like they were on their way to go dancing. And not at the Jerusalem Academy or the Lonely Fellows' Club, where you had to pay for the girl. They each had one of their own, all of them, girls who loved to press their bodies against theirs for the sheer joy of it.

"It's all right if you look like a farmer," Jack reassured Laurie. "Burnside is the country. You got a cow around the back? Can we milk her? I've always wanted to learn how."

"Knock it off. And don't call me Layb or I'll bust you one."

The five brothers drew back in mock fear.

"All right, all right, we'll do anything you say. Just don't slug us. We're not fighters, we're lovers!"

They fell on Laurie, tousling his hair and giving him Indian burns on both wrists.

Sam lifted the box of preserves and thrust it into Laurie's arms.

"Our mother wanted your mother to have this. It's a little gift from our house to yours."

"Thanks."

"The family's got to stick together," Rudy said. He had the gift of making a cliché sound like criticism.

He wheeled Bella's bicycle down the gangway and into the backyard, then leaned it next to Bluma's. The girls owned the same style of bike with the exact same wicker basket attached to the handlebars, and the exact same bell: Schwinn bikes from the West Side factory not far from their apartment.

"You're a couple of sharp girls," Rudy said admiringly. Then he wolf-whistled at the bikes.

His brothers followed him into the yard. They peered through the screen door into the Coop, the place their mother talked about in low tones of trepidation and disapproval. Bootleggers did not particularly impress the brothers. Half their neighbours on Lexington Street had portable stills in their closets or on their back porches, courtesy of local commercial interests. And they knew any number of priests and rabbis with permits for sacramental wine, including a Negro rabbi who supplied the Jerusalem Academy. But a real blind pig was a step up from the small operators they knew.

"Don't go in there," Laurie advised. "He doesn't like it."

"We wouldn't go," Izzy assured him, "even if he invited us."

"And not because we don't care for a drink from time to time," Sam added.

"Or even from time to time to time," Harry finished.

"We can't stay," Rudy told Laurie, cutting the comedy. "We gotta see a man about a dog. But when Sabbath is over, which is tomorrow, as you well know, our mother will come and visit your mother and make sure everything's copasetic."

"Assuming she's invited," Izzy said.

"Or even if she's not," Rudy added, ending the comedy on a sour note, which was what the brothers preferred, despite their hijinks and vaudeville routine. They liked to laugh, but not because things were funny. They laughed with bared teeth.

"MY SWEETNESS!" BLUMA YELLED. SHE ran down the stairs as Bella burst into the house. Bella might have been skinny, but she practically took the screen door off its hinges.

The girls hugged in the kitchen next to Bluma's mother, who stared at them in disbelief. The girls ran to Bluma's upstairs room and slammed the door. They did what they always did every time they got together: they stripped down to their undies and pulled on each other's clothes. Bluma took a look at her cousin. A carpenter's dream, flat as a board. Bella pulled off her sleeveless T-shirt, something handed down from one brother or another, or maybe from all five of them.

Her nipples were as dark and hard and closed as two nuts.

"When you gonna get real titties?" Bluma asked.

"For my next birthday," Bella told her. She put her hands over her breasts, then drew them away. "My brothers promised me a pair. Brand new ones too, not hand-me-downs for once."

They laughed and Bella threw her T-shirt at Bluma's head.

"Your brothers don't give you breasts. Your mother does."

Bluma pulled on Bella's shirt. "I don't know if this thing is gonna fit. And you can see right through it."

"You'll stretch it with what you got."

"Jealous?" Bluma teased her.

Bella shrugged.

"Don't be," Bluma advised.

They pulled shirts over their undershirts and put on each other's trousers. Bella's were boys' pants whose hem her mother had let out. Satisfied, they admired each other in their ill-fitting clothes.

"Now we're just right!"

"We're perfect!"

"I better go say bye to my brothers."

The girls ran into the yard to soak up the Lexington Street admiration.

"Now I can't tell who's who," Rudy said.

"That's the idea," Jack reminded him.

"You girls be all right," Harry told them. "We're going."

"Going, going …"

"Gone!"

The Lexington Street gang climbed into the Packard. Izzy started the engine and put it into gear.

"What are you girls gonna do?" Sam asked.

"Ride our bikes," Bella said happily.

"And you got nice ones," Rudy complimented them, and was rewarded with a punch in the biceps from his brothers.

"Back to civilization!" Izzy said with heartfelt enthusiasm as the car lurched into action.

"See ya, Hayseed!"

"Bye, Layb!"

Laurie watched them pull away. Layb, my ass, he thought. Hayseed, yourself. He was as jealous as jealous gets. It was worse than with Mary Anne who kept promising to come to the lean-to. He wouldn't have been this jealous over her.

That's because this was the better kind of love: family, unconditional. He'd never known that kind, and it galled him when that gang of monkeys descended on his house to deliver Bella to his sister. His sister's best friend's brothers — he could hardly force himself to say what relation they were to him: cousins. His blood. They showed up his revolt for what it was: play-acting. His lean-to was like a kid's tree house. They were in the world and he wasn't. He'd better do something about that.

His sister and Bella were riding circles in the yard on their bikes, getting on his nerves with their one-note kid bells. They were laughing, but it wasn't carefree. They were getting ready for the big transgression. Laurie had given them the idea. Don't go in there. He doesn't like it. That's what they were going to do. Go in there. They didn't need to plan or discuss. It was a thing they could do and maybe get away with.

Bella hopped off her bike and leaned it again against the Coop. The place ruined everyone's life, or so she heard, but it felt pretty fragile to her. The pieces of wood plank would come off in her hand if she yanked hard enough, and she wouldn't have minded doing just that. She went to the screen door. It was on a tight spring to make it shut fast and keep out the flies. Flies like sugar, and that's what booze is. Candy for grown-ups. She found a brick on the ground and wedged it against the bottom of the screen door so it gaped open. This was for Bluma. She was doing what Bluma wanted to but couldn't without her.

They bounced their bikes over the low threshold and rode into the Chicken Coop. It was like that Jewish story, the Chanukah one they heard when they were kids. They came in and desecrated the temple. There were bad guys, the Greeks, who conquered Jerusalem and entered the temple with pigs and stone gods. That was bad, like the Irish kid who crapped in Miss Reilly's desk drawer and got caught. Bluma and Bella desecrated the speakeasy with their bikes. With her cousin's strength, Bluma pedalled straight into the place that made her guts churn and rode circles on the plank floor and yelled at the top of her lungs.

"My sweetness!"

When I'm with you, I'm strong.

Their fat tires left dust tracks on the floor. They couldn't get up much speed, which meant they didn't have a lot of balance; they banged into the round-backed chairs and the scarred tables, tipping them this way and that. When Bluma saw how easily a table turned over, she rode right into one and kicked it so it toppled over like a drunk. When they were good and ready, and not one minute before, they rode into the backyard, up the gangway and all the way to the stores along 95th Street.

They stopped alongside the curb. They were out of breath.

"How come he didn't come and yell at us?" Bella asked. "I thought he was bad that way."

"I don't know where he is."

"I thought we weren't allowed."

"Oh, I'm allowed, but only when he wants me to work."

"You work there? You work in a speakeasy?"

"Sure. You wouldn't believe the stuff I do. I serve drinks to coppers and act charming. I cut the cards and deal."

"That's like real life!"

"I sure hope not," Bluma told her.

"Sorry." Bella shrugged. "That just sounds so grown-up, like something my brothers would do."

She looked down the street, then scuffed at the curb with her shoe. The Coop came between her and Bluma. She should have done it more damage.

"What do we do now? It's got to be something good for our first day."

"Good and far is more like it," Bluma said. "I know. Let's go dip our tires in the lake."

"How far is it?"

"I've never been. But I know which way it is."

They started east on 95th, following the streetcar tracks. They wobbled down the middle of the street with the trolley driver banging on his bell behind them to scare them off the tracks.

"What did the German boy say to his mother? Look, Ma, no Hans!" Bluma called to Bella, and lifted her hands off the bars.

"Last time I heard that I fell off of my dinosaur," Bella yelled back.

The shopkeepers heard the bell and looked up. They recognized the bootlegger's daughter who'd been hauled out of school and carved up by that drunk of a quack doctor who made his living off railroad accidents. She was making a spectacle of herself and holding up the streetcar, nothing like the beaten puppy-dog she usually was with her schoolbooks clutched against her stomach.

The streetcar veered off and Bella and Bluma kept going. They bumped over the sets of railroad tracks that guarded Burnside.

"I've never been this far," Bluma told her cousin.

"We might fall off the edge of the world. What'll happen then?"

"What always happens to girls."

It was a happy fear, the kind you go looking for. The bells on their handlebars rang by themselves when they went over rough pavement, and there was plenty of that. They pedalled hard to climb the bridges that crossed the canals and slips and turning basins, bridges red with rust. Bluma thought of the kids who lived in the caves hollowed out of the banks of the canal. She didn't want to live down there; she wanted to be on Lexington Street, with Bella.

The girls coasted down the slope of the bridge. Bluma wondered what her father would do when he saw the turned-over tables. He couldn't blame her. He had no proof. But he did: the tire tracks on the floor. Maybe he wouldn't see them. And if he did, maybe he wouldn't imagine that his mousy daughter had ridden her bike into his speakeasy.

"Don't pedal," Bella shouted. "I'll pull you!"

She grabbed Bluma's hand to tow her, pedalling like mad on the heavy bike. Bluma took her feet off the pedals and stuck them straight out. A Schwinn was a bull of a bicycle and it took good legs to ride it, especially pulling another girl.

Standing on the sidewalk were coloured people with nothing to do than watch them go by. Bella dropped Bluma's hand. The Negroes were curious, or angry, maybe; the girls couldn't tell which. A boy their age stepped into the street and made a move to grab hold of Bluma's handlebars.

"Let me ride in your basket, white girl!"

Bluma dodged him. The boy's buddies laughed. He wasn't really trying to make her fall.

"Who says we're white?" Bella challenged him as she rode past, so close she slapped him on the shoulder.

That shut him up. No white person would ever say a thing like that. She caught up to Bluma and took her hand again.

"Were you afraid?" Bluma asked.

"Naw. I didn't have time to be. I just kept pedalling. As long as you pedal, you won't fall."

"Would you kiss a black boy?"

"If I was close enough."

"They got such lips," Bluma said in wonderment.

"You try it and tell me what it's like."

The girls laughed at the absurdity of the idea. First kissing, then being able to tell. They crossed more rail lines and stood on their pedals to protect their behinds and the rest. No one lived around here. There was scruffy prairie with oil drums lying this way and that, and the street petered out into broken pavement. The air was grainy with coal dust. A city in a garden — that was Chicago's motto. But the garden hadn't reached down here.

Then the lake appeared, and it was a little disappointing after all the effort: a flat expanse of grey water, smelling of dead alewives that floated along the shore. The girls dropped each other's hands to steer across the industrial wasteland. A rock jetty thrust into the lake and they headed that way.

They jumped off their bikes at the foot of it.

"My nut-sack aches," Bluma told Bella. She rubbed her crotch with her eyes closed, the way she saw boys do.

"Imagine having one," Bella said.

"Must be inconvenient. Always getting in the way."

"They probably say the same thing about us!"

"I don't think so," Bluma told her. "All they think about is getting their hands on it."

Fishermen were sitting on the flat rocks of the jetty that served as a breakwater for the entrance to the harbour. The men were bent over their lines that disappeared into the flat surface of the lake, and they paid the girls no attention.

"Wonder what you can catch."

Bluma shrugged. "I don't know. Carp, maybe?"

"I'd rather catch a smoked fish."

"Let's dip."

On Passover you dipped your herbs in salt water. Even Bluma's father did it, though he never explained why. The girls were supposed to know the story, instinctively, ancestrally. Instead, they changed the ceremony: they dipped the pudgy front tires of their Schwinns into the waters of Lake Michigan.

It wasn't easy. They eased the heavy bikes over the edge of the jetty and lowered the front tires toward the water. They had to hold their bikes by the back tire and bend their knees and roll forward slowly so the bike wouldn't end up at the bottom of the lake, and them with it. Bluma was bigger and her weight made her more stable. Bella was more agile. They both managed to dip their tires in the oily lake water, then grapple their bikes back onto the jetty.

"We did it!"

"We always do what we say we're gonna."

They laid their bikes down and sat on the edge of a rock. For a minute they were as intent and silent as the fishermen around them.

"My mama's coming tomorrow."

"Your brothers gonna drive her?"

"No. They gotta work. She'll take the streetcar."

"All the way out here?"

"It's a straight shot. That's what my brothers say. She'll sit there in the car and worry the whole way she doesn't miss her stop."

"That's your brothers talking!" Bluma laughed.

"Yeah, you're right."

"You talk like they do."

Bella shrugged. "Maybe so. It makes sense: they taught me English."

"Tell me a story from your house," Bluma asked her.

"What do you mean?"

"You know, a normal story. Something your family does. Your mother, your brothers. What's your mother do?"

"You know what."

"I don't know anything. You'd be surprised at the stuff I don't know."

"Even if you do all kinds of things no other girl does."

"Even if I do."

"My mother keeps the store."

"See, I didn't know that. What else?"

Bella told Bluma as much as she could about the store on Lexington Street and what life there was like, a world so fantastic to Bluma, so absolutely normal, that it glittered like Ali Baba's treasure house. Taube's store was always open since they lived above it, but they might as well have lived in it. Anyone could drop in at any time. Neighbour women left their kids there when they had a doctor's appointment, people stopped by to play cards with her brothers, and once a wedding was celebrated in the back. The whole neighbourhood had credit at the store, but you had to know how to ask for it. Bella's mother Taube spoke only Yiddish, and she had no letters, only numbers, so Bella helped her with the men who brought the merchandise.

"What about your father?"

"I've never seen him work. But he goes off every day."

"The opposite of my father. I always see him work. And he never goes anywhere."

Bella didn't like talking about family because it separated her from Bluma, the way their families were so different. Her father made no problems for her. He did nothing wrong because he didn't do much at all. In the morning he went to schul to think about God, which was a demanding, full-time occupation. He did odd jobs in a cemetery that kept him busy, tending graves and cutting the grass that grew around the stones, and Bella imagined he was paid for that because she'd seen him give her mother dollar bills. He never raised his voice or his hand. He was the rarest thing in the world, the kind of man women are always looking for: a man with no vices.

"Tell me a funny story with your brothers," Bluma said.

Bella had one of those at the ready.

"My mother's always busy with the store. When I was a little kid she used to make my brothers take care of me. 'Take your sister for a walk in the carriage! And while you're at it, stop at the fish store! They've got my order.' So they did. Except they wrapped the fish in the blankets where I was supposed to be, and my brother Rudy carried me on his hip. They pushed the carriage down the sidewalk, real slow and proud, and all the ladies stopped to lean over the carriage and gawk at the brand-new baby. But when they opened the blanket, there was a carp staring back at them!"

Bluma bent double laughing. She'd heard the story plenty of times, and it was her absolute favourite.

"I'm gonna piss myself!" she declared.

A panicked look crossed her face. For a second Bella was afraid her cousin would do just that. You couldn't rule out her wetting her pants, which would have meant going back to the house. But Bluma caught herself in time.

One of the fishermen turned in their direction.

"Shut up, you're scaring the fish."

"What fish?" Bluma said. "You'll catch a rubber boot."

"If you catch a smoked fish," Bella promised the man, "I'll buy it from you."

"Go away," the fisherman told them. "The both of you."

Bella and Bluma weren't impressed. If there were fish in this lake, they'd know about it.

"I'M DEAD ON MY FEET!" Taube declared the next afternoon.

The energy she used to throw herself into the kitchen chair said otherwise.

"How can you be exhausted?" Rachel asked her sister. "All you did was sit."

"Yes, for hours, it felt like. I was worried I'd miss my stop. I was concentrating the whole way."

"You know it's the last stop. The end of the line. You can't miss the end of the line."

Taube shrugged. "How would you know? You never go anywhere."

"I don't need to. I've already been."

When the two sisters sat down, it was the signal for their daughters to make themselves scarce. They were out the door and down the street in no time.

Taube and Rachel were two studies in how to handle immigration. Taube made no concessions to America. She would not learn the language. She would not change her name to something other people could pronounce. She acted as though she'd never left Shukyan. Not that she was prone to fantasy: she did know, objectively, that she was living on the West Side of Chicago, in a neighbourhood called Lawndale, on a street called Lexington. But in her store, she recreated Shukyan, and there, with her family and neighbours and language, she lived a life untormented by uprooting.

Her American life went splendidly. Every Sabbath, after lighting the candles, she would say in a low voice, so as not to awaken the envy of the evil spirits that gathered around every happy occasion, "I'm all right here, aren't I?" Her husband, who never missed a candle-lighting, grunted his approval.

Taube applied the art of denial to her sister's husband, that *zhlub*, that low-life, that animal. She never referred to him by name or admitted that he played any role in her sister's life. Hearing Taube speak, you'd think her sister was an unmarried spinster who miraculously had children, or a widow whose husband had died in infamy, his name never to be spoken again.

She would never have come to America if it hadn't been for the man whose existence she would not acknowledge. When she learned that Rachel had been sent for, and was leaving Shukyan, she made plans to do the same. She came to Chicago to be with her, but Rachel lived so far away she might as well be in another country. And when she did travel the hours it took to come see her, Rachel acted so fatigued Taube wondered if the trip was worth it.

Once Rachel offered her an excuse. "America wore me out."

Taube didn't contradict her. "The truth is as clear as the nose on your face," she countered.

"You can't see your nose," Rachel said. "Unless you squint like this." She demonstrated for Taube. "But that gives me a headache."

That's as close as they came to a confrontation. If her sister wanted to live in blindness, Taube thought, that was her life. But the girl, Bluma — she should be spared the suffering. And as far as she, Taube, could tell, Bluma was spared nothing. The least she could do was get her niece out of that house for a while.

"I appreciate you taking Bayla for the weekend," she told Rachel. She refused to use the American name Bella's brothers had chosen for her.

"It's nothing. They're good together. Better than sisters."

Taube picked a piece of poppyseed cake off her plate with the tip of her finger. The cake was not very good and the tea was watery, and Rachel had not provided the sugar cubes Taube liked.

"Yes," she agreed with her sister. "Better. That's why when Bayla and I leave today, Bluma should come with us."

"On the streetcar? All that way?"

"Bayla knows the streetcar. We won't get lost. She and Bluma can ask for directions. And my sons wrote everything down on a paper."

They sat for a while. In the silence, Taube could feel her sister mustering her arguments.

"You need time to yourself," Taube told her.

"What would I do with it? Time weighs heavy as bricks."

"Bluma should get some fresh air. We're going to the Dunes and we'll take her with."

"Here in Burnside, it's practically the country."

"Burnside is the city," Taube corrected her. "Your daughter needs fresh air and plenty of it."

"So that's why you came. To take Bluma back with you."

"Is there anything wrong with that?"

"I suppose not."

They sat in silence a while longer. Taube drank her tea the way they used to in Shukyan. She poured it from the cup into the saucer and drank from it. But the sugar cube she liked to hold delicately between her front teeth was missing, and with it, a big part of the pleasure.

"All right, Bluma can go."

Taube wondered what her sister saw and knew, and what knowing and seeing meant in her case. Didn't she know her husband was a criminal? Imagine the effort it must take not to know that. No wonder she was tired all the time.

Taube stood at her side and hovered as Rachel packed a little bag for Bluma. But all Rachel did was turn circles, and she got nowhere near putting together the things her daughter would need. Taube watched, and was frightened for her sister. So this is what they mean by disorganized. Her boys had brought that word home. It was on everyone's lips in Lawndale.

"You could stay here tonight, sister. Go back with the girls tomorrow."

"I can't."

"Now it's you who can't."

"I can't because of the store. The boys are looking after it, but they're boys."

"They're men," said Rachel. "They drive around in a car."

Taube would never spend a night in that criminal's house.

"WHAT DO YOU THINK THEY'RE talking about?" Bluma asked.

"Us — of course!" Bella laughed. "What else can they talk about? Everything else is off limits."

"My mother's ashamed when your mother comes to visit."

"Then you should visit me. You come to our place."

"If you only knew," Bluma said dreamily.

"Come and live with me. That would solve a lot of problems."

"Would it ever!"

A day into Bella's visit and they were still in their mismatched clothes. They stuck out, even in a neighbourhood of scruffy kids wearing hand-me-downs. Bella's tomboy shirt scarcely held Bluma's breasts in check, and Bella floated inside Bluma's. But they wouldn't have it any other way.

They went along 95th Street, holding hands. They looked in the shop windows and speculated on the merchandise, the dresses they would never wear and the shoes that would never go on their feet. They'd never wear grown-up dresses and tight-fitting shoes because those were for ladies and they'd never turn into that. And why venture into a shop when the shopkeeper knew they had no money, and would chase them out — why have your feelings hurt on purpose?

Bella pointed to a mannequin wearing a coat. It looked ridiculous on a summer day.

"My mother wore a coat all the time when she was big with me."

"Yeah? Even in summer? How come?"

"She was ashamed."

"Ashamed? She was married!"

"Ashamed of being pregnant and being so old," Bella explained. "She was too old to get pregnant."

"How come you know that?"

"My brothers. They tell me all the stuff I'm not supposed to know."

Her brothers had brought up Bella, and it showed. She was a stickball champion and she could still run like the wind on legs so skinny they seemed to have no room on them for muscles. With five brothers teaching her, she never learned how to act like a girl.

Farther along, where the street ran parallel to the train yards, there was a strip of prairie where a bunch of bored Irish kids were looking for something to do. She spotted a boy from her class. His cop father drank at the Coop, but that wasn't the kind of thing you mentioned.

"Hey, Tommy."

"Hey. If it isn't the class dunce."

"You're a dunce, you. I bet you don't know what a pyramid is."

Tommy looked at her, suspicious. "Sure, a pyramid. They got them in Egypt. I studied them."

"We can make one here," Bluma told him.

"Yeah. Sure we can. A pyramid in Burnside. And I got a camel in my garage. But I only take him out for a spin on Sundays."

Bluma counted the kids. There were eight of them. That made ten with her and Bella. They had enough.

"I'll show you how. A human pyramid. We'll build it ourselves. But you got to watch me and do what I say."

"Like I'd take orders from you."

Bluma ignored him. She wiped her palms together and got down on her hands and knees on the straggly grass.

"You're a big guy," she told Tommy, making a grab for his leg. "Get down on the ground next to me."

Tommy pulled away. "Hands off!"

"What are you afraid of?"

"Not you."

No kid in Burnside wanted to be touched. When someone went to put a hand on you, it meant punishment. Bluma couldn't stand that scaredy-cat way the kids had, but she needed them. Two girls don't make a pyramid.

"If you're not afraid, then do what I do."

Tommy couldn't refuse a challenge, especially not from a girl, and the class dunce to boot. He kneeled down next to her in his dungarees. His clothes smelled like cabbage, an Irish smell. She hoped she didn't smell like him.

With the two of them kneeling side by side, Bella climbed on top. She weighed no more than a leaf.

"See? Nothing to it."

She hopped off.

"Okay, you guys, pile on like she did," Bluma told them. "I'll be the keystone."

"More like the Keystone Kops," said Tommy on the ground next to her.

"I told you there aren't no pyramids outside Egypt," one of the kids said.

"Not that you'd know what a pyramid is," Bluma told him.

"If I didn't know, I wouldn't let on."

"If I knew, I wouldn't tell you."

Finally she got everyone to do as she said. Two kids got down on their hands and knees next to her and Tommy. Three more climbed onto their backs, tottering, trying to keep their balance. Then two on top of them and, at the very top, Bella, the lightest and most agile. The kids hollered and insulted each other about the way they smelled and how they were too weak to play this game, but the rickety construction stood.

"Now what?" Tommy said, struggling next to her.

"Nothing," Bluma told him. She felt the effort he was making to hold up the weight. It was nothing for her. "This is it."

"This?"

"What more do you want?"

"Now that's a duncey thing to say. No wonder, coming from you."

"That's what you think. I'm great with figures."

"What are you talking about?"

Tommy gave her the eye. His father spent more time at the Coop than in his own house. Bluma might know something about him that he didn't.

"Your father says no one can deal cards like me. He calls me Angel Fingers."

"You lie — my father would never say something like that. You, a girl, dealing cards? That makes you a double dunce. No wonder you can't get anywhere in school. You spend all your time in a speak-softly shop!"

He burst out in noisy, self-conscious laughter.

"Ask you father, if you dare. You'll see I'm not lying."

Then she lifted one hand from the ground and slugged Tommy in the shoulder. He tried to hit her back but she dodged him. The kids on the rows above them started hollering and crashing down on top of them.

Bluma and Tommy glared at each other. She'd gone too far. The rule was never to talk about what people did in the Coop. Now she had an enemy forever.

All that was her father's fault.

Bella was lying in the grass at her side, pulling burrs off her shirt. "That was great!"

"Come on," Bluma told her as she shrugged off the kids lying on top of her. "I've had enough."

"You hit like a boy," Tommy told her.

"Don't worry, I won't say nothing about your father."

"And I won't say nothing about yours."

"I don't care about him," she told Tommy.

She grabbed Bella's hand and pulled her to her feet.

"Let's go. We had our fun."

The two girls turned their backs on the kids and went down the street, parallel to the tracks. In the yards down the embankment, the trainmen were assembling a freight, banging the cars together to couple them.

"Why'd he tell you that you hit like a boy?"

"Don't you think it'd be better to be a boy?"

They walked together, hands clasped.

"I don't know," Bella said. "I'm already sort of a boy."

Bluma looked at Bella's nearly flat chest under her loose shirt, and her heavy jeans and the Buster Browns on her feet. Her haircut was courtesy of her brothers and an inverted bowl.

"Yeah, you are now," Bluma told her. "But just you wait."

Bella knew a girl had to get married. It was inevitable, something unpleasant but that wouldn't kill you, like a trip to the doctor's office. There were worse things than marriage. You could be the girl nobody wanted to marry.

"I know. We'll probably have to get married," she told Bluma.

"That's what girls do. But we won't let that change us."

"No. We won't let a man separate us. Even if we do get married."

"Right," said Bluma. "Any man that'll have one of us will have to have both of us. Swear?"

"I swear."

They spat on the ground, then stepped on each other's spit and ground it onto the sidewalk. Then they shook on it. Bella and Bluma cemented their sacred trust with what came from their bodies.

Walking along 95th Street they began to sing:

> *As I was walking down the street, a billboard met my eye*
> *The advertisements written there would make you laugh and cry*
> *The wind and rain had come that day and washed the sign away*
> *And what was written there would make the billboard say,*
> *Come smoke a Coca-Cola, drink ketchup cigarettes*
> *See Lillian Russell wrestle with a box of Oysterettes*
> *Pork and beans will meet tonight to have a finish fight*
> *Chauncey DePew will lecture on some polio tonight.*

They sang loud and tunelessly and were happy with the results.

"With a song like that, for sure we're gonna be stars," said Bella. "But we need a name."

"Don't worry, I've been thinking. We'll be The Fledglings," Bluma announced proudly.

They couldn't carry a tune, but they had a song and a name, and that was a start. Neither of them knew where the tune came from, but they did know it was called "The Billboard Song." Bella heard it from her brothers, who had pulled it out of the air.

"What's a fledgling? Funny sounding word."

"It's a baby bird," Bluma explained. "I looked it up. A baby bird that's just learning to fly. Like you and me."

Bella hugged her. Bluma knew all kinds of things. How she ever got to be class dunce, Bella would never understand.

The Fledglings, they decided as they walked through the neighbourhood, swinging their clasped hands, would be famous. They would appear on radio, tour New York and Los Angeles, ride across the country on the train, in sleeping cars with polished brass fixtures, wear furs and change their names into something like Betty or Peggy. They would be escorted to their shows by gentlemen who were exquisitely polite to them. They would not get married. Their families never appeared in their Fledgling fantasies; they were each other's only family.

"I think we can go back to the house now," Bluma said.

She didn't say "home" or "my house." It was "the house": a building. Around the front, Bluma kicked at the fence her father had built for Libby. She did that every time. One kick at a time, she would tear it down.

When they walked in the door, Taube and Rachel were standing in the kitchen. Taube had her handbag, and Rachel was holding Bluma's kit bag.

Bluma understood. She hugged Bella. Her cousin grabbed the bag from her aunt and looked inside.

"You don't even need that much. In the Dunes you can run naked like a Red Indian and wash your clothes in the lake. Or not even. You don't get dirty with sand. Not that anyone's watching."

"You're going with your cousin," Rachel told Bluma. "Your Aunt Taube will take care of you. They're taking you on vacation."

Rachel spoke in mournful tones, as if her daughter were being sold into slavery, instead of going off to enjoy the freedom of not having to serve in the bootlegger's house. Bluma understood she was to show no further joy, and she did not, out of respect for her mother who was losing her companion in misery for a couple of weeks.

SEVEN

Sand in Their Shoes

IN THE SOUTH SHORE LINE train carriage, after waiting circumspectly in the station, their hands clasped in front of their bodies like parodies of their parents, Bella told Bluma they were going to play a game. The first one to see sand wins.

Bluma stared intently out the train window at the sooty Bronzeville tenements. The inhabitants glared back from behind their streaky windows.

"Not yet," Bella told her. "You're wasting your time. Wait till we get out of the city."

"What's so good about seeing sand?"

"You can go barefoot in it. It doesn't hurt your feet like pavement. And it means we're getting close to the beach."

"I never saw sand, I don't think."

The train rounded the edge of Lake Michigan, past the steel mills that darkened the sky with their chimneys. Bella's father coughed at the sight, then got up to find the smoker and have a cigarette. In the swaying train car, he climbed over the barrier of suitcases and bags his wife had erected around them to keep strangers away. A needless precaution, since the smell of smoked fish and green onions that hovered like a cloud over their position was barrier enough.

Bluma watched him move down the aisle, steadying himself on the backs of other people's seats. Bella's parents did everything in perfect, harmonious silence. Something must have been the matter with them. Something was missing; that something was fighting. They never spoke a word of criticism to each other. Their edges fit together flawlessly, pieces of a jigsaw puzzle fresh out of the box.

She went back to staring out the window. Bella's mother was pushing strips of smoked whitefish on her from her bottomless picnic basket, with cucumber and tomato to balance out the salt. Bluma wasn't hungry. Her breakfast was still balancing on the top of her stomach.

The telephone poles flashed by at close range, almost close enough to touch. What if one reached in and touched her? The pole would be like a visitor you opened your door to but who intended you harm — like marriage for a girl. She thought about the oath she swore with Bella. What chance did they have of making it stick?

She closed her eyes to shut out the telephone poles. The trip to America could have been like this, her half asleep and knowing nothing of where she was going. She remembered none of it. All she knew was what people told her. The seasickness, the illness, the arrival that was supposed to make it all worthwhile. The memories she had weren't even hers.

Except for one: the sardine sandwich. She had a sardine sandwich in her bag when she got on the boat, and she swore she wouldn't eat it until she got to the other side. When her father came to get her she had the sandwich in her hand, inedible by then, and he got mad at her for wasting food.

What good was memory? Discard things that can do harm. She couldn't discard her stomach so she put it outside her body, where it couldn't hurt her, even if that meant she had a hole in her middle. She was going with the person she loved most to the place she most wanted to go, and still it kept up its campaign against her.

"I see sand! I win! I win!"

Her mother shushed Bella.

"*Dos meidele shloft*," she told her.

I'm not sleeping, Bluma thought. I'm pretending.

Bella shook Bluma's arm. She knew her cousin wasn't asleep. She made her look out the window at the patches of yellow sand between the skinny trunks of birch and cottonwood.

Bluma didn't want to look.

"What's the matter?"

"Nothing. I feel seasick."

"Trainsick," Bella said.

"Yeah. Trainsick."

She put her head against the back of the seat. Bella combed her hair with her fingers.

"Go to sleep. We'll be there soon. You don't have to look for sand anymore."

Bluma closed her eyes. She thought of using the toilet but it was too far. She heard Bella's father coming back from the smoker where he'd spent most of the trip. The smell of tobacco rolled off him in waves. Bella's mother was making small talk with him, and he made sounds that weren't exactly words, but they were answers of a kind because they showed he was paying attention to her and had no objections to what she said. Bluma listened to his sounds; they entered her body. He should have been her father. Then Bella could be her real sister, not just her cousin. If she couldn't reach back and get a different father, she would go forward and get a different man. That was called a husband.

Bella was right. They'd have to get married. No one wanted the humiliation of being an old maid. But men were walking collections of vice, the Coop had taught her that much; she had to find one with the fewest flaws. There were men who drank and men who beat their wives and men who couldn't hold a job. They had to be avoided. Better to marry a man who made soft reassuring noises like Bella's father, and who didn't explode in shouting and clenched fists. As a rule, men didn't talk, at least not to women. The best kind of man would make warm animal sounds.

If she had a choice, she'd marry Bella. That wouldn't be so hard. They were already good as married, minus the wedding night skirmish. If she married Bella, she could be with her day and night — which was what she was going to do in the Dunes, so why was her stomach acting up?

I want to be well, just for once, she prayed to Bella. If you love me, cure me!

BLUMA AWOKE TO BELLA AND her parents gathering up their bags. She got to her feet. The train stopped with a great grinding lurch and she lost her balance and fell onto Bella's father. He held her steady, then urged her forward with a hand on her shoulder.

Bella helped her swing down from the car onto the platform. She had the knapsack with their things in it, one bag for the two of them. The sun was hot and the air smelled of tar and smoke. Bella's father herded them down the platform.

"I see sand," Bluma said.

Bella laughed. "Sure, you do. It's everywhere. But I still win."

The station had big letters that read CHESTERTON. In the shade around the side, men in straw hats dozed on horse carts. Bella's father set down his cardboard suitcase and chose a cart-driver. In his most formal, flowery language, the kind he used to address Gentiles, he spoke to the man.

The farmer glanced around for help. He was afraid to ask the man with the suitcase to speak English, because what if he already was — then he'd be insulted. The farmer was just trying to make a little money ferrying people to the beach, and he ended up stuck with this ceremonious little man in black speaking double dutch.

That's when Bella stepped in. It was part of their unspoken family routine. She walked up to the farmer and patted his horse on the nose, then asked him, to his great relief, how much he wanted to take them to Johnson's Beach.

He hadn't finished naming his price when she told him, "Too much."

The farmer was no match for Bella. He was so grateful to this kid who spoke some kind of reasonable English that he agreed to what she wanted to pay. She knew he would. She'd done this before. The Chesterton farmers were lousy hagglers.

They began hoisting their things into the cart.

"Feature those watermelons," Bluma whispered to Bella.

"We'll be the best customers you have all day," Bella promised the farmer. "Ten cents for the ride, and we'll take a watermelon while we're at it."

Besides being a lousy haggler, the farmer was generous with his wares. With the parents sitting stiffly in the back and the two girls on either side of him, he reached around and grabbed a melon off the pile. He took a bread knife from his pocket, wiped it on his overalls and cut off slices for them.

"Good, huh, girls? My prize-winning melons are the pride of Chesterton. What do you say?"

"The best," Bluma said.

"You kids staying at the big hotel there?"

"No, that's not for us," Bella said. She glanced back to see if her mother was listening. Taube hated it when she confided things to strangers. "We have a little house all to ourselves."

"Well, isn't that nice?"

The girls bit into their watermelon slices, cheek-deep in dark pink fruit. They pulled away from the station and rolled along sand roads that were smoother than freshly laid asphalt. Bella and Bluma leaned over and spat watermelon seeds off the edge of the cart to see who could spit farthest, trying to make sure the seeds didn't blow back in their faces.

"You fixing to start your own watermelon patch?" the farmer asked.

"Sure. We'll pave the road with them. Sounds like paradise!"

"They won't grow in the sand."

"Then where do you grow yours?" Bluma asked.

"I've got some land right where the sand gives out and the dirt takes over, not too far."

"We'll come and visit," Bella promised. "We'll work in the fields."

"I bet you will! City girls!"

Bluma clamped her hand over her mouth. "Uh-oh, I swallowed one."

"A watermelon's gonna grow in your stomach," Bella teased. "You're going to have a watermelon baby. Isn't that true?" she asked the farmer.

"I don't rightly know," he said, not wanting to take sides. He had never met girls this sassy, and he figured he'd better watch his step.

Bella poked at Bluma's stomach.

"Oh, I can feel it already. It's growing fast. And it's going to be a girl!"

"That's the only kind of baby I'll ever have."

"Don't be so sure, cousin."

THE JOHNSON'S BEACH HOTEL WAS a great rickety wooden vessel leaning on the shifting sands of the Indiana Dunes. It looked as if it had been beached during a Great Lakes storm and taken over by squatters. It was a honeymoon hotel, a getaway for unmarried couples, the kind of building that one misplaced cigarette would burn to the ground in a minute. From the wraparound veranda, the guests could sit in the porch swings and contemplate the lake. The hotel was unheated and stood empty in winter. In the summer, people fought for a room.

The farmer pulled into the hard-packed sand lot at the side of the building, where the road ended. Bella's parents climbed down laboriously, stiff knees and tangled skirts. On the ground, steadied by her husband, Taube took out her change purse and made a great show of hunting for the right coins.

"A dime and a nickel," Bella told her.

Taube placed them in the farmer's hand like a noblewoman bestowing alms.

"Maybe you have something else to offer us?"

The farmer stared at her. He even took off his hat, as if that might help him understand her. Didn't this woman know she wasn't speaking English? He'd never been to Chicago, but if it was full of people like this, he was in no hurry.

"What else have you got to sell?" Bella repeated.

The farmer listed the contents of his garden. Bella looked to her mother, but she was paying no attention, even though she'd asked the question. The usual routine, Bella thought. Fear of the unknown ran her mother's life.

"You come this way sometimes?" she asked the farmer.

"I deliver to the hotel, two-three times a week."

"Leave us whatever you got in a crate with the bill, and tell us where to leave the money. Don't worry, we're good for it."

The farmer shook his head. "You certainly know your way around the world."

Bella supposed that was a compliment. "I'm an all-American girl," she told him.

She thrust out her hand and she and the farmer shook on it. He didn't look like he shook hands with a lot of girls. Then he disappeared into the hotel kitchen to get the cook's order.

Bella kicked off her shoes and started dragging her cousin toward the lake.

"I sealed the deal with the hayseed. At least we won't have to eat sand."

They ran to the water's edge. The horizon was a thin, hazy pencil line.

"It's like the ocean," Bella said. "It goes on forever."

"We crossed the ocean once."

"Would you believe it? I don't remember a thing."

"Who would? We were babies."

The two girls approached the water carefully and put their toes in it. Freezing. That didn't bother them.

Then Taube called to them, and they ran back to the cart with their shoes dangling from their hands to unload the watermelon. Bella's father stood by the cart, glowering at the lake. He didn't like water. He had sailed across it during the great traumatic voyage of his life, and he remembered every sickly minute of it.

A wheelbarrow stood along the side of the hotel. Taube tipped it over briskly and shook out the sand. Then she took the suitcase from her husband and put it in with the food basket and the girls' knapsack. Her husband looked on approvingly, almost admiringly. Taube grasped the handles and began piloting the wheelbarrow down the narrow plank walkway laid out in the sand. The unlocked wheelbarrow and the plank path were provided for the greater good by the people who lived in the shacks along Johnson's Beach. Without the wheelbarrow, they couldn't carry their things to their shack. Without the plank walkway, pushing a wheelbarrow through sand would be an ordeal.

The shacks were scattered across the sand like dice. Some stood on stubby stilts made of cinder blocks, but most squatted flush on the ground. Except for the hotel, Johnson's Beach belonged to anyone willing to take a chance on their place not being there the next time they showed up.

The plank walkway ended at the foot of a great bluff. Taube set the wheelbarrow down and let out a sigh of biblical proportions. She leaned against a weathered post and dabbed at her forehead. Two rough signs were nailed to the post. "Falcon House" and "Donnell," with letters chiselled into the wood. Taube was running with sweat, but taking off a layer was out of the question. She had been born in these clothes.

A steep wooden stairway made of hundreds of tarry steps led up the side of the dune.

"Don't tell me we're going to walk up with all our stuff," Bluma asked.

"No. We're going to race. Whoever loses has to sleep on the floor!" Bella looked into Bluma's face. "Come on, take a joke! We won't walk, you'll see."

Attached to the post was a mailbox, though no mail was ever delivered here. Taube opened it. Inside the box was a Mason jar set upside down to keep the water out, and in the jar two bare wires dangled.

"Do it," she told Bella. "But be careful."

Bella touched the wires together like a thief hotwiring a car. A spark jumped but she didn't flinch.

"Magic," she told Bluma.

Bella shaded her eyes and looked up the stairway. "Here she comes! Old Faithful!"

A lift came lurching down a single rail in their direction. When it reached them on the flats, Bella separated the wires and the lift bucked to a halt.

Bella threw their knapsack onto it, along with her parents' bags.

"All aboard!" she called. "Get on, Bloom. You'll see, it's like something out of Rube Goldberg."

"Dr. Donnell made this. Have some respect," her mother told her.

Bella climbed onto the platform and pulled Bluma on with her.

"Who's Rube Goldberg?" Bluma asked. "Is he family?"

"Come on, you know him, he's in the comics. Everybody knows him! Anyway, you're no more Goldberg than I am, and he probably isn't either. No Goldberg ever started out life as a Goldberg."

Bella's father touched the wires together and the lift took off, carrying them and the family baggage up the steep grade on the rail that ran parallel to the stairs. Far below, Bella's parents began climbing, two figures in black in the shimmering sun, advancing slowly up the steps, their shoes sticking to the creosote blooms in the wood. Then something happened that Bluma had never seen before. After several steps, her uncle took her aunt's hand.

"You scared?" Bella asked her.

"It's scary, admit it."

"Just don't look down."

"You shouldn't have said that!"

"There's no reason to be afraid. A real scientist built this machine. Look here."

Bella lifted her behind and showed her a metal plaque screwed into the wooden platform. "Capacity, two children," the plaque read.

"That's you and me!"

She squeezed Bluma's shoulder.

"Hey, don't do that, you'll push me off! Anyway, we're not children."

"No, we're not," Bella agreed. "But what are we?"

"I don't know yet."

"We're certainly not young ladies."

Bella made young ladies sound so proper and hoity-toity that Bluma couldn't help laughing despite her fear, which was the idea. How could they be young ladies when they were sitting cross-legged on a piece of tarred wood being yanked up the side of a sand bluff, Rube Goldberg style?

Then Bluma did what Bella told her not to do. She looked down. An ocean of shimmering nothingness beckoned her. Dive into me, the air urged. She remembered something she'd heard about a man who left his family. Thin air. He'd disappeared into thin air. How could a person disappear into the air like a bird flying out of sight?

Bella tapped her on the shoulder.

"I told you not to look down."

"Sorry. I got curious."

"First you were trainsick. Now you'll be liftsick."

"I don't get it. I feel like I'm falling over the edge, but I'm not moving a muscle."

"Nerves," Bella concluded.

"Yeah, nerves. That's what everybody says. I'm getting sick of that word."

"I don't blame you."

The lift creaked and bucked, and with one final lurch, it reached a platform at the top of the stairs.

"End of the line — you survived!" Bella called.

She jumped off the lift and started dragging off the bags. Bluma was the last piece of luggage to go.

"There. Solid ground."

"Next time I'm taking the stairs."

"You'll get used to it. It's like everything else."

Bella pulled her along the sandy terrace toward the cottage.

"See those vines over there? That's poison ivy. Whatever you do, don't touch it. Don't get it mixed up with grapevines. It's easy: 'Leaves three, let it be.' You'll see. Grape leaves don't have that shiny look like an oilcloth."

"Don't tell me now, I'll never remember."

"And see how I'm walking on the boards? Walk the same way. If you drag your feet you'll get plenty of slivers. I'll have to pull them out with a pair of red-hot tweezers. You'll love that!"

THE STAIRWAY, THE LIFT AND the house were the work of Dr. Donnell, the man Taube did not want her daughter calling Rube Goldberg. Like the real Rube, Donnell was an engineer, but unlike him, he made useful things. His creations looked like they would never hold up, but like the lift, they always came through.

Dr. Donnell was part of the family on both the maternal and paternal side, which happened often enough in Shukyan. Bella's family called him "Doctor" out of respect for his superior social status.

The man applied all his genius to the Dunes colony. In the Old Country, a person of his talent would have spent his life building scale models of the Kremlin out of toothpicks on the kitchen table, or designing a fishpond if he was lucky, which was the only occupation available to someone from the wrong religion. But in the New World, .

all of nature was his canvas. He was the first person from the West Side to walk past the shacks on the Johnson's Beach flats and discover the wilder nature of the Dunes. He carved out a ledge at the top of the bluff, then solidified the terrace by planting cottonwoods that thrived in sand, and shored up the whole thing with railroad ties. Not only was he an engineer, he was an expert scavenger, and that trait comforted the poorer members of his family who saw he was one of them after all. Most of his building materials were either scrounged or had fallen off a truck.

Once his terrace proved trustworthy, he poured a sturdy square cement floor and built a house made of cinder blocks on it. That meant transporting materials to the top of the bluff, which was where the stairway and its one hundred and sixty-two creosote-smelling steps came in. It was built out of railroad ties too. Dr. Donnell had a weakness for them; they were made to last forever and could always be found on the cheap. The next step was the lift that had hauled a cement mixer and the cinder blocks up the side of the dune, but was now used for the pleasure of children, though he and his wife had none of their own.

On the desk in his study, lined with engineering manuals in several languages, in his apartment in a neighbourhood more genteel than Lexington Street, he kept a register with the names of family members, when they had last used his cottage and for how long.

"You are now ready for your period of decontamination," he informed Taube and her husband when he came to visit them in the old neighbourhood.

Taube wrinkled up her nose. "What are you saying — that we have lice?"

"No. In America there is another word for it: vacation. Happy now?"

Taube was. She was happy to take her daughter away from her sons' rowdy influences. She was afraid they were turning Bella into a boy, and she had boys enough already. She was even happier for her niece Bluma, who needed decontamination if anyone did. The visit ended with Dr. Donnell writing their names into his register and blowing on the page to dry the ink.

There was one house higher up the bluff than Dr. Donnell's: the Falcon House that belonged to an ancient Russian couple named Fialkov. He paid them a visit during the construction of his cottage, and offered them the use of the lift. They thanked him, then made him promise never to build higher than where they were. "We were the first ones here, you understand. It is who we are," they told him.

He promised. Reassured, they began to talk. It wasn't long before they told him they'd known Dostoevsky; in fact, he still owed them money. When Donnell suggested they were unlikely to collect the sum — a gambling debt, no doubt — they interpreted that to mean he thought they were lying. They sprang to their feet, suddenly spry when there was something so important to prove, and went to the bookshelf and produced an armful of first edition Dostoevsky novels in Russian, inscribed by the author, dating back to the last century. Merely signed, or dedicated to them? Donnell read Russian laboriously, and to take the time to read the inscriptions would have been a further insult to this imperial-looking old couple. It must have been an honour for them to have the great writer welsh on a debt. It assured their distinction, all to way to America.

Dr. Donnell had a communist architectural vision. The cottage had one door, and it led to the outside. Otherwise, on the inside, no one room was closed off from any other. Donnell's guests washed and cooked and slept in one large space, though a partition did set the bathroom apart. All rooms belonged to all people, at all times, for all functions.

WITH THE KNAPSACK ON HER back, the suitcase in one hand and the food basket in the other, Bella led the way into the cottage. There were paintings on the walls, above the sink, spattered with water stains, and on the ends of bookshelves. They weren't paintings, only pictures of paintings, but what mattered were the colours. All the colours the girls didn't have in their houses were here in the engineer's cottage.

Bluma looked at the pictures.

"Imagine getting married to a goat."

"What goat? That's a sheep."

Bluma pointed to the paper pinned to the bookshelf.

"Look, don't you see? A woman in a wedding dress, and there's a goat above her in the sky."

"I think she's getting married to that man."

"I don't know, I think it's the goat. Look how he's smiling. More than the man is. The man's all dewy-eyed like he just got through crying."

"You're right. The goat looks like the cat that swallowed the canary."

"If I could have a wedding like that," Bluma ventured, "maybe I'd take the plunge. Look at how sweet the man looks with those big wet eyes."

"Yeah. But it's only a painting. We'll get married when smiling goats fly up to heaven."

The girls broke up laughing. Talk of love and courtship and marriage ended that way.

Taube and her husband found the girls laughing for no good reason when they stepped out of the glare of the sunlight and into Dr. Donnell's dacha. When her daughter laughed, it always sounded to Taube like she was laughing at her. Her husband cast a dark eye at the pictures. He knew, as every person in his right mind does, that goats can't fly. And anyone who tries to make you think different is a danger to himself and society.

Despite the flying goats, ten minutes later Bella's mother had transformed the Donnell cottage into a sandier version of Lexington Street. She couldn't do anything about the paintings cut out of magazines with their offensive bright colours, so she counterattacked with something tangible: food.

She spread her supplies across the table. Smoked fish, pickles, apples, tomatoes, salted tongue, cucumbers, tins of sardines. She brought the entire contents of the larder with her in her wicker basket. Those everyday objects would make the place hers.

Her husband was at home wherever he hung his hat. He took a wooden chair from the kitchen table and went outside with it, onto the terrace. The screen door slammed behind him. He set the chair on the flagstones, another tasteful touch provided by Dr. Donnell, who had come upon the stones behind the hotel, where some contractor had dumped them. By propping the chair backwards, Bella's father could keep himself out of the sunlight. Little by little, he became one with his surroundings. He took off his shoes, then a few minutes later his socks, and a few minutes after that he let his bare feet touch sand. He rolled a cigarette and smoked it, licking the paper first so it would burn more slowly.

That night, Bella and Bluma hesitated about what to wear to bed. They talked in whispers. Bella's father was on the screen porch smoking, and her mother was there too, watching him smoke, but the girls took their precautions. They couldn't count on Bella's parents' ignorance of English forever.

Bella was the youngest of her family, and when she was little, her job was to share her bed with whatever female boarders her parents took in to meet the rent. She was used to the intimacy of a body in the bed next to her. It wasn't the same for Bluma.

"I suppose we gotta wear something," Bella said.

"Yeah. Nobody sleeps naked. But don't wear the same dirty shirt you've had on all day."

Bella sniffed her shirt that was actually Bluma's.

"It's not dirty."

Nothing was ever dirty as far as Bella was concerned. Her brothers were snazzy dressers, regular clothes horses, but she hadn't gotten to that point, and it didn't look like she would.

"Oh yeah?" Bluma asked. "You rolled around in the prairie with the

Irish kids, then you rolled around in the sand. Not dirty? Phew!"

Bella got the message. She unbuttoned her shirt and threw it on a chair. Bluma did the same, then took off the undershirt that her mother made her wear.

They hugged each other under the covers. Bella felt Bluma's breasts against her chest, warm and foreign and as different to her as a boy was from a girl. She smelled like dust and sweat to Bluma, even without her shirt. It was a tomboy smell, and Bluma wished she had it too.

Bluma's appendix scar was rough against Bella's skin. Bella reached down and prodded it gently.

"What happened to you?"

"Didn't you hear?"

"Nobody tells me anything. It looks like you don't either."

"I got appendicitis," Bluma said proudly.

"Yeah? Is it catching? You still got it?"

"No, they cured me. They took it out."

"Took what out?"

"My appendix."

Bella nudged the scar. It was rubbery and puffy. "Does it hurt?"

"Not really. Not there."

"Then where?"

Bluma put Bella's hand over her stomach. "There. Right in the middle."

"I can't feel anything."

"That's 'cause it's inside."

"Are they gonna take that out too?"

"No. They can't."

"How come?"

"Because it's me."

A lot of time Bluma talked in riddles about invisible things. Bella believed in what she could see, which meant a lot about Bluma was beyond her. She didn't like not understanding everything about Bluma.

"Dr. Bella's gonna fix you, but she won't cut you up with a knife. But she will give you the laughing gas!"

She started in tickling Bluma. Her cousin curled into a ball and laughed and swatted at her. Bella swatted back and they rolled in the covers. Their parents, lawfully and legally married, never showed bare skin to each other, and they certainly didn't laugh in bed, where everything had the gravitas of duty. Bella and Bluma were miles ahead of their time.

THE NEXT MORNING, TAUBE SENT the girls back down the stairs to return the wheelbarrow to the hotel.

"Go see if anyone's selling fish," Taube told them. She gave Bella her change purse. "You talk to them."

"Sure thing."

At the top of the stairs, Bluma looked at the lift.

"I'm going to walk. I want to count the steps."

"There are exactly 162 of them."

"I want to count them myself."

"Whatever you say, scaredy-cat."

Bella followed her cousin down the stairs, and wondered what it must be like to live in the shadow of your fears. She thought of the times she'd been afraid. There was a tornado once when she was young, and the wind broke the kitchen window and showered her soup with slivers of glass — she'd been afraid then. Another time a chicken got loose in the poultry shop and flew into her face, and she still didn't like being around birds. But those fears were different from Bluma's because they came from outside.

"You're right," Bluma said when they reached the bottom. "There's 162 of them."

"I bet you didn't even count!" Bella turned over the wheelbarrow and set it on the plank path. "Get in, I'll give you a ride."

"Forget it, I weigh a ton."

"Yeah, a ton of feathers."

Bluma climbed into the rusty wheelbarrow. It wasn't as easy as Bella's mother made it look, balancing the soft tire on a narrow plank. You needed arms of steel. Bella sang as she wheeled Bluma toward the hotel, her voice lusty and tuneless.

"The streets were so bad, the lanes were so narrow, I had to bring my wife home in a wheelbarrow."

"I am not your wife," Bluma protested as she lay on her back with her legs over the edge.

"You are now — I'm taking you home! I'll carry you across the threshold."

"Good luck!"

Bella raced down the plank walkway. Bluma raised her head and saw they were getting near the hotel where they wouldn't be able to play this kind of game. She started squirming and pitching herself from one side to the other, and with a little help from Bella, the wheelbarrow ran off the plank and into the sand. She rolled out of it as Bella flew over her and landed nose-first in the sand.

Bella got up and brushed herself off. Bluma was lying at her feet, laughing and crying at the same time.

"You're hysterical," Bella told her.

Bluma wiped her eyes and blinked the sand out of them. "What's that?"

"Hysterical. You know."

Her brothers said that all the time. But it wasn't a word you could define.

"You know, when everything's too much. When you laugh so hard you cry."

Bluma sat up. "I'm not crying. I got sand in my eyes."

They walked the rest of the way to the hotel and left the wheelbarrow in its spot. Bella turned it over. Her arm muscles leapt under her olive skin.

"Do you know," she asked Bluma, "that the best ice cream cones in the world come from right here?"

"No kidding?"

"Strawberry."

"I'll take watermelon. Do you have any money? I don't."

"Money, always money, that's all people talk about. I have an idea, and that's just as good."

"Right," Bluma said, incredulous. "Ideas are as good as money. Since when? We'll have to use our female charms. Especially you."

"Very funny! We'll sing," Bella decided. "You'll see."

The two girls made their entrance into the sweetshop in the cool, dim parlour on the ground floor of Johnson's Beach. The screen door slammed on its spring and the owner looked up. It was a slow time of day for ice cream.

"We're The Fledglings," Bella announced.

"Though some call us the Gold-Dust Twins," Bluma chimed in. "And you can see why."

She flipped her wavy hair with the back of her hand.

"We're here to entertain you," Bella warned.

Before he could object, the sweetshop man found himself being entertained. He had never seen anything like this. Two olive-skinned girls, one with baby tits and a wavy brunette with great knockers, materialized out of nowhere and started squeaking out a song, though it wasn't one he'd ever heard:

> Bay rum is good for horses
> It is the best in town
> Castoria cures the measles
> If you pay five dollars down.

Their voices were pure torture, a creaky shutter in a Lake Michigan squall. He wouldn't have minded getting the one with the knockers into his back room for a quick feel — he figured she could use a little fun. But the two of them looked inseparable. He raised his hand and they stopped in mid-verse. A little too quickly in his opinion, as if they'd been waiting for a cue.

"I've got a deal for you. You stop singing and I'll give you each a baby cone."

"Strawberry," Bluma told him.

The sweetshop man obliged. "Two baby cones for two real sweet babies. Now if you could only carry a tune. But you can't. Not even if you had a bushel basket."

There were whole strawberries from the nearby fields in the ice cream. Bluma dug hers out with her sandy fingers.

"Look, they still have their little hairs on them."

"I bet they do," the man said. "A little bit of fur, just like you."

"I know you're just trying to get rid of us," Bluma told him, "but it's not that easy."

"This stuff is heaven. We'll come back whenever you want us to," Bella offered.

"That's all right. There's no hurry."

"See you soon, then," she said.

"With money in your pocket, next time."

Bella and Bluma walked along the beach in front of the hotel. The water was slack, slate grey and smelled strongly of alewives.

"See? We put our considerable feminine charms to good use."

"I thought I'd have to kiss him, but he was a pushover." Bluma shook her head in wonderment. "This place is something."

"That's because no one's ever seen Fledglings like us before. We're one of a kind."

"Do you think we'd make it this easy on Lexington Street?"

"Why not?"

"I'd like to live there."

"You could."

"I'd need an excuse," Bluma said.

"School," Bella told her.

"What about it?"

"You could go to school where I'm going to go. People's Junior College, on the West Side. It's way too far to go back and forth every day from Burnside, so you'd have to live in my house."

"People's Junior College? What kind of place is that?"

"One I can get into and that I can afford. It's free. I'm gonna study Spanish. I'm gonna be a Spanish teacher and nobody can stop me!"

"Where'd you ever get an idea like that?"

"All the places where they speak Spanish," Bella told her, "are a long way from here."

"You want to leave Lexington Street? It's paradise."

"Don't make me laugh! I wanna see the world!"

Bella ran ahead, down the beach, and drew a wide circle in the sand with her toe. She slid an imaginary rose between her teeth and slipped make-believe castanets onto her fingers. Kids building sandcastles looked up and stared but Bella was beyond self-consciousness. She was a Fledgling, a born performer. She launched into a new song in her croaking voice:

La cucaracha, la cucaracha,
Ya no puede caminar
Porque no tiene, porque le falta
Una pata par' andar!
Cha-cha-cha!

Bella finished with a bow. Bluma applauded, and so did the sandcastle kids. Bella removed the rose and took off the castanets and ran back to where Bluma was sitting.

"How do you like it?"

"Okay. But I don't know what the words mean."

"Either do I. But I'm going to find out. I'm going to learn." She threw herself onto the sand next to Bluma. "You could go to my college."

"I don't want to be a Spanish teacher."

"You don't have to. Be something else."

"I'll probably go to Washburne."

"To secretarial school? You want to?"

"I'll learn a skill, something useful. I'll get a job. What does it matter; you're going far away, where they speak Spanish."

Bella put her arm around Bluma, then got up and pulled her to her feet.

"Come on, we got to look for fish. With all this water there's bound to be some."

In a little wood building that looked like a guard post, and that stood by the back of the hotel, they found a fisherman with a bucket full of whitefish. He was willing to sell them one, wrapped in newspaper, on one condition. They had to take it back to their house and the icebox as fast as they could.

"Otherwise it'll go bad," he warned. "And I don't want anyone saying that my fish aren't the freshest around. When I look at you, I see a couple of girls who aren't in a hurry to get anywhere."

"We're in a hurry," Bella told the fisherman. "Just look at us."

They walked along the wheelbarrow path, balancing on the planks, Bella carrying the fish under one arm.

"We should have got a smoked fish," Bluma said. "I don't like being in a hurry."

"I eat smoked fish every day. Anyway, they don't have it out here."

Bella stopped and put a hand on Bluma's shoulder. "You know, you can study anything you want to at Junior College."

"You're the one going there. I'm the class dunce, remember? I'm going to take shorthand and do steno and type letters."

"You're the class dunce only because your stomach hurts."

"I know that. But it still hurts. And I'm still the dunce."

They went past the shacks, rentals for people not lucky enough to have a Dr. Donnell in the family.

"Let's see what's inside that place."

"I don't think we ought to." Bella looked over her shoulder, toward the bluff, in case her parents were watching with a spyglass.

Bluma rattled the screen door of a cottage.

"You sure you should be doing that?"

"There's no one home. They would've answered by now."

Bluma wormed her fingers through a tear in the screen and unlatched the door. If this was breaking in, then being a thief must be easy.

"What do we do?"

"Nothing," Bluma told her. "Have a look around."

She lifted the latch from its eye and pulled the screen door open, then knocked on the loose front door.

"Company's coming!"

The flimsy door opened on its own. Bluma hardly had to nudge it. The place was waiting for them.

The shack made Dr. Donnell's cottage look like luxury. The floorboards sagged in the middle and in some places they didn't even meet. Bluma knelt down and looked through a crack. Below, the sand was cool and shadowy and damp.

"I see sand."

"Don't fall through."

A jelly jar stood on the kitchen table. The previous tenants must have left in a hurry.

"Why would anyone leave this behind?"

Bluma opened the jar. The contents were covered in a white fur of mould.

She dropped the jar onto the table. "This jelly is haunted!"

"Right. Haunted jelly."

"Look, there's white ghosts on it."

"Take a bite, I dare you."

"You go first!"

Bella laughed, dropped the fish on the table and threw herself onto the bare mattress of the day bed. The metal springs protested.

"I'm the papa," she announced. "I'm the king of the house."

"If you're the papa, that means you can't talk," Bluma told her. "You just grunt. And that means I'm the mama. The mama's the real king." She thought about that a second. "The mama's queen."

"Come sit on my lap, Big Mama," Bella beckoned her from the creaky bed.

Bluma crossed her arms over her chest and stamped her bare foot.

"I can't. It's that time of the month."

Bella sat up, intrigued. "It is?"

"Of course not, silly! Otherwise I couldn't be on the beach and all that."

"Then come and bounce on the bed."

"Let me explore first."

Bluma wandered over to the kitchen area, scuffing at the shreds of torn linoleum that clung to the floorboards in spots. Bella jumped off the bed and went to do her own exploring in the bedroom. They were living in Donnell luxury, with real glass in the windows. Here there were just wooden shutters over torn screens.

Bella looked into the closet and pulled open the chests of drawers. They were empty except for beetles and ants and sawdust. Bluma came and looked over her shoulder.

"Nothing for us to wear," Bella told her.

"Everything's empty. We can move our things in."

"Sure. What do we say when the people show up?"

"Sorry, too bad for you! We got here first."

We could live here, Bluma figured, the two of us. Put some stuff in the drawers, hang some things in the closet. That way Bella wouldn't go to college.

The room had a Murphy bed in the back of the door. Bluma pulled on the rope. Obediently, the bed descended, then folded open, creaking and sighing as it reached the floor. She sat on it and ran her palms over the mattress. Who had laid their bodies on this bed? She might lie down on a bed like this one day, but love would never come to her.

"A penny for your thoughts," Bella said. "You look all dreamy."

"Me, dreamy? I don't dream."

"Impossible! Everyone does."

Bella bounced onto the bed next to her. A mouse bolted from a hole in the mattress and streaked across the floor into an open knot in the boards. Bluma screamed and jumped off the bed.

"Bluma, it's just a mouse. It's more scared than you are."

"How do you know?"

"I'm guessing."

"Let's get out of here," Bluma said. "I heard someone outside. A man with a wheelbarrow come to cart us away."

"We'd better put the bed back."

"Come on — you want to get caught?"

They were worse than thieves. They broke in, but not to steal. They did it to snoop on people who weren't even there.

Bella grabbed the fish on the way out and the screen door slammed behind them like a gunshot. They fled into the dunes, slipping and sliding and falling in the loose, burning-hot sand. Bluma tried to put her shoes on as she ran, but that wasn't working. When they figured they were high enough up the bluff to be safe, they stopped and looked down. There was no one, of course.

"We got away!"

"We really are a couple of girls," Bella laughed. "Scared to death of a mouse."

"There could have been someone," Bluma said.

They collapsed onto the sand. Below, the lake sparkled with silver diamonds.

"We might as well pick some grapes," Bella decided.

"What about the fish?"

Bella unrolled the paper and sniffed it. "He says he's all right."

They climbed the face of the dune toward the wild, untended, dark purple grapes growing on tangled vines.

"They're Concords."

"You know everything about the great outdoors," Bluma said.

She stripped a handful of grapes off the vine. Their skins were as tough as the cover of a baseball, and so sour she spat them out. There was more seed than fruit to them.

"No one can eat these."

"My father makes wine out of them."

"We have nothing to carry them back in."

"Watch this, world," Bella announced.

She pulled off her shirt and stretched it out on the sand, then started dropping grapes onto it by the cluster.

"Someone'll see you! You're not decent! A girl's not supposed to advertise."

"I got my undershirt on."

"It's no bigger than a handkerchief."

"So what? Who's gonna see?"

"Someone," Bluma promised her cousin.

"The man with the wheelbarrow, maybe?"

Bella looked like a Concord grape herself with her taut dark skin. Her ropy muscles moved eagerly along her arms and shoulders, and sweat stood in pools in the hollows of her collarbones.

"You don't have to look at me," she told Bluma.

"You're the one who's advertising."

Bella crossed her arms over her chest. "So I'm not like you. So what?"

"I'll trade any time."

"You would not. You got all the men looking at you. Don't think I can't see it."

"I don't want anybody looking at me. I want to stay the way I am."

"Good luck. Your body does what it wants and you have to play catch-up. You have to make do, one way or another. There's no use trying to stay the way you are."

"You know all sorts of things, cousin."

"I listen to my brothers."

"I can't imagine Laurie talking to me like that."

"My brothers don't talk to me. They talk around me, and I make it my business to listen. I'm just their mascot."

Bella went back to picking grapes. Bluma dropped onto the sand to watch her. Her cousin was a wonder of the world. She didn't even know she wasn't wearing a proper shirt.

After a while Bluma picked herself up and wandered along the crest of the dune. The sun heated the sand like a desert, and the breeze off the lake didn't come this far. Her head spun and she headed for the meagre line of shade under the cottonwoods.

From her spot, Bella lifted her head and wiped the sweat out of her eyes.

"Hey, keep away from that plant!" She stood up. "The one you're standing next to. That's poison ivy — remember, I told you!"

Bluma edged as close as she could to the plant to rile up Bella and make her stop picking grapes. It was a dare, and she liked dares. But the sand tricked her. It slipped away beneath her feet and she stumbled onto the poisonous leaves.

Bella watched it happen.

"You'll get poison ivy."

"I didn't see it."

"You did so. I was watching."

"I can't see anything in this sun. It's too bright. It's too hot out here."

"It's summer, dumbbell, that's why. You've got the whole dune, and there's one little poison ivy plant, and you step right on it. That's what I call bad luck. Let's go. I've got all the grapes I need and my fish is getting hot."

That evening, Bella's mother fried whitefish and the girls watched trails of ants as they marched in and out of the cupboards. Bluma's foot began to itch. She swore she would keep it to herself. She had years of experience doing that. It took discipline and she had it. But of course Bella caught her scratching on the sly.

"I'll fix you," she told her. "Dr. Bella to the rescue."

She slipped behind the partition where the toilet was and came back with a bottle of viscous, sickly looking compound.

"It stinks. And it's pink. I don't want any."

"Doctor's orders. Otherwise the poison ivy will spread up your leg and eat you alive."

"Right!"

"You stepped on it on purpose." She spread calamine on Bluma's foot. "Don't touch it. Let it sink in."

Bella washed her hands.

"You didn't tell her about that plant?" her mother asked.

"I did."

Taube turned, looked at Bluma and shook her head. Bluma attempted a smile. Did she step on it on purpose? If she did, that meant she had a strategy. She had her reasons. She felt proud as she watched the ants march over the threshold and out the door, bearing bread-crumbs past her pink foot. She wasn't just some poor innocent girl things happened to, who didn't know what she was doing.

In the evening, Bella caught Bluma sweeping sand off the sheets with the palm of her hand.

"Talk about a useless thing to do!"

"I'm cleaning house."

"The floor is covered with sand. There's sand between your toes. There's sand in the cupboards and sand in your ears. Why shouldn't there be sand in the bed?"

Bluma stopped. "Aren't you afraid you'll catch my poison ivy?"

"I don't catch it. I'm not allergic. Now let me see your foot."

Bluma lay back on the bed and stuck out her foot. Bella took it, turned it this way and that, murmured, "Not so bad," then shook the bottle of calamine lotion. The stuff was thick and dark pink and had a medicinal smell, not exactly a stink, but bad enough to make you think it was going to work. She spread calamine on the red welts on Bluma's foot.

"Try not to scratch yourself."

"You're sure you're not going to catch it?"

"Not from you." She narrowed her eyes. "You wouldn't give it to me, would you?"

"I'll try not to."

They laughed. It was worth catching poison ivy to be on the same side of laughter.

IN THE MIDDLE OF THE night, the itching returned. Bluma slid her hand down the length of her bare leg to her right foot, trying not to disturb Bella. The problem was the sand. It woke her up, and that brought the itching back.

Her hand reached her right foot. I'm not scratching, she told Bella, sleeping next to her. I'm just holding. She stayed in that position, bent, her muscles cramping. She listened to the waves hitting the beach, each time with a different rhythm. She knew because she counted the seconds between waves. They did this everywhere around the world, night and day, and it didn't matter who heard or who didn't.

She thought about Laurie. What would he say if she told him she was leaving Burnside for Lexington Street? As if she could do that. Class dunce. If anyone was going to leave, he would. It wouldn't be long. All she could hope for was a quick goodbye and a vague promise for the future.

She'd be alone in the house with no ally against her father. Caring for Libby was out of the question. She could barely bring herself to look at her half-sister. Half-sister, half-there. She didn't care how impolite that sounded. The thought of Laurie leaving made her foot itch. He would have bawled her out for not falling asleep. If you can't sleep, there must be something wrong with you. You have a disease, and it has a name, insomnia, not like the other disease she had that didn't have a name, only a symptom: nervous stomach.

Some nights Bluma was sure she'd never sleep again. But she must have fallen back asleep, because suddenly she was awake and her eyes open. There was a presence in the room, a blurry pale form. A kitchen match flared and Bella's mother appeared above her, a kerosene lamp in her hand. She lit it and trimmed the wick as low as it would go. Light splashed across her body as she turned to set the lamp on the bookcase. Bluma looked. Her aunt was naked. Her heavy breasts rose as she lifted her arms and untied the clip that held her hair. Two dark nests curled in her underarms. Bluma had never seen a naked woman. She didn't think women were allowed to be naked outside of the bath. Her aunt's hair fell on her shoulders and down her back. A tangled shadow gathered between her thighs.

Taube turned and Bluma had just enough time to shut her eyes and pretend to sleep. She felt her aunt leaning over her. "Poor child, such pain." Then Taube picked up the lamp and moved behind the partition, where the adults had their bed.

Bluma opened her eyes in the darkness. She spent the rest of the night awake.

"HEY, MR. MELON MAN!"

The girls spotted the farmer coming out of the hotel kitchen, about to drop his straw hat back onto his head. When he saw Bella and Bluma, he kept his hat in his hand.

"I bet you don't remember us," Bluma said.

"How could I forget you, young lady?"

"We were supposed to be your best customers," Bella added. She thrust her hand into her trousers pocket and jingled her change. "Money talks and nobody walks."

The farmer chuckled. When had a girl last talked to him that way?

"You certainly have quite the tongue in your mouth," he told her.

"I'll take that as a compliment."

"Let's just look. I might have something left in the cart for a customer like you."

His cart was on the shady side of the hotel. Bella patted the horse on the nose as they went past.

"I bet you remember me," she said to it.

"Whew! That horse smells strong," Bluma marvelled.

"Smells of horse," the farmer said.

"I bet he's got horse sense too," Bella chimed in.

"You girls never let up, do you? I don't think I could keep pace."

He climbed into the cart and handed down a crate, something he'd never do with other customers, but these girls were different. He reminded himself not to favour one over the other, but it was pretty hard for a man, even a quiet-hearted one like himself, not to let his eyes linger on the well-developed one who thought his horse smelled strong.

In the crate, there were runner beans and sugar snap peas and leaf lettuces as wide as home plate in a ball game.

"Is the quality guaranteed?" Bella asked.

"How did you like my watermelon?"

"I'd take another if you had one," Bluma said.

"This time, don't swallow the seeds!" the farmer teased her. "How are you going to get it home?"

"We have a system."

"If you go swimming, you don't want to leave the produce out in the sun."

"The sweetshop man will keep it for us."

The farmer shook his head in admiration. "The world is your playground. You got it all figured out."

"It only looks that way," Bluma told him.

Bella sized up the choices from what the farmer had in his crate. She'd learned a few secrets about food from her mother, and the first one was that the purpose of eating is to fill up. That meant potatoes, lots of them. But the Americanization worker who came to her school told them that eating green vegetables was the American way, though they never showed up on her table, except for cabbage, but it wasn't green by the time it got there. She didn't know what snap peas and runner beans tasted like, but she would find out. Lettuce was useless according to her mother because it was made out of water. But watermelon was good, even though it was nearly all water too.

"You're quite the shopper," the farmer complimented Bella once she'd paid him. "Tell you what. I'll leave everything in this crate and you can get it home easier that way. But you have to give it back to me afterwards."

"I will, I swear."

"You don't have to swear. I trust you girls."

"You do?" Bluma asked.

"Just leave the crate with your sweetshop man, or in the hotel kitchen."

The farmer climbed onto the buckboard and urged his horse forward. Bella and Bluma walked toward the rambling wood-frame hotel with their crate of vegetables.

"People are so nice here," Bluma said.

"Why wouldn't they be?"

"They're nice because we're The Fledglings."

"I'd rather be a Fledgling than anything else."

"Naturally," Bluma told her. "A fledgling is just starting out. Nothing's happened to you yet. You can do anything."

WITH THEIR JOHNSON'S BEACH CONNECTIONS, they kept the icebox at the Donnell cottage full. They moved in and out of the hotel like paying guests. They left the farmer's crate in the hotel kitchen, because when the sweetshop man saw them come through the door, he shooed them away. But the kitchen staff and the social director, whose main job was to keep everyone's glass full, loved their wise-guy talk.

"What would you say to a little nip?" the social director asked Bluma one late afternoon when the girls were at the hotel buying fish.

Bluma looked the man in the eye. His getup was ridiculous: white pants, white tennis shoes and a white jacket with a flower pinned to it.

"My father's a bootlegger," she told him. "I've seen enough booze to last me my whole life."

The man laughed and pulled at the sleeves of his jacket. "Well, isn't that the darndest thing? That explains a lot."

"Besides," Bella added, "she's underage."

"If drinking's illegal, then there's no age for it."

"That's the kind of stupid thing we'd say," Bluma told him.

"All right, all right." The man put his hands in the air. "I get the message."

They headed out the door, Bluma leading the way.

"See you girls again," the social director called after them.

Taube went to the beach with the girls once. The sun's generosity poured mercilessly down upon her and her armour of black shawls. Showing your body was for her daughter and niece, not for a grown woman. She looked like the grim reaper, walking across the sand as streams of sweat ran down her body, trapped underneath her black woollens. Her religion was born in the desert, but along their wanderings, her people had forgotten how to dress for hot weather. She strode up to the water and glared suspiciously at the lake. Its meek wavelets broke docilely at her feet. She turned her back on its harsh reflection, uncomfortably aware of her body. The hotel veranda provided the only shade, but she was certainly not going to sit there with the Gentiles drinking whisky out of teacups. To the girls' relief, she soon retreated to the cottage to sit in companionable silence with her husband.

This was the freedom Bella and Bluma were waiting for. They charged into the freezing lake in the standard-issue gym shorts they wore for physical education. The shorts looked like bloomers — "Blumas," Bella called them, a mass of shapeless cotton that both girls liked. She was wearing their knapsack high on her back. When they were waist-deep, they stopped.

"I'm gonna make a proper young lady out of you if it's the last thing I do! Now get to work and wash this stuff!"

She started pulling dirty shirts and underthings from the knapsack and throwing them at Bluma's head. Bluma grabbed them out of the air. She dunked the clothes and squeezed them out, over and over again, her job because she had complained about the lack of hygiene. When she finished, she dipped into the lake neck-deep and squealed.

"There! I washed my last thing!"

In a soaking shirt clinging to her body, Bluma was advertising something fierce, but Bella decided not to point out the obvious. They dashed out of the cold water and threw themselves onto the sand to dry.

"I told you we could wash our clothes in the lake!"

Bluma sniffed the edge of her shirt. "Smells like herring."

"As long as it's fresh."

Bluma wouldn't have said no to a cake of soap. But she was studying to be a tomboy which, she figured, was the only way to keep men's eyes off her. If Bella washed herself in the lake without soap and dried herself on the sand, then she would too.

"It's time for your appointment with Dr. Bella."

She picked up her cousin's sandy foot and inspected it.

"Try not to scratch. It'll get infected."

"I know, I know. Ever try not to itch?"

She turned Bluma's feet so she could inspect her soles, and gave a low whistle.

"You got it bad. Luckily I have just the thing."

She pulled a pair of tweezers from a side pocket of her knapsack, and spit on them to clean them off.

"If it hurts, you're allowed to scream."

Bluma howled and moaned and rolled in the sand in mock agony as Bella grimly pulled out one splinter after another.

"I told you not to drag your feet on the boards!"

"Help, I'm dying! Put me out of my misery!"

Bella was pitiless. She had Bluma's feet in a vise-like grip.

THE HOTEL'S SOCIAL DIRECTOR HADN'T given up trying to get into Bluma's good graces. Women were suggestible, and though she might be underage according to her friend, she was still a woman. The way she hung around the hotel with her friend gave him plenty of openings.

One afternoon, the girls marched into the kitchen.

"It's our last day," they announced. "We came to say thank you."

"All good things have to come to an end," said one of the chefs.

"How come?" Bluma asked him.

He looked up from his cutting board. "I'll let you know when I get the answer!"

He went back to his slicing, attentive to his fingers.

The social director wandered into the kitchen. He liked the camaraderie of the place, and the cement floor was cool beneath his tired feet. The cooks didn't drink on the job, but they didn't give him a sideways look if he took a little nip.

"You gave up on the ice cream man? Now you're on to us?" he asked Bluma.

"Watch out or we'll sing for you," Bella threatened.

The social director got a genius idea. "Tonight we're going to have a nice big bonfire on the beach at sundown. It'll be my send-off for you," he said to Bluma, "only I don't have time to collect the wood. Find me driftwood, logs, branches — anything that burns. You two want to do that? I'll make it worth your while."

"We work for union wage," Bella told him.

"Union? These days a man's lucky to have a job! You see the burned spot on the beach in front of the hotel? Dump the wood there."

"You're the boss, Boss," Bluma told him.

The girls slipped out the door before the social director could make his move.

"What do you think? Do we do it?" Bella asked a minute later.

Bluma looked up and down the beach. "Not a lot else to do."

"We don't know how much he's going to pay. And you'll have to kiss him goodbye."

"I'll take my chances," Bluma said.

They strolled up and down the beach in search of driftwood. Carrying it was the problem. The sand closest to the water was solid enough to hold the wheelbarrow, and Bella ran to get it. With the lake lapping at her ankles, she pushed it along as Bluma hunted for anything burnable.

She came back with an armful of branches and jumped into the wheelbarrow with them.

"You want to be part of the fire?" Bella asked.

"The flames danced higher on my funeral pyre." She put her hand over her heart and rolled her eyes backward, a teenage Sarah Bernhardt.

Bella steered the wheelbarrow into the lake and dumped Bluma in. The way her shirt clung to her body was wonderful. With Bluma chasing her, she came across the ruins of a wooden chest, half sunk in the sand.

"I can't believe the stuff people throw away."

"Maybe it fell off a boat. Maybe there's a body inside."

They rocked and twisted and pried at the top of the chest until the cover popped off. Inside was a small school of dead fish.

"Ho, ho, ho and a bottle of rum."

"Drink and the devil had done for the rest!"

"You're not the class dunce after all! That would make a great Fledglings song."

"Right. And we're supposed to be young ladies!"

DAVID HOMEL

Bella and Bluma piled the driftwood in the fire pit on the beach, then brought the wheelbarrow back around the side of the hotel. The sweetshop man was there, sharing a cigarette with the social director.

"A beach bonfire's good for business," he told the sweetshop man. "Look at that heap. Those girls did a hell of a job. You should give them a touch of the sweet stuff."

The girls absolutely refused to take the bait.

"Strawberry," Bluma said.

"They don't know what blushing is," the sweetshop man marvelled.

"We're city girls," Bella explained.

The man came back a minute later with two small strawberry cones.

"You may be Hebes, but you're good kids," he told them.

"We feel the same about you," Bella answered.

"And you give as good as you get."

"No, not quite," Bluma told him. "We're not allowed to. But one day we will, and then you'll see."

"How much you gonna pay us?" Bella asked the social director.

"It doesn't feel right giving money to girls."

Bluma stepped in. "Don't bother, we did it for fun."

She pulled on Bella's sleeve and they walked away, licking their ice cream.

THAT EVENING AT SUNDOWN, THE social director set the heap of wood on fire with the help of some low-grade booze. Whisky was cheaper than gasoline, and there's nothing like the sudden whoosh of flame to thrill the crowd. The sweetshop man circulated with his wares among the young marrieds and couples beyond the bonds of wedlock who came out of their rooms to gaze at the fire and take a break from each other. The social director didn't sing much better than Bella and Bluma, but that didn't keep him from leading the assembled multitudes in song. Everyone around a bonfire, singing in one voice — if this wasn't good clean fun, what was? "Michael, Row the Boat Ashore." "Pay Me

146

My Money Down." "The Rock Island Line." They were all slave songs and the guests might not have sung along if they'd known where they came from.

> *Pay me oh pay me*
> *Pay me my money down*
> *Pay me or go to jail*
> *Pay me my money down.*

Bella took Bluma's hand. They were standing as close to the fire as they could. Bella snuck a glance at Bluma. Her cousin was chewing on the inside of her cheek.

Bella squeezed her hand to make her stop.

"I'd stay here forever," Bluma said to the fire.

"Dr. Donnell's coming tomorrow. We were lucky to get the place when we did."

"Yeah. Sure. Lucky."

"Don't forget what I said about college. There's room at our place. And I don't want to hear about you being class dunce. We don't tell that story anymore."

Bluma pulled her hand from her cousin's grasp and wiped the sweat off her forehead. Decontamination was a temporary measure.

EIGHT

Right Ventricle Hypertrophy

LIBBY CAUGHT COLD EASILY, AND breathing was a labour for her, so she was rarely allowed out in winter. But with the warm days, the door onto the front yard was left open so she could get some air behind the tall fence her stepfather had built for her.

Where there's a fence, there's always some way to wriggle under it or climb over it. Someone is going to get curious and want to know why it's there and what's on the other side. The Burnside kids who went past the Goldberg property had plenty of opinions about the Chicken Coop, since their fathers spent a good part of their time and pay there. When the fence went up, they naturally started climbing on it, figuring it had something to do with booze. Maybe there were barrels of the stuff behind it. Maybe they could get their hands on the hooch and find out what all the excitement was about.

The fence was built by a jack-of-all-trades carpenter who rewarded Abe Goldberg's meagre pay with a quick and sloppy job, with plenty of uneven boards for footholds. The kids were on the fence in no time. When a pair of red-haired boys popped their heads over the top and peered down, Libby thought her unspoken prayers had been answered. Here were playmates; here was affection. Libby beckoned to the boys to climb over and come to her.

"For the love of Jesus!"

They fell back from the top as if they'd been shot, then scattered down the street with Libby's anxious mewling in their ears. Her appearance scared them, but worse was her naked need to share her affection.

Their terror lasted half a block. When the boys stopped to catch their breath, a grand idea visited them. The next day they were back. For a penny, they would boost their friends up so they could get an eyeful too, especially since Libby had a way of pulling at her clothes so they hung loose around her body. Pretty soon every boy in the neighbourhood was clinging to the top of the fence for as long as his muscles would hold him.

Libby was enchanted with their company. But the visits never lasted long, and no one came over to her side of the fence. She wished for more boys who would stay longer and come closer.

From an upstairs window, Rachel watched the spectacle. "Savages!" She tapped on the window glass to chase the boys away, but they heard nothing, and Libby paid her no attention. She cursed Mr. Reisz, which did no good. He'd already paid the price.

The Midwestern heat was Libby's accomplice. Doors and windows left open in hopes of a breeze, Bluma off somewhere else, her mother sitting facing the electric fan with her eyes closed and the front of her dress open. When Libby tried to get her attention, Rachel murmured, "Savages!" and made a great show of mopping her forehead.

Libby went out the open door and found herself in the backyard between the house and the Coop. It was evening and the air was heavy with humidity and coal dust. The elms were limp and the nervous rattle of the freight yards came riding up from the end of the street.

The door to the Coop was open. Libby heard bursts of joyous laughter and she followed the happy sound.

A man was leaning against the doorjamb, whisky in one hand, a glass of ice water in the other. He turned to his friends in the room behind him who were leaning back in their chairs, drinking and sweating.

"I do believe I'd better give up the sauce," the man announced.

His friends laughed. Anyone who threatened to break the bonds of fellowship deserved to be scoffed at.

"No, this time it's for real. I'm beginning to see hallucinations, right in front of me, clear as day."

The man rubbed his eyes. Libby did not disappear.

"Were I to be seeing pink elephants and green snakes, I'd understand. But I'm seeing the strangest little girl."

"It's Goldberg's daughter. What about her?"

"No," the man insisted. "This girl is something completely different."

He extended a hand through the shimmering air.

"Come, my beautiful hallucination. Come, my fearful monster, show me you're not real."

Libby was delighted. She went to the man's side. When she got close enough, he brushed her hair with his hand.

"Why, child, you are completely real. Of all the damned things!" He rubbed a few strands of her hair between his fingers as if it were fine cloth. "What manner of creature are you?"

Libby began to sing. She loved music as long as it had no words. In Shukyan, on market days when she would stand at her mother's side at her stall, an ancient man would come and sing to her. Di, di-di-di, di-di-di, half-song, half-prayer, and she loved it, and loved how the old man bent and bowed to her as he sang his wordless song. At the door to the Coop where she wasn't allowed to go, she sang that beggar's song for an Irish drinker wilting in the heat.

"Come," he said to her. "There are many good people here in need of your song."

She went no farther than the open door. The men would have to come to her, and they did. They gathered with drinks in their hands as she sang the Shukyan alms song.

"What a wonderful place this is, this Chicken Coop," the man said. "One girl cuts the cards and serves you whisky, and brings good luck to all, each in his turn. Then comes this musical hallucination, a monster you might say, but of absolutely the best kind. She's a spirit, I'm telling you, a will-o'-the-wisp, a good banshee, a spirit from the lost country."

"Shut up with your poetizing, O'Connor, and lend an ear."

O'Connor did. Libby's song transported the men to a gentler country, better than the one they were living in, where they were paid slave wages to keep the peace from being troubled by others with even less in their pockets than they had. Hallucination or not, they began to sing with her. Their inhibitions were loosened, but something more was at work than Chicken Coop whisky. Their songs and Libby's had nothing in common outside of unending sadness. The Irish tenors rose to shore up Libby's wavering voice. Often she could not control her muscles, they cast her this way and that in waves of palsied confusion, but now she was calm and concentrated. She bent and bowed like the beggar in the market, and the Irishmen imitated her in encouragement.

Abe returned from the backroom with a keg of whisky on his shoulder. His arrival broke the spell. He was mortified by the sight of Libby, his secret weakness standing there for all to see in the early evening light.

He set the keg on the floor, something two men together would have had trouble doing. The weight of his secret was double the keg's. Every Mick cop in Burnside could read his passion for this strange girl who wasn't his. He was like Mr. Reisz who had come before him: he heard accusations that weren't there from people who couldn't have made them. No man in the room was in the mood to poke fun. They were all under Libby's spell.

Abe went to her.

"Come with me," he ordered.

His voice was harsh in the midst of the wonderful music. She obeyed with a stifled cry of protest. It was no more than a squeak, a mouse caught in a cat's paws. Abe led her across the yard and into the house. The Irishmen's song faded. It took a great shock to make a roomful of Irish drinkers stop singing, but that's what happened.

In the kitchen, Abe found his wife sleeping in her chair, lulled by the heat and the noise of the table fan.

"You let her get out!"

Libby whimpered. She hated it when a man raised his voice.

Rachel opened her eyes. She didn't bother waking up completely.

"You don't do anything. You don't pay attention. You don't watch her. She went into the Coop with the Irish. You want that? She's your child too!"

Rachel didn't hear the "too." Abe's routine rages exhausted her and she'd stopped listening, even when he said something incredible. Abe Goldberg might have been a bootlegger, a low-grade gangster, but in his mind he was Libby's protector, and he loved her better than her own mother. He was proud of that. Another man might have planted his seed in his betrothed while he was off with the Czar's men, but his love for Libby wiped that stain away.

Rachel stood up heavily. Libby grabbed at her breasts through her open dress. Rachel brushed aside the girl's hand.

"Come," Rachel told her.

She led her away, out of the kitchen and the circle of hot wind stirred by the fan. Rachel had no place to go, but away from her husband was a start. She couldn't stand the airs he put on, the way he boasted about being better with Libby than she was.

He was better with her, but she didn't care. Finally she was rejecting her first-born. It was America's fault. The enormous fatigue she felt, the loneliness. In Shukyan, the village watched out for Libby. In Burnside she was a monster, a hindrance, an embarrassment to stick behind a fence. The village wasn't there to care for her. Her husband's care was just for show. He was in it for himself.

Rachel pushed open the door to Libby's room but her daughter wouldn't go in. She stood in front of this luxury — her own room — and acted like she didn't understand what was expected of her.

"Have it your way," Rachel told her. "Stand here for the rest of your life. I should care."

The upstairs was an oven. She couldn't wait to get back to her chair in front of the fan and close her eyes, and retreat into sleep, though it wasn't real sleep because it brought no relief.

The problem was America. She was always tired here. In Shukyan she was a miracle of energy. Everyone in the village agreed on that. The child, the business of being a widow after Mr. Reisz's accident, keeping house, dealing with the farmers, running the stall on market days — she did it and never thought twice. But America had made her immensely fatigued. She didn't know what being tired was until she came to Burnside, where she wasn't doing a tenth of the chores she did in Shukyan.

Maybe immigration isn't for everyone, she thought. Maybe it's not for anyone. But plenty of people made it. There were new success stories every day.

From across the darkened yard, where the men usually shouted and slugged each other in the face until they fell down in a heap, Rachel heard something strange. The Irish were singing a wordless Yiddish tune she recognized from her days in the market. The old beggar who had his spot by her stall had come to visit her in Burnside.

By the time Abe got back to his business at the Coop, the Irishmen were in full and glorious song, singing Libby's melody.

COLD KILLS; HEAT DOESN'T. ABE believed that. But summer was the tougher season for Libby. She stood behind the fence in full sun in the front yard and waited for her visitors. Streams of sweat ran off her body and her pale skin burned. She didn't drink the glasses of water her father told her she was supposed to in this heat.

Libby was in deep sadness. She had been torn away from the Coop at the height of her triumph and the boys had stopped visiting. Her stepfather had threatened to kill anyone who climbed on his rickety fence. As she waited for the boys who did not appear, her heart beat harder with anticipation and disappointment.

Right ventricle hypertrophy was killing her. No one was there to notice her breathlessness, her listlessness, her weakening limbs. In the middle of the afternoon, her oxygen-starved legs bent lifelessly under her as she stood by the front door, staring across the yard at the fence. She dropped to the ground. Her forehead struck the concrete step and her skin split open neatly. She was too weak to call out, too fascinated by the blood that streamed from her head. She'd been so well cared for in Shukyan, and so closeted in Burnside, that she'd never suffered even the most ordinary childhood scrape, and she didn't know how to react to this one.

Abe Goldberg found her several hours later. By then the blood had stopped and dried, closing up the wound. He picked Libby up in his arms and marched into the house.

"Look at this! This is how much you care."

Rachel gazed at him, unimpressed. "You know full well she wasn't made to live forever."

"What do you know? Nothing! I'll cure her myself," he promised.

Abe swept out the back door on his way to the Coop. The slam of the screen door stirred her.

"The moral conscience of Burnside!" she called after him. "If you only knew how bad those clothes fit you!"

IN THE AUGUST HEAT, THE thirst for a cold beer drew the Burnside drinkers to the Coop, but to their unhappiness, Abe announced he was closing early. His customers did not take him seriously. They ordered another round. Instead of lining up the glasses, he chased them out of his place. Grumbling, some still sober, they filed out into the evening, threatening to take their business elsewhere.

"Go home to your wives!" Abe yelled at them.

The men stopped in the dusty alley behind the Coop.

"Of all the damned things for a bootlegger to say," O'Connor remarked. "Something must be wrong with his mind."

He shook his head and led his fellows into the night.

"We'll have to start drinking with the polacks if this keeps up," they lamented.

Once the customers were gone, Abe locked the door, doused the lights and went into the backroom. Libby lay on the pallet he had made for her among the barrels. The speakeasy became a sickroom, its air heavy with the antiseptic smell of whisky. Everything was still and quiet and dim. Abe stood above her and listened to Libby's noisy, shallow, rapid breathing. She was agitated in her half-sleep, she moaned and tried to push something away in her dreams, but her arms had no strength. He didn't know what to do, or how to help her. He believed that being there was help enough. He was a man of will: he would will her back to her poor life despite her furiously pumping heart and her blood that didn't carry the oxygen it should and the infection from her head wound she couldn't fight.

Abe lowered himself onto a chair at the foot of her pallet. On the back of the chair hung her bloody clothing. He was cramped and uncomfortable, but that was as it should be. He would share in her suffering. He would take it from her and carry it himself, since he was strong enough for two. As he kept his fierce vigil, he thought of what he could say to make her want to cling to life. A story — he would tell her a story. That's what fathers did, and he would too, even if he wasn't her father. He would be better than her real father, and better than her mother, which wouldn't take much. He would tell her a complicated story that took forever. He'd make it good so she'd want to stick around till the end.

The best story he knew was how he came to America, and all the things that happened along the way. It was one story he hadn't told anyone.

Until then he'd never figured his life contained any kind of story, let alone a good long one to tell Libby, who could never tell anyone else. It can't be, Abe told her, that I was born bad. People aren't born bad. They get that way. So something must have happened.

Okay, he admitted to Libby, back in Shukyan I was no angel. I wasn't much for books. I could read, but I never understood what I read. People would stare at me and say, "You read it, right? So understand!" But I didn't. Reading something doesn't mean you understand. What was there to understand in the first place?

He stopped. He was afraid he didn't know how to tell a story. That it was beyond his power, the way people told him it was. Then he remembered something that could make a story. Only an audience like Libby would do. A strange event had befallen him on the road between Shukyan and Danzig. It wasn't the kind of thing that would turn a man into a bad man, but neither was it a story you'd volunteer to tell, unless you were Abe Goldberg trying to save a sleeping Mongoloid girl you inexplicably loved more than your own blood.

He had sojourned among the Czar's men once, and been a pliant soldier. That had cost him dearly. Another man had known his wife before he had, a secret shame that galled him. He knew the Czar's press gangs would return for him, and when they did, he swore they would find empty space. He packed his bag and rehearsed the farewell words. The summons to the army was his signal to leave for America. He began walking west with little idea of where he was going. Columns of men were doing the same thing for the same reason, but he didn't want to walk with them. They seemed too conspicuous, and he was afraid of getting caught.

After three days of walking, he came to his first big obstacle. He had been expecting it, since Shukyan was rich in tales about men escaping this way. It was the end of the afternoon, and the shadows were gathering. A wide river lay before him. A couple hundred metres further along, he saw a bridge. Judging by the soldiers and other men in uniform gathered there, he was at a border, though he didn't know what the next country was, only that he had to get there. He walked to the water's edge. The river was muddy and slow moving. If the soldiers saw him, they made no move. Only people who wanted to cross the bridge mattered. Abe retreated from the riverbank and found shelter in a copse of trees. They were birches, bigger than the ones he knew in Shukyan, where the land was acidic and made life difficult for trees and every other thing that tried to grow. He leaned against the silver-white bark and immediately fell asleep.

He awoke sometime later, in darkness. He was pleased: his plan was working so far. He took off his boots and put them in his sack, which he tied around his neck. As quietly as he could, he began to swim across the river. The current didn't bother him. The water was lazy, slow and heavy with silt. There was no spring runoff. He wasn't afraid of water, not like most people he knew who were afraid of everything. Dogs barked in the distance, but there were no signs of life from the bridge or the opposite bank.

When he reached it, he took off his clothes to wring them out. When that was done, as if she were waiting for him to finish his domestic routine, a woman spoke to him from the darkness.

"You must be tired," she said in Polish. "Come and lie down."

"No, I'm not," he answered in Russian.

"Come and lie with me."

In Tabiliak's view of the world, sex was a capricious act that put a man in danger. "I can't," he told the woman.

He heard laughter in the dark.

"You'll get pregnant," he warned her.

He could think of no better argument. It should work on whoever she was, since it often worked on him.

"Is that so?" the woman's voice asked. "What are you, such a potent bull? Let me see! Anyway, I decide whether I get pregnant or not."

The woman stepped out of the darkness and stood before him.

He put his hands over his privates. She pushed his modesty aside.

"And you're a Jew, as I suspected," she said.

Abe Tabiliak looked at the ground.

"Look at me," she ordered.

He glanced at her, briefly. She was older than he was, with a handsome, weathered face, colourless eyes and something he had never seen before: long, loose hair hanging to her shoulders.

"I can't," he repeated.

"What can't you do?"

"I can't."

She listed the reasons why he would.

"You're a Jew. You just swam across the river. You don't have papers. Maybe you ran away from the army."

As she spoke, his hands returned to cover his privates. She reached down and uncovered him, and with one sure finger, she made him respond to her touch. To his everlasting shame, his body eagerly answered. A woman had never done that to him.

"Get me pregnant," she told him. "I dare you." She weighed his organ in her hand, as if calculating the chances. "Fill me to the brim, Yid."

He discovered that night that it was better not to be a Jew. A Jew was a plaything of the fates. For one endless night, that's what he was — her plaything. He was ashamed how the Polish woman showed him things he didn't know existed and couldn't have imagined, the way she exposed his ignorance and conducted his body. Her compliments shamed him. He did not want to hear that he had a dick like a donkey. That didn't seem like a desirable thing for a man. And he didn't like the way she panted like a horse and scratched like a cat and bit like a dog.

In the first light of morning, foggy and grey but with the promise of blue skies above the mist, he contemplated the face of his tormentor. Like him, she hadn't slept much, and what sleep she did enjoy was on top of him, keeping him prisoner inside her. Through the night, her muscles would clench around his penis, clench and let go, hold and release; even as she slept, another woman seemed to be awake within her, a possessing spirit that would not stop making love to him, the helpless refugee. In the Czar's army he'd heard stories about this kind of thing, tales of a lascivious spirit that inhabited a woman's body and visited men in their sleep, leaving them drenched and exhausted. Unfettered by imagination, he had not believed in those stories.

The morning light showed him something he hadn't seen the night before: her pudgy, doughy body and flattened face, the way her hair hung flat against her skull. A Tatar, a tribe from the East. This was too much laughter, even from God, who made him the victim of a woman with the same enormous need for affection that his stepdaughter had.

He threw her off and got to his feet. His damp clothes lay on the ground in a heap. As he pulled them on, she grabbed for her dress and covered her breasts and the spot between her legs, as if she'd caught his modesty. That was not a Mongoloid thing to do. Her features were like any other woman's.

Once he was dressed, his clothes smelling like mushrooms, and had his pack on his back, he didn't know what to do next. The woman had all but taken him by force, but he felt he should say something to her, a few polite words of farewell. Abraham wasn't devout, but he was superstitious, and he worried about the seed he was leaving behind. She could take those wayward children and bewitch them, turn them into monsters that would track him down and torment him, even on the other side of the ocean.

"Good day to you, madame," he said.

She declined his outstretched hand.

What could I have done? he wondered as he walked across the meadow that rose from the riverbank. He turned and looked back. The woman was sitting on the ground, still clutching her dress, and from where he stood, he could see she was crying.

"I made it to Danzig," he told Libby, "without anything else happening to me except a dog bite. The dog wasn't rabid. I'm a lucky guy!"

In the silence, he lifted himself from his chair and went into the main room of the Coop. Stale cigar smoke hung heavily there, and he opened the door to let it out. Kids were shouting and dashing down the alley. The noise they made came from another planet, where children played in the dusty twilight.

He sat down at Libby's feet and put his hands in his pockets.

"You leave the place where you were born. You lose everything you had and everything you were. But that saves your life."

Libby had no opinion. She had experienced the same losses, but got nothing in return.

"Pretty good story, huh?"

It wasn't good enough. Libby's heart gave out as Abe sat by her side, satisfied with his story that no one would ever hear.

ABE GOLDBERG WAS NOT GENTLE in his grieving. When he understood that Libby had slipped away on him, he felt rage and rejection. There was no resignation in his mourning. Libby had died on him; it was a slap in the face and for once he couldn't pay it back. He had done so much for her, and she had responded with nothingness.

Abe sent word via the Burnside precinct station that the Coop was open for business again, with apologies for having inconvenienced his best customers. Some returned, but others, the singers and storytellers who gave the place its charm, had taken up new habits elsewhere. Abe was at loose ends, already bored with his grief.

The day after Libby was buried, Abe came into the Coop and found Laurie there. The boy didn't look up. He was deeply absorbed in the sports section of the newspaper his father kept for the customers.

Abe went to the cabinet and produced a bottle and a glass. He set both on the paper his son was studying.

"It's time you learn to drink."

"I'm busy," Laurie told him.

"Yeah, reading the paper. You got nothing better to do."

"As a matter of fact I do, just as soon as I finish the scores."

At first Abe didn't care. Then he wondered whether his son might have something going that was better than what he had.

"What can that be?"

"I've got someone to see, and I don't want to be stinking of whisky."

"Anybody you would be seeing," Abe Goldberg told him, "shouldn't be fussy about that."

"Don't be so sure. Girls don't like it. Or don't you know that by now?"

So it was girls. His son was going soft on him.

"Why should you care what they think?"

The reason was so obvious Laurie didn't bother answering. It was like asking why a sunny day is better than a rainy one.

"Women!" Abe Goldberg spat. "It ain't all it's cracked up to be — get it? You go in hard, you come out soft. They take your strength. You're a man, then afterwards you're a mouse."

Laurie couldn't argue with him. He had no knowledge of the subject. All he had was desire, and he was sure that his desire, pure and true and strong, would lead to knowledge — the sooner the better.

He raised his eyes from the paper. His father was a disgrace, a temple to vulgarity, the very opposite of romance.

Abe put a glass in front of him. He poured a couple of inches of his best Canadian poison into it. The fumes rose and stung Laurie's eyes. Laurie knew about whisky; he'd snuck drinks more than once after chaotic nights at the Coop, when his father left a loose bottle outside the strongbox cupboard. Whisky burned your eyes, it deadened your tongue, it bit at the roof of your mouth, it scalded your throat, it ate your guts. Why people would go out of their way to drink it was something Laurie couldn't fathom. It was like standing in front of a streetcar.

Laurie looked at the glass. "Real pretty colour."

"Who cares about the colour? Drink it," his father told him.

"You drink it."

"That's an order."

"So's mine."

"You're ordering me?"

"You figure it out."

Laurie had seen men go through this, on the street and in this very room, the bombastic preparations for a fight. He thought the ceremony was stupid, all this "Sez who?" and "Sez me!" and "You wanna say that again?" If you were serious, then you just got it over with.

His uppercut caught his father completely by surprise, though Laurie was the more surprised of the two. His fist drove Abe's bottom teeth upward. They trapped his tongue against his top teeth and practically split it in two. Blood flew from his father's mouth, and Laurie jumped back. He was wearing his best shirt.

His fists were still clenched, and he was ready to go for the soft spot behind his father's ear, but he didn't have to. His father was bigger and meaner, the old man had way more experience, but all he could do now was hold his hand over his mouth. Laurie had righteous anger on his side, and Abe couldn't beat that.

Laurie turned and walked out of the Coop. He checked his shirt and pants. No blood. He moved down the gangway by the house, and looked up at the kitchen window to wish his mother goodbye, but he couldn't catch her eye. "You wouldn't want to know anyway," he told her. "You never did." That would have to do for goodbyes.

Laurie was in a complete state of shock. My right hand betrayed me, he thought. He looked at it. His fist was still clenched.

With his left hand, he unrolled the fingers of his right. They were cramped and painful.

No. My hand did not betray me. It spoke for me. Though I didn't know what it was going to say until it said it. It spoke for my mother and my sister too.

He headed across the prairie, broke off from the main path and walked toward his lean-to. As he came closer, he saw the grass was freshly parted. His heart filled with joy and desire. He hadn't thought Mary Anne would come, she would change her mind the way she had a dozen times before. But she was waiting for him, his just reward.

He parted the tall grass with both hands the way she had. He was walking in her footsteps, toward manhood.

Mary Anne had brought a blanket and covered the floor of the lean-to with it. She got up when Laurie came through the door. They kissed, briefly at first. He kept his right hand hidden. He didn't know hitting someone could be so painful.

"Lie down on the blanket," Mary Anne told him.

He did as he was told. When he pictured how this might happen, he was doing the leading. But he didn't mind as long as she was here, as convincing as a miracle. Mary Anne kneeled above him and unbuttoned her blouse. She had a determined look on her face. When all her buttons were undone, she pulled up her foundation garments and showed him her breasts.

"There," she said.

"They're nice." He liked looking at them better when they were covered.

"Irish breasts," she told him.

"Is that a special kind?"

"They have freckles."

It took him a few moments, but he understood that was an invitation. He reached up to touch the freckles with his left hand. They were like tiny dots of pale rust on her skin. He wanted to touch her nipples, but he didn't know if the invitation extended that far.

"You're my baby."

She was whispering, though there was no one around to hear.

"You're my baby too."

"Then be my baby," she told him. "Do what a baby does."

She swung low over him and made it clear what she wanted. He took her nipples into his mouth and sucked at each one. Her little sighs and starts guided him, what was too rough and what was just right, but he wasn't sure he liked this so much. He wanted to be a man. He was a man, now that he'd punched his father's lights out. He didn't want to do what a baby does, and suck some girl's breasts. Then he remembered what his father said about women, and wondered if it was true. But Mary Anne wanted him to do this thing and she made it clear she liked it, so he followed. It was a useful lesson to learn so early on.

Then it was over. She pulled away and buttoned up her shirt and told him she had to go home.

"You're lucky."

"About what?"

"I can't go home," Laurie blurted out.

He told her about the punch he'd thrown, and how well it had connected. He heard the pride in his voice and knew it was wrong.

Mary Anne reached for his right hand. He tried to hide it, but she found it and kissed it.

"It'll be all right. Just tell him you're sorry. My father and my brothers are always fighting and they're still family."

"But I'm not. I'm not sorry."

"You don't have to be. Just say it."

"You don't know my father."

"They're all the same. Trust me. They want to believe everything will be all right."

But Laurie didn't want to go back. He'd done the thing that made it impossible to return, and he wasn't going to let the opportunity slip away. Just as well Mary Anne stopped when she did, and they didn't go all the way. Otherwise he'd have to stay in Burnside.

She stood up, gathered her blanket and brushed the wrinkles from her skirt. They left the lean-to and he walked her across the prairie to the street. They came to the sidewalk and stood at a proper distance from each other.

"You can be my baby anytime you like. You want to keep the blanket?"

"No. I'm leaving. I'm going out west."

Mary Anne winced as if he'd slapped her. It was like when he hit his father. He didn't know what he was going to do until he did it. He wanted to leave Burnside, only he didn't know it till now. No place but far away would do.

"I show you my breasts, I let you touch them and kiss them, and all you want to do is leave? How do you think that makes a girl feel?"

Laurie touched the inside of her wrist, even though they were in public view.

"You're the nicest thing that's ever happened to me."

"Not nice enough, by the looks of it."

He left her on the sidewalk. Now that he said he was going out west, he had to do it. He started walking toward the rail yards. He climbed over the fence and scrambled down the embankment. He knew people travelled on the railroad without paying, but he didn't know how that worked. And he didn't know which way west was. He reached the freight yard and looked at the tangle of rails going off in every direction.

That's about the size of it, he thought.

He had a fifty-fifty chance of going the right way, which was better than his odds if he stayed. Then he slowed down to think. The lake was east. The sun came up from there. Which meant west was the opposite direction.

He turned his back on Lake Michigan. A train was creaking along on the track next to him, no faster than he could walk. He grabbed the door lever on a boxcar. The door slid open. It was easy, a regular invitation. He made himself comfortable. His father had fled Russia and walked across Europe and sailed the Atlantic all the way to Burnside, and his father was a lesser man. Laurie knew he could do better.

WHEN BLUMA CAME HOME FROM the Dunes, her foot still raw from poison ivy and her shoes full of sand, she found the population of her house reduced. Her half-sister was dead. Her brother was gone. Her father was apparently still alive, but the victim of some mysterious disease. Terrible sounds came from the Coop. Once the home of merry Irish drinkers, the place was haunted by a single sick bootlegger.

I go away, Bluma thought, and all hell breaks loose. Maybe I should go away more often.

Her mother couldn't tell Bluma anything more than Bluma could deduce. From her spot in the kitchen, Rachel hadn't seen her daughter grow weak and die. She hadn't heard the buildup to the fight between her husband and her son.

"I can imagine what happened," she told her daughter. "But I prefer not to."

"Talk about useless," Bluma said. "That's got to be some kind of record."

"Go look for yourself. I've had enough of those men."

Bluma went upstairs. The windows were closed and the place was an oven. In her room, the air was stale and dead. She took off her right shoe and examined her foot. It was still scaly, but the sores had closed up; new pink skin was coming in underneath. She held up her shoe and slowly poured its contents onto her bed. There, sand in the sheets, just like with Bella.

She put her shoe back on and went into Libby's room. She wanted to feel sadness, but it eluded her. Libby had to be more than the person her father used, but what was she? Unknowable, Bluma thought. The living proof of her father's negligence. Dead proof now. Sometimes the best plays are the ones you don't make. Now she could make that play. She could become Libby without anyone being the wiser. But she needed a reason, an occasion to take Libby's dates.

In the empty room, Bluma laughed out loud, an alarming sound because she wasn't much for laughter on her own. Was Libby's death the special occasion, or did she need to get used to being her first, like breaking in a new pair of shoes? She went into her mother's room and jerked open the drawer she once explored so fearfully. She found the paper. Libby was older than her by seven years. What the hell, Bluma figured, I look older than my age, every man is always telling me that. And a lot of people's dates get mixed up when they cross the ocean.

I can do it. I can be my half-sister. I can be a Mongoloid retard. She laughed at the audacity, taking on the identity of someone at the bottom of the heap. It was like Bella telling that black boy she wasn't really white. It was the perfect crime, the place no one would ever think to look.

She had no paper or pen to note down Libby's dates. The hell with it. Bluma folded up the naturalization paper and stuck it in the back pocket of her pants. Then she headed down the stairs, past her mother and into the yard, almost an American now.

NOURISHED BY FEELINGS OF DESERTION, Bluma dreamt great adventures for her brother. The more magnificent his adventures, the more bitter she felt.

Bluma knew that men rode the rails west. The ones who weren't going out west had already been there, and returned with tales of failed dreams that no one wanted to hear. From the embankment above the rail yards, she would look down and see hobos huddling around their garbage-can fires. A hobo was someone who travelled, not necessarily to get somewhere, but because he had an itch.

Her brother wasn't a hobo. He had a destination, at least in her story.

She knew that men slipped and fell as they tried to grab hold of the freight cars, and the wheels would pass over their bodies two hundred times, because a train could be a hundred cars long. How many cars did it take before you stopped feeling anything?

That wouldn't happen to Laurie. He was too fast, too strong. God helps those who help themselves.

He would make it out west, Bluma decreed. Not just anywhere west — to Texas. The train would stop in Lubbock and he would jump off. The heat would be so strong it would nearly knock him down. His knees would be stiff and he'd shake off the pain. She knew nothing about Lubbock except that it was on a list compiled by Bella's brothers of places in America that had Jewish-sounding names. He would walk down the main street of Lubbock and his shadow would stretch out tall in front of him. There would be a water tower with "Lubbock" written on it in huge block letters. Tumbleweeds would bounce past.

Everything Bluma knew about the West came from Tom Mix cowboy serials.

It would be lonely on Main Street. The wind blew past him, hot and stinging with sand. The train that brought him pulled away. He wished it farewell. He began to sing *Aleyn in Veg*: "The desert hears God talking, Why, then do I feel so sad and heavy of heart?" That sad song, maybe the saddest of all, made Laurie feel better. You could sing a Jewish song in Texas.

He walked into the Crystal Saloon, through the double doors. He would be a man among men drinking whisky and gambling. He would order a beer and drink it off in one swallow. A man standing nearby would size him up and offer to buy him a steak, after telling Laurie he looked like something the cat dragged in, which wasn't necessarily a compliment. He made fun of his name when they shook hands, because "Laurie" sounded like a girl's name, but her brother stood his ground.

An enormous steak arrived on a chipped blue plate. The man who bought him the steak asked Laurie if he wanted to come and work on his ranch. He would sleep in the dormitory with the other cowboys. Laurie would ride a horse, wear a hat, dig his boots into the stirrups, and would change into somebody else. What was left of Burnside in him would wash away. As she pictured Laurie becoming someone new, she was rehearsing her own transformation.

Laurie would turn into one tough hombre. There were Mexicans out in Texas who spoke Spanish, and he would eat their food out of a pan over an open fire. Maybe Bella was right to want to be a Spanish teacher.

On the ranch, the cook was a Mexican señorita named María Jesús with long, lustrous hair and a low-cut blouse. She had a gold front tooth. No, her father had the gold tooth and a leathery face that looked like it had been cut from a saddle, and he looked daggers at Laurie because he was in perpetual mourning for his wife, killed by the rancher in an accident, and his daughter was all he had. But in the end Laurie won him over, even if the man was as mean as a scorpion.

In the dormitory one night, her father spoke threatening Mexican words to him, and Laurie didn't understand them, though he knew he was in danger for his life. From out of nowhere he got a crazy idea: he answered in Yiddish so the leather-faced man would see they were on the same side. What did Laurie say to him? "You're not the only foreigner around here." It worked. They fell to laughing and the Mexican slapped him on the back because he understood they were both foreigners on a Texas ranch, and they had to stick together because there's strength in numbers. They celebrated their alliance by drinking together, but just one glass. Laurie would learn to speak Spanish, and for his troubles he would win the heart of María Jesús.

As long as Laurie was still alive, he could always come back. That was the main thing. He could come back with María Jesús on his arm if he wanted to.

But he would never come back. Laurie would throw a shroud over the past and it would cover her. He wouldn't even notice her underneath it, trying to wiggle free. He had no idea of her secret life.

THE NEXT DAY BLUMA WENT to say her goodbyes to Laurie. She crossed the prairie and headed for his lean-to. The grass and weeds were higher than ever. She didn't like having to break the trail. The grass scratched her legs and made the poison ivy sores burst into furious itching. The stuff was called crabgrass. The crabs pinched and grabbed onto her on her way to say goodbye to her brother.

Bluma could feel his absence. Twigs and leaves were scattered across the floor. That wouldn't have happened if he'd been here. Bluma bent down to pick them up for him and saw a handkerchief in the corner. A girl's handkerchief. Laurie brought girls to the lean-to. And all the time she thought this was his refuge from their father.

She tossed the twigs back onto the floor and kicked at the handkerchief.

She had to fight her way back across the prairie, through the crabgrass. It was an obstacle course, and everything was an obstacle, a test of how much she could take. Her feet and ankles were on fire. Her stomach had her bent double like an old woman and it laughed at her when she told it to stop. It took her forever to make it back to the sidewalk. She hated Laurie for not letting her say goodbye. She'd always hate him, even if he came back, even if he sent her a train ticket to Texas.

Bluma found her mother in the kitchen. She was holding a wooden spoon, though there was no pot on the stove.

"I want to go live on Lexington Street," she told her, "with Bella and her family."

"Your father needs you."

"He does not."

"There are chores. I can't do everything."

"Chores? Like serving Irish cops?"

"There are no policemen in this house."

Bluma stared at her mother. The spoon was quivering ever so slightly in her hand.

"We should have stayed in Shukyan."

"Yes. Maybe. But what's the point of saying that now?"

ABE GOLDBERG PULLED HIMSELF OFF Libby's pallet in the Coop's backroom and raised himself into the standing position. The infection had taken hold the minute his son slugged him. His forehead burning, his swollen tongue filling his mouth like a piece of rotting meat, Abe half-walked, half-crawled from the backroom to the salon. He locked the windows and the door. He tried each window twice, and rattled the doorknob so hard it broke off. He looked at the knob in his hand. Both were foreign objects. He couldn't control his muscles. He dropped the knob, and it took an unusually long time to fall to the floor.

Once he figured no one could hear him, he began to howl at the top of his lungs. He clenched both fists above his head and bellowed. He purged himself of as much humiliation as he could. He didn't bother with words. They would have taken too much effort. If he used words, he would have to say something, maybe even what was wrong with him. Tell a story, like with Libby, the story of his son, and everything that happened between them. He wasn't in the mood to admit to anything.

Once he voided his humiliation, he turned to the real problem: the wound inside his mouth. He knew alcohol had a variety of uses besides its main one, which was to make glad the heart of man. Alcohol was a solvent. You could clean counters with it. And it was a powerful antiseptic. His throat sore from howling to the point he could barely swallow, he filled a teacup full of whisky. He held it in his mouth and didn't swallow. He let it lie against his tongue, where it burnt like the devil. His eyes teared over with pain. For the first time, outside of providing him with a living, booze was actually doing him some good.

Once the tissues were anesthetized, he spat the whisky onto the floor. He looked at the stain: rust-coloured from blood. His life was a shameful thing that needed changing, but he had no idea what that would involve. It was changing without his consent. It was unravelling. First Libby came to the Coop. Then she spited him by dying. Then the business with Laurie.

Those were just the local changes. Bigger ones were happening in the world outside. He didn't read the papers or listen to the radio, but he couldn't avoid the talk around the Coop. The great age of the speakeasy was about to end. He voted against Roosevelt because he was told to, even if he didn't know who the other guy was. But his vote had done no good. The supplier had been very patient about explaining the nature of democracy to Abe Goldberg. Elections. Candidates. How Roosevelt would put an end to Prohibition. No Prohibition, no Coop. Abe Goldberg would have to find something else to do. He couldn't imagine what that would be. He wasn't a flexible man. He didn't know how to go legit. Abe Goldberg's services would no longer be required. He would disappear, all because of democracy.

Normally he paid little attention to his body, but he noticed worrying changes there too. When he howled, sometimes he couldn't hear himself, but when he did, his voice reached him from far away, as if it were a radio playing out in the yard.

He repeated the alcohol treatment over a number of days. Each time his tongue burned less. He began to negotiate with the pain, a good sign. During the first set of treatments, he spat the stuff out, but now he was swallowing the whisky. It helped him separate himself from the wounded, humiliated man he had become.

Then he stopped getting better. He was going backwards. The feeling of his tongue lying heavy and inert in his mouth tormented him. His tongue was a foreign body, a slug, a loaf of decaying meat.

He tried to form words. That's what a tongue is for. But what should he say? He pondered a moment, then began reciting all the words he knew for the male organ, first in English, then in Yiddish, then Russian. He didn't hear himself slurring the words with his fat tongue, sounding like the drinkers who used to fill the Coop. Next he cursed out Laurie and pronounced him dead — dead to him. What a wonderfully useful thing speech was!

After schmuck and putz and all their dreary brotherhood, and You are dead to me, I have no son, I didn't even enjoy the act of making you, the sentimentalist in Abe Goldberg made a sudden appearance.

Standing unsteadily in his storeroom, the pallet swaying far below, the floor stained rust-coloured, he began to sing *Aleyn in Veg*. Alone on the road. The words ambushed him and made him cry. He got mad at them. I expect nothing more from life, he sang, and yesterday doesn't bother me much either.

It was the same song Bluma had Laurie sing as he walked down the dusty street in an imaginary Lubbock.

In the middle of his cure, the supplier showed up. He parked in the alley behind the Coop and came around the building into the yard. He had one helper with him, and two more in the car to guard the merchandise.

When he saw the Coop's closed door and drawn blinds, he drew his pistol. His helper did the same. The supplier, a man named Daley, turned the doorknob carefully. It came off in his hand.

The shades were pulled down in the house too. Daley hated standing in the open in front of blind windows. He felt like a sitting duck, and wished he hadn't left the shotguns with the two helpers guarding the stuff. But those were his orders: the firepower was supposed to protect the booze from hijackers. His life was worth less to those Cicero gangsters he worked for than a couple barrels of their headache whisky. "If you smell gunpowder, you're in Cicero" — they loved that joke. But there was plenty of gunpowder in Burnside, he was willing to bet.

He banged on the back door of Abe's house. Rachel stuck her head out the kitchen window. He'd never been so happy to see a Jewess in his life.

"Go away! Don't bother me! He's in the Coop!"

The window slammed shut.

The supplier walked across the yard to the Coop with the slow step of someone who knows he's cornered his prey. He banged on the door with the doorknob.

"Hey, Goldfarb, open the door; I'm asking nice."

"You hear us, Goldstein?" his helper chimed in.

"Open up, Goldgelt."

Daley was proud of his joke. But it was more than a joke. It was a way of flushing out his man. He knew how sensitive Jews were about their names.

Then the inside door opened and there was Abe Goldberg, looking like death. He kept his hand on the screen door. Daley knew something was wrong with him. What kind of man would think a screen gave protection?

"It's Tabiliak. There's no such person as Goldberg. Never was."

That's what Abe thought he said. But his visitors heard gibberish.

"What in hell happened to you?" Daley asked.

"Something die in your mouth?" his helper put in.

"You're going to take delivery, Goldberg. No matter what your name is."

"The bar is closed," Goldberg got out.

"Today is delivery day."

Daley nodded to his helper, who trotted off toward the alley.

Goldberg and Daley stood staring at each other, a screen door between them. Through it, Daley could see the other man's mouth was crusted with dried red spittle, and that his face was hanging to one side.

"What happened to you? You get mad and beat yourself up?"

Goldberg took the trouble to answer the question, but Daley didn't understand a word.

"You've got to get the marbles out of your mouth, buddy."

Daley wondered what sort of man would try and talk when he knew he sounded like that. But maybe Goldberg didn't know — that was a possibility. Since the bootlegger couldn't talk, Daley decided to do the talking for both of them.

"They say by the end of the year, Prohibition will be a thing of the past," he told Goldberg. "Fucking Roosevelt is acting fast. Let me tell you a little secret. We were all supposed to vote for Al Smith, but I voted

Roosevelt anyway. I don't care. I'll find something else to do. I'm sick of this job. But don't start dancing in the streets just yet. Things are going to get worse before they get better."

Goldberg let go with a burst of gibberish. Daley was happy for the screen that shielded him against the spray of bloody saliva. The helper came back with another man, carrying a whisky barrel. A third trained his shotgun on the imaginary hijackers hiding in the backyard.

"We'll bring it inside. Then you can pay up."

Goldberg showered the men with meaningless noise. Then he made a writing motion with his right hand.

"Chalk it up? Now that's a good one!"

"You're a funny guy, Goldstein," the helper said. "Having a dead rat in your mouth doesn't keep you from being a real funny guy."

The helpers set the barrel down just inside the door.

"You're as strong as an ox, that's what they say, but maybe it's not true anymore," Daley told him. "We'll leave it right here. Just sign the paper."

Goldberg did, and Daley herded his helpers out of the yard, toward the car.

"You're going to let him off without paying?"

"We're delivery, not collection. If we can collect, good. If not, someone else will. Anyway, it doesn't matter. You were looking at a dead man."

IN THE STOREROOM, ONCE THE car had pulled away, Abe tried to lower himself onto the pallet, but he fell onto his side instead. The effort of talking to Daley had burst the abscesses on his tongue, and his mouth filled with pus. It was time for another alcohol treatment. But he was lying on the pallet, and the counter with the bottle seemed miles away. It belonged to another lifetime, when he would whisper to his muscles and they instantly did his bidding. He slumped back. The cure would have to wait.

He thought of calling for help. Maybe Rachel would take pity. Women did that sometimes. But when he tried saying her name, he sounded like an idiot, even to his own ears.

He lay on his side, telling the parts of his body what he wanted of them, and getting no reply. He wondered how long he'd been like this, and why no one came to look in on him. "I'm convalescing in my sickroom," he told the world through his hanging mouth. "You're supposed to bring soup." Hunger finally moved him. He rolled across the floor to the cabinet, pulled a bottle off a low shelf and drank until the pangs were stilled.

Maybe I really am dead, like those Cicero hoods said. If I'm dead, how come no one's sitting over my body and celebrating my life? No one came to the Coop. It was like everybody had stopped drinking, all at once. Could Roosevelt have put him out of business that fast? Maybe Roosevelt killed him. When he went into the trade, Abe figured he'd never be short of work. He'd always be the centre of attention. Selling alcohol was like being a rabbi. There would always be a need.

NINE

Good Rubber After Bad

SOMETHING STRIKINGLY NEW TOOK PLACE at the end of the summer: Rachel and Bluma had a full-fledged conversation. Bluma thought of her mother as a fixture, an inert piece of furniture like the kitchen chair, the way any child feels about her parent. But behind the outward paralysis, the woman had a strong will to spread her unhappiness.

"Sit."

Her mother pointed to a chair at the kitchen table.

"Your brother is gone and your father can't work. How do you think I'm going to keep this house together?"

"You could get a job," Bluma told her mother.

Rachel laughed.

"You used to work. That's what you told me. You worked in Shukyan."

"That was in another country. Back then I could do anything. I could work from sunup to sundown."

"Now you can't get out of the chair."

"Now I don't want to," her mother corrected her.

"I decided I'm going to secretary school. I'm going to Washburne."

"Why do you need school to learn secretary when you can have a job right now? Sadow is hiring."

"How would you know? You never go out."

"People come to me," Rachel said, full of self-important mystery. "I hear things."

"Sadow? Tires? I'd rather be a taxi-dancer." Bluma burst into song. She was a member of The Fledglings again, but a more vulgar version:

> *Everyone works but Papa, he sits around all day*
> *Staring into the fireplace and smoking his pipe of clay*
> *Mother takes in laundry, Sister is a whore*
> *Everyone works but Papa, I can't take it anymore!*

Her mother cut her off with a shriek.

"My own flesh and blood, a *kurva*! Men pushing their bodies against you so you feel their things. And you liking it!"

"A taxi-dancer isn't a *kurva*. She's a dancer. She dances with guys. She makes them feel better about themselves. I heard about a girl who works at the Lonely Fellows' Club. She makes plenty of money, she has nice things and she doesn't have relations if she doesn't want to."

"A kurva!"

"Stop saying that."

They sat in silence a moment as Rachel regrouped. Bluma waited for the next assault, and her mother didn't let her down.

"Take the job, at least for a while. We need money. We have to pay for the whisky your father ordered. It's just sitting there, and he won't open his business and sell it. You know what happens to people who don't pay what they owe."

"You want him to open the speakeasy again, and have a house full of drunks next door?"

"It's easy for you to criticize. It's a job, a living. And now it's gone."

"Why don't you go see what's wrong with him?"

Rachel smiled wanly. "I'm too tired. You can't imagine."

"Make an effort."

"I have made efforts," her mother defended herself.

She and Bluma sat for a while more. Bluma felt inertia coming over her. It was contagious. She was catching it from her mother. "All right. But it's only temporary."

"Of course."

The following week, Bluma started at Sadow's Vulcanizing. The job was her class-dunce destiny, and her first outrage against the sacred oath she'd sworn with Bella. The two girls were breaking up, and they didn't need a man to do it.

CARL SADOW, THE BOSS OF Sadow's Vulcanizing, stood five feet two in his Cuban heels, but his height was no handicap. The Little Napoleon of retreads with the barrel chest and the big voice conducted his business from a backroom where he went unseen. His height, or lack of it, was no problem, but he did have a handicap for someone in his line of work: English was completely out of his reach. He had to practise what he was going to say before he said it, and no one had the patience to wait around till his rehearsal was complete. Life was just too fast-paced. And if someone did bother hanging around, he wouldn't understand a word unless he knew ahead of time what Sadow wanted to say. He was hopeless even when it came to talking tires.

Bluma's job was to be the voice of Sadow's Vulcanizing. A ventriloquist's dummy for an illiterate midget — now that takes the cake.

In an act of mockery, the Almighty blessed Sadow with a wife nearly six feet tall. Esther, the queen of retreads, had a favourite bit of mischief. When he was standing in his back office, giving orders or defending his sub-par work to a dumbfounded customer, she would come up behind him, make a pillow on the top of his head with her two hands, then lie her head on his and act like she was catching forty winks. A wide, satisfied smile crossed her face. All business would halt as everyone stopped to watch this mismatched miracle. Sadow took it as a display of affection; other people saw something different.

Bluma had no plans to hang around Sadow's for long. A paycheque or two for her mother, and the family debt would be erased, the whisky paid off. If she taught Sadow a few simple phrases, he wouldn't need her anymore. But it took her a week to lead him through the words "We fail to understand."

"Say that," she instructed, "then add whatever you want at the end. When someone calls up or comes by to tell you how lousy your tires are, and how they want their money back, just say those words."

After a week's practice, he could more or less reproduce the phrase, but his heart was not at peace.

"Will people really understand?" he asked in some shredded language that could have been Bessarabian.

"It doesn't matter. You know you're saying it, and that's what counts. It's a real class sentence," Bluma assured him. "It'll set them back on their *tuches*."

"Okay, okay, good." Sadow beamed. What a deal he'd got with this girl. "But write it, write it down."

Write it? Bluma wondered. You can't read. But she wrote it down anyway.

A few afternoons later, she heard him on the phone.

"We fail to understand," he began. There was a long hesitation. Sadow was clearly no improviser. "We fail to understand ..." He switched into Bessarabian and shouted into the receiver, "We fail to understand what you're bellyaching about, all right, already?"

He slammed the phone down. He walked over to Bluma's spot. He was radiant.

"It works! Just like you said!"

He wandered away from Bluma's desk. "We fail to understand," he repeated like an actor rehearsing his lines. "We fail to understand." What a babe she was! What a looker! What a find! His saviour!

Sadow's Vulcanizing crouched low and smelly in the 95th Street industrial zone, not far from the South Shore Line tracks. Vulcanizing was a technology for times of no money. The shop's rubber artists, all black men who had to be hidden from the white customers, melted worn tires onto the backs of other worn tires to make supposedly new tires that quickly threw off their acquired tread like a wet dog shaking itself dry. Naturally the customers weren't overjoyed, but they couldn't afford new tires. So they paid for another session at Sadow's that cost a little less than the first, and whose results were never better.

Though he'd learned to say "We fail to understand," Bluma remained Sadow's first line of defence. She turned into a first-class rejection artist.

"Those tires cost me money I don't have," was the complaint she heard most often. "Good money."

"There's no such thing as good money," she would answer. "And if you didn't have the money, you couldn't have bought the tires."

"If I could have bought tires, I wouldn't have to come to you."

"Exactly my point."

No matter how rude she was, Sadow would not fire her. The ruder, the better.

The very inefficiency of vulcanizing made it good business. It was something everyone could afford — over and over again. That was its advantage. The disadvantage for those who dealt in it was that it stank, and the barrier between the shop where the black men worked and the office was no more impermeable than a bamboo curtain. Bluma smelled like burning rubber, weekday and weekend, even after she'd scrubbed her skin and poured perfumed shampoo over her hair. The smell was acrid, gritty and sour. She complained about it to her mother, who claimed she couldn't smell it. But coming from Rachel, that was no guarantee.

One day when Bluma was sitting at the counter in the Greek luncheonette down the street from Sadow's, eating an egg salad sandwich that tasted like burnt rubber, a smooth sucker came up behind her.

"See this gal?" he asked no one in particular, and no one in particular answered. "I'm gonna marry her."

She didn't pay him any mind. Here was a guy, claiming he was going to marry her, and he couldn't talk to her face to face or look her in the eye. He had to tell a counter full of strangers first. Typical, she thought.

Then he made his move: he slipped onto the stool next to her. She didn't bother with him. Her egg salad sandwich required all her concentration.

"Yes, I am. I'm gonna marry her. Mark my words, fellas."

His hand lay on the counter next to her plate. If he put it on hers, she would slap him.

She looked up from her plate. Waves of burnt-rubber stink rose off her hands. It didn't matter how many times she washed them. If she could smell it, he could too.

"Go away," she told him.

Bluma pushed the rest of her sandwich into her mouth. She wiped her mouth on the back of her wrist and told the owner, who was also the cook, to put it on her slate till next payday. She headed for the exit. As the luncheonette door with its out-of-tune bell closed behind her, she heard the guy bragging.

"You don't know me, boys," he was telling the indifferent counter. "You don't know that I don't take no. Let me introduce myself. They call me Eddie."

"Go to hell," she told him through the closed door.

SINCE SHE WAS THE REJECTION artist of Sadow's Vulcanizing, Bluma figured that getting rid of this smooth-talking braggart who preferred to talk about her instead of to her shouldn't be much of a challenge. But she was an easy target. She went to the Greek luncheonette every day, sat on the same stool and ate the same thing. The Greek was the only one who would give her credit.

No man had ever paid attention to her this baldly. Sure, there was the cook and the sweetshop man and the social director at Johnson's Beach, but she had been with Bella, and her cousin deflected them. The idea that she could have feelings for a man was completely foreign. No other man, she decided — no new man — would hurt her.

A day later, Eddie and his gift of gab slipped onto the stool next to her and flagged down the Greek.

"Give me what she's having," he called.

The Greek eyed her suitor suspiciously. The lunch counter customers were his family, and he watched over them jealously.

"No more egg salad," he told Eddie.

"Then give me what you have — fried baloney."

Fried baloney, like you, he grumbled to himself in stage-whisper Greek. Then he threw a slice of industrial meat onto the grill and set about crushing it with a wooden spatula.

Bluma snuck a look at Eddie as he was ordering. He had no obvious defects like that customer at Sadow's who liked to come and stand by her desk, and blew saliva bubbles whenever he tried to talk. No drawbacks or handicaps visible to the naked eye, which could only mean he'd learned to hide them.

Don't go away mad, she told him in her imagination. Just go away.

By the time his fried baloney arrived on a plate of dubious cleanliness, she was stuffing the remains of her sandwich into her mouth and heading for the door. Back at Sadow's, she spent a half hour in the toilet. That was the blandest item on the menu, she berated her stomach, so what's the matter? But she knew what the matter was. Avoiding Eddie was making her sick.

When she came out of the toilet, Esther Sadow was waiting for her, six feet of female solicitude. Bluma got a creepy Miss Reilly feeling.

"You all right?"

"Better now. Got rid of it."

"You allergic to some man?"

Bluma laughed. "I never thought about it that way."

Sadow's wife put her arm around her shoulders. Bluma wanted to collapse into her embrace. The older woman smelled of burnt rubber too, but on her, the stink was perfume.

"You're a real looker, honey. You get out there in the world, men are going to notice you. And they're going to like what they see. Plus you got something hurt about you that definitely draws them like flies."

"That's not my fault."

"I know. I know it's not."

Then Sadow's wife told her a few other things. She laid out her theory of love and marriage. Bluma had heard it before. A good man was a man with no vices, or at least as few as possible considering he was a man. A man who didn't beat you, wasn't a drunk, didn't two-time you and give his money to some other woman, a man who knew how to hold down a job. Who even bought you a present once in a while.

"This one's got a vice," Bluma said. "He's persistent as hell."

"That's the way men are. They have to be. Otherwise we wouldn't pay them any attention."

"If you say so."

"What's he look like?"

"Search me."

"Is he good-looking at least?"

"I don't know what he looks like."

Esther shook her head in wonderment. "You really aren't very far along in the game, are you?"

"No. And I don't want to be."

Bluma wondered what kind of leg Esther Sadow had to stand on. She married a guy who needed a stepladder to kiss her. But maybe she didn't like to kiss. Maybe she married the midget so she wouldn't have to kiss him. Anything was possible.

THE NEXT TIME THE GREEK set down her egg salad sandwich on a pristine white plate, he told Bluma, "You don't want him bothering you, I'll tell him to stop. And he'll stop."

"Thanks. I'll take care of it myself."

Like clockwork, Eddie showed up. "Fly-Paper Eddie," she called him. He slid onto the stool next to her and called out his order. His fried baloney with mustard did not show up. The Greek was ignoring him.

"What's a guy got to do to get some service here?"

Bluma turned and gave him the once-over. She owed her new friend Esther Sadow that much. Now she'd be able to tell her what he looked like.

Not like very much. Like every other man. There was nothing distinguishing about him.

She listened to Eddie bawling out the Greek for his slow service. "You're not from around here, are you?"

She spoke to him. That was her fatal mistake.

He turned and looked at her. Surprise was written in block letters on his face.

"No. I'm from New York."

"Like hell you are. What are you doing here? In Burnside, of all places."

"My father's in furs. He's got a shop on Madison Avenue. He wanted me to be in furs too. But I didn't want to. So I left town."

"You had to leave town? You couldn't just tell him no?"

Eddie shrugged and squirmed on his stool. "It's complicated. Like a long story."

"Yeah? Too bad, nobody here has time for long stories. We're too busy watching the clock. We all got bosses that need us something bad." That was one thing she could tell Esther about him: he was a liar, and not a very good one. "Where do you live?"

"In a hotel."

"They got hotels in Burnside? That's news to me, and I've been here a long time."

"Sure they do. They got them for the executives that travel and look after things."

"Executives in Burnside. That'll be the day."

She stood up and pointed at the clock. Her mouth was full of food.

"Yeah, go ahead. See youse tomorrow."

"Youse? Nobody says youse here."

He didn't understand her through her mouthful of sandwich. She gulped it down. "Sure thing, Fly-Paper."

Eddie laughed. He couldn't believe how easy this was turning out to be. In the old days, a man had to go through channels. There was protocol to respect, barriers made of priests and rabbis. Parents and wary, hostile older brothers stood between men and women. In New York, village alliances survived the trip to the New World and tied a guy's hands. A suite had to be presented in the proper way. But Burnside was the Wild West, open and lawless and free. Anybody could talk to anybody any time they felt like it, without worrying about whose toes he was stepping on, and whether he was going to get a knife in the back.

She could call him Fly-Paper all she wanted.

Back at Sadow's, Bluma had something for Esther.

"I called him Fly-Paper," she reported, "and he didn't even take it the wrong way!"

"You mean there's a right way to take getting called Fly-Paper?"

The two women laughed at the thick-headedness of men. Their conspiracy brought Sadow from out of his back office.

"You're keeping my employee from working," he told his wife.

"She's laughing, she's happy. Happy employees work better — don't you know that?"

"I don't know what I know," Sadow said sententiously.

"You don't know anything about your employee. She's a looker, every man can see that. But she's not brassy like some, and she's hurting inside."

Sadow headed back to his lair.

"I fail to understand," he told his wife. "As long as you're all right, that's all that matters."

Bluma and Esther watched him retreat. "I never saw a man like that," Bluma said.

"The strangest part is that he means it."

"I told my mother I'd rather be a streetwalker than work in an office. But then I wouldn't have met you."

"You, a streetwalker?" Esther burst out laughing. "Let me tell you, it's harder than you think. That deep, abiding inner pain business you got? That's the last thing they want to buy. Take it from me!"

Bluma sniffed at her shirtsleeve. "At least I wouldn't stink so much."

"Oh, you'd stink all right!"

"HOW COME YOU EAT THE same thing every day?"

Now that he had her talking, Eddie pressed his advantage.

"That's the only thing my stomach will take. And even then ..."

"Even then what?"

He's the kind of guy you've got to spell everything out for, Bluma realized. And she did. Maybe that would drive him away.

"Even then sometimes I can't keep it in me. I got a nervous stomach."

"Is that so? Well, bland isn't for me. Give me a hot pastrami with a kosher spear. I want to taste my food."

That was another thing she could tell Esther. Eddie's ears were so stopped up he couldn't hear anything she said. In some circles, that was called self-confidence.

"I want to get to know you," he declared suddenly, though the opposite seemed true. "You got a best friend? You live with your family?"

"I got a best friend," Bluma told him. "She's my cousin."

"Ain't that nice! I'd like to meet her."

"Oh, you will. We've been best friends forever. We made a promise to each other a long time ago."

"A promise is a promise," Eddie mouthed.

"We swore, and we spat on the ground, that any man who'd have one of us would have to have both of us."

Eddie drew back like he'd touched a hot stove. "Now what the hell's that mean?"

"Just what it says."

"I'm not in the business of marrying two girls."

"I don't think she'd like you either, Fly-Paper!"

Bluma's courtship was off to a rough start. She'd throw this sucker off her scent. She'd become a wild woman if that's what it took to unstick Fly-Paper.

"I'll introduce you two," she promised Eddie. "The day I made that promise with her was the best day of my life."

"You're kind of young," Eddie told her, "to be getting nostalgic."

"What's that mean?"

"You know … Having the best day of your life behind you. That doesn't seem natural."

"Oh, I'm not natural, that's for sure!"

BLUMA WAS THE HERALD OF her own misfortune. She carried the story of her courtship to Bella after the endless ride through the South Side, and the Loop transfer over to the West Side. The trip took all day, and proved what Bella had said: if she went to People's Junior College, she'd have to move into Lexington Street.

She'd never had any intention of going to college. That was for Bella, not her. But she would have gone to secretarial school. To Washburne. That was enough of a trek. Excuse enough to move into Bella's, now that her brothers were setting themselves up in haberdashery and moving out of the family flat. One of those free rooms could be hers. Bella could learn to be a Spanish teacher if she had to;

Bluma would learn shorthand. No more Sadow, no more stink. No more Fly-Paper.

The streetcar driver startled her when he called her stop. She got off.

Bella was waiting for her on the stoop of their building in the cool autumn air. They hugged each other.

"Hey, Fledge, welcome back!"

"I don't think I'm a Fledgling anymore. A Fledgling is just starting out. I'm too tired to be at the beginning."

"That's the working world for you." She sniffed and wrinkled her nose. "You smell like a car on fire."

"It's my new perfume. No man can resist it."

They laughed at the prospect of attracting suitors with stink. It was original, a real Fledgling idea.

"I see you came on Sabbath," Bella teased her.

"Otherwise known as my day off," Bluma answered. "God doesn't go all the way down to Burnside, though the streetcar does. Who told him to invent Sadow's Vulcanizing anyway? A couple of paycheques and I'm out of there."

Bella sniffed at the collar of her cousin's jacket. "Smells like the devil in hell."

"Thanks a lot, Fledge! What would you know about hell?"

They laughed. Bella pulled out a bag of monkey nuts.

"Remember when you used to be crazy about these? I bought them for you."

"I remember. I was always jealous because you had them and I didn't."

Bella stared at her cousin. "Jealous? Why would you be? I always shared with you."

Bluma shrugged. "I don't know … You had the store and you could get all you wanted."

"My mother wants to get rid of it. She can't take the hours anymore.

My brothers say she's worked enough. They'll take care of her."

"You could take it over."

"Me? I got school."

Bella slipped the invisible rose between her teeth and slipped on the make-believe castanets.

La cucaracha, la cucaracha,
Ya no puede caminar ...

"Hey, did you know they have two different ways of saying 'to be' in Spanish?"

"Why bother?"

"I like it. It's more complicated."

"You would!"

They broke open the monkey nuts with their teeth and spat the shells down the steps and onto the sidewalk. It was a ceremony from their earlier days, when time stretched on forever. They had no way of measuring it then, and no reason to, either. Now, time for Bluma was the oversized clock at the Greek's lunch counter. For Bella, time was about verbs. In Spanish, one verb meant you changed over time, and another meant your state of being was fixed. "An essence," her teacher told the class. Bella figured her cousin was the second verb, and she was the first, and that was a problem between them.

They emptied the bag of monkey nuts. It didn't take them as long as when they were kids.

"There's this guy who's been hanging around the place I eat lunch. A regular fly-paper."

"Sounds appealing."

Bluma glanced at her cousin. She was beginning to get some curves. Maybe she'd start understanding now.

"You know what he did?"

"I can't imagine."

"I'm sitting there minding my own business, eating my sandwich, and he starts telling everyone he's going to marry me."

Bella laughed. "He told everyone, but he didn't tell you?"

"I overheard."

"Tell him to scram."

"I did."

"And?"

"It doesn't work with some guys."

"I wouldn't know," Bella admitted.

"Okay," Bluma said, "what if that happened to you? What would you do?"

"I'd get my brothers on him. Nobody can just come up and start talking to you like that — unless you opened the door for him."

"All I was doing was eating a sandwich. I don't have my brother. I'm unprotected."

They sat on the top step, brushing the monkey-nut shells off the stoop with the soles of their shoes.

"I guess I'd better meet him," Bella told her cousin.

"I don't think you'd like him."

"If that's true," Bella said slyly, "then you'd better forget about him. Don't you remember our sacred oath?"

"Of course I do! Our promise! And you know what? I told him about it."

"And?"

"He told me I wasn't natural."

"What does that mean? Our oath is the most natural thing in the world."

They hugged each other and laughed on the stoop by the family store, as the Sabbath foot traffic crunched over the shells on the sidewalk in front of them.

"If I don't like him, then you can't have him. If he doesn't want me, he can't have you." Bella thought it over. "Hey, Fledge, we've got all the angles covered!"

"So that settles that," Bluma agreed.

The machine of Bluma's courtship was defeated, just like that. Bella had a magical way of remaking the world. Life was lightness for her, and when they were together, Bluma shared in that blessing. Where do you get a life like that? she wondered.

Part of the answer came rolling up Lexington Street in the form of the nine-passenger Packard, big and heavy as a hearse. It slowed and came level to where Bella and Bluma sat, the horn sounded and arms waved wildly from the open windows. Bella's brothers were arriving for their visit. They drove past the house and parked on the next block out of respect for their parents, who could tell themselves that, against all logic, their sons had walked all the way to Lexington Street, obeying the law about not operating automobiles on the Sabbath, while transporting cakes and bottles of schnapps and smoked whitefish and a sack of apples from the Michigan orchards, those wonderful, resourceful boys with their nose for business, so devoted.

They came up the sidewalk with their bundles, laughing over some private joke. They're like a shield around Bella, Bluma thought, while I stand alone.

"Look at the elegant young lady!"

Bella's brothers gathered in comic, awed contemplation. They would have devoured her if they'd been allowed to.

"Of course you walked here like us," one of them was saying, Rudy, maybe. "So as not to use a motorized conveyance on this day."

"We don't care how you got here, as long as you got here. Our sister couldn't wait to see you!"

That could have been Jacob, or Jack, extending a hand and pulling her to her feet. He wrinkled his nose and sniffed.

"Such original perfume!"

"Essence of retread," one of the brothers agreed after putting his nose in her hair.

Before Bluma could act offended, the brothers ushered her and Bella through the door to pay a visit to their parents, who would beam with pride at their bunch. Bella's father would be so moved he would almost speak. For Bluma, the scene was as unreal as a fairytale.

THE NEXT WEEK AT THE luncheonette, Eddie the masher, the fly-paper, slipped onto his usual stool.

"I hear your mother's taking in boarders."

"Yeah? Where'd you hear that?"

Eddie waved his hand in the air. "In the neighbourhood. I'm a neigh-bourhood boy now."

"You're a roomer in a transient hotel."

"She must need the money," Eddie deduced.

"Who doesn't? You think I'm here for fun?"

"I'm going to make an application. You know, get out of the hotel."

"If you're doing that for me, remember, familiarity breeds contempt."

"You trying to tell me something?"

"Don't tell me you never heard that expression. I thought you New Yorkers were so sophisticated. I guess not."

Bluma got to her feet. She didn't have to look at the clock. Her inner lunch bell was ringing. Sadow would be needing her for the usual important business: the denial, the brush-off, the outright refusal of responsibility.

"We could see each other more often," Eddie said. His puppy-dog eyes gave her the creeps.

"I fail to understand," Bluma said, and moved toward the door.

Bluma sought out Esther as soon as she got back to the office — the stink factory, she called it. She was used to it now, and had stopped smelling it on herself. But the minute she stepped into the outside world, where no one else smelled like burnt rubber, she realized how bad she stank.

"I can't believe it!" Bluma told Esther. "My mother's renting out a room and not even telling me, and I'm here working for peanuts. If

Fly-Paper takes it, he'll be all over me like a dirty shirt. I don't get it. What does he want from me?"

Esther's laughter was loud and vulgar and incredulous. "Come with me. I want to show you something you've never seen."

She took Bluma by the hand and led her into her inner sanctum. The woman had an office the size of a washroom, but at least it was hers, with a door that closed and a mirror for touch-ups. Esther switched on the light. She had no trouble turning Bluma this way and that.

She pulled back Bluma's hair from her face and twisted it into a bun, then combed it with her fingers.

"That's what they see. That look, like you're waiting for the next blow to fall. Who could resist?"

"I'm all-right-looking, I guess."

"You're not listening."

"What can I do about it?"

"Nothing. That's the point. It's you."

Bluma turned away from the mirror. "Then what can I do? I don't want it!"

"Knowledge is the best defence."

"Against what? I tell you everything, and you say the cruelest things."

Esther took her in her arms. "I'm trying to help you."

"Everyone's always trying to help me," Bluma said bitterly. "Do I need that much help?"

"I'm trying to help you see yourself the way they do. So you'll know what they want from you." Esther stroked her hair. "You're a real looker, you know."

"I hate that word."

Sadow knocked at the door. "What are you two doing in there?"

"It's her ladies' time. Leave us be!"

He did. Esther released Bluma from her pitiless, feminine embrace, but kept hold of her hands.

"It's not just you. It's all of us. There's no sense trying to make believe we don't know what's happening. Forewarned is forearmed."

Esther brought Bluma's hands to her mouth and kissed them, stink or no stink. Then she sent Bluma back to her desk.

"I'M MOVING IN," EDDIE TOLD Bluma a few days later at the lunch counter.

"You're moving in on me, I know that much. But it won't do you any good. Familiarity breeds contempt."

"I'm moving in. That's what I'm telling you."

He stood in front of her like a boxer, shifting his weight from one foot to the other, ready in case she reached out and tried to poke him one.

"I don't think you get it. I'm moving into your house. Your mother is renting me the room."

"You dirty rat!"

Bluma didn't finish her sandwich. The lunch-counter door slapped back and forth as she hit the sidewalk.

"Hey, mister, you really know how to treat a dame," one of the diners told Eddie. "What's your secret? Everybody here wants to know."

Eddie picked up the abandoned sandwich from her plate and pushed it into his mouth. "We'll see who laughs last," he told them. Chewing on Bluma's sandwich, he headed for the hotel where his packed bag waited.

That afternoon, when she returned from work, Bluma heard someone moving around in Libby's old room. For a moment she felt a leap of irrational joy: Laurie had come back. He'd disappeared without a word — why couldn't he return the same way, even if he was in the wrong room? He could have changed rooms. A man who's been to Texas can do anything.

She hurried down the hall and threw open the door. There was Eddie, standing over an open suitcase.

"What the hell are you doing here?"

"I told you I was moving in. Your mother rented me the room, like I told you."

Bluma slammed the door so hard plaster fell from the ceiling. She rushed to her room, then stopped halfway. Who cares, let that leech hear everything! She banged down the stairway to the kitchen, where her mother sat, sorting lentils.

"How could you do that?"

Her mother looked at her blankly. Stones and pebbles on one side, lentils on the other.

Bluma pointed to the ceiling. "You rented out her room! Don't you have any respect for the dead?"

"The dead," Rachel told her, "don't have to eat." She slid a piece of gravel from out of the heap of lentils. There were more and more stones in the sack these days. "Your father can't work, not in his condition."

"What do you know about his condition? You never see him."

"You go, then come back and tell me. Listen, daughter. Your brother left us. And your salary isn't enough to live on, especially the way you spend it on your pleasures. What do you want me to do?"

"You rented Libby's room. What about Laurie's room? Who're you gonna put there?"

"God willing, Layb will come back."

"Like hell he will."

Rachel paid no mind. She concentrated on her lentils.

"I'd rather be a streetwalker than have that man in the room next to me," Bluma said. "At least I'd get to choose instead of having one shoved down my throat."

"Do as you like, daughter." The word streetwalker had lost its power to frighten her. "No one chooses in life. Did I choose?"

"You could have stayed in Shukyan."

"Maybe I should have, with the three of you. But he sent for me, and I never thought to refuse. It was an honour not to be forgotten. I could have been an immigration widow, working in the market. Libby would have died, but I would have had you and Layb. Sometimes when I sit here, I amuse myself with that thought."

"It must be very amusing."

"You wouldn't understand."

"You're selling me into whoredom, only it's called marriage."

"I don't know what you're talking about."

"Rent out Laurie's room while you're at it to some other man who wants to marry me. Let the two of them fight it out. The one with the most cash wins."

Bluma stomped back up the stairs. In the hallway, she listened to Eddie moving around in Libby's old room. It was his room now. What's he doing in there? How can he make so much noise in a room that small? It sounded like he was pacing, walking from door to window, bed to wall. Was he nervous? Him, nervous? Now that was a joke.

Then she heard the drawers opening and closing, and understood he was putting away his things. It hit her: he really had moved in. He was here to stay. She retreated into her room. There was nowhere to go.

Eddie was a trap that was set the day she was born.

The next morning, she told Sadow she needed extra time for her lunch break. The king of vulcanizing was not happy.

"I have a doctor's appointment," Bluma said.

She thrust out her chest and rolled her shoulders to make Sadow understand it was ladies' business, which meant it was none of his. The suggestion worked. Everything that had to do with the mysterious workings of women terrified him.

"Just don't make it too long. I need you here. And stop spending so much time with my wife."

When she stopped in front of the building where the doctor had his offices, Bluma realized how foolish her plan was. She looked up at the three storeys of brick. The building backed onto the rail yards, and its facade was sooty and dark. How could she expect sympathy in a place like this?

On the door that led upstairs, Dr. LaRue's name was written in stencilled letters that imitated gold, but had faded to a jaundiced yellow. General Medicine. She pushed open the door and climbed the stairs that smelled like cigars. The building trembled and shuddered as freight cars were coupled in the yards out back. She imagined Laurie in that crash of metal. If he had stayed, this wouldn't be happening. Eddie wouldn't be pacing in the room next to hers.

Dr. LaRue, General Medicine. The same faded gold stencilling on the pane of opaque glass. Knock and Enter.

Bluma stepped inside. It was amazing she'd survived the encounter with LaRue's knife. The sheet on the examination table had seen its share of bodies. The sink had rust spots on it. Pills were scattered across the desk like a losing hand of cards.

Dr. LaRue came tottering in from the backroom. He looked at her, blinking his eyes like a man emerging from a cave.

"Are you in trouble?"

"You don't remember me?"

"Young lady, I've had so many patients."

"Not by the looks of this place."

LaRue sniffed the air. "What's that smell? Is something on fire? Is this building finally burning down?"

He considered the long trek to the hallway to look for signs of smoke.

"It's me," Bluma told him. "It's from my job."

"Well, that's a relief." LaRue smiled.

Bluma pulled her blouse from her skirt and showed him the scar on her belly. "You remember this? The poor little schoolgirl and her teacher, Miss Reilly, and the so-called appendectomy?"

The doctor put his hands in front of his face. "Please, put that away, don't tempt me. I might not be able to control myself."

She looked at the wreck LaRue was and thought of passing a comment, then thought better of it. Why dare a man to prove he was an animal?

"You cut me open, but you only made me worse. You were supposed to fix things, but I never got better. And I'm still not better. And you call yourself a doctor!"

LaRue tried to remember the girl, but couldn't bring her back from the past. His knowledge of anatomy was still intact, even if his memory was shot. He pointed at her belly.

"That's an appendectomy scar. If I was so bad at my job, you wouldn't be standing here. You'd be at Waldheim."

"You owe me a favour," she told him. "I've come to collect."

"So, you're in trouble," he deduced. "Here, sit down." He showed her a chair, then sat behind his desk, acting medical all of a sudden. "Tell me what you want."

Bluma sat down, even if the chair's arms looked sticky. She'd come this far, but now she was out of courage. How could she explain the problem without talking about her feelings, which she did not want to do? Since she couldn't say what she was, she said what she wasn't.

"I'm not pregnant," she told him, "if that's what you think."

"Well, that's a relief."

A relief for her, but not for him. Making angels was an important sideline.

"I couldn't be pregnant."

"Good. Then what's the problem?"

"I don't want to get married."

In an embarrassing gush of bitter confession, she told the whisky doctor the whole story about Eddie.

"How can I feel anything for him?"

LaRue surprised her. He didn't tell her to go ahead and get married, that girls grew into marriage like an ill-fitting suit of clothes, and she would too, in time.

"If you don't want to marry this man, then don't. What's so difficult about that?"

"I want a letter from you, saying I'm unfit for marriage. Say you examined me and I'm not a virgin."

LaRue laughed. "From my practice, I can tell you that's no distinction. I can't write a letter like that. From the medical point of view, it's meaningless."

"Not to me."

"I'm sorry."

"Then say I have a social disease."

"That's patently not true. I'd risk losing my licence."

"For what it's worth."

The doctor stood up and moved heavily around his desk to where Bluma sat. He did what she'd been expecting him to do. He placed his two heavy, unclean hands on her breasts.

"Get your mitts off me, you rat," she told him in an even voice.

He leaned over. His formaldehyde breath washed across her face. "I'm going to make you the happiest girl in the world."

"You're out of your goddamned mind!"

LaRue drew back and crossed his hands over his chest.

"Very good, young lady! If you can say that to me, a person of authority, a doctor of medicine no matter what you think, then you can say that to him — whoever he is. You came marching in here, very bossy, you pulled up your blouse, you showed me a thing or two. Very nice, by the way — smooth skin is always made better by a slight imperfection. So I'm sure you can find the strength to tell your pressing suitor to go take a hike. I have faith in you. If you'd like to rehearse on me, please do, if you think it will help. I'm happy to be of service."

"That won't be necessary."

LaRue took her hand before she could draw it away. She hated how he played games with her. It was cruelty at its worst, worse than Esther Sadow telling her why she attracted men.

He looked her in the eye and pointed a finger in her face with his free hand.

"No," he told her. "I won't marry you. Get out of my life and stay out." He dropped her hand. "Now, say it: I won't marry you."

"It's not that easy!"

"I did what I could for you," he said in his defence.

Bluma was crying by the time she turned the doorknob and ran into the hall. If it were only that easy. LaRue didn't understand: Eddie wasn't the problem.

Esther Sadow was hovering by her desk when Bluma got back. The woman stank of solicitude, a less decorous version of Miss Reilly.

"You all right?"

Bluma shrugged.

"Something the matter? Fly-Paper bothering you?"

"You don't know the half."

"I can help, you know. I wasn't born yesterday." She leaned closer to Bluma, full of mischief. "The tire man wasn't the first. Not by a long shot. I've been around."

What was it with everyone? Why did they feel they had to help when she never asked anything from them? Didn't they have lives of their own? Did they really need her so badly?

"There's nothing new," she told Esther.

"You don't look so hot. What you need," Sadow's wife decided, "is to get out and have a little fun. Meet some people."

"I'll try," she promised.

"There's plenty of clubs." She nodded her head toward the back office, where Sadow ruled. "I used to go to Dreamland, before I got serious again."

Dreamland, Bluma repeated to herself. Now that was a place she'd never been.

TEN

The Lover's Couch

EVEN IN HER ADVANCED AGE, every morning Bluma Krueger awoke
from a shallow, Restoril-induced sleep with a bitter chemical taste on
her tongue. She kicked off her day by vomiting. Her nervous stomach
was still nervous after all these years; a lifetime had resolved nothing,
and she had given up trying to converse with it. She didn't rush to the
toilet the way a sick person would. She lifted her legs out of bed, leaned
on the stabilizer bar bolted into the wall and went off wearily to the
bathroom. Once that ceremony was over, her day could begin.

Joey knew this because his mother didn't spare him a single detail.
Listening to her, he wondered if there was ever a time when she had
been a normal, carefree girl. Imagine a life of not getting better, where
you cling to the illnesses that defines you. From four legs to two to
three, as the Sphinx had it, existence went unchanged. As a member of
the therapy generation, for whom self-improvement was the goal of life,
Joey was terrified by the prospect.

He had a disloyal thought. What if his mother was making her
life sound worse for his benefit? When they finally reached the contem-
porary era, when he was alive and aware, he would play his memories
off against hers and see. But they weren't there, and it might take them

a while. In the meantime, she was all too eager to please. You want me to dish the dirt? she asked him a few days back. He hadn't protested the word dirt. Silence was consent. She'd do anything to make her boy happy.

From beyond the parking lot, the oceanic hum of the I-95 washed over him, urging him toward sleep. His mother had exhausted him once again.

She was still insisting on him writing everything down as she watched, but he was cheating. He had bought a high-tech tape recorder smaller than a pack of cigarettes, and taped all their conversations. Of course, he still used pen and paper. Bluma loved watching him scribble on pads of Office Depot canary paper. But as he wrote, his backup never missed a word.

At the Ecological Solutions offices, he reached into his jacket pocket, reversed the tape and pressed play. Bluma's voice issued from the machine in surprisingly rich quality.

"The bitch ruined his life," she was saying — about whom, he couldn't remember. She laughed at the prospect of a ruined life. "What a buncha deadbeats, all of them."

Joey clicked off the recorder. With her vulgarian's voice and rich chuckle, she didn't sound like a woman who had spent her life being miserable.

He retrieved the thimble-sized glass from the corporate cupboard and began the first stage of the decompression process. It takes the edge off. That had been just another barroom expression until he began his sessions with Bluma. Now he knew exactly what the words meant.

He wiped the glass dry on his shirttail. One good thing about doing his own laundry was he didn't have to explain why certain articles of clothing smelled certain ways. Caroline liked to laugh at his collection of T-shirts from various baseball teams from cities he had never been to, with the logos of teams he knew nothing about. "Who the hell are the San Diego Padres?" she asked as he pulled their T-shirt over his head. He got his revenge by slipping it over her head, where it hung from her shoulders like a pup tent. He made her keep it on as they made love, and she was delighted when he put the shirt back on at the end of the night.

After his stop at the office, he moved on to the second stage of decompression with Ozzie at their usual spot. He was waiting for Joey, faithful as ever.

"How goes the battle?"

"That's exactly what it is. Sometimes when I get out of there, I'm so exhausted I can hardly walk. I'm shell-shocked. It's like battle fatigue."

"Bluma fatigue," Ozzie offered.

"Yes," Joey allowed. "And I've got it even on days I don't see her. It's this fear … The family mould cannot be broken. There's more of her in me than I care to admit."

Then, a glass of Chianti in his hand, Joey confessed to Ozzie about Caroline.

Ozzie took it all in. Joey could feel him working hard not to react.

"What is she to you?" Ozzie asked.

"Well, she's not my girlfriend. And it's not exactly an affair. I don't know what it is." Joey smiled sheepishly. "She's my miracle."

"I hope you told her so."

"I did."

"You? Say something like that?" Ozzie shook his head in admiration. "Your inner Joey has truly come out."

"I never imagined 'inner' and 'Joey' going together."

"But you do have an inner Joey," Ozzie insisted. "You must have."

"Let's change the subject, okay?"

Joey Krueger hated compliments. He would screw himself into the floor to avoid one.

"Anyway, I didn't exactly set it up with Caroline," he said. "Nothing was planned. It was the fireflies' fault."

"When you say something like that, I know you're a changed man."

"I am unaccustomed to change," Joey admitted.

"How long have you been with her?"

"A couple of weeks."

"What do you know about her? She's married, she has kids, she has a job, a car, visible means of support?"

"She's nervous. She kept rubbing her skin, like this." Joey performed her tic and didn't like how it felt. "Like hurting herself."

"And that's attractive?"

"Hardly!"

The conversation was the opening Sheila the barmaid was looking for. She leaned forward from her side of the bar and provided Joey and Ozzie with an eyeful of tanning salon cleavage, a move meant to assert her authority over this pair of amateurs.

"If she's not attractive, why are we so fascinated by her?" she asked.

"We were fascinated?" Joey asked innocently.

From his vantage point, it looked like she took her tanning sessions in the nude. "We were talking about something," Ozzie jumped in. "The usual thing: love."

"Love, right. When it's not ripping gas tanks out of the ground."

"Wait a minute, Sheila," Joey reminded her. "A good barmaid listens, but never admits she's listening. And she never repeats. Ever."

Sheila slapped her left wrist with her right hand. "You're right. I done wrong. I owe you one."

She brought over the bottle of well-brand bourbon and splashed a refill into their glasses.

"Let the games begin," she declared.

"To your love life." Both men lifted their glasses to her.

"To yours," she said to Joey.

"I'm married," he reminded her.

"Famous last words." Sheila thought a moment. "Then let's drink to the broad that's hurting herself. May she be cured once and for all — or am I being indiscreet again?"

After the toast, Sheila drifted away to torment other customers. Ozzie and Joey stared into their drinks that looked insurmountably deep.

"Jesus," said Joey, with Sheila safely out of earshot. "Every barmaid cliché in the book."

"But with a heart of gold."

"If you drink all that, Ozzie," he predicted, "you'll fall asleep in front of Helen Mirren. You'll hurt her feelings. You know how actresses are."

"My wife falls asleep most of the time she's watching."

"I thought she was wild about those shows."

"She says she can watch," Ozzie said, "even while she's sleeping."

"Women can do that," Joey agreed.

"Wives can," Ozzie corrected his friend, then took his glass in hand. "On the count of three, we drain these suckers. Then we leave."

In the parking lot, leaning against his car as his friend leaned against his, Ozzie had a flash of alcohol-induced wisdom.

"You know, Joey, you're doing this for your mother because you hope someone will do the same for you some day."

"My life is completely mediocre. It wouldn't make a good story. I lack nobility."

"That's what you think. What about Elke? What did she say?"

"About what?"

"The fireflies, Dumbo."

"She didn't say anything."

"I find that hard to believe. Maybe you weren't listening."

"Well, there was something. A few days later, she told me she was seeing someone."

"Seeing someone?" Ozzie repeated. "Like a therapist or something?"

"No. Seeing someone like … like a man."

Ozzie shook his head. "It sounds too neat. She's making it up."

"What can I do about that?"

"Nothing, Joey. You're in the clear. That must be what she wants. She's giving you her blessing. Her permission."

Ozzie got into his car. A second later, Metallica was pouring out of the sound system, advising them not to waste their hate on anyone else, and to keep it for themselves. The car trembled with the rage of a sixty-something rock band.

"Come on, Ozzie, that stuff's for kids."

"The guy singing is your age, if he's not older. And his words are immortal."

Ozzie slammed the door shut, threw the car into reverse and backed in a tight circle so he was facing the strip mall exit. He peeled onto US 1, tires squealing like a slapped baby. The man was not an experienced drinker, and Metallica awoke his inner teenager.

Joey watched him go. He had failed as a friend; he hadn't told Ozzie everything. There was more about Elke. The day after his first night with Caroline, in the living room by the front door, with the dachshunds waiting warily, Elke stepped into his path as he was heading out to his office. She had her hands on her hips and her elbows out so he couldn't slip past her.

"I'm seeing someone," she told him. "I think you should know."

Joey had the same reaction as Ozzie. He thought therapist and told her as much.

"No, seeing — fucking! Remember fucking?"

Then Elke made an earthy gesture of remarkable crudeness. Coming from her, it was so incongruous Joey laughed.

"Now that you know, do you want a divorce?" she offered.

"No," he told her. "I already have one." Then he asked, since she wanted to tell him, "What's it like?"

"I feel like a woman again."

She turned her head slowly to one side and exhaled languorously. "Jealous?" she asked hopefully.

"Jealous ... Let me think."

Joey considered the possibilities as the dogs milled around anxiously by his feet, hoping for some marital discord they could interrupt. God, they could use a good shampoo! Focus, he told himself, and he did. He could have been jealous because the person under his roof was up to something without him knowing it. Worse still — without him even being able to imagine it. If she'd changed, he hadn't felt the difference. He was ungifted when it came to intuition, but then again, man's intuition was not a common expression. Not knowing what she was doing on the sly and her not telling him — that could have made him jealous.

But physically jealous in the red-blooded, murderous American way, raging over his lost sexual privileges with Elke? What had they been? He couldn't quite remember. Lovemaking was a distant province at the far reaches of an empire called marriage. Indifference had become a habit. Like so many habits, no particular decision stood behind it. People forget to do the things they used to do. He couldn't remember which of them had forgotten first.

"No, not jealous," he told her. "Just surprised."

"Violently surprised?"

"Me? No. Mildly surprised. Well, quite surprised." He raised her eyes to hers. "So, who's the lucky guy?"

"See? You care!"

"Of course I do," he allowed. "You're still my wife. So, are you taking precautions?"

"Are you nuts? Don't you know how old I am? But I still lubricate like crazy — that's what he says."

Followed by the satisfied dogs, she swept out of the living room without bringing up his late return the night before. That was an accomplishment, and he gave her credit for that.

WHEN JOEY DROVE THROUGH THE Branfords on the way to his office or a job site, the soothing cultured voice of National Public Radio went with him. Public radio was his one concession to New England intellectual life. You had to listen in once in a while to find out what the culture vultures were up to. On the road, even on a short drive, their confident, knowing chatter was easier to take than the rap of wannabe gangsters, or the three power chords of the metal bands his partner Ozzie worshipped.

On the radio on this day, a dour man with an Irish accent was being interviewed. It turned out he was a writer who'd won a coveted prize with an impressive purse, hard to believe considering how irretrievably gloomy he sounded. Maybe that was the way you had to act if you were a writer, the way Joey had to sound enthusiastic and competent when it came to pulling gas tanks out of the ground.

The writer was being asked about memory. Joey turned up the volume.

"There isn't any such thing as memory," the writer claimed. Then he abruptly went silent, filling the radio waves with dead air.

For the benefit of the puzzled interviewer, he added, "What people call memory is really imagination. We make it all up."

With the volume up, in the Volvo's quiet interior, Joey could hear the guy scrape his chair on the floor as he got up and filed out of the studio: the interview from hell.

The writer's comment was more a riddle than an answer. If he was right, Joey figured there were two ways to take it. He could feel immeasurably free — free to make up his mother's past to suit himself. Or tremendously despairing because there was no past to reach back and capture. What happened to her story then?

He had not listened to NPR until he met Caroline. She worked for the local affiliate in some administrative position, and probably wasn't responsible for putting the writer with the peaty accent on the air. But he would ask her anyway. If there's no such thing as memory, but only imagination, was a person just a leaf in the wind, a flash of sunlight on a fast-flowing river? What about our past that brought us to this point, into each other's arms — is that made up too?

A woman who works welts into her skin as her lover looks on — that has to be a message from the past. The sort of behaviour a person might indulge in private, she did right in front of him. The red marks disappeared as quickly as she made them, but that wasn't the point. Caroline didn't recognize any border between what she did when she was alone and what she did when she was with him. It was a privilege to know a woman like that.

Bed was the only place her hands didn't reach compulsively for some part of her skin to punish. Joey had known two marriages, and in both, his wives remained rigorously unchanged once they had their clothes off. Lovemaking didn't change them. If anything, it made them more themselves, the way aging is said to do. Caroline was different. Her hands reached for him, and not some vulnerable spot on her body. All self-punishment stopped. Her caresses were quiet and contemplative. Together, they talked about the baggage they brought to bed — the past again, not imagination but a real territory. The books they'd read that had been the guides of their age. Caroline confessed to never having read *The Joy of Sex*, though she did belong to the demographic. *Our Bodies, Ourselves* was another story. She paid closest attention to the chapters about cancer.

"I read it too," Joey volunteered.

"And?"

"I felt on the outside, looking in."

Caroline laughed indulgently. "Well, my love, it wasn't written for you."

"Tell me something," he said. "Why did you choose me?"

She laughed at him. "My God, we only just met! You sound like some old grey husband waxing nostalgic on his wedding anniversary."

"Sorry."

"Anyway, I didn't exactly choose you. All of a sudden you were there. You know, some enchanted evening." Caroline did a pretty good

Sinatra imitation, or was that Perry Como? "And you wanted me. That hasn't happened since … since a long time. I acted on impulse. I never do that."

"Never?"

"Besides, you're a goofy guy. I like that."

"Me, goofy? I'm melancholic."

"You told me you work in ecology. That is absolutely the baldest pickup line going."

"But it's true," Joey protested.

"Tell it to the Marines!"

Caroline was full of brassy expressions, but she wasn't brassy herself. A brassy woman is a hurt woman who wears a brass shield against her own bad choices. Caroline wasn't like that.

They spent the nights after their first one talking at the coffee table, enjoying the foreplay they skipped the first time. They sat with their glasses of bourbon and ice sweating circles on the glass surface. After the first night, when he had read her thoughts, Caroline made sure they had their own glasses.

Joey brought over a bottle. Caroline noted the brand. Maker's Mark, one of the premiums.

"Does that mean you're moving in?"

"I wouldn't feel right about drinking yours all the time."

"We'll put it in the cabinet. It'll be our security blanket. Though you're not much of a drinker."

"Look." He held up his glass. "I'm drinking."

"You are. But you can make love to me without getting high first."

"I hope so!"

"Not all men can."

Drinking and men: that must have been a trigger, one of many. Caroline reached up and began rubbing her temple. She'd worked that spot the first time, with the geraniums. Joey wanted to stop her. What she was doing looked like self-injury. On the radio, he'd heard about people who did that. She was hurting herself and if you love someone, you don't want that person doing that. But he didn't reach out and still her hand. That would make her self-conscious and set a border between who she could be when he was around and who she couldn't. That was who she was: a woman with tics. He would love her that way.

As he watched, he felt his dick stir. Dick and tic — they rhymed. Her tic was a kind of foreplay. She was telling him to be good to her, better than she was to herself.

When he looked up next, the red spot on her temple had disappeared.

"You're somewhere else," she told him.

"No. I'm here. Thinking how wonderfully quiet it is."

"Oh, yes, those horrible dogs of yours." She smiled guiltily. "Sorry for badmouthing them."

"Of hers," he corrected. "They trained themselves to bark every time we have a fight."

"They trained themselves? Pretty smart animals."

"Do they bother you?" he asked Caroline.

She thought of answering, but raised her glass instead.

"To the quiet."

JOEY HAD HAD ENOUGH OF Elke calling him a mama's boy; he decided to leave Bluma out of the picture when it came to describing his schedule to Caroline. A grown man spending his days in his mother's apartment, taking the dictation of her life story sounded a little deviant.

That will be my secret garden, he decreed. At long last, I have one.

But he couldn't keep Caroline a secret from Bluma, even at the risk of admitting he'd turned a Commandment into a Suggestion.

His mother interrupted his elaborate explanation of how it began. The fireflies and the ice cubes, crossing the lawn barefoot, he who never took off his shoes and socks, even on the beach.

"Spare me the details, okay? Good for you, I'm happy! I'm glad you're finally getting some satisfaction."

"You're not ... You don't think ...?"

"You expect me to defend the bonds of holy matrimony? Haven't you been listening all this time? I told your father to take a hike. Go find yourself — that's what I said, and I said it years before finding yourself got fashionable."

"It's just that ... Forget about it." He shook his head.

"Your wife — wife in name only — is wasting your time. You're not going to live forever, you know. And there's no pleasure after death, no matter what they say about the seventy-two virgins."

Joey had never heard about the seventy-two virgins. They sounded like a real headache.

"You must have had fun in your day," he said hopefully.

"Fun? The fun I had was when I was a girl. Bella and me used to stand on the sidewalk and look at the dresses in the dress-shop windows and laugh at the proper ladies who were going to wear them. We'd laugh ourselves silly! When it came to your father, there were no fireflies and barefoot in the park."

"Once he left to go find himself, didn't you have any fun then?"

"Depends on your definition of fun. Sure, men pursued me. But they were usually my boss. And I wouldn't call it romance. If you were lucky enough to have a job, you had to keep it."

Joey leaned back in his chair. On the wall of mementos and photos in her apartment, there wasn't a single picture of Bluma with a man. Satisfaction. He wondered what the word meant to her.

"WOULD YOU BELIEVE," JOEY TOLD Caroline that evening, "I told my mother about you and me."

Caroline sat up, alarmed.

"I hope I won't have to meet her. I'm too old for the meet-the-parents ordeal."

"Don't worry. She told me she was happy for me. She's happy I'm finally getting some satisfaction — that's what she said."

"How does she know I'm satisfying you? You tell her?"

"Of course not. We don't talk that way. That's her word. She's got a mouth on her sometimes."

Caroline mulled that over, then lay back, her arms behind her head. "So that means," she concluded, "if you can tell your mother about me, you're pretty much married the way I am."

"Maybe. But probably not as free."

"Free? I heard that word somewhere before."

The lovers' bed possessed some of the qualities of the analyst's couch. In Caroline's arms, Joey began to remember shreds of his own story. Memory or imagination — he didn't care which, as long as the story intrigued. Lying down with her opened the doors to the past. The sting of bourbon helped too. Sometimes at the Italian place, before the crowds showed up, Sheila would play a side or two of Leonard Cohen. Once Joey heard the old poet whisper the words *A visionary rush of alcohol.* He didn't get it. Alcohol doesn't give you visions, unless they're the pink elephants and green snakes of the terminal phase. But in Caroline's bed, Maker's Mark brought forth details from his past.

"My mother used to talk to the moon," he said into the warm cloud of perfume that hovered over the nape of Caroline's neck.

"Did the moon talk back?"

"I don't think so. It was a one-way conversation. She would stand by the window and part the curtains just enough to peer out, then she would have her little conversation."

"About what?"

"I don't know. I never understood what she was saying."

"She could see out but nobody could see in," Caroline deduced.

"How's that?"

"The curtains. She opened them just a little. She could look out, but she thought nobody could see her."

"Hey, you're good! You could be a shrink."

"That's because I've done that myself. And you know what? People can see you. If you can see them, they can see you. That's the first thing you should learn when you're a kid."

So it was about detection, Joey realized. His childhood living room was like a doll's house. He could take the roof off and the actors, his mother and himself, would spring to life and play the scenes he needed them to. "So many terrible accidents," Bluma would tell the moon, as if it didn't know what was going on below. She'd repeat the small disaster stories from the daily paper, the child drowning in the swimming pool at his birthday party, the golfers struck by lightning at the eighteenth hole. Death showing up when people were least prepared.

His mother, he thought, must have been waiting for a similar catastrophe.

After a last cigarette, her husband toddled off to bed, and she would go to the window and search for the glowing ball of light, as blank as an untouched sheet of paper. When she found it she forgot all else, including her son Joey, wakeful and vigilant, who stood a few steps behind her, at the entrance to the living room.

"What do you see, moon?" she asked. "Do you see it?"

It? Joey wondered.

He couldn't ask her since he wasn't supposed to be there.

ELEVEN

The Gun Girl

"A WOP'LL BEAT A JEW any time when it comes to class!"

Bluma recognized the girl with the big mouth. Agnes, her name was. She usually came in when Bluma was on her way out, and all she knew about her, besides the size of her mouth, was that the Greek made a big deal about her.

"If a wop gots something, she'll share it with you. But Jews are just in it for themselves."

Nobody contradicted her at the counter, but nobody agreed either. They were all waiting to see where Agnes was going with her little number. Bluma didn't wait.

"How come you know so much about the subject?"

"Finally somebody wants to talk to me."

"Impatient, aren't you? A real hothead. Isn't that what they say about you smouldering Italians?"

"We're passionate," Agnes said.

"Good for you."

"That's why we share everything."

"Including your hare-brain opinions?"

"Yeah. Them too." She laughed. "Especially them."

Agnes proceeded to tell Bluma the scientific evidence she based her opinions on. She was at a club the night before; she wasn't too sure because she'd been on quite a whirl lately. It was a black and tan. She was with her gang and one of the girls conned a guy out of twenty bucks. It wasn't conning, really, it was stealing, because the guy was drunk and didn't know the girl was making his pockets. When they got outside on the street with the loot, the girl, who was Jewish, wouldn't share the take with Agnes, even though they were supposed to be in it together.

"That's what I'm saying," Agnes concluded.

"It sounds like you got the wrong friends," Bluma told her. "Which means maybe there's something with you. No offence."

Agnes considered the possibility.

"You want to be my friend, is that it?"

"We could go to a club together." It took all her courage to get the words out.

"For sure I'm not going with that Jewish girl anymore!"

"I'm Jewish," Bluma told her.

"We'll see how that works out."

"Ever been to Dreamland?"

Agnes gave her the once-over. Bluma didn't know what Dreamland was and it showed.

"If you want to, so do I," Agnes said. "We just got to make sure you don't get broken in. A girl like you."

Bluma had no idea what Agnes was talking about.

"I got a new shift," Agnes was telling her. "I'll be at lunch same time as you."

"We'll have plenty of time to talk. Plus there's someone I'm trying to stay away from."

"I'm warning you, people don't usually want to stay away from me!"

On their way to lunch from their jobs — Agnes worked at a stamping plant, making Caruso records down the street from Sadow's — and at the counter with their sandwiches, Agnes made it her business to educate Bluma. Bluma liked the attention, and she liked looking busy when Eddie came around. "You need training," Agnes was telling her. "You got to use your wits. Otherwise, a girl like you, you'll fall into a trap. You know what I mean?"

"Sure."

Agnes looked unimpressed. "You'll end up giving them something and getting nothing back."

The something, the nothing — it was all about her body. The unknown zone between her legs. Bluma never imagined her body as anything more than a playground for pain. But Agnes made her see it was a precious commodity she could trade for money and favours. "But never trade it all the way," she cautioned. Not going all the way was at the heart of the con game.

"Now that you know, don't forget it. That's what I mean when I say you need training."

Agnes moved on to the subject of riding in cars. Going to a club wasn't like going to any other place. You couldn't just take the streetcar and get off at the corner and walk right in the door. You needed a car. Which meant you needed a man. But not just one so he wouldn't get ideas — a bunch of them together. They were your company for the evening, but you absolutely could not trust them. They couldn't trust you either, but sometimes them wanting to have relations so bad and the alcohol in their blood made them forget that fact. If you could get their watch or make their pockets while you were with them, that was all right too.

"So, you're stealing," Bluma said.

"Conning isn't stealing. Conning is using your wits. You use your wits to outwit somebody."

"And your body too."

"Yeah, yeah. So what?"

Agnes was in no hurry to talk about her body outside of its

potential for trade. She was like Bluma that way, which was why they were starting to be friends. Neither of them could understand the excitement their bodies caused in men. That was a good thing, because it kept them from getting carried away the way a man would.

"Why do we even need men?" Bluma asked.

"You know a girl that's got a car?"

"No," she admitted. "Not yet."

"Not yet?"

"Yeah. Not yet."

Agnes gave her a searching look. She had better keep her eye on this one. Bluma could imagine things she couldn't, even though she'd had months of the high life and the other girl was a greener.

It was more complicated than just cars, Agnes explained. You had to know where the club was, who was working the door, what the password was if there was one — it was a regular science. She'd never seen a girl keeping the door at a club. There were plenty of them on the dance floor or on stage, singing, being light and gay and decorating the premises. But the business part, never.

"Conning is a business, right?"

"You really got a mouth on you," Agnes said admiringly. "Were you born that way?"

"Hell, no. I was born a mouse. I had to learn. I had a good teacher."

"Yeah? Who was that?"

"My father."

Agnes nodded. That was their shared secret. "I get it. In that case, you'll go far."

Bluma turned out to be a pretty good conwoman. First, she conned Agnes into thinking she could be part of her gang. It was a two-girl gang so far, like in the better days with Bella. Conning a bunch of drunk-up guys in heat was nothing compared to getting Agnes to take her seriously. Then came the hardest part: she had to con herself into thinking she could do all the things a gang girl was supposed to do.

The word "con" came from confidence, and she had none of that. But she discovered that a lifetime of covering up paid off. It was a Friday, and Agnes was late for lunch. When she did show up, she threw herself onto the stool next to Bluma's ten minutes into the break.

"Fucking wop," she growled.

"What's up?"

"The boss tried to put his hands on me. I told him where to get off. I don't even know if I'll have a job when I go back — if I go back. If I can't meet the rent … Hell, I'll ask my brother to move in."

It was the break Bluma was waiting for.

"I'll share with you. You don't want your brother. You'll just end up doing his laundry."

Agnes turned to Bluma as her egg salad sandwich arrived. "Yeah, you're right. Yeah, maybe … But first we're going riding tomorrow. You in?"

"Like Flynn."

It was a test, and Bluma was ready. Everything was going according to plan.

BLUMA WAS READY FOR EVERYTHING except the car ride through the West Side that took her right past Lexington Street. She sat in the back with Agnes, and two Italian guys with greased hair and parts as sharp as knives were in front. One of them was called Manny. The one who drove didn't seem to have a name. Agnes was babbling away about how West Side girls always wore such pretty dresses.

"Maybe," Manny answered without turning around. "But in Lawndale, the girls wear rags."

Bluma looked out the window at the three-storey, red brick walkups of Lawndale, Bella's neighbourhood. Bella could be out there, standing on a street corner. She'd look up and see her in the car with Agnes and wonder what she was doing there, why hadn't she told her she'd be in the neighbourhood, and now that she was here, was she finally going to move in and go to school with her?

Bluma slumped down on the seat and her leg rubbed against Agnes.

"Where you going?" Agnes asked.

"Nowhere. I get carsick sometimes."

"Nerves," Agnes diagnosed. "Don't worry."

"That's the way I am. One time I even got trainsick."

Agnes went on with her talk about pretty dresses, as subtle as a punch in the mouth when it came to what she wanted from the two guys. Finally they drove out of Lawndale without Bella appearing on the corner at a red light and peering into the car, her face dark with disapproval. Guilty, Bluma thought. Guilty of what? Do you have to be guilty of something to be guilty? It was the kind of thought that made her crazy.

They crossed Austin Avenue into Oak Park. The streets widened and the sky reached down unimpeded to the ground, to brick sidewalks straight and orderly under wide oaks, past the dollhouses that Frank Lloyd Wright built for grown-ups. Bluma heard church bells ringing lustily, making iron waves of sound. Church bells on a Saturday?

It must have been a wedding. Some nice girl was getting married to a man. Love, honour and obey. How did she even know those words? The thought of loving, honouring and obeying Eddie made her bowels turn liquid.

"See that dame with the fur?" Manny asked as they passed a woman on the sidewalk. "We're gonna let you off at the corner. You're gonna walk back in her direction, and when you get up next to her, you're gonna ask nice and pretty where the Lake Street El is. We'll take over from there. Got it?"

Agnes and Bluma climbed out of the car at the next corner. They smoothed their clothes and combed their hair with their fingers.

"If I had a pretty dress, I'd feel better," Agnes said.

"I thought that's why you're doing this. So you can buy yourself one."

"Oh, yeah, the money. I almost forgot. Nothing wrong with money. But I'm doing this just for something to do. You know, to get out of the house."

The girls began walking down the sidewalk toward the woman. Bluma slipped her arms through Agnes's. Agnes gave her a sidelong look. She didn't like being touched.

"You're not that way, are you? You rub my leg in the car, and now this."

"We look sweeter this way," Bluma explained.

"Sweeter?"

"Like we're innocent. The mark won't get suspicious."

"Maybe."

When the woman was a dozen paces away, Agnes whispered, "I'll do the talking. You sound too much like a Jew. That won't work in Oak Park."

Agnes stopped in front of the woman and asked where the Lake Street El was. Her eyes were wide, she batted her lashes, her voice was saccharine and the question made no sense because they could practically hear it rattling past one block over. A hundred percent fake, Bluma thought. But the woman with the fur stole went for it. She was at home in the world, she was confident. Maybe that's why they called it conning.

"You go to the next corner and turn left." The woman patted her fur as she gave directions, like she was comforting it, though it was the other way around. "You'll see the station —"

Then Manny was behind her, quiet and quick as a cat, for a big guy. He grabbed the stole off the woman's neck. She screamed and turned around. With his free hand, Manny knocked her pocketbook out of her grasp and Agnes picked it up.

"Help! Police!"

"Scream all you want," Manny taunted her. "There's nobody around but us."

The woman's high-pitched voice grated on Bluma. She hated her. She was too easy a mark, a real nobody, just somebody she had to use to get free of Eddie. Bluma slipped her left leg behind the woman's and threw her backwards. The move worked in Burnside, and it worked in Oak Park too. The woman lost her balance, fell backward with her legs in the air and hit her head on the brick sidewalk.

The driver came level with them and they jumped in. They drove in tense silence till they crossed Austin Avenue and were back on the West Side, on Douglas Boulevard. Manny pounded the dashboard.

"Good work, girls! She didn't know what hit her!"

"The sidewalk did," Bluma said.

"Yeah. Somebody call a cop!"

Manny laughed at his own joke, and his voice broke like a kid's. Nerves, Bluma thought. I'm not the only one. He started tearing through the woman's pocketbook.

"That was Thelma McClintock," Manny said, holding up the woman's card from the Oak Park Public Library. "Say hello to Thelma. A book reader, what do you expect? Goodbye, Thelma."

He threw the card out the car window and rifled through the money compartment. There was a ten and two fives. A real haul.

He turned around and handed Agnes a five-dollar bill.

"Your share," he told her.

She took it gratefully.

"What about me?" Bluma complained.

"That is you." Manny pointed his chin at the bill. "For the both of you."

"It's all right," Agnes told her. "I'll make change."

But it wasn't all right. Twenty divided by four is five, five bucks each. Sure, they were girls, but Manny couldn't have done the job by himself. That Oak Park woman would have run screaming the other way when she saw him coming at her. And what about the fur? Manny would fence it and make plenty.

Bluma kept the injustice of it to herself. Unless she had Agnes on her side, there was no sense raising a ruckus. Anyway, the money didn't really matter.

"Take me to Dreamland," Bluma said. "I can make change there."

Manny laughed. "They don't give change at Dreamland. And you're not dressed right."

"We can fix that," the driver said.

"You talk after all," Bluma told him. "I thought you were a deaf-mute."

"I only talk when I have something to say."

He turned off Douglas Boulevard onto a side street and pulled into the alley.

"You missed it with all your chattering, girls, but on Douglas there's a real nice dress shop. Go pick yourselves out something pretty. Take your time, get a good look at the merchandise. When you're happy, come back and we'll be waiting for you."

Bluma and Agnes got out of the car.

"You think they're trying to get rid of us?" Bluma asked.

"I know what they're up to. Hey, you didn't have to do what you did back there."

"What did I do? Back where?"

"You didn't have to knock that woman down."

"She was screaming. It hurt my ears."

"Oh, yeah, I forgot about your nerves. You're the sensitive kind."

"The cops would have come. You think I want to get pinched?" Bluma looked at her and narrowed her eyes. "You're the tender-hearted one here, is that it? What does that make me?"

"We don't know yet," Agnes told her. "We're going to find out."

They went into the store that was right where the driver said it would be. The wooden floor squeaked as they walked up to the rack of dresses.

"I admire you, that's all. I couldn't have done that," Agnes said.

"I didn't know I was going to do it till I did."

Agnes pulled a dress off a hanger.

"Here; blue." She held it against Bluma's body. "It looks good on you."

"Too tight in the bust."

"You're full-breasted. I wish I was like you. The guys must hang around like flies."

"I don't need guys hanging around."

Agnes drew the dress away and put it back on the rack. "You really are that way. I never met one like you, but I heard about it."

"I'm not any way."

Bluma was going to tell her about Eddie to prove she had a man after her, which meant she wasn't that way, but she changed her mind. The story could have just as well proved the opposite. The worst way was no way at all, which was how she felt. The shop owner came up to them, licking his chops over a sale. A Jew, she saw. She should have known: Douglas Boulevard. She didn't want to knock over a Jewish store.

"So what do you ladies need?"

"Something blue," Agnes said. She took the dress off the rack again and held it up.

"You're getting married? Congratulations! Who's the lucky guy?"

"She doesn't know yet," Bluma told him.

"I'm sure she'll have her choice. And blue's just the colour for you. The changing room is at the back." He eyed the two girls. "One item at a time."

A bell rang in the back of the store.

"That must be the delivery truck," the man said. "I'll be right back to serve you. Take your time. Looking's free."

The delivery was Manny and the driver, and the shopkeeper did not come back. Bluma chose the same blue dress in the next biggest size and held it against her body. She didn't bother looking in the mirror. Agnes started sweeping dresses off the rack and throwing them over her arm.

"Just one," Bluma told her. "To wear at Dreamland."

Agnes stared. The dresses slipped off her arm onto the floor.

"This time I'm the tender-hearted one. Come on."

The girls left the store with one blue dress each.

"Manny's gonna kill you," Agnes warned. "All that trouble for one measly dress."

AGNES YANKED ON THE CORD and the Murphy bed descended from the back of the door. She threw herself on it, face first.

"I'm in a daze. I don't know what I'm doing."

"You drank too much. You're just like the guys you con."

"First I con, then I drink." She lifted her head and looked at Bluma. "I got to let my hair down once in a while. When you're conning, you always got to be on the lookout. I wanna have fun sometimes. Not just work."

"The things people called work!"

"It is so work!"

"It's a job. That's not the same thing."

Bluma looked around the flat. Dirty dishes in the rusty sink, dresses and slips thrown over chair backs that made it hard to find a place to sit, Agnes's underthings waiting to be rinsed out in the bathroom. The place looked like the green room in a burlesque theatre.

Agnes rolled onto her side. "I got to get this dress off or it'll look like hell tomorrow. Help me, why don't you."

Bluma unfastened the snap in the back, a simple act Agnes could have done if she'd been in better control of her fingers. The smell of smoke rose off her short black hair, along with cologne and sweat from the men she danced with. Bluma figured she must smell the same — of smoke, in any case. Dreamland was a black and tan, which accounted for the Negroes on the stage playing their music made for dancing, which Agnes could do like a pro. It didn't occur to Bluma that dancing would be involved. She stayed off the big round polished floor in the middle of the club.

"Thanks, sister." Agnes eased out of her dress and lay back in her slip.

"I'll hang it up. It'll air out better."

"You really want to do everything for me."

"Let me come and live with you," Bluma called from the bathroom. "Not forever. Just long enough to get this guy off my tail."

"I don't know as I want to live with a Jewish girl."

"You can't say I don't share," Bluma said. She came back to the room. "And I'm not asking for anything in return."

"That's impossible."

"Just time."

"Time to do what?"

"Time so they'll know I'm not theirs."

"Theirs? Who's that? I thought it was some guy." She rubbed her temples. "You give me a headache with your riddles. Anyway, I promised my brother ..."

Bluma looked around the room. There was the Murphy bed and the shallow couch she was sitting on. Agnes had to see the same thing she did. There was no place to put a boy in this flat.

"All right, all right, you win. I got to sleep now."

The deal wouldn't be complete until they did a stickup, the two of them together. That's what Bluma told Agnes the next morning over a cup of something the Italian girl called coffee.

"A rat died in my mouth last night while I was sleeping," Agnes announced. "How the hell did that happen?"

"You drink as much as any man."

"Thanks for the compliment."

She closed her eyes. An hour or two later, she woke up again. Bluma had spent the time watching her. The one-sided intimacy kept her vigilant. The predator in repose, the merchandise out of public view: it was a thrill to see Agnes spread out that way, her slip in an unbecoming ball around her hips, in an attitude of sheer uncaring — this from a girl who made everyone pay full price for every smile.

It was like being on the inside of some secret.

"You can't do no stickup," Agnes told her through half-closed eyes.

"Training," she reminded her. "Any girl can learn."

"You need instinct."

"I showed you I have it."

Agnes laughed from the depths of her hangover. "You showed me you got a mean streak, that's all."

Like a snake, she sprung from her languorous position on the bed. In her hand was a chrome-plated revolver a foot from Bluma's face.

"Stick 'em up! Now!"

"Where did you —"

"Now!"

Bluma did as she was told.

"Look how I'm doing it. Keep the heater close to your body. Don't hold it up like the Statue of Liberty. They'll knock it out of your hand. Get it?"

"Got it."

Agnes lowered the gun.

"Where did —"

"I never sleep alone," Agnes told her.

"You had me there," Bluma admitted.

"I get bad dreams sometimes. I need to protect myself." Agnes sat up and eased down her slip. "I'll make us more coffee."

"No chicory this time."

"You want real coffee, we'll have to stick someone up."

She caught Bluma reaching for the revolver as she was busying herself at the gas burner by the sink.

"Don't touch it. You'll get prints on it. Use a hankie."

"So you're not a con girl. You're a gun girl. How come your brother lets you do something like that?"

"If your brother's Italian, you can't do anything without hiding it. That's one thing about Jews. You're lucky that way. You don't have your family always breathing down your neck."

Bluma rubbed the nape of her neck underneath her hair. "I never pictured myself as lucky."

There were any number of things the girls could have said about luck, but they kept their thoughts to themselves.

That was part of the training. You avoided saying things that were obvious just to show how smart you were. You avoided admitting anything that might give someone an advantage over you down the road. And if you had to talk, and everybody did sooner or later, you made it sound like a wisecrack. That part got on Bluma's nerves, though she understood the method. Agnes and Manny and the driver had a smart remark for every occasion. They were like a vaudeville act, or a burlesque emcee paid to keep the unruly crowd in stitches.

"You've got a gun," Bluma told her. "We don't need anyone else. We'll keep the money ourselves."

Agnes tried to imagine doing a job without the help of a man's natural violence. The gun would be the equalizer, which is why guns were invented, including this ladylike model she'd never tried out. But if word got around that she'd done a job on her own, just her and the Jewish girl, there'd be hell to pay.

She was already paying, so why not?

"We'll knock over a gas station," she told Bluma. "Wear your pretty blue dress."

"WOULD YOU MIND TELLING ME where the ladies' room is?"

The attendant gave Bluma the once-over, liked what he saw and slipped his greasy rag into his back pocket. His eyes stopped at her breasts, stayed there awhile, then moved up briefly to her face. He didn't know the word vulnerable, but even a gas station attendant can feel the hurt in a woman.

"Come with me, honey, I'll show you."

He walked her toward the back of the station. Heaven had answered the prayer he would never have dared put into words. He'd break her in, right here, on the heap of tarps by the motor oil cases. Hurt once, hurt twice — you don't miss a slice off a cut loaf. Then he'd take off. The whole neighbourhood could serve itself free gas — he'd be long gone.

He turned his back to the entrance and put his hand on Bluma's shoulder. Agnes came up behind him through the open door and put the gun barrel against the nape of his neck.

"Stickup," she told him.

"Come on, quit your kidding."

He wouldn't put his hands up.

"I got advice for you, mister," Bluma told him. "She's worse than a man."

For a second the attendant wondered about what could be worse than a man, and that was hesitation enough for the girls. They pushed him past the heap of tarps into the bathroom. Agnes grabbed a chair and wedged the crosspiece of the back against the doorknob.

"You come out before we tell you to, you'll get it in the neck."

"Two broads sticking me up," he wailed from behind the door. "How am I gonna tell my boss?"

"Don't tell him it was broads," Bluma advised.

That bought them a few seconds of silence. Agnes did the till. Singles and fives — hard times hadn't visited this place.

The door rocked on its hinges.

"You stay put!" Agnes ordered him.

She raised the revolver, aimed high and shot. The bullet tore through the wooden door like butter. The girls headed for the entrance. The gun was still hot when Agnes put it back in her purse.

"I never shot the thing before. That felt good! And it didn't even kick."

"What if you got him?"

"The only way I'd get him is if he was hanging from the ceiling like a spider." Agnes laughed. "Hey, I had to show I got a mean streak too. I can't let you outdo me."

Bluma stopped on the sidewalk and looked at her shoulder. "Shit, I got grease on my dress."

Agnes pushed her along. "Come on, now's not the time. I'll buy you another one."

They jumped on the first streetcar they saw. Bluma threw a handful of change into the fare box. She didn't have to count now. They didn't bother checking where the car was heading. They rushed to the back, giggling like two girls who'd just got their first valentine.

"This has got to be a first," Agnes told Bluma. "Two girls doing a stickup without a man and getting away clean!"

"On the streetcar of all things."

"We could have got caught."

"Yeah. But we didn't." Bluma grabbed Agnes by the shoulders and pulled her close. "We're a real team."

"I guess we are now." Agnes's voice dropped. "You had a close call back there. Another half a minute and he would have had you on your back with your legs in the air. That would have been the real stickup."

"I don't want to think about it."

Bluma looked out the streetcar window. They were heading north on Western Avenue, with no destination except away from the scene of the crime. Each block took them further into safe territory, but it didn't much matter. She figured the attendant would never say that a couple of girls had stuck him up. What man would admit to that?

They could get caught or not. Either way was all right with her. The goal was the same.

"Now what do we do?" she asked.

"Spend it," Agnes told her. "What else? Put it in the bank?"

Night after night, they returned to Dreamland. The nightclub wasn't far from Agnes's flat by the Marshfield El stop. Living with Agnes was like going to a party you couldn't refuse to attend, and once you got there, you couldn't leave. Agnes didn't exactly say it outright, but she didn't want Bluma in her place when she wasn't there. Bluma paid half the rent with her share of the take, but the flat wasn't half hers. So it was Dreamland and the pursuit of pleasure, whether she wanted it or not.

Bluma didn't know how to pursue pleasure. She couldn't dance, and no one stepped up to teach her. She tried drinking, but drink ate holes in her stomach. Through glassy eyes, Agnes gazed at her with pity, but no commiseration, and introduced her to people as her little sister who needed looking after.

One thing in Dreamland gave Bluma pleasure, and that was the music the Negroes played.

She had strange thoughts as she watched them. Their music freed her mind to wander. The Negroes were decorative, the way the women who danced in the club were. They weren't people, they were adornments, and both were necessary for that atmosphere of heady excitement everyone was looking for. But the Negroes had an advantage over the women. They had their music that they played for them-selves, and they had togetherness and an alliance that Bluma couldn't imagine having with Agnes or any of the con girls who worked the club. Bluma stood by the side of the stage and gazed at the musicians as the room danced and whirled around her. The musicians saw her watching, but none of them would meet her eyes.

When Agnes decreed that the evening was over, they retreated to the flat, with Bluma steering her toward their destination. One night Agnes pulled away and stopped under a streetlight. Her eyes were wild.

"I know what you're thinking," she accused Bluma. "You think I've got no inner life."

"I don't know what you mean."

"Sure, you do. You Jews are the kings of inner life."

"You should meet my father. He's a regular philosopher!"

Usually the brutality of fathers was the cement that made them sisters, but tonight it didn't take. Bluma went to her side and took her arm.

"That stuff you're drinking is poison."

Bluma slumped on the couch and pretended to sleep. Agnes got sensitive when she drank, and didn't want Bluma looking at her as she slept. Bluma had to fall asleep before Agnes did, or make it look that way.

Once Agnes was unconscious, Bluma would open her eyes and watch her in her disarray. She could smell men on her skin and clothes from across the room. A wad of crumpled bills lay on the night table beside her head. Agnes conned hard for the money, but once she had it, she didn't care where it ended up.

Bluma's vigil lasted the whole night. She never slept, but that must have been the dreams. Her mind's eye brought up images that irritated and bored her: stacks of banknotes with missing denominations or ones that didn't exist, like the dream of the seven-dollar bills; travels in Manny's car where they drove in circles and never went anywhere, which was close to the truth; the clash of the Dreamland band that provided the rhythm for the futile, frenetic action. The report of the gunshot through the gas station door jarred her awake. She opened her eyes. She was still on the couch of torments, exactly where she'd left herself some time earlier.

From there, she gazed enviously at Agnes's bed, where there was easily room for two.

If I go there, she thought as she looked at her friend lying on her stomach, her arms thrust forward like she was swimming, her bare legs parted, she'll throw me out. And she hadn't been here long enough to be ready to leave.

The first time Agnes talked about being in a daze, she thought the girl was making excuses, since she had the willpower of a cork on the waves. But Bluma was beginning to understand. She had forgotten how long she'd been with Agnes, first as a friend, then as the girl she shared a flat with. She said friend, but of course, Agnes was no friend. She was the person who occupied the place a friend should. Agnes wanted someone to complain to. She wanted an audience for her dramas, and there was the convenience of having someone around to take the edge off the loneliness that was as inevitable at the end of the night as drunkenness was after drinking. That wasn't friendship. Bluma knew what friendship was. What she had with Agnes was a kind of bandage you taped over the hole in your life.

The one thing she could say in Agnes's favour is she shared the proceeds fifty-fifty. She never pulled rank because she had the gun and could shoot it, or because she got them into Dreamland without paying. She was true to her word from the lunch counter. A wop shared what she had.

Through the long nights in Agnes's flat, Bluma thought back to Bella, and blamed her for the mess she was in.

Bella wasn't there for her. Bella didn't protect her. Bella let her drift. Bella went on with her life as a Spanish teacher. If Bluma was here in this flat that stank of cigarettes and undone dishes and acidic tomato sauce, shivering and curled up on a couch that was too short for her, it was Bella's fault.

She considered what there was to go back to. Not much. The job at Sadow's was a vague memory. Money was no issue. With Agnes, she earned in an evening what she made in a month with the vulcanizer. And she didn't have Agnes's burning need to spend. The Italian girl couldn't ride past a red-hot stand without stopping. She was proud of her bad habits and irrational moves, like buying drinks for guys whose money she'd just stolen for the pleasure of hearing them call her a good sport.

That was the difference between them. Agnes went riding with guys and did con jobs and stickups for the excitement. Bluma had a mission. Lying on the lumpy, shallow couch, her head heavy with the night's racket, the one glass of whisky she drank beating up her stomach, she decided that her mission was complete. She didn't need to hang around any longer.

How long had it been? By now Libby's room would be empty. Eddie would have taken the hint and packed his bags. What was he going to do — stick around and sort lentils with her mother?

The next morning, once Agnes got her bearings, declared herself part of the world again, made the beverage she insisted on calling coffee and rinsed out her stockings, Bluma told her she was going back to Burnside. The whole thing was more painless than she feared. She was expecting accusations of desertion and infidelity, and figured Agnes would call her a dirty rat and who knows what else. But she didn't react any more than if Bluma had told her she was going to the movies with someone else.

"You were never really one of us, even if you had some good ideas," Agnes said.

They embraced. Agnes held on until Bluma started to feel nervous. It wasn't just the Dreamland smell on her. With Agnes, she never knew what was for show, and what was real need, and not knowing gave Bluma the willies.

"I'll be all right without you," Agnes told her as she went out the door.

IT WAS A CHANGE RIDING the streetcar after seeing the city from an automobile. Which was better? Everyone would say "automobile," but at least in the streetcar she didn't have to swap smart conversation with hoods.

Bluma walked through Burnside in the raw autumn wind. She heard bells from the polack church and realized it was Sunday. She tried to figure out how long she'd been away. There had been bells in Oak Park too, but that was from a wedding, though now she wasn't so sure. She tried to count the number of Saturday nights at Dreamland, but every night was Saturday night there. That's what put her in a daze. By the time Bluma got to the house and went up the gangway to the kitchen door, she still didn't know how long she'd been away.

Her mother wasn't at her usual spot at the kitchen table. Bluma climbed the stairs. She would sit in a hot bath one hour for every night she'd stayed with Agnes. There would be the sweet silence of an empty house.

She walked past Libby's old room. The door was closed, but not all the way. She pushed it open. Eddie was sitting on the bed in stocking feet, legs apart, hands on his knees.

He looked up.

"I was waiting on you," he told her. "Nice dress you got."

All her sacrifice, all that time — for nothing. She slammed the door and ran into her room.

Even there, she could feel his poisonous presence. He was taking over. He probably slept in her bed when she was away. She wouldn't be able to sleep there, no matter how exhausted she was. She jumped up and went to the window. The grass had turned brown in the prairie. If Laurie was here, he'd turf Eddie out on his ass. But Laurie wasn't here and he wasn't coming back. Burnside was frozen in time. Eddie had no sense of time either. He didn't care how long she'd been gone. He would wait forever.

A couple of weeks hadn't been enough to discourage him. She needed something stronger.

She went down the hall and pushed open the door. Eddie was sitting right where she'd left him.

"I was a gun girl on the West Side with a wop."

"Is that so?"

"Yeah. A wop girl. Me and her. We had this driver named Jerry. Jerry Yale. What a dream! The poetic type. The kind I like."

"A poet driving for a couple of gangster girls?"

"What's wrong with that? He wanted to see everything life has to offer."

Eddie didn't answer. The story was too foolish to believe.

"A poet type, but smart too. Knows his way around. One time we were making love in the park, and all of a sudden I open my eyes and I see this pair of shoes, right by my head. Policeman's shoes, you know, with the big toes. The cop starts threatening to run us in. Jerry jumps up and gives him five bucks to get lost."

"If you need to see him one last time," Eddie told her, "I'll drive you. I'll wait for you."

"You'll drive me?"

"I got a car now," Eddie said, as if transportation was the issue. "I just don't want to see him."

Eddie's gentlemanly *délicatesse* solved the problem of there being no Jerry Yale. She could relax. She'd take a ride over to the West Side with Eddie in a few days, when she felt like it, maybe on the weekend. She'd find something to do over there. Who knows, maybe she'd even find the real Jerry Yale.

"We like to meet in Douglas Park," she told Eddie.

"I can find it."

"I have to be ready, though. I'm not ready yet."

Bluma turned and went downstairs. Her mother was at the kitchen table.

Rachel looked up. "Well, here comes a stranger!"

"Did you put him up to this?"

"I don't know what you're talking about."

She pointed to the ceiling. "Why is he still here?"

Slowly, her mother turned in Bluma's direction.

"You've been away God knows where. You must have had a very exciting time, but here, life goes on as usual. The lights, the groceries, everything else — do you think your father is going to help out? He's locked in the cage he built for himself, roaring like a madman. Go look in on him."

"So, he's a saint?"

"No one ever said that of your father."

"I mean Eddie."

"A saint?" Rachel stared at her daughter as if she were just as mad as her husband. "No. He's not a saint. And neither are you."

"That's a relief!"

Rachel was not much for irony. "I don't know why we bring children into the world if it's only for them to abandon us," she said.

"I didn't ask to be born. I didn't ask to come to this place."

"I think we had this conversation already."

ON THE DAY OF HER excursion to Douglas Park, Bluma put on her pretty blue dress with the grease spot on the shoulder that was barely visible now. She decided to take her mother's advice: she walked across the yard to the Chicken Coop. The air was cool. Goosebumps rose on her arms. She would need a jacket for the park.

She pulled open the screen door. The inside door was unlocked and the knob was missing. She didn't knock or call her father's name. She had come to see the enemy in his lair.

She closed the door quietly. It was the kind of respect you show when entering a sickroom.

Dust lay visible on the overturned chairs, as if a barroom brawl had taken place here, long ago. The sugary odour of spilled whisky had leached away and been replaced by the closed-in air of neglect.

Once I cut the cards here, Bluma thought. I cut and dealt for the cops. Their grateful good humour and flowery red faces and soppy songs oppressed me. That was a lifetime ago.

Nostalgia came to an abrupt end. Her father lumbered out of the backroom and appeared in the doorway, one hand on the wall. His face was divided in two. One side was alive with anger and surprise. The other hung lifeless.

Bluma stared at him, unafraid. He doesn't know who I am. He doesn't recognize me. Her father began to bellow like a wounded animal. Bluma waited for him to rush at her and pummel her to the ground — to kill her the way she thought he always wanted to. "I'm going up to Douglas Park," she told him.

She didn't know what to say next. And she didn't know what Douglas Park really stood for.

Her father bellowed and slapped his forehead with his good hand.

"I'm going with Eddie. He's driving me. You probably don't know who Eddie is. He's the sucker who pays the bills. I got to marry him so he'll keep forking over the cash because you can't work."

Her father lifted his head and roared. Bluma saw what the problem was. He couldn't form words with his half-dead mouth. The sounds he made came from his chest and throat, unformed animal noises.

"He's taking me to see Jerry Yale. I told him Jerry and me made love in the park. He didn't seem to care. I guess he's playing it cool. But you know as well as I that it never happened. There's no such a person as Jerry Yale, and that's a crying shame."

She wondered how much her father understood. Nothing, probably. He'd never understood anything before, so why would he start now, in the state he was in? She could tell him everything because he couldn't talk. It was a terrible emancipation after all she'd suffered under his weight. He was just a sounding board now, a way to hear herself think. Finally, he was her victim. It was about time.

"That's the worst part. I made up Jerry Yale, and now I want him for real. But he doesn't exist. What can I do?"

He stared, his eyes wide, half his face hanging like a baggy frock on a bent hanger. She had a crazy thought: he understood everything she was saying, and miraculously he was on her side.

"That's what I'd like," she confided in him, "a poetic type like Jerry Yale. A sensitive guy with big brown eyes. Imagine that! There's no end to the shit I can dream up."

Her father grunted, a softer alternative to bellowing. She imagined he was giving her advice, or even a blessing. "So long," she told what was left of her father.

She closed the door, not much freer than when she'd come to say her farewells.

SHE AND EDDIE DIDN'T TALK much as they drove through the South Side, then up toward Douglas Park on a Saturday afternoon. He held the scribbled directions in one hand, and the rest of his attention was dedicated to his cigarette. He smoked one after the other. She knew that smoking was a sign of nervousness, though not the only one, since she didn't smoke and she was twice as nervous as everyone else.

She wondered what was behind his devotion. It was not like any man, or any human being she could think of, to accept abuse and respond with equanimity. Turning the other cheek was a fairy tale. She insulted him in public and in private. She left her own house so she wouldn't have to hear the sound of his footsteps. And the whole time he waited for her with a disposition so even it was unnatural.

Is that what love is?

The idea that Eddie might love her was fantastic, like the arrival of Martian tripods in Burnside. He was trying to light one cigarette off the other while holding his directions to Douglas Park in his hand and keeping the car on the road. Eddie could love her if he wanted to. Loving her only made him ridiculous. Who did she love? Certainly not him. Once she'd loved Bella. Now she loved Jerry Yale.

She ordered Eddie to drop her on the 12th Street side of the park, not far from the clothing store she and Agnes had knocked over. She was wearing the same stolen blue dress, but her sense of guilt wasn't what it had been the afternoon she made Agnes limit herself to one item. Today, she would have cleaned off the rack.

Eddie stopped the car at the corner. He must have spent all week rehearsing his lines.

"I'll wait right here. I'll park the car, and I'll be here waiting for you when you come back. Don't come back till you're good and ready and you've got it out of your system."

Then a trolley was on their back bumper, and the motorman was banging away on the bell to get them to move off the tracks. Bluma jumped out and slammed the door.

She disappeared into Douglas Park on the gravel pathway. A minute later, she stopped and turned around. Eddie could have been following her. If he was hiding behind the trees and bushes, she'd never spot him. Well, what of it? Bluma retraced her steps and headed north on Sacramento Avenue. She didn't bother looking for Eddie's car. The Saturday afternoon idlers were lined up along the storefronts, and they called to her as she passed. She didn't look in their direction. Before, she would have told them where to get off. It was amazing how many things she didn't care about now.

The autumn air was cool, but she was sweating by the time she got to Lexington Street. The last time she was here it was a Saturday too. The whole family united — it had galled her. The way Bella's brothers treated her, like they wanted to jump her bones. Look at the elegant young lady, then making fun of her burnt-rubber stink. They might have been Bella's brothers, her cousin's protection, but they were men all the same.

Then she stumbled onto them, the whole bunch, and they did look like a gang with their sleeves rolled up and their caps on crooked. They were supervising men from a moving company who were carrying crates into the store. They had sold the place. Someone else was taking over.

One of the brothers spotted her. It took him a moment to realize who she was. That was okay. She couldn't have said who he was either. Jack or Rudy or Sam or Harry — all the same.

"You all right, cousin?" he asked.

"Yeah. Why wouldn't I be?"

He shrugged. "You look like you've been running. Somebody chasing you?"

"Is Bella around?"

"Upstairs. You know the way."

She went up to the flat. She reached out her hand to ring the door-bell, then stopped. What was the rule again? No electricity on the Sabbath? Meanwhile, the brothers were working away downstairs.

She opened the heavy front door and stepped inside. It was a stranger's house. Bella's house, but Bella was a stranger now. Who was to blame? The floorboards creaked under her weight. The smell of roasted meat was in the air, a homey smell. She didn't dare call Bella's name. She would stand there and wait in the hallway until someone noticed her.

A minute later, Bella stepped into the hall.

"Hey, Fledge, it's you! I knew I felt something."

"What did you feel?"

"I don't know, something in the air."

"That's me all right."

"Oh, go on! What are you doing on the West Side? And unannounced, on top of it?"

"I'm going to the park to meet a guy who doesn't exist. Want to come?"

"Sure! I've been waiting forever to do that. It'll be like the old days when we were free to pretend."

"Back then was somebody else's life."

Bella went to Bluma's side and held her in her arms.

"You don't smell like burnt rubber."

Bluma tried to pull away from Bella's embrace, but she wouldn't let her.

"A man who doesn't exist," Bella said. "That would be the best kind."

"That's what I thought too."

"So we don't have to worry about whether both of us want him 'cause both of us do."

"And we don't have to worry about whether he wants us," Bluma agreed.

"So that means you got rid of Fly-Paper?"

This time Bluma pulled away from Bella's arms.

"No. It's worse."

"Don't tell me …"

"He's boarding at my house. My mother rented out Libby's old room to him."

"Where did she go?"

"She's gone."

Bella took Bluma by the shoulders. "What's happening? You're not telling me anything. You're hiding from me. That's not the deal."

Bluma looked away. "There's too much to tell."

"Next thing you'll be telling me you're marrying Fly-Paper."

"I'd never tell you that."

"You're going to let that man lie on top of you, any time he wants. I know what's gonna happen — you're gonna get married," Bella burst out. "Then you might as well do it in this house. At least I'll be able to keep an eye on you — and you'll need me to!"

Taube stepped out of the kitchen and into the hall to see what the commotion was about. She had a dishrag over her shoulder and a wooden spoon in her hand. Her daughter ran past her with tears in her eyes, toward her room at the back of the apartment.

"I see you are still best friends," she said to Bluma, then went to comfort her daughter.

BLUMA SAT ON A STONE bench that was covered in dry leaves beneath the great, bare, spreading trees of Douglas Park, holding her stomach and rocking back and forth. Who was make-believe and who wasn't? Maybe she was make-believe, like Jerry Yale.

She was in mourning for Bella. Her stomach told her that. But it didn't tell her anything else she could use. She knew one thing. She didn't care what Eddie knew or didn't know about the things she did. Maybe that made him the man to marry after all.

Sitting on the park bench, she laughed. Was that what love is? That couldn't be true. She'd learned that much from Bella. She cared what Bella thought, even if Bella ran away from her and hid, and left her standing stupidly in the hallway.

A few old men who looked like they'd melded onto their benches turned to examine her. A good-looking girl, holding her stomach and rocking back and forth, laughing to herself.

"You all right, sister?" one of them asked.

"Never been better."

"You could have fooled me."

She stood up. They were old men, grey and shabby with disappointment. No sign of Jerry Yale here. She moved down the gravel walkway deeper into the park, hands on her belly as if she were pregnant, but all she was carrying was pain. She came to a lagoon. A cop stood by the water's edge, tapping his foot in his big brogans and rubbing his nightstick against his thigh. He was guarding the fish from hungry people who wanted to catch them. She knew the cop. He was the same one Jerry paid off with a fiver so he'd take a hike and let them get on with it. What did it feel like, having Jerry lying on top of her? She had no way to imagine that.

She climbed the grassy slope that led up from the lagoon. At the top, the bushes grew together. Sticker bushes, she saw. They formed a fence to keep people from getting through. Bluma knew about fences. She bent low and with her forearms and elbows she pushed her way through the branches, careful not to let them scratch her eyes. A meadow stretched out before her. On the grass, at the foot of the scattered trees, couples were lying on blankets. They had a second blanket thrown over them for privacy.

Bluma didn't have a blanket. She spread out her jacket and lay down on the grass, alone on lovers' lane. She turned on her side to watch the couples moving under their blankets like snakes in a jute sack, but covered the way they were, she didn't learn much. She looked away, embarrassed by her own ignorance. The rocky ground dug into her backside.

The ground was cool and damp. The couples must not have felt the whisper of winter in the air and the humidity rising off the earth. She stared at the sky through the great elm trees. The watery autumn sunlight stung her eyes and she closed them. It was easier to think of Jerry Yale that way.

He came to her at last. He spread a warm blanket over her. Then he lay down next to her and his warmth was good. She kept her eyes closed when he kissed her because that's what she was supposed to do. He touched her breasts, but not the way Dr. LaRue had. After a time, he slid his arm beneath her and began easing up her blue dress. It was probably getting dirty underneath but it already had an oil spot on the shoulder. With all of Agnes's talk about getting broken in, and the gas station attendant's plan to throw her onto the tarps, she imagined something violent, like a stickup. But Jerry Yale wasn't like that at all. Everything was calm and measured and tentative, at least at first.

When the pain came she was not surprised. She expected it. But she'd never felt pain in that part of her body.

"You're a good girl," he whispered into her ear. "A good, good girl. You're my girl."

It wasn't the first time a man had probed the inside of her body. But no man had done it with his own flesh.

"I love you," he said into her ear.

"I love you too, Jerry."

"I'm not Jerry. I'm Aaron."

She lay down with Jerry but somehow Aaron took his place.

"You won't get in trouble," he promised. "I used a sheath."

She kept her eyes closed as he slipped away, leaving her open to the autumn wind when he took his blanket with him.

BLUMA KNEW SHE'D BEEN GONE awhile by the pile of cigarette butts on the corner where Eddie was waiting. He had painted a self-portrait in ashes on the sidewalk at his feet.

"You ready?" he asked.

She nodded.

"You see him?"

"Yes," she said softly.

"And it's over?"

She couldn't deny that.

He steered her toward his car parked across Douglas Boulevard. An army of butt-pickers descended on the treasure he left behind.

Driving back to Burnside, out of cigarettes and already suffering from withdrawal, Eddie made her an offer.

"You've got to do something about your father," he told her.

Neither of them had said a word until then. Bluma was busy shifting her weight on the seat, searching for an acceptable position, wondering how stained she was and if it would show, negotiating with the newfound pain between her legs. She liked the dull throb of stretched tissues. A change is as good as a rest, and it was a pleasant change from her stomach.

"What do you want me to do about him?"

"Not you, me. I can give him a job."

"You, give him a job? You're hiring? Nobody's hiring anybody."

"I told you I'm in furs," he said, acting hurt.

"Your father's a furrier in New York City. On Madison Avenue, wherever that is. That's what you told me. And you told me you came here because you didn't want to be in furs."

"I didn't want to be in furs with him. That's not the same thing. I'm going to open a business. Cold storage. I'll be in furs, but not exactly."

"Cold storage? That sounds like somebody getting bumped off."

"That's where rich ladies put their furs during the summer for safekeeping."

"I suppose you know a lot of rich ladies with furs?"

"I don't have to know them personally. You advertise, you find business. Nothing to it."

Bluma looked out the car window at the people of Bronzeville standing around garbage can fires in their thin coats, rubbing their hands together. There wasn't a fur-wearing rich lady in sight, but coloured people didn't wear furs, or if they did, the men were the ones sporting them. She'd seen a man in a fur coat on the dance floor at Dreamland. She thought of telling Eddie that, then figured she should save it for later.

"Cold storage is quiet, there's nobody around. I'll need a watchman, someone to keep an eye on the place. Your father can do that, can't he?"

Bluma laughed. The idea of her lurching, bellowing father following somebody else's orders, actually working and doing what he was told, struck her as the funniest thing she'd ever heard. She pictured him in cold storage, a giant hall of ice, with mink collars hanging all around like the one she and Agnes grabbed off that woman in Oak Park. In the middle of it stood the ex-bootlegger Abe Goldberg with his droopy face. Eddie was roping in the whole family and reserving the idiot's job for her father. Amazing how well the strategy was working.

When they got to Burnside, Eddie went to park the car in a spot he figured was safe from junkers, thieves and other hoods. Bluma found her mother in the kitchen.

"The sucker is giving your husband a job," Bluma announced.

"He said he would," she told her daughter. "His word is good."

"So it's a complete package, is that it? He gets me, and in return Dad gets a job. What do you get? The rent? Or does getting me mean he's got a free ride?"

"If you don't want to marry him, don't. Marry someone else."

"It's like a fairy tale. The poor daughter gets given away to a foreign potentate. Then she's carried into exile and spends her life pining away." Bluma laughed unhappily. "But sooner or later, she'll return to claim her due. What happens then?"

Eddie came in through the door. He saw his fiancée standing angrily at her mother's side, and he knew he was the subject of their argument. Bluma met his eyes and he looked away. He's afraid of me. I can do whatever I want. I'll hang out with Agnes if I feel like it. I'll go looking for Jerry Yale. He won't even lay a hand on me.

It wasn't exactly love, honour and obey.

When it came time to get the marriage licence at City Hall, Bluma put Libby's birthdate as her own, and Libby's date of naturalization as a citizen of the United States of America, along with the number of the certificate. The licence was Bluma's first official American paper outside of her report cards, and though every three months they declared she wasn't working up to her capacities, they didn't say whether she was a citizen. Now she was a legitimate member of the nation. She made the play she'd been waiting to make. All that worrying, all that carrying on with Laurie, and in the end there was nothing to it, just a lying stroke of the pen. She'd been waiting so long she didn't have to check the dates. She knew them by heart.

That was one good thing she'd get out of this deal.

At the licence bureau, Eddie looked over her shoulder and read her birthdate. He didn't think she was that old. She didn't look it, but it was too late to ask questions. When it comes to women, you can never forget their birthdays, but don't ask how old they are. Anyway, he told himself, you're only as old as you feel. And on that day, Eddie was feeling pretty good. He'd just secured himself a cozy little situation with the bootlegger's daughter.

ON A SATURDAY EVENING ON Lexington Street, after sundown and with Sabbath over, Bluma had a serious talk with her stomach. There had been many of them during her lifetime, but none this earnest. She felt she needed to explain to her stomach what was about to happen.

To hold the conversation, Bluma slipped away into the bathroom. It was the only safe place. She looked at herself in the mirror. She looked at the looker in the pink dress. She had no interest in her face or the wavy curls that framed it or her breasts that were so irresistible to so many strangers. She talked to her guts instead.

"Shut up for once, will you? I've given you all I got. What more do you want?"

I want you, her stomach told her.

"You've got me," she retorted. "If you kill me, you'll die too. Ever consider that?"

Her stomach had not considered that.

"You ought to."

Her stomach should have realized that though tormenting the vessel that carried it was its business, the vessel's death meant its death too. But her stomach was too single-minded to be capable of that sophistication.

"Shut up! Just this once! Let me be!"

"Open up!"

Her maid of honour was at the bathroom door, calling her name, wanting to know who she was talking to in there.

Bluma opened up.

"I heard you yelling," Bella said.

"Sorry."

"When you get married, that's when you'll be sorry. You can still tell him no. We'll send the guests home and eat the food ourselves."

Bluma tried to smile. Bella closed the door behind her.

"So why are you doing it?"

"Marriage," Bluma told her unwilling maid of honour, "is the first step to divorce. I'll be out of the house, I'll have my mother off my back, I'll be free. But only if I get married first. It doesn't really matter who to."

There was more anxious knocking. "What are you girls doing in there?" Rachel called. "The ceremony is supposed to begin."

"Bluma can't get married," Bella shouted through the door. "It's her lady's time. She's unclean!"

The word unclean brought Rachel pushing her way into the bathroom with Taube behind her.

"What am I hearing?" Rachel demanded of her daughter. "You'll do anything to stop this."

"It's not true," Bluma said. "I'm all right."

"I made it all up," Bella admitted.

The two women pushed their daughters out of the bathroom and into the living room, where the witnesses had gathered.

A FEW DAYS LATER, EDDIE drove her father to the cold storage facility in Garfield Park, had him fitted for a uniform and got him the necessary tools to be a night watchman. Bluma was spared the sight. Abe couldn't lurch home on his own from the West Side every dawn after his shift, so Eddie found him a room on the premises that she called "your father's apartment." She was spared the sight of that place too. But her imagination didn't hold back when it came to the picture of her father staggering and bellowing as he moved through a giant hall of ice like a monster in a horror film, through a dense forest of mink and sable and silver fox.

Her father got a night watchman's job. She got citizenship. She wondered what was in it for her mother.

Bluma didn't have to wait long to find out. Rachel was moving to the West Side, to her sister Taube's flat. She'd gone straight to the point with Taube. She couldn't stay on in Burnside, alone in that house, with the Coop mocking her every time she looked out the window. Taube couldn't say no and Rachel knew it, not with the empty rooms going begging now that her sons had set themselves up elsewhere. Bluma heard the news from Eddie. The injustice sickened her. All this time she'd wanted to live with Bella, and her mother ended up taking her room.

TWELVE

The Teller and the Tale Have a Falling-Out

FINALLY, THE IT BLUMA HAD been telling the moon about arrived. It took the shape of a letter Joey wasn't allowed to see. It must have been explosive. The atmosphere in the house went from the usual unspoken discontent to open panic.

Joey didn't have to read it. His father's lamentations told him everything.

"I married a Communist!" he wailed. "And I didn't know it."

"Well, that spares you," Bluma answered. "You're innocent of all charges."

"Couldn't you have just been a fellow traveller? Joined the socialists or something?"

"I guess not. I had to go all the way."

"You should have known. You should have imagined this could happen."

"What?" Bluma was outraged. "I should have imagined Joe McCarthy and Roy Cohn and crazy people looking for Reds under the bed back when I was a girl?"

"Is there anything else you're not telling me?"

"I can't remember."

"That's a hell of a defence!" Eddie paced and fretted and bit his nails, then lit a cigarette. "Of all the damned stupid things to do! Couldn't you have joined something that wouldn't have got you into trouble, since you had to join one of those lefty things?"

That was one insult too many. Bluma hated it when Eddie repeated himself, and he did that a lot. "Jerry Yale sold me the membership," she told her husband. "I remember that. He was so sweet about it, I couldn't resist. He made the Communists sound so poetic."

"You mean you were seeing him after we got married?"

"I don't know. I can't remember dates anymore. It was too long ago."

"And now you got us into this mess!"

"They were the underdogs. So were we. Maybe not you — we were."

"Yeah, your father the bootlegger, the gangster — some underdog!"

Joey looked on in fascination as his parents fought. He liked to hang around and see what wonderful comebacks his mother would produce.

"Okay. What are we going to do now?" Eddie was a man of few surprises, and he didn't like being the butt of the unexpected, be it the Red Squad or the ghost of Jerry Yale.

"Nothing," Bluma said.

"Nothing?"

"They're gonna come here. I'll have to talk to them."

"They're going to make you name names. You're going to have to."

"Who do I know? I don't know anybody."

"Make up a name," her husband told her. "Otherwise they'll never leave. They'll sit here forever. We'll have to feed them dinner."

"I'll work on it," Bluma promised, and walked away.

Naming names. What did that mean? She was a housewife with a kid, a dull husband and a completely undistinguished life, a nobody in the purest sense of the word. A nobody who knew nobody. In her opinion she'd never done anything out of the ordinary, like plot to overthrow the Constitution of the United States of America. Until the letter showed up, she didn't know she was a Red. She'd forgotten she joined the Party. She didn't know how it happened — beyond Jerry Yale sweet-talking her into taking a membership.

Sometimes she forgot he didn't exist.

Now, all of a sudden, she was a somebody. The FBI was interested in her — what a distinction! Only the paranoid opportunism of McCarthy could have turned Bluma Krueger into an object of intense federal interest.

"WHEN THEY COME, WE'LL HAVE to keep the kid out of the way," Eddie said as the date grew nearer. "He shouldn't hear, he shouldn't know."

Yoo-hoo, I'm here! Joey felt like shouting and waving his hands in the air. Of all his father's hateful habits, the one Joey hated most was the way he talked about him as if he wasn't there, as if he was an idiot and couldn't understand everything that was laid out before him.

He watched his mother as she prepared for the visit and the naming of names. Compared to his father, who shrank in size with every fretful word and butted-out cigarette, she was cool-headed and in complete possession of herself. She was heroic; she didn't seem to realize she was about to face the most fearsomely efficient truth machine in the world, the very equivalent in horror of Stalin's Russia.

Joey wasn't ready for the evening she burst into tears over her soup. The event fascinated him: his mother crying. That hadn't happened before. When his father caught him watching, he averted his eyes and stared at his soup: pale green Campbell's Cream of Celery.

"I missed the bus stop on the way to work," his mother wailed. "How could I have missed the plant? It's only a mile long and I've only been going there for years. I had to walk back. The noise and the smoke of the trucks on Harlem Avenue gave me such a headache. Then I spilled a cup of coffee on the filing."

Joey looked up. His father was triumphant. He wasn't the only one who was afraid.

"What if I get the sack? Then who will work?" Bluma turned to her husband, her face twisted by sobs. "You'll have to get a steady job!"

Joey's eyes met his father's. The boy knew what was expected of him. He got up, left his soup uneaten and went into his room.

ONE AFTERNOON, EDDIE CAME BACK late from work, more fretful than usual. A bad smell hovered around him. It wasn't the classic one of the wayward husband, whisky and cheap perfume. Bluma crossed the kitchen where she was preparing supper and sniffed at him. A charred animal stink rolled off him like a wave.

"I know, I know." He shooed her away.

"What do you know?"

"We had a fire."

"A fire?" She stared at him uncomprehendingly.

"Yeah, a fire." Eddie acted insulted the way he always did when she asked too many questions. "You know, fire, with flames and smoke and stuff burning."

"How can you have a fire in cold storage? The place is below zero! There's nothing in there but coats."

"Coats burn."

She turned her back to him and put both hands on the counter in front of the sink where a heap of vegetables lay. The vertigo she felt was the exit door swinging open. If she had to face the G-men, she'd rather do it on her own. Eddie was like a weight she had to carry, and at a time like this, she didn't have any strength left over for him.

"It's possible, it can happen." He wrung his hands, but even with her back to him, she could feel how artificial his distress was. "There was a problem with the electricity."

"We had insurance at least?"

"I had some."

"Some? But not enough," Bluma concluded. "If your insurance was no good, at least they can't accuse you of arson."

"No one is accusing me of arson."

She wheeled around and faced him. "Then what are they accusing you of?"

Eddie reached for his pack of cigarettes. The cigarettes, the fire — Bluma had the crazy notion that he'd set the fire himself.

"It's your father. He didn't make it. The smoke got him."

It took Bluma a moment to understand what her husband was telling her, and not because the news was so terrible. Her father had been gone from her life for so long she could scarcely remember him.

"Is this your way of telling me he died — by saying you had a fire in the cold storage?"

"Sorry," Eddie said. "I didn't know how else to do it."

"Well, it's done. Congratulations. So what are they accusing you of — murder?"

"Negligence. They're saying he wasn't mentally responsible. They say he couldn't carry out his duties. He shouldn't have had the job, so that's my fault."

"How did they find that out if he's dead?"

Eddie drowned his cigarette in the sink. Bluma was past caring.

"Somebody ratted me out to the fire marshal. One of my employees. The guy never liked your father on account of him staggering around and bellowing all the time."

"Don't speak ill of the dead. At least have that decency."

"You're defending him?" Eddie lit a new cigarette and blew smoke at the ceiling, covering one stink with another. "He's better off now anyway."

Bluma turned on him. "You can't say that. You can't decide for people."

"I sure can say that. You didn't have to spend all day listening to him hollering and carrying on. The echo was hellish in that place.

But don't worry, I'm not avoiding my responsibilities. I'll pay for the burial."

Bluma turned away and went to the window. Joey was on the sidewalk in front of the house, scribbling away furiously on the cement with a piece of chalk. He was too old for sidewalk art. Then she saw he wasn't holding chalk, but a sharp-edged stone. He was an angry boy; that anger was hers against Eddie. Living in this house, with her husband's uselessness and her anger at him, was no good for him.

Then she realized what that meant.

"You're my husband. A husband is supposed to be the provider. All you provide me with is headaches. My father dies on the job you got him and you can't be bothered to say you're sorry."

"I didn't set the fire. For all I know, he did. I wouldn't put it past him. He could have done it out of spite. All those furs, up in smoke. I don't know what I'll do now."

"It's over, Eddie. I'm walking." She watched Joey punishing the sidewalk with his stone, and took strength from his young revolt. "I'm taking the boy. I'll find some place for him and me." She made herself turn and face her husband. "Everything we have we'll split fifty-fifty."

"It's more like what we don't have."

That was as close as he got to begging her to stay: asking her to be miserable in his company.

"I said all I've got to say," she told him.

Eddie watched her from the dining room table as she went about the business of dividing the family holdings. As she worked on their accounts, he fiddled with his latest invention that was still at the prototype stage: a tabletop dishwasher. Rubber hoses and metal switches littered the table, which had the family eating off the kitchen counter most of the time. Eddie had still not defeated the greatest challenge: piping the hot water into the machine and evacuating it at the end of the cycle without flooding the room.

He was anxious but passive, the worst of both worlds, though part of him hoped, since his wife was leaving him anyway, that she'd clear out before the G-men came visiting. She had picked up a few notions of administration in the offices of the International Harvester plant where she worked, and they stood her well. The car, the insufficient insurance, their meagre savings, the little money squeezed out of his New York family. Everything was done in cash. She had never seen a chequebook. Eddie looked on as she sleepwalked through the procedures, splitting up the assets. Eddie was right about one thing: there was precious little to divide.

At the end of the week, she handed him six hundred dollars in cash. She didn't bother with an envelope and didn't ask for a receipt. She slapped the money into his hand like the West Side gun girl she briefly was.

"Six hundred dollars, your share. Fifty-fifty. Now go find yourself. I'm giving you two years."

"Then what?" Eddie asked.

"Then nothing, if you can't figure it out."

"How will I find you?"

"I'm going to Bella's. Remember her?"

Joey stood by the front door with their bags. Bluma had decided: when it's time to leave, we go out the front door. Joey watched the transaction eagerly. He was in rapt admiration of his mother. She was a hero out of Marvel Comics who could turn his life upside down with a single wave of her hand. Suddenly they were leaving the house where he'd lived his entire life. His father was disappearing in the distance behind their taxicab, and they were being driven to another house — all because it was his mother's will. And that stack of money she'd thrust on his father — she had the same amount in her purse. The last thing he'd do was snivel and cry for his papa and blame his mother for losing him. Bluma didn't have to explain it to him, even if she did a few days later. Joey understood it was no loss at all.

Bluma had another reason for leaving Eddie, as secret as it was irrational. The FBI knew she lived here. When they showed up to question her, and maybe even deport her to Soviet Russia, that's where they'd come knocking. When they did, they'd find Eddie, wringing his hands and smoking two cigarettes at once. Maybe he'd tell the cops that he didn't know where she was. They could sit in her old apartment forever. Eddie could serve them coffee, then dinner, they could sleep on the couch, but he wouldn't be able to help them.

Of course, the FBI could find her if they wanted. Knowing Eddie, he'd probably squeal on her out of spite. But it would take them a little extra time to track her down. In the meantime, she would prepare. She would live.

ON THE DAY THE G-men visited, Joey was herded into the room where he slept. He was disappointed, but not surprised; from the very day the letter arrived, he wasn't supposed to know what was going on. That didn't change here, in this new apartment that belonged to a woman he was instructed to call Cousin Bella. He had never met the woman before, and didn't know what a cousin was. Eddie had not been much for family, and he kept away from his mother's relations. His cousin Bella was an oddity: she had no husband and went off to teach school every day. Though he had plenty of lady teachers at his school, he never thought one could come from his own family.

What was different in this new apartment was how his mother handled the visit. With his father, she rattled on endlessly about the FBI and the Reds, about people naming names, about finks and rats and honourable people. She didn't say anything about that now. The visit had become a secret subject. Joey had never seen a G-man outside of television, and now one, probably two since that's how they worked, were going to come to the place he was staying and sit in the living room, on the other side of a closed door, with their notepads and bad suits and IDs in plastic cases, threatening demeanours and muscles. He wouldn't have the chance to see them. His mother ordered him to stay in the room until she came to get him. In case he had a mind to disobey, she locked him in. She didn't trust him, and that hurt his feelings. Didn't she understand they were allies?

Once the key turned in the lock, Joey went to the door and put his ear to it.

There were two G-men; he heard their voices. So they did travel in pairs, just like on TV. There must have been a Good Cop and a Bad Cop. One of them asked Bluma to name names and she did. She had done her homework. Her husband used to tell her she was naive and scatter-brained, out of touch with reality and unprepared for the world. Nothing was further from the truth. She'd researched, she talked things over with Bella, she did a little recollecting in private, free from his anxious fretting, and when the fateful question was asked, she volunteered the names of people who had already received visits. She gave them names they already had — or so she hoped. That way she wouldn't hurt anybody who hadn't already been hurt. The last thing she wanted to be was a stool pigeon, a canary, a fink, a rat. She wanted to be on the side of honourable people.

Since Jerry Yale had never existed, or only for a few fleeting moments, he couldn't have invited her into the Party. A Jewish man was behind the invitation, that's all she recalled. She couldn't do any better for the Good Cop who was trying to get her to remember that apparently strategic piece of information.

"Honestly, it was more than twenty years ago. So much grief has passed since then. I have trouble enough remembering what happened last week with these sleeping pills they have me taking."

"Make an effort," the Bad Cop sneered.

"I was another person back then. Honestly, I told you all I know."

At the word "honestly," the Bad Cop shot an incredulous look at the Good Cop, as if they'd never heard that one before.

The cops pushed her to ratchet up the fear factor, but that was just for show. They looked at Bluma Krueger and saw her for what she was. A middle-aged woman with a spreading butt, a Yid broad, aging badly, a clerk in a factory who seemed to have lost her husband recently. A visit from them had that effect on a lot of couples — that was the point. They decided that Bluma Krueger did not represent a clear and present danger to the Constitution of the United States, a document they had sworn to uphold, but had never read. They got to their feet. Bluma stayed on the couch. Her legs wouldn't let her get up.

"We'll be back," the Bad Cop told her. "You never know when."

But the G-men never bothered to return. The preparation for their visit was worse than the visit itself. It was like going to the dentist's. You worried, you got anxious, but the pain was never as bad as you thought it would be. The federal agents folded up their notebooks, put their badges back in their pockets and moved on to the next ex-Commie.

A few days later, Bella announced to Bluma and her son, "All right, it's over. Now we can go back to living again."

But Bluma's anxieties did not depart. It was impossible now to go back to living like before. She had a secret that she wasn't about to tell anyone, except the moon: she wasn't a real American. She had stolen the date of birth of someone who was a real citizen and was dead, but sooner or later the FBI would find that out. She'd lived with Libby's dates so long she'd forgotten about the play she made, that little cheat, until the G-men showed up. Now her very existence was in danger. Her life in America depended on a lie easily discovered. They could send her back to Stalin's Russia — they could if they wanted to. They could do whatever they wanted and no one could do anything about it, assuming that anyone cared. She was helpless. Getting deported to the USSR would be just the dose of medicine a Commie like her deserved. How stupid can you get? she asked herself. She tried to picture the life that awaited her in Stalin's Russia. She had very little to go on outside of a few black-and-white photos from *Life* magazine. She put herself into one of those grim propaganda stills. She would wear a headscarf like those old women, she would sweep the streets with a twig broom, her fingers and the tip of her nose would fall off from frostbite, the cold-country version of leprosy. Bluma's fear of being deported grew more intense every day. She went to work and did her filing, she managed not to spill any more coffee on the paperwork, but fear took over her life. She had lost her routine. Nothing was routine for her now.

In the evenings after the meal that Bella prepared for her and Joey, she would stand by the window, behind the heavy drapes with their floral motif. To put off gazing into the street and the dangers waiting for her there, she studied the pattern of the drapes. They were cream colour, and when she asked Bella how they got into her house, Bella looked at her strangely. "Don't you remember? I had them on Lexington Street. You saw them a hundred times when we were young." Bluma couldn't recall them, but she couldn't trust her memory. Had they always been with her, like the other afflictions from girlhood? The drapes had a pattern with wide, dark-crimson leaves with stiff veins as solid as bones scattered across the cream fabric in no particular order. No leaf had veins like that. They reminded her of the one or two times she'd glimpsed her husband's cock at the beginning of their marriage: upright, pumping, absurdly eager. The leaves were wide and concave. When she told Eddie to take a hike, she lost the only person she had ever dominated. With Bella, she was back to being a mouse. One evening Bella came up behind her as she was keeping her vigil.

"Go to bed," she told her.

Bluma wheeled around in terror. She hadn't heard her cousin come into the room.

"Still nervous as ever?" Bella inquired.

Bluma said nothing. She turned to the parted drapes and the street beyond. This will not work, she thought. I can't live in a place where people see me. Where they watch the things I do.

She pulled herself away from the dark street.

"I appreciate you taking us in," she told Bella stiffly. "For old times' sake."

"Not just for old times' sake," her cousin told her. "I'm happy to help out. But you need to put what happened behind you. You have to relax and start taking care of yourself, and taking care of your son."

"I can't put that behind me. It is me."

Bluma turned her back on her cousin and parted the drapes again.

"You could try living in the present," Bella told her. Bluma was sure her cousin had gone, but she stayed in the room to torment her, and keep her from keeping watch. "You could try living during the day, not just at night."

Bella retreated to her bedroom. Neither of them wished each other sweet dreams.

Go to bed. The words stung. Come to bed — that might have made some difference. An invitation. She thought of Jerry Yale. It was getting late for him to show up and love the body she had now.

Bluma could watch the street for hours and see no one, but the quiet landscape brought no relief. She refused to take comfort. There were plenty of bushes, trees, parked cars and darkened windows out there. Each was a shelter, a blind, a place for trouble to hide. Anyone who cared to could find out how she stole Libby's dates. She wasn't so sure she could count on nobody caring.

Laurie said it all back then, but she hadn't listened. Maybe it doesn't matter if you're not a citizen. It seemed so important to be included.

Included in what? The right to vote? She didn't vote anyway. Included in her father's love and esteem? What a joke!

At the window, with the moon her witness and confidant, the moon that strangely enough always shone in the sky like a blank slate to write her troubles on, she considered the pattern of her life. The men in her life came in pairs. Opposites. Laurie and Abe. Jerry Yale and her husband. There was a good man and a bad, like with the cops. She always ended up with the wrong one.

She had Jerry Yale, but he loved her only once. It was her first and best time.

Every day the FBI didn't come knocking at her door with the deportation order was one more day of waiting. Bluma considered confessing and getting it over with. She pictured the Burnside precinct, the bored, irritated policeman kicking her out and sending her packing.

"No one would believe me anyway," she complained to the moon. "I'm just a girl."

The next day at work, she put out word among the women in the office that she needed lodgings, and fast. The situation was desperate. Her husband had tracked her down at her new place and was threatening to make trouble. The man had gone off his rocker.

The network of divorcées and separated women got busy. No one doubted her word. By the end of the day, she had a new place to hide. It was out of town, perfect in a case like hers. The place belonged to the Barone family; they were cousins of a woman who worked in bookkeeping a few offices over. The woman wasn't separated or divorced, she'd had an annulment. Bluma didn't know what that meant, and it didn't matter to her. It didn't matter either that she hadn't met Mary Barone. She'd show up with her suitcases and Joey's bag, and they'd all get to know each other. That's the way the network moved.

CAROLINE WIGGLED OUT OF JOEY's embrace and looked him in the eye.

"'I married a Communist,'" Caroline said. "Just like the Philip Roth book. Wow, you guys are authentic!"

"I never knew why she spent all that time by the window. I thought it had something to do with the drapes."

Caroline raised herself on one elbow. As a woman of her time, she

believed that everyone carries a dreadful repressed memory clamouring
to escape.

"Maybe there's something else involved," she told him, "that you're
not remembering. Or almost remembering."

"You mean repressed memory syndrome? I heard that it was all
made up."

"You heard that where? In a men's magazine?"

"No. On NPR. On your radio station."

"I'd never take you for a denier. Not with your interest in the past,"
Caroline told him.

"The strangest thing is that the house is all wrong," Joey said. "My
memory has me in a room that didn't exist. The apartment wasn't
like that, and the door didn't lock from the outside. It feels more like
a dream than a memory. There's something off-kilter about the whole
thing. Maybe I imagined it."

"Maybe someone told you about what happened. A lot of our
memories come from other people."

"I don't remember my mother telling me any of that before."

Joey lay back with his head on the pillow, discouraged. Even his
intimate memories weren't really his and couldn't be trusted. The
Irishman's comment on the radio, that gloomy, dour, prize-winning
author, summed up the melancholy of his project. Memory is no more
than the stuff you make up, a complacent fiction, whether good or
bad. In which case his time capsule project was next to useless.

"Maybe I was too young to remember," he ventured. "Maybe there's
an age when you can have memories, your own memories, and before
that they come from somewhere else. So if the FBI memory isn't mine,
not authentically mine, then whose is it?"

"Maybe you could ask your mother," Caroline said, trying to help.

"Maybe I could ask the moon."

Caroline leaned over him. "It's all right, baby. You're in the present
now, with me."

"Right."

Later in the night, still disquieted, he rose from Caroline's bed and went to the living room window. There was a cool, brilliant half-moon high above, emitting the kind of light that gives that lump of stone its reputation for sterility. Joey considered the moon a moment, then wrinkled up his nose at it.

"No," he said in his very approximate Robert De Niro imitation, "I'm not talking to you."

He opened the door quietly and stepped outside. The autumn air was cool. He stood on the front walk of her house and looked at his body in the moonlight. Naked in the Branfords. I look like a statue. No — I look like I'm dead. My body is as pale as a corpse. He stepped onto the grass. The dew was cold and fallen leaves moved in the wind around his feet.

He stood on the lawn, needing to piss — the middle-age alarm clock. He crossed onto his side of the grass. It was more decorous to urinate on your own lawn than on your neighbour's, especially if you're sleeping with that neighbour. But I am not sleeping, he defended himself as he pissed away in the moonlight. I am standing here naked in the autumn moonlight.

When he realized, as he stood emptying his bladder, what the missing piece in Bluma's story was, he couldn't believe it had taken him this long. It was Bella, the constant companion, and the constant absence. He would find her. Everyone is findable. She'd been a Spanish teacher in Chicago under her maiden name. He'd start there.

Considering how she and Bluma had parted, he figured he'd have to find her without his mother's help. That was all right. It would be his little surprise for her, for all she'd done for him.

When he went back gratefully to Caroline's bed, he felt that old entrepreneurial rush again. He had a hunch to play.

ON A DREARY AFTERNOON A few days later, with the rain falling on the leaves in the wooded ravine outside Bluma's building, Joey reached for his pile of Office Depot notebooks on the floor. The subterfuge allowed him to slip his hand into his sports jacket and switch on the miniature tape recorder. Another session was about to begin.

"How's it going with the firefly lady now that the fireflies are gone?" his mother asked.

"We're still seeing each other."

Bluma wasn't going to let him get away with a simple answer.

"She's not calling you a mama's boy like your wife did?"

Joey grimaced. Some things he should have kept to himself. Maybe his mother felt the same way.

"No," he told her. "She likes that I'm doing this."

"That's got to be a first! Boy gets girl with a story about his mother." Bluma clasped her hands over her heart. "I'm the subject of pillow talk! I never thought I'd see the day. Well, they do say love is strange."

Joey didn't like where the conversation was going. "Why wouldn't a woman want to hear a story like yours?"

"Look at me. I'm hardly an inspiration for a girl."

Joey smiled. For a girl. He'd tell Caroline that tonight.

"A lot of women would like to have a life like yours," he told his mother. "Hell, sometimes I wish I had the life you did."

"Are you nuts?" she burst out in a loud, outraged voice. "My guts have been eating me alive since I was ten. Every day when I was a kid, I prayed for my father to die. Maybe if I could have said it out loud, that might have helped. My spine is fused, I can hardly sit down, and when I'm sitting down I can hardly get up. I can't sleep without pills. I can't sleep with them. I throw up every morning before breakfast. And I'm walking around with just one breast. Is that strength and nobility and inspiration and whatever else you've been saying? You want that? You want to live like that?"

No, Joey told her. He didn't want to live like that. He mumbled an apology that wasn't convincing because he didn't know what he was apologizing for.

His mother got to her feet, suddenly spry, considering the history of ailments she'd rattled off.

"All those things and things worse than that, things I'm not telling you — I'm supposed to reveal everything for the sake of a tall tale?"

"Things you're not telling me? Wait, you're not supposed to hold out on me. That's our agreement."

"Hold out on you?" she echoed. "I'm your mother, and I have to keep up some semblance of decorum, no matter what you think. I'm not just a story. I'm a real person."

Joey closed his notebook as Bluma made a brave attempt at stalking out of the living room in the direction of the toilet. Halfway there she faltered and leaned against the wall, exhausted by her own anger. With her back turned, he clicked off the tape recorder and pushed it deeper into his pocket. The day's session was over. It was short, but rich in many things.

He had to suppress a nagging feeling of relief.

His mother returned a few minutes later. A fecal smell hung in the air. He recognized one of the health issues she'd neglected to mention.

"Death," she told him.

"Death?"

"That's why you're so interested in my story. Or what you're making of it. You're afraid of death."

"We're afraid? It seems like that's all we talk about."

"No," she told him. "Not mine. Yours."

She sank into the easy chair across the room. "And now, I'm tired. Beat. It's time to retreat to our neutral corners."

"This is a boxing match? We're in the ring?"

"Yes, we are. Work on without me," she advised. "I'm sure you can. The story is tired. You've squeezed every last drop out of me."

He stood up. He didn't know what to say. Next time, he told himself, if there is a next time, shut up and stick to recording.

Joey stood in the parking lot of his mother's building with his hand on the car door, letting the soft rain fall on his shoulders. In the marshy woods below, nature had gone quiet. Lines of overweight trucks rumbled over the aging road out front. If his mother chose to withdraw to her neutral corner, he had no choice but to do the same. But he had no idea where his corner was. His brief sense of relief gave way to loss. With the session aborted, he didn't know what to do next.

He began by getting in his car, starting the engine and turning on the radio. Maybe it would supply a hint about what he'd apparently done wrong. But NPR was carrying soothing classical music that conveyed nothing, and he was not in the mood to be soothed. He pulled out of the parking lot with the building's security cameras on him. He knew they were watching him, since he helped pay for their maintenance.

He was on Bluma's bad side, and he didn't know how he'd gotten there. Things had been going too well; that was the problem. Until now, he had traversed the minefield of memory unscathed.

He was in love with his mother's story and he'd told her as much. That was his misstep — that, and turning her, a real person, into a character. He should have kept his declarations to himself; he should have kept Caroline a secret. Satisfaction. That word sounded obscene in his mother's mouth.

He drove through the Branfords on automatic pilot, feeling guilty for hurting his mother's feelings. But he was unhappy with her. She had broken their bond. Suddenly they weren't accomplices. She made his work look sordid and unseemly after everything he had done to create that bond. What was wrong with the project all of a sudden?

He pulled into the parking lot at the Italian place. The middle of the afternoon is no time for a productive member of society to be moping around a bar, but that's where he ended up.

"Welcome," Sheila called as he pushed open the door. The place was empty and she was wiping down glasses in preparation for the after-work crowd. "Got a meeting?"

"With myself."

"Where's your partner?"

"Minding the store."

"The very picture of glumness," Sheila said. "You had a falling-out with the woman in the flame-coloured dress?"

"Worse. My mother."

"That's tougher. So you came to Our Lady of Good Counsel."

"The usual," Joey told her.

Sheila brought him the antipasto plate and a glass of Chianti.

"What happened, golden boy? I thought you could do no wrong."

"I told her how much I admired her. She said we ought to stop talking. 'Neutral corners,' she said."

"Maybe you're missing something," Sheila suggested. She put a ball-point pen in her mouth instead of a cigarette. She had grown used to the smoking ban, but it ruined so many perfect moments. "Did you tell her about your new love interest, by any chance?"

"I mentioned something a while back. She said she was happy for me."

"I bet." Sheila took the pen out of her mouth and held it like a cigarette. "She's jealous," she said.

"How could she be? I'm the one who's jealous."

"You, jealous? Jealous of an old lady who's your mother?"

"Jealous of how good her story is."

"I think you need to work on your emotional intelligence, like most men. Don't you get it? You broke the solemn oath. Not only solemn, but unspoken."

"What's that?"

"That you'd stay unlucky in love together."

Joey took a large sip of Chianti and contemplated the beads of fat glistening on the surface of the industrial cold cuts on his plate. Between Bluma and him, which of them was jealous, and of what? Both of us, he decided, but of different things.

He looked up. Sheila was gazing at him incredulously. He realized she was expecting some kind of answer.

"She told me I was afraid of death."

"Welcome to the club."

"Not her death. Mine."

"I'm not sure I follow," Sheila admitted.

"It sort of makes sense," Joey said tentatively, "though I can't say why."

"Well, look at it this way. You tell a story and you live forever, isn't that what they say?"

"But I'm telling her story, not mine."

Sheila shrugged. "What do I know? I'm just a barmaid. But maybe you peeked somewhere you weren't supposed to."

Joey took another sip of wine, more velvety in the afternoon since it came from a fresh bottle, and thought of everything he would want to keep hidden if someone was looking into his life. There was no end of things, failure of every kind, starting with the bad hair dye. Luckily, no one wanted to tell his story.

He toyed with his eggplant and wondered what his mother wasn't telling him. The answer to that would make a story in its own right.

JOEY DIDN'T KNOW WHAT TO do with himself. His sessions with Bluma were like cardio workouts for other men: they gave him energy for the rest of his day. Without them he had less enthusiasm. If his breakup had been more conventional, with a girlfriend, he could have gone out with Ozzie and commiserated. But a misunderstanding with his mother? There was something deviant about his problem.

A week without a session had him feeling fidgety. Apparently, he had developed a dependency. Who would have thought that recording your mother's story could have that effect? He knew one sure way to get back in her good books, and it didn't involve a dozen long-stemmed roses, a box of chocolates and dinner and a show. The surefire remedy was an outing to the Indian casino along the interstate, and he decided to play that card.

The casino was no more Indian than Joey was. It owed its existence to a businessman who had a stroke of genius. He dug around in the mouldy old treaties and discovered that parcels of land still belonged to people who had disappeared long ago. The man bought up the rights that belonged to those lands, since their rightful inhabitants couldn't enjoy them anymore. Among the rights was the privilege of living outside the petty rules that governed the rest of the state: taxes, gaming, that sort of thing. Next to the Indian casino was an Indian gas station featuring cut-rate prices, and an Indian trading post that sold untaxed cigarettes. A smart guy with the Lebanese name of Khoury was behind the whole thing.

Bluma loved to gamble. She used to ride out to the casino on her building's senior bus, thanks to the social director who organized excursions to coincide with the arrival of the monthly pension checks. But Bluma dropped out of the group. Either they stayed too long and she got exhausted, or they didn't stay long enough when she was on a winning streak.

Joey phoned her from Ecological Solutions.

"I'll take you to the casino," he offered.

Her voice brightened. "That would be great. I haven't been there in a dog's age. The only thing I'm gambling on are those two-dollar lottery tickets from the tuck shop. And I've even cut that out. That Mrs. Dong who's running the shop — I can't understand a word she says. The last time I went in there, my mind played a trick on me, and I thought I was in Bella's family's store, and I started talking Yiddish to the poor Korean lady. I must be losing my marbles. Well, it's high time!"

Joey smiled to himself. She was. talking again. He could hear the pages of her good books turning.

"You still like to gamble, right?"

"But not with just anybody. If you think I'm going to forgive you that easy, you've got another thing coming."

"Who said anything about forgiveness? I'm like you. I've got time on my hands. And I'm treating."

"Let me check my busy schedule."

He hung up the phone. Her little vice was so likeable and easy to cater to. He made a note to stop at the ATM on his way to her place.

At his desk, Ozzie busied himself with paperwork, trying not to listen to the phone conversation.

"I'm going to the Indian casino with Mama," Joey told him.

"Say hi to Tonto. I hear the place is good entertainment for the old folks."

"She's a real gambler. I don't know where she got that vice."

"Probably from you. You could ask her about it. Put it in your story."

"Not today. I'm not after confrontation. We could use some quality time together."

Ozzie looked up from his papers. "Isn't that all you have?"

"We had so much that now we need reconciliation."

"Well, they do say familiarity breeds contempt. I hope you get lucky."

A FRIENDLY SECURITY MAN IN a golf cart was waiting to shuttle them from their spot in the underground garage to the casino door. Joey's Volvo fit right in among the luxury utility vehicles. "You're in good hands here," a large sign informed them, describing the security procedures in place. Joey doubted he'd have to worry about anyone holding them up for their winnings on the way back.

"You folks have good luck now," the golf-cart driver said.

"Lady Luck doesn't know I exist," Bluma assured him.

Joey liked taking chances on the next ecological catastrophe, but his taste for gambling ended there. He loathed the casino. When a person stepped inside, all other life disappeared. The end of the world could come and they'd never know it. There wasn't a single window, just rows and rows of slot machines as far as the eye could see.

That was the game Bluma favoured. It was simple and easy to follow, with no need to remember anything. Buttons to push, a handle to manipulate if she wanted to get more complex. A gerontologist must have invented the one-armed bandit.

Joey stopped at the bill-changing station. Bluma looked away showily as the machine spat out smaller denominations than the ones the ATM had delivered. He stacked the bills into a neat pile. The casino was one of the few places in America where you could walk around with hundreds of dollars in your hand and not worry about someone trying to snatch it.

"What'll it be?" he asked. He looked at the banks of machines. "Hearts of Rome or Riches of Venice?"

"I like the ones upstairs."

Bluma was right in the heart of the casino demographic. The place offered entertainment for retirees, nothing too strenuous like hiking up a hill or straining to hear the actors at a matinee. They boarded an escalator and let it do the work. At the top, under a plastic tree, a man was sitting in an armchair, reading a novel as thick as a brick, indulging the missus, no doubt. The rattling soundtrack didn't seem to penetrate the shelter of his book. Bluma started down an aisle, casting suspicious looks at the machines, searching for the one that had given her good luck in the past.

She stopped.

"Payday," she said, and settled in on a high-backed chair. The machine was the simplest model, with three images to align instead of five.

Joey pulled a second chair next to hers and laid the packet of bills by her hand.

"Not all at once, silly. It's all about suspense. Don't you know that?"

"No," he admitted.

She shushed him, afraid he would bring her bad luck. He picked up half the stack of bills and stashed it in his pocket where he kept the tape recorder.

His mother started feeding the machine, building up credits and spending them, keeping up a running commentary about the unfairness of it all — the machines, the oddsmakers, the people conspiring behind these gaudy contraptions. She was here to complain about being here. When she wasn't complaining, she sat in a trance — or was it meditation? Occasionally she won more credits, which didn't strike Joey as much of a victory, but he kept his mouth shut. Bluma was happy. He fell into an empathetic trance: the sameness of the spinning dials, the noises of pleasure and disappointment around them, the convivial offer of the man who pushed the coffee cart down the aisle. After a while, his mother began slowing down. Some fierce, initial need had been satisfied, and now she was just playing out the string. Discreetly, he produced the second half of his money. At one point, a middle-aged Asian man alighted at the machine next to theirs, as graceful as a dragonfly at the end of a reed, and threw his money into the machine. He activated the handle on the side, apparently going for higher stakes, but he was not rewarded. He exhaled and dismissed the machine with a wave of his hand so Joey and Bluma would know that he'd never had any real hope.

Bluma won more credits, but no payout. A group behind them was more fortunate. A man with a white surgical glove on his playing hand and his two lady companions squealed with pleasure. Their machine had just delivered.

"All you get now is a payout slip," Bluma said, disabused. "I used to love the old ways, when the coins would gush out the chute and roll across the floor. A regular horn of plenty!"

She turned and glared at the group that looked happy enough with their paper.

"Nowadays, when you go to cash out, they look at you like you found the paper on the floor."

"Are you thirsty? Hungry, maybe?"

"Hungry? Spare me! Why, are we all out of cash?"

"We're still solvent."

"Okay, let's play."

Joey dipped into the reserves he hadn't intended to spend, but a treat was a treat. He was paying for her pleasure, and her pleasure was his. No sense stopping before she was sated, even if he was deeply bored by the casino effects, soporific and kitschy, designed to enchant children and old people, all those flashing lights and electronic beeps. He had come here often enough with her to be used to the strange ways of the place, like the members of the party behind them who had struck it rich. They wore magnetic cards on strings around their necks, and they plugged the cards into a narrow slot on the face of the machine, making themselves extensions of it. Privilege, the card read.

Bluma tired. She tried to sit back, but her chair was not forgiving.

"It wins, I lose. I quit."

He helped her to her feet off the treacherous swivel chair.

"You didn't lose. You had fun."

They exited the section along the stain-concealing, pumpkin-coloured carpet. The reading man was still immersed in his novel by the top of the escalator. They passed the bar, remarkably small for a casino.

Bluma veered off toward a table in the lounge that was empty except for the barmaids. The garish, jangling decor raged unabated there too, with the music and racket from a bank of TVs loud enough to cover the most aggressive marital dispute. But who went to a casino to talk?

"I want a drink," Bluma announced.

"You know it won't agree with you," Joey warned.

"Don't think I don't know. I want one of those sweet drinks with a silly name. A Sidecar, a Pink Lady, a Grasshopper, a ... whatever."

"Sex on the Beach," her son suggested.

Bluma looked at him sideways. "I suppose we didn't win. We didn't come out ahead."

"We didn't come here to win."

"I know. But I like the idea of winning. Just for once."

"Let's just say we cut our losses. We were entertained. We reached our limit and stopped. At least that's one problem we don't have."

"Speak for yourself. I'd come here every day if I could."

The waitress appeared. Joey ordered a glass of Chianti and stuck with his order even after she wrinkled her nose at his selection. Bluma reeled off her list of antique drinks. The waitress hadn't heard of any of them. But she was smart enough to see that the name was what mattered, so she suggested a Rusty Nail. That tickled Bluma's fancy.

"With my luck, I'll step on it," she told the waitress.

"Now, now, I'm sure you had fun."

"Right," Bluma told the waitress. "So much fun I want to forget."

"At least you knew what to expect," Joey said.

"Now what did I tell you about suspense?" she scolded him.

They watched a herd of seniors moving down the aisle past the lounge, making slow progress, their chaperone urging them on, threatening them with missing the bus.

"That was me, before, when I used to go with the group. They shouldn't tell them they'll miss their bus. They'd like nothing better."

Joey and Bluma were the only customers in the lounge. The drinks arrived in no time, preceded by cardboard coasters and swizzle sticks. The Indian casino was the last facility to offer the old-time drinking paraphernalia.

The first sip of Rusty Nail loosened his mother's tongue.

"So, you want to kiss and make up?"

"I'm just happy to be here," Joey said.

"Disingenuous kid that you are. You know this place is my little vice."

"If I can do something to make you happy, why not?"

"Right!" Bluma sipped her drink through the plastic straw, unimpressed by her son's good will. "But there are limits," she told him.

"Limits to what?"

"Don't play dumb! Everybody wants people to be interested in them. But there's a limit to that interest."

"And what is it? That seems to be the problem."

Bluma gave him a long look. Joey could see it in her eyes: she was about to say something that would put kissing and making up beyond reach. But she surprised him.

"What you need is to put yourself in the story. And leave me out."

"But your story is so much better than mine."

It was his standard line, but his mother didn't want to hear it anymore. She sat back in her chair and toyed with her drink.

"Are you still beating a path across the lawn to the girl next door?"

"I opened my heart," Joey said grandly, "and love came in."

"Is that so? As long as you don't get sued for divorce."

"Elke has someone too."

"Now, isn't that convenient?" Bluma took a healthy sip and grimaced. "This isn't agreeing with me. Life, liberty and the pursuit of gisms — women work so hard at it these days!"

Gisms? Joey wondered, then caught on to his mother's pronunciation.

"Didn't pleasure exist in your day?"

"It hadn't been invented — not for us. We were too afraid of getting pregnant. It was the worst thing that could happen to a girl. Getting in trouble! Oh, some girls rubbed their betrothed's ... you know, to relax them, as men put it so elegantly."

Joey recognized his mother's strategy. He wanted to know about her life? She'd punish him with too much information. But he refused to be embarrassed.

"Maybe I could sue my mother," Bluma mused.

"For what?"

"Being a bad parent. For abandonment, breach of contract, for not teaching me about the birds and the bees, for not giving me proper self-esteem. Don't you read the papers? You should. Start reading something besides the business section. Children are suing their parents these days and winning."

"You can't sue a dead person," Joey said earnestly.

"And you can't take a joke."

"Sorry."

"But you're right, I was too slow. Such a wonderful invention: suing your parents for not being good parents!"

"I'm sure they'd come up with some defence."

"And I know what it would be. 'We brought you into this world. That's where the contract ends.'"

Joey and Bluma heard squeals of joy from a bank of machines not far from their table. Three ladies somewhat younger than Bluma had hit a modest jackpot.

"Some kids did sue, in their own way. Laurie, for instance. He disappeared and never came back. Never sent word. Too afraid of being traced, maybe. Or too guilty. That's how he handled it. I should have done like him instead of hating him for leaving. Funny — I never found out what happened to him." Bluma laughed unhappily. "I used to tell my mother I was going to be a streetwalker. *Streetwalker*. No one says that anymore. That word used to terrify my mother. She'd look like a snake had slithered out of her grocery bag."

She slapped her knee with her palm. "Maybe I should have been a streetwalker. I wonder what they do to not get pregnant. All those men, one after the other, the way that must smell after a while … And that horrible makeup, that smeary lipstick, all that hysterical drama you have to put on to attract the customers!"

"That's a lot of self-punishment just to get back at your mother. It seems a little extreme."

"I would have been punishing myself, sure, but what else is new? It might have worked."

"I think you need to forgive," Joey advised.

"What Cracker Jack box did you find that one in? Forgive! Not forgive — sue! Oh, of course, you're right. My mother didn't exactly have the best personal life. Though I suppose she was no different from any other woman back then."

Bluma finished her drink, then went trawling through the shredded ice for the last drops of alcohol.

"No, that's not true," she decided. "My mother was Superwoman."

"That's a change of pace!"

"Yes, Superwoman. Like in the comics. Because it must have taken a superhuman effort all those years not to see what was right in front of her, like the nose on her face. Not to see the Irish cops passed out in the yard, not to hear the shouting and fighting that scared me so much, not to notice her son had disappeared. My mother was Superwoman. No, actually, she was Barnacle Woman — that's a new kind of superhero. She hung around at her sister's flat, unwanted, but they didn't have the heart to get rid of her, until finally she died."

"What did she die of?" Joey asked. "I never knew."

"How could you? Gangrene. Yes — gangrene. Her own body poisoned her."

Bluma glanced around for the waitress, then spotted Joey's glass on the table, barely touched.

"What's your excuse — you're a teetotaller now?"

He took a sip of acidic Chianti to show her he was in on the good times. "Sorry, I was too busy listening to drink."

"I was afraid of that. Well, it's my fault too. I signed up for this. Did I know what I was getting into?"

"Neither of us did, really."

Mother and son sat a moment in the blaring lounge. The three lucky senior ladies had cashed in, and they came in to celebrate their good fortune.

"Dumb luck," Bluma concluded.

At the table behind them, the ladies were demanding drinks with paper umbrellas in them.

"You know," Joey began, "I keep having this memory."

"You mean I'm not the only one with the disease?"

"Of course not."

"Well, dish the dirt. Don't hold out on me."

Joey took a swallow of his Chianti. The waitress was right: it tasted like vinegar. Who drank wine in a casino?

"I keep seeing myself in a lettuce patch. I'm unhappy, I'm crying. There's no one around, though someone is supposed to be there, someone who went away. I start pulling leaves off the plants. Maybe I'm hungry, or maybe I'm mad at the lettuce. There are heads and heads of the stuff, all in rows. Then I bite into something and it crunches beneath my teeth. I pull it out and look. It's a snail. A snail in a broken shell and it's still moving."

"That's a memory? It sounds like a bad dream."

"How come I have it?"

"I don't know. You shouldn't. You were too young."

"Tell me what's going on."

"We were living in the basement at Mary Barone's. Somebody at work fixed me up with her. It was after we left Bella's. Mary's kids were supposed to look after you in the garden. It wasn't a garden, it was more like a field. They grew vegetables for the market, you know, what's that called? A truck farm."

"What was I doing in the lettuce patch if I was too young?"

"Too young to remember. Well, maybe too young to be there too. But there wasn't much choice."

Bluma crossed her arms over her chest, the old protective measure from the cancer. The biopsy, the rush to ablation, the analysis of the tissues that showed there'd been no cancer after all. It was the Miss Reilly story all over again, though with a greater loss of self and a bigger scar.

"Who was Mary Barone?"

"A saint. An angel from heaven. And the closest thing I ever had to a mother, even if she wasn't much older than me. She took us in after Bella started minding my business, and after I told your father to go find himself. A single mother back in those days, I don't need to tell you …"

"You were brave."

"A single mother was like a whore back then. Worse than a whore: a whore with kids. I didn't have a stick of furniture. I left everything with your father. Mary took us in, she let us live in the basement, she took care of you when I went to work."

"I didn't know any of this."

"You were too young. That's what everybody thought back then: the kid's too young to remember, it won't hurt him. But it wasn't all torture. You had your fun. You used to run wild on the farm like a Red Indian." Bluma clapped her hand over her mouth and looked around.

"The lettuce," Joey said. "What was I doing there?"

"You were the youngest of the bunch. Mary's kids probably left you there. Or you wandered away. But you didn't get lost, and nothing bad happened, because here you are today, in tip-top shape."

"It isn't a very happy memory. I keep seeing myself crying, I'm watching myself from above, and then I bite into the snail, and it's like I wake up."

"I told you it was just a dream!"

"No. I wake up from the past, and here I am."

"I don't know what to tell you. Go into analysis," his mother offered.

Bluma watched Joey take a sip of sour wine.

"Afraid of death," she told him. "Just like I said. That's the kind of scene anyone would want to stay away from. You tell my old age to keep away from yours."

"And I end up there anyway."

"In the lettuce patch as a kid. Not exactly old age."

"No. But not very pleasant."

"Serves you right! Anyway, what do you expect? How did you think you were going to stay out of the picture?"

"I didn't really think about it."

"You were going to tell my life story and keep yourself out of it?"

"It does sound unlikely."

"My story is your story," Bluma said triumphantly. "Welcome to it!"

She cackled with laughter and rubbed her hands together, a witch at her cauldron in the casino lounge. To hell with tomorrow, to hell with her roiling gut — she was tired of crunching ice. She glanced around the lounge, caught the waitress's attention and waved her glass in the air.

"Is that why we're here?" she asked. "So you could tell me that memory?"

"Maybe so. And I wanted to be back on terms with you."

"Terms?"

"Better terms. Speaking terms."

"Well, we're there. We're speaking. About you, of all things. Well, why not?"

The waitress showed up with another Rusty Nail. Bluma sat back and played with her swizzle stick, turning the ice in her drink. She had a way of making him twist in the wind. The poor little Burnside girl had learned a few tricks along the way. That was inevitable, and healthy.

They would both be better off when he finished her story.

From the winners' table behind them, the three ladies were raising their glasses in victory, paper umbrellas and all. Bluma cast a disdainful look.

"I think I've had enough of this place. You can take me home."

"What about your drink?"

"You finish it."

"Waste not, want not."

Joey drained the Rusty Nail, negotiating around the crushed ice. The Drambuie stuck to his palate and quarrelled with the Chianti dregs. Laboriously, Bluma pushed her chair away from the table.

"Don't move. I'll go pay, then I'll help you."

By the time Joey rushed back to the table, his credit card still in his hand, his mother was standing unsteadily, one hand on the chair back and the other on the table. Her hold on life was tenuous despite her courage. Everything depended on her taste for the fight.

"Can you make it?"

Joey offered his arm, something she usually did not accept.

"I'm not dead yet. And I'm not going till I'm good and ready."

Suddenly her spark returned.

"You haven't finished my story. You still need me, right?"

"More than ever."

THIRTEEN

The Unveiling

THAT EVENING, IN A STATE of post-Bluma stress disorder compounded by the sensory barrage of the casino, Joey took refuge at Caroline's.

"When I listen to her, I wonder what else I don't know about me," he said.

"No doubt many things. It's like canoeing: there are always snags beneath the surface."

"I knew I could count on you for words of comfort."

Another question went unspoken: What do I not know about you? The week before, Caroline's husband had come visiting. Until then, he'd been a shadow, a launch pad for her jokes about how free she and Joey were, or weren't, to be doing what they were doing. She volunteered no information about his visit, and no assurances about what she and her phantom husband had done during his short stay. Joey wondered whether he had the right to ask, but the question sounded prurient and petty in equal measure.

That night, as Caroline slept, he rose from her bed. "I'm such a macho pig," she'd laughed as she laid her head on the pillow an hour earlier. "Once I'm satisfied, I just roll over and start sawing wood." Joey had no such luck. A dream had interfered with his sleep again.

He was writing, it was a charge he'd been assigned, like a scribe or an illuminator, but he was writing on granite, as an engraver would. Then the perspective widened and he saw he was working on a gravestone. But the letters he was engraving, dates and a name presumably, kept slipping off the face of the stone and sliding onto the ground. The frustration woke him up.

He moved down the hallway toward the unused spare bedroom, a place he hadn't explored. He flipped the switch and his eyes were punished by the unshaded glare of the overhead light. From the threshold, he saw the bed was rumpled and unmade, but nothing in the room showed that two consenting adults had shared that space. There was no evidence of anything, one way or the other. It was like the question he couldn't ask.

Joey shut off the light, then retreated to the couch in the living room and lay lengthwise on it. Love knows no retirement, no tranquility. Its torments are forever young. Maybe that's a good thing. He opened his eyes a minute later and found Caroline standing before him with a shawl around her shoulders. Satisfied or not, in her sleep she'd sensed trouble.

"What are you doing here?" she asked.

"Thinking about what I don't know."

She shrugged off the shawl and it fell from her shoulders onto his chest, trailing perfume. She stretched out her hand in the darkness.

"You could do that just as well with me."

He gathered the shawl in his hands. "What did I do to deserve you?"

"Nothing. You're just lucky." Caroline's laughter lit the dark room.

"I'm the luckiest man on earth."

"Then it's all right if there are things about you that you don't know."

THE DACHSHUNDS FORCED THE ISSUE of Joey and Elke's cohabitation, which they had been successfully putting off. No surprise there — the stinky, querulous sausages had been ruling the roost for years.

With their master and mistress away from the house more often, busy pursuing happiness — "gisms," as Bluma called it — the dachshunds were left to themselves. They were unhappy, bored, at loose ends. They were social animals that demanded admiration and attention. When Joey returned to the house, the dogs followed him into his room and insisted on staying there, curled up in a heap under the single bed. What was this change of heart, he wondered. Normally, the dogs hated him and he hated them. But when he tried to kick them out of his room, they whimpered so pitifully that even he was moved.

The first time that happened, he had all the symptoms of a bad cold the next morning. Mysteriously, the stuffy head, the runny nose, the sore throat vanished a few hours after he vacated the house. A curtain lifted and he was himself again, without the benefit of echinacea or Advil or any other patented cure. He described what happened to Caroline the next evening.

"You're allergic," she diagnosed.

"To what?"

"To your house. Or something in your house. What else could it be?"

"After all this time?"

"You can develop allergies later in life. You don't have to be born with them."

It all seemed too neat, as if Caroline were trying to pry him away from Elke, which didn't add up, since she hadn't made a single move in that direction. He spent the next night with the dogs in his room, breathing in their wet manure stink in the increasingly hostile air. By morning he was sure he had double pneumonia.

His doctor, who had once prescribed Viagra to combat his sexual indifference to Elke, even after telling him the drug would not create desire where desire was lacking, sent him off for tests. He placed high on the scale for intolerance to dog dander.

"I guess I've got my dander up," Joey joked through puffy eyes.

His doctor ignored him. Jokes took time, and time spent joking was not billable. His advice was unambiguous. The patient was intolerant to something in the environment. Either a change of environment or full environmental cleaning was called for.

"You should first carry out decontamination," the doctor told him with an insincere smile. "Then get rid of the irritant."

"My wife and her dogs," Joey lamented. "She loves them."

"You could get her a pet without dander."

"Like what?"

"There are certain short-haired rabbits that don't provoke the same reaction."

"Right. That would never work. Aren't there shots for this? Insensitivity therapy or something?"

"I'm not going to recommend inoculation for a condition that can be easily solved in a non-medical way," the doctor said, getting to his feet.

At the door, he clapped Joey on the back. "A lot of men your age are having much more difficult conversations with their doctors than this one. Tell me, are you very attached to the dogs?"

"Those two Kraut stinkpots?"

"Then you should be happy to change the environmental factors."

They shook on it as the doctor called for his next patient. At least this time, Joey thought, he didn't ask me about my morning erection. He still hadn't got the point of that question.

Out in the parking lot, in the cool sunshine, he contemplated the natural world with pleasure. The fog of allergy symptoms was lifting like morning mist. Like so many patients, he had been dishonest with his doctor. He had invited the dogs into his room the previous night to worsen his state.

"You always hated the dogs," Elke told him that evening.

"No one could love them more than you. But I do spend plenty of time with them. The proof? I spent so much I developed an allergy."

"A fake allergy."

"Look, I brought in a doctor's note, like back in school."

He waved the test results from the allergy clinic in front of Elke. She looked away. He put the paper down on the kitchen table as the dogs charged into the room, barking excitedly, sensing the coming storm.

"Here, it's even readable for once. Look at the check marks in the little boxes, then tell me I'm faking."

"I didn't say you were faking. But you planned this. Your brain changed itself on purpose."

"My brain changed itself," he repeated. "Wow! I didn't know I had it in me."

"Either did I, frankly. I underestimated you."

"It's my inner Joey," he told her, "coming to the surface."

"I'm afraid so. Who would have thought?"

They stood together in the kitchen, a dark, close, low-ceilinged room with a bank of narrow windows that gave directly onto a dense cedar hedge. With their superior training, the dogs milled around at their feet, whimpering and melancholic, unhappy that there might not be open conflict to interrupt after all. Neither human was in the mood to pay them any attention.

Elke pointed to the dogs. "Are you suffering now?"

"Not particularly."

They stood side by side at the counter, like the team they no longer were. The team, Joey thought. They had teamed up. That's what Elke had called their arrangement when he'd first moved in with her. Into her house that overlooked her garden. Years later, both remained in her image.

"I suppose you want to go live with the neighbour lady?"

Joey had no ready answer.

"Go ahead." Her voice was calm. "You can wave to me in the morning when you go off to work. And you can still be my husband.

You can take out the garbage and cut my grass in the summer."

"Don't be silly. I'm just telling you I can't be around the dogs for very long."

"Do yourself a favour, Joey, and do me one while you're at it. There's not enough passion under this roof to start a good fight. We faded in. We'll fade out. We can both do better elsewhere."

In spectacular fashion, Elke proved how little he knew her.

"You surprise me," he admitted.

"It's about time. And it's a shame we had to wait this long for that to happen, at the very end."

She exited the dining room, the dogs following her. Joey's head was spinning. A permission, a free pass — that easily? It made him wonder what he didn't know about Elke.

She turned his way before her final exit.

"And please don't be so impressed with me that you'll have a change of heart," she told him.

JOEY REMEMBERED THAT CHRISTINE, OF the Saran Wrap dress fame, and the other women of the architecture school used to complain about a special affliction that affected them. It was called fear of completion. Apparently there was some flaw in the women candidates in technical fields that kept them from finishing what they started. They procrastinated and self-sabotaged until they reached the point of failure, which had been their destination all along.

Joey considered the pile of canary pads on the glass surface of Caroline's coffee table and wondered if he hadn't fallen victim to the same syndrome. He was avoiding finishing his mother's story. But at least he knew why. The thing that defined him was coming to an end.

But where was that end?

It was a bright, cold Friday afternoon. The door opened and Caroline came in from raking leaves. She stood inside the front door, holding her rake in her gloved hand, a picture of domestic satisfaction with one surreal touch: a woman in her living room holding a large gardening implement. A dozen bright-red maple leaves clung to the green metal tines of the rake. Her face was flushed with autumn wind.

Joey looked up at her. "Will you love me if I don't have this story to work on anymore?"

"Will you still love me tomorrow?" she sang in a tuneless parody of him.

"I'm serious."

She looked at the blank yellow page of his pad. "Running out of things to say?"

"When you're out of things to say, I guess you have to call it The End."

"Then you'll be more available."

"I could help you rake leaves."

"Exactly. You could hold the bag open."

"That sounds like fun."

Then his nattering cellphone attempted locomotion across the table. The spectacle, like a beetle fallen on its back trying to right itself, rescued him from his quandary. There were rare times when he was grateful for the irritating little device.

"Joey, my boy." It was Ozzie. "We just signed the contract of the century."

"Imagine that. And the century has only just begun."

"I suppose you haven't been reading the papers."

"I live in the past. You know that."

"Remember the old Housatonic Railroad freight yards?"

"Don't tell me!"

"Yup. Condos up the ying-yang. And who decontaminates?"

"Catastrophes Are Us?"

"Yes, sir!"

Joey put on his little boy's voice. "We're rich! We're rich!"

"This calls for a celebration."

"Like someplace really fancy?"

"Better not. Sheila brings us luck."

"You're right. Be modest in victory." Joey paused. "Jesus, the business practically runs itself."

"Right," said Ozzie. "You paid me that compliment once before."

Joey stowed his canary pads in their legal-sized file folder, happy for the diversion, though he knew it was only temporary. He looked up and caught Caroline's evaluating gaze.

"The dilemma has been put off," he explained. "That was my partner. He wants to talk business." He caught himself. "Ecology business."

She shook her head. "The memoirist and the businessman. Whoever thought they could go together?"

AT SHEILA'S BAR, THEIR ONLY concession to success was ordering champagne. She looked at them suspiciously.

"You don't even like champagne."

"How would I know?" Ozzie said. "I've never drunk it."

"He only uses it to bathe in," Joey added. "Pour a glass for yourself while you're at it. Today we're big spenders."

"If I drank everything that every customer in this bar told me to … Okay, just this once, because it's you. So, what's the occasion?" She clapped her hand over her mouth. "Right, trade secrets. Mum's the word."

She opened the bottle with scarcely a pop for discretion's sake. Sheila toasted them. "To the occasion, whatever it is."

She took a gulp and set the glass down on the unoccupied end of the bar, out of harm's way. Then she executed her Don Ho imitation, complete with the line about the tiny bubbles. She did a terrible Don Ho, but so did Don Ho. Then she went off to nose around in other customers' business.

The bar was filling up. The Sox had folded for the season, and some less storied team had taken their place on TV.

"Remember," Ozzie began, "when there was a gas station on every corner?"

"The world has become a dangerous place, and that's good for us."

"The bad news is that you'll have to come out of retirement."

"Unfortunately, I'm not ready. I have to finish the story."

Ozzie took in that information, but said nothing. They drank.

"Sheila's right. I don't know about this stuff. There's something feminine about it."

Ozzie filled their glasses. "How's the inner Joey?"

"How do you get from femininity to that question?"

Ozzie shrugged. "Nothing. Just a slip of the drink."

"You haven't drunk enough, Ozzie. Okay," he admitted to his friend, "I do have a problem."

Ozzie held his breath.

"I can't tell if I've got to the end of my mother's story or not."

Ozzie breathed out. That was no problem at all. "And I can't wait till you finish it. You'll be free to think about something else."

Joey reached for the champagne bottle.

"Actually, I have been. I figured we'd have a little ceremony for the time capsule, and I wanted my mother's best friend to be there. Thanks to the association of retired Spanish teachers, I found her. She's going to show up."

"That's not what I'd call thinking about something else."

Joey gave a guilty smile.

"Is this friend a real person or just someone in the story? And what ceremony are you talking about?"

"The time capsule, what do you think? You never seal a time capsule without some kind of event. You know, a small crowd of interested people. I wanted my mother's cousin to be there. They were best friends growing up, but they got separated."

"So, she's a real person."

"She sounded real to me."

"Everyone really is findable," Ozzie said.

"Even old ladies. I'm going to make it a surprise," he told Ozzie. "A treat I'm springing on her."

"A surprise? At her age?"

"Why not?"

"I can think of a few reasons. But it's your call."

"A reunion of two best friends, separated for years ... I like that."

Ozzie looked dubious. "I don't know, Joey, that sounds too much like a movie. Tell you what: I'll skip that scene and work on Housatonic instead." He raised his empty champagne glass. "I'll see you back at the office."

A FEW DAYS LATER, JOEY settled into his usual spot across from his mother. His hands and his pockets were free of all recording devices. He gazed at her swarm of tchotchkes and realized he would not miss this place one bit. Questing after her story day in and day out, its truth forever just out of reach — he was exhausted. A healthy sense of resentment accompanied his fatigue, which wasn't what he planned to feel when he first started this noble project.

"I think I've finally reached it," he informed Bluma. "The page where I write 'the end.'"

"If you finish my story, what will I live for?"

"But I'll still pay as much attention as before," Joey stammered. "I'll still come every morning."

Bluma laughed uproariously at his discomfort.

"Oh, you calm down! That's from *A Thousand and One Nights*, one of those Arab fairy tales. Scheherazade — everybody knows that one."

Bluma looked at her son as if he were the most illiterate curse who ever crossed the threshold of her apartment.

"Sorry. Everybody but me."

"You should read more."

"Right now I'm preparing estimates on decontaminating the Housatonic rail yards."

"Sounds fascinating!"

"Thanks. That wasn't what I had in mind. I had in mind getting out of the business."

"So what happened?"

"Ozzie. He wants me to come back and help him."

"Well, you can do that for him after everything he's done for you."

"That's what I'm doing. And I can, now that I'm just about finished with the time capsule. All finished but the finishing."

"I've heard that before."

"Sorry for being predictable."

"Eddie used to say that every time I asked him when he was going to start selling his tabletop dishwasher." Bluma's hand grazed the brown Social Security envelope that still lay on the table. "Eddie, of blessed memory."

"Well, I'd better finish. I don't want to remind you of him."

"Don't worry about that. You take after me."

"So, you won't die if I wrap up your story and move on to something else?"

She crossed her arms over her chest, and Joey winced.

"There are no guarantees," she declared.

"Not even in Scheherazade?"

"Read it yourself and find out."

The rain pelted her windows, whipped by a northeaster. Half rain and half sleet off the Atlantic, much too soon for his plan, stripping leaves from the branches in the marshy woods beneath her window. Mother and son sat in rare silence and watched the raindrops streaming down the pane. Winter was threatening to arrive, always too soon, like every year.

"I think we should have a little ceremony," he told her, "when we put the time capsule in the ground."

"We'll need better weather than this. I don't want to catch my death while celebrating my life. I can't stand the cold anymore."

ON A PRE-WINTER ERRAND he was doing for her, Joey went into Caroline's garage with a gallon container of grape-coloured windshield washer fluid and its impossible-to-open plastic cap. He saw it there, leaning in a corner, its metal blades gnawed on by rust, clearly unused and unloved: a post-hole digger. The tool had gone out of style years ago. There were easier mechanized ways to dig holes for planting shrubs. The awkward-looking, archaic double handles brought back a detail from Bluma's story of her one childhood vacation. That detail had stuck with him because it held an ecological question: would a sack of organic household trash in a paper bag decay into nothingness if it were dumped into a hole in the sand?

He had something like an inspiration. With this outmoded tool, and the little-used muscles of his shoulders, he would dig a hole in the soft ground of the Branfords and deposit the time capsule there. All he needed was Caroline's permission. With her windshield washer container filled to the brim, he went back into her house to seek it.

"The earth at the far end of the flowerbeds was turned over a while ago, but I never got around to planting anything there. So it'll be easier for you to dig there. Just don't get too close to the geraniums."

"I won't hurt them. They're my lucky flower."

"I'm happy you'll be using that tool. It'll represent me."

"You mean ..." There was no sense stating the obvious. "Everyone is dropping out."

"Maybe this is one of those things that you have to do on your own." She paused to choose the way to say it. "I know your mother well enough from what you've told me. I don't have to meet her."

Joey started to protest, but Caroline cut him off. "Don't worry, I won't be far. I'll be waiting for you after the ceremony."

HE AND BLUMA STOOD IN the front yard, by the flowerbeds that were mostly dormant. She was draped in her winter coat in the radiant sunshine. Next to her were two lawn chairs he had set out. The extra chair was for the surprise guest who was late. The time capsule tube lay on the first chair where, when she tired, his mother would sit.

Joey felt the assembly should have been grander. Many were absent, and not just his Branford friends: Miss Reilly, Dr. LaRue, Laurie, Abe and Rachel, Eddie and Jerry Yale, the one who really should have existed.

Joey was lucky. He had been hoping for a crisp, clear autumn afternoon, and nature delivered something better. Bluma had insisted on her winter coat, but she was sweating underneath it. During the night, a burst of Caribbean air swept up the eastern seaboard, and for the ceremony they were blessed with an Indian summer day, unseasonably warm and humid, with a patina of hot particulate blowing off the interstate.

Joey was dressed for outdoor work in his rough mustard-coloured construction boots. They were too clean, and no amount of scuffing from the post-hole digger would make them look honestly come by. With his hands protected by gardening gloves, Joey picked up the tool, jammed its blades against the ground, twisted its arms and brought up a first bite of earth. His shoulders ached after the first minute, and he slowed the rhythm, to spare his muscles and to wait for Bluma's cousin. She watched him as if he'd stepped out of a foreign universe. The tool brought back no memories, and she had forgotten why he was digging the hole in the first place.

The pain in his shoulders convinced him that the hole was long enough for the tube to be laid on its side, and deep enough to be respectable. He set down the tool and pulled off his gardening gloves. His mother stared at him, bewildered by the proceedings, and unsure what she was doing here on a stranger's front lawn.

He had prepared a speech, but now he was afraid it would sound painfully sentimental, despite all the embarrassing clichés he had removed from it. And giving a speech to a single person, his own mother, struck him as ridiculous. It was like throwing a birthday party for yourself, and having nobody come.

Suddenly he was saved. A car pulled into Caroline's driveway, moving so fast it stopped half on the grass. The car had rental plates and that neutral, I-don't-belong-to-anybody look.

The passenger-side door flew open.

"Hey, Fledge, I made it to your party! And I'm only a little late." She nodded toward the driver still behind the wheel. "He got lost, what do you expect from a kid?"

An old lady stepped out and strode across the lawn.

"My sweetness!" she croaked, and her voice broke. She opened her arms.

Bluma stared at her. She knew that hoarse tomboy voice. And she knew the words. She'd spoken them herself. They came from a story and they belonged there, in the past. My sweetness.

Too bad she was in such terrible shape. If she could have run, she would have.

"Fledge, I'm here! What do you think about that? Are you happy?"

Her worst fear come true: Bella peering into the back seat of the car the day she rode with Agnes to Oak Park. Bella grabbing her and ripping her away from the ordinary life she was heading for. Her boy liked to call her extraordinary, but he knew nothing. Hers was the most ordinary life imaginable. She felt mortified, ashamed of what she had become, with this decrepit body she dragged around.

Then she remembered it was Bella's fault, and everything switched around. Bella hadn't looked into the car and stopped her from going to Oak Park. Bella let her spend those endless nights on the couch at Agnes's place. Bella hadn't forced her to do the hundred things that would have kept her off the path that led here.

Bella stopped in front of her and waved a mischievous finger in her face.

"Any man who'll have one of us will have to have both of us. I want to meet your husband. Where is he?"

"He didn't come back, so I guess he never found himself. He smoked himself to death — though I've got no actual proof."

"So we're together at last!"

Bella threw her arms around her. She felt her cousin's body freeze. She stepped away.

"You don't look so bad. I heard how sick you were. But you're all right!"

"Who says?"

"I do."

"I look like hell," Bluma told her, "and you know it. It's a good thing I've got my clothes on or you'd run screaming from the premises. But you — you look great. Time hasn't found you."

"I stay away from mirrors." Bella shrugged off the compliment. "But that's not the point. I'm here to celebrate you."

Bluma turned to Joey. "Why didn't you tell me she'd be here?"

"I wanted it to be a surprise."

"At my age there are no good surprises." She stared at the shallow trench her son had dug. "I don't have a choice, even when it's supposed to be my day."

She turned to Bella. "You've come to watch my life disappear into a hole in the ground."

"I don't know about holes. You're lucky someone cares enough to write down your story. I came to see you for the occasion. And I came a long way."

Then she caught sight of the post-hole digger lying on its side. "Hey, I remember that thing. My father dug holes with it in the sand at the Dunes for the garbage. It was the only work he would do. You and I had to do everything else."

"I don't remember anything like that," Bluma told her cousin. "You're making it up."

She stared into Bella's face.

"Don't you know who I am?" Bella asked her.

"I have to sit down."

Bluma lowered herself into a lawn chair. "A trip down memory lane. Sounds like a nightmare." She looked up at Joey. "I'll never forgive you."

She rummaged through the pockets of her winter coat and found a pair of oversized sunglasses with giant white plastic frames. She put them on, but her hands were shaking, and the glasses ended up on an angle on her face. They looked like something out of Elton John's wardrobe.

"Where did you come from again?" she asked Bella.

"Chicago."

"You're still there? I couldn't go back if I wanted. I can't travel."

Joey felt a presence at his side. He turned and looked into the face of Bella's son. He had the frizzy hair that afflicted nearly everyone in the family, but he was darker, almost olive-coloured, and had the unwrinkled skin that goes with that complexion.

"No offence," the man told him. "But this isn't the world's greatest idea."

Bella came to her son's side.

"This wasn't what I was expecting," she said to him. "She's so withdrawn, so unresponsive. It's like she doesn't know me — my best friend."

"She's just surprised," he consoled her.

"No. She's mad at me. Why did I come here?"

Bluma heard the hurt in her cousin's voice. She took off her sunglasses and squinted at her.

"Sing that Spanish-teacher song for me."

"No," Bella told her. "You'll only get madder than you already are. You used to get mad as hell at me for wanting to be a teacher."

"Go ahead," Bluma ordered. "Sing it."

"I don't want to."

"I promise I won't get mad."

Bella took her chances. She croaked out the refrain:

Porque le falta, porque no tiene
Marihuana por fumar!
Cha-cha-cha …

"So, you actually stuck with being a Spanish teacher?"

"When the kids got older, I went back."

"What about your husband?"

"Gone."

"You didn't respect our sacred oath either."

"Who got married first? And who told who not to do it? I bet I was the only maid of honour who told the bride not to walk down the aisle. I didn't want to lose you."

"We got separated after we swore we never would." She pointed at Joey and Bella's son. "Look at our kids, staring at us like we were museum pieces."

"The museum of women of the twentieth century," Bella agreed.

"You were normal," Bluma accused her. "You had a normal life with a normal husband."

"Now he's dead, and I've never felt more alive. It's a shame to have to say it that way. It wasn't his fault. That's just who men were."

Bluma laughed unhappily. Bella took advantage of that laughter to go to her, and Bluma let herself be embraced briefly. She let Bella pat her on the shoulder, the unsuccessful contestant receiving consolation.

Joey chose that moment to hold up the metal tube with the time capsule in it. The story he had recorded and that lay curled inside didn't seem to matter anymore.

"I was going to give a speech, but the ladies beat me to it. I'll put this in the ground, then we'll have a little drink for closure — I think they still call it that these days. Then we'll let them get back to reminiscing."

"I don't call that reminiscing, do you?" Bella's son told him.

"No," he answered. "But I have to call it something."

He bent down and laid the metal tube in the earth. Everyone stared at it as if this were its funeral. With a plastic snow shovel from Caroline's garage, he started filling the hole.

As he did, his mother raised her face to the sun.

"I remember everything," she said to Bella. "I was just pretending I didn't."

She began to sing the Fledglings' song. It came out like a dirge:

> *Come smoke a Coca-Cola, drink ketchup cigarettes*
> *See Lillian Russell wrestle with a box of Oysterettes*
> *Pork and beans will meet tonight to have a finish fight*
> *Chauncey DePew will lecture on some polio tonight.*

"Why on earth did we sing that? It doesn't make a lick of sense."

"It did at the time," Bella told her. "It made all the sense in the world for us girls."

Joey considered his mother, defiantly clinging to her pain, and her ex-best friend. When did his mother's friendship with Bella start falling apart?

At birth, he decided.

He went to the porch where a cooler sat, and returned with two bottles of champagne. He opened them and handed out the glasses that came from Caroline's kitchen.

"Better than a Rusty Nail," he told his mother.

"I can't not," Bella told him when he handed her a glass.

Bella's son caught his eye. The man raised his glass to him in a silent toast. I could get to know him, Joey thought. We probably share a couple of things.

When he looked back to Bluma, her glass was empty. She was losing her inhibitions. This was the time to do it.